FLIRTIN

"Entertaining and lively. . . . A compelling romance that will leave readers breathless."

—Publishers Weekly (starred review)

"Take a wonderful jaunt through time with likable characters and some excellent humor."

—Romantic Times (4½ stars)

SEDUCING MR. DARCY

Winner of the 2009 RITA® Award for
Best Paranormal Romance

"Sexy fun."

—BookPage

"Hot, adorable, and irresistible. Rip its sexy white shirt off and have your way with it."

—DarcyWars

TUMBLING THROUGH TIME

"Tackling both time travel and the concept of authorial intent in fresh ways, this romance debut is a joy and its author is worth watching."

—Publishers Weekly

"Ingenious! This heartwarming, laugh-filled ride through time has everything a great novel needs."

—Romance Junkies

11   2021

These titles are also available as eBooks

For Jeanne Lowther, Janet Parish, and Lee Parish.
Thank you for helping to keep the memory
of my parents alive and giving me
the gift of feeling like a daughter.

ACHING
for
ALWAYS

GWYN CREADY

POCKET BOOKS
New York London Toronto Sydney

Pocket Books
A Division of Simon & Schuster, Inc.
1230 Avenue of the Americas
New York, NY 10020

This book is a work of fiction. Names, characters, places, and incidents either are products of the author's imagination or are used fictitiously. Any resemblance to actual events or locales or persons, living or dead, is entirely coincidental.

First Pocket Books paperback edition October 2010

POCKET and colophon are registered trademarks
of Simon & Schuster, Inc.

For information about special discounts for bulk purchases,
please contact Simon & Schuster Special Sales at 1-866-506-1949
or business@simonandschuster.com.

The Simon & Schuster Speakers Bureau can bring authors to your live event. For more information or to book an event contact the Simon & Schuster Speakers Bureau at 1-866-248-3049 or visit our website at www.simonspeakers.com.

Cover design by Lisa Litwack.
Cover illustration by Gene Mollica.

Manufactured in the United States of America

10   9   8   7   6   5   4   3   2   1

ISBN 978-1-4391-0728-7
ISBN 978-1-4391-7148-6 (ebook)

ACKNOWLEDGMENTS

So many people have given me their support: Teri Coyne, Manuel Erviti, Wileen Dragovan, Nick Cole, Donna Neiport, Mary Parish, Mary Nell Cummings, Katie Kemper and Scott DeLaney, Bill Slivka, Joe Gitchell, Betsy Tyson, Jean McCloskey, Annie and Mitchell Kaplan, Todd DePastino, Vince Rause, Karen Rumbaugh, Jean Hilpert, Lynne Crofford, Beverly Crofford, Dick Price, Kate and Mark Zingarelli, Kathi Boyle, Mary Bockovich, Doris and Lloyd Heroff, Betty Jean Pyle, Kim and Wayne Honath, Kelly and Mike Brown, Marie Guerra (going for the hat trick!), Valli Ellis, Dawn Kosanovich, Theresa Gallick, Michele Petruccelli, Ellen Genco, Tory Ferrera, Alison and Jeremy Diamond, Ted Kyle, Mark Prus, Caroline and Richard Holme, Garen DiBartolomeo, Alan Schaefer, Jennifer Davidson, Barb Herrington, Christine Lorenz and Norm Goldberg, Julie Pastorius and Dale Hostavich, Louise Larkin, Gudrun Wells and Stuart Ferguson, Scott Cready, Sally Kay, Pam Maifeld, Cassandra Ott, and Mary Irwin-Scott and Grant Scott.

Three books provided invaluable guidance: Miles

Harvey's marvelous *Island of Lost Maps: A True Story of Cartographic Crime, How to Lie with Maps* by Mark Monmonier and H. J. de Blij, and *Maps: Finding Our Place in the World,* edited by James R. Akerman and Robert W. Karrow Jr.

The Dollar Bank lions are magical, though probably not in the way I've suggested. You can see them at 340 Fourth Avenue in Pittsburgh, a block or so from Rogan's house, in reality, the Burke House at 209 Fourth, Pittsburgh's oldest surviving office building, built in 1836.

The alley in question does exist, in exactly the form I've described (save the invisible dome, of course, though as with all things invisible, how does one really know?). It is Strawberry Way, and I encourage you to walk its enchanting length.

· I have to thank Judy Hulick again for her inspiration and infectious joy. I hope she doesn't mind being immortalized in these pages. Thanks as well to Diane Pyle, who loves maps as much as I do and who cuts quite the literary figure as the can-do best friend.

India, the kitten, left her paw prints, literally and figuratively, on this story. She was with me every step of the way, motor running.

Joy Balentine and the folks at the Heinz History Center were very kind to let me check out the sightlines from their outdoor balcony, especially a week before the G-20 conference, when the urgency of my mission undoubtedly gave me the air of a terrorist.

A special thank-you to the Historical Center of Mt. Lebanon, especially Margaret Jackson, its go-go president, who has shared her passion for the past as well as the present with me.

Mega thanks to Lisa Litwack at Pocket Books, who envisioned the scrumptious cover, and to photographer Gene Mollica and dress designers Shirley and Victor Forster, who brought the vision to life.

I've raved about my copyeditor, Judy Steer, before and I'll do it again (I wonder if I should have put a comma before the "and"?). Without her amazing work, my readers would be considerably less happy.

A special shout-out to the all-powerful Megan McKeever, whose unflinching support and expert direction is very much appreciated.

Thanks as well to Claudia Cross, who is the Sacajawea to my Meriwether Lewis (apologies to Meriwether Lewis) on this intriguing expedition.

Finally, I am surrounded by three wonderful people who give me many, many reasons to be grateful every day. Lester, Wyatt, and Cameron—I love you so much, it hurts.

PROLOGUE

"Captain," Mr. Fallon said, "the island's in sight."

Young Monk, stealing a glance from the smudged columns of numbers that served as his punishment for larking in the sheets when he should have been scanning the horizon for sails, watched as the captain—a man privately nicknamed Granite by his crew—actually laughed. And though Monk dared not look out the gunport while disgraced, he thought he knew the reason for this surprising outburst. The island, as Fallon had called it, was no more than a rock, a barren rock with sheer, slippery sides, looming like the gray tower of Newgate Prison above the wild, crashing sea. No man could climb it, and Monk was certain Granite would allow no man in his care to try. What could the men who'd chartered this beleaguered voyage have been thinking?

"Thank you, Mr. Fallon," Granite said. "I spotted her a moment ago myself. Keep her dyce. I'll be up when I finish here."

"Aye, sir."

Fallon closed the door to the captain's quarters, but it opened again a moment later. Alfred Brand, the leader of the men who'd hired Granite out of his unemployed naval captain's existence to find this isolated rock, stepped inside.

"How soon until we can make our approach?"

"I beg your pardon," Granite said. "I didn't hear your knock."

Monk felt a shiver go down his back. But Brand, a rat-faced man with long pink nose, dark eyes and shining teeth, had no experience of Granite at his most polite, the becalmed sea before the earthshaking fury of a North Atlantic squall.

"I suggest we hurry," Brand said, "while there's still light."

Granite cut his gaze toward the table with a look of such modulated benevolence, Monk's mouth went dry. Granite was a handsome man, with dark hair like Monk's, but he was capable of silencing an entire watch without a word.

"Monk?" Granite said.

"Aye, sir?"

"Step up to the deck to see if the ship's master can use you."

Monk jumped to his feet, relieved to be released from both his unhappy task and the budding storm, but as he scurried out, he heard Granite's chill tones.

"Mr. Brand, I believe I made it clear when I accepted this assignment that the safety of this ship and my men would be paramount. Your objective, whatever that may be, can wait until the weather lifts."

"I have paid well over—"

"I am aware of what you have paid. Crowns can buy a voyage, but they cannot induce me to smash my ship upon the rocks. We shall wait."

Monk finished the last of the splicing. The rough work seemed all he was good for, and even for that he was slow and of unremarkable ability. He would never make a sailor, and for a long moment he wondered if the path laid out for him was the one he should be on. With a sigh, he slipped his hands under his arms. They were bleeding and nearly numb from the cold. The rain had stopped half a watch ago, and now the immense darkness of the clouded night seemed ready to consume the ship in one easy swallow.

He gazed at the island, an inky blackness against the sky. It was nearly as high as the main mast, with sheer sides that ended in a blunt top from which another, smaller peak rose. He'd heard Brand and his two traveling companions talk when they thought they were alone, though the words they used—"through hole" and "unbound event"—made no sense to Monk. There was a secret there. One that involved the map Brand kept locked away.

"My poor, dear Monk," a soft voice cried. "Let me see you. You're hurt."

Mrs. Brand took his hands and turned his palms up to look. The unexpected touch made him think of his mother. He believed, though he could not rightly remember, that her hair had had the same moonbeam sparks to it and her eyes the same wide, knowing gaze. How a woman like Mrs. Brand could be married to such a man as Mr. Brand, Monk did not know, though Yannick, the carpenter's mate, had said, "Gold buys more than an unemployed sea captain," when Monk had asked.

"How old are you, Monk?"

"Ten, m'um."

She shook her head. "Has the captain seen your hands?"

"I shouldn't like to bother him with such things."

"Aye, he does seem to be quite busy as of late." She cast a gentle look in the direction of the captain's quarters. "Nonetheless," she said firmly, "you are in his care." She took Monk by the shoulder, guided him toward the door and knocked.

"What is it?"

"Mrs. Brand, sir, with Monk."

Instead of a terse "Enter," or an angrier "Not now," Monk heard the remarkable sound of a chair being pushed back and the approach of footsteps. He barely had time to wipe the surprise from his face before the door opened.

"Mrs. Brand, good evening."

"Are you aware, sir, that your charge has been worked until he bleeds?"

Monk shut his eyes instantly, waiting for the explosion.

"I-I am generally not told of such things."

Monk slitted a lid. Spots of color had appeared on Granite's cheeks, and he stood as meek as a mouse.

"I know you have much on your mind in the running of this vessel, sir, but the boys are in your care, this one most specifically. I believe the matter warrants your attention. How many hours have you been working, Monk?"

Monk, who had been working six and had many times worked more than twelve, said, "Four, m'um. A standard watch." There was a brotherhood amongst sailors, after all.

Granite cleared his throat. "He may clean up in my washroom."

Monk rounded the corner into the captain's tiny privy at a clip, pausing only to see if the sailors in the passageway were witness to this unimaginable privilege. He dumped the pitcher's cold contents into the basin.

"It has grown into a beautiful evening," Mrs. Brand said, her voice carrying on the thin night air.

"Indeed. How is your little one? I hope the storm did not bother her."

"My daughter can sleep through anything."

This was decidedly untrue, thought Monk, whose hammock hung outside the cabin Mrs. Brand shared with her husband and one-year-old daughter. Many a night, he had heard the angel-faced girl singing nonsense words to herself in her crib while her parents talked in tense undertones on the deck above. He thrust his hands into the water and shook them.

"I am sorry for my husband's driving insistence. I fear he has no more understanding of the intricacies of running a ship than I."

"Please do not trouble yourself on that account, milady. My only wish is to see the ascent of the islet accomplished quickly and safely so that I may return you—that is to say, you and your family—to England."

"I thank you for that."

There had been an odd tone to her words, and Monk, who was now rolling the small ball of soap against his palm, paused to be sure he could hear what followed.

"I should do anything, I think," Granite said softly, "to ease your burden."

This was hardly the first time Monk has seen the two speak. Mrs. Brand appeared regularly on the quarterdeck when her husband and his companions took over the officers' mess, whispering over their map. But it was the first time Monk had noticed this curious import. It was as if each sentence had a meaning apart from the words being spoken. As always, he found it unsettling adults had the ability to appear to speak plainly without actually doing so.

"Is there anything, anything at all, you can tell me about your husband's intentions at this place—only so that I may make the effort more efficient?"

Again Mrs. Brand hesitated. "I cannot in all honor say anything."

"Nor do," Granite added after a beat.

The pause that followed was so long, Monk wondered if one or both had been struck by apoplexy.

"Nor do," Mrs. Brand agreed with evident sorrow.

"Hear me," Granite said in a hoarse whisper. "I do not censure. I do not judge—except to judge you honorable and true. But, oh, if I could only see you happy."

Monk held himself very still. A ship lived hour to hour on the mood of its captain, and theirs could be determined, disappointed, angry or serene, but he was always in control, and this gush of florid emotion shocked Monk.

A confusing silence followed, filled with the rustle of

clothes. Then Monk heard the cabin's main door bang open.

"I've found you at last, my dear," Monk heard Brand say. "Our daughter is making an unmerciful racket."

"I should go," she said in a choked voice.

"Aye, please do," said Brand. "Captain, the storm has lifted. Let us proceed."

The sea rocked the ship. Even with every anchor laid, the approach would be something close to fantastic. Monk held the mast top easily and listened to the men far below.

"We cannot get a rope across," Granite said, his voice raised to be heard over the rising wind, "nor the ship any closer."

"You gave me your word, Captain. Are you saying you will not uphold it?"

The infernal bugger! Monk's blood boiled. He gauged the distance to the islet. At this height, he was nearly eye level with its small, flat ledge and the peak that rose from that. "Begging your pardon, sir," he called, "but I can do it."

Granite glared into the top sheets. "Who spoke?"

The crew fell silent. Talking out of turn was an offense.

"Monk, sir," he said. "I think I can do it."

"Come down here."

Monk caught a shroud and sailed to the deck. In an instant, he was staring into a pair of fiery eyes.

"What nonsense are you spouting?"

"Sir, if I can catch the ship as it rolls toward the island, I can swing in on a rope. I can catch the top, or at the very least the edge."

Those steely eyes traveled up the mast and over to the islet. "Good Lord, you'd have to be as high as the crosstrees."

"I can do it, sir. Have done. Or something very like it."

"Let the boy try. At least someone here is willing to make an effort."

It was Brand's associate, Spears. Spears and the other man—Collingswood—gazed at him from the rail. Monk dearly wished he were grown. He wanted to pop each of them square in the nose for their blackguardly insubordination.

Brand said, "The boy says he can do it. Surely, Captain, you can't object."

For a moment, Granite looked as if he were about to fulfill Monk's wish himself, but with evident reluctance he relented. The order was given, and in less than a quarter hour, Monk stood on the edge of the extended foremast, outfitted with the tools necessary to anchor the rope were he to find himself lucky enough to land without breaking his neck. He clutched the line, which was attached to the crosstrees above his head. The end of another rope, one much thinner, whose length lay curled into hundreds of neat, wide loops on the deck, was tied around his waist. He observed the immense roll of the ship, sending him in dizzying circles high above the sea, and even at this height felt the spray of salt upon his cheeks. He would have to jump as the ship swung away, praying the forward movement that followed would carry him over the island's flat top, then release the rope and drop. If he let go too high, he would batter himself upon the unforgiving rock. If he let go too soon or too late, he would fall into the sea, and while he was a capable swimmer, he had no wish to exercise his skills in the churning darkness below. If he were able to avoid all possible dangers and land on the narrow flat surface, he would anchor the rope around his waist in the island's surface, and the crew, still in possession of the other end, could rig a makeshift seat and use a pulley to deliver the men safely to their destination.

He wanted to do this for Mrs. Brand, who gazed worriedly at him from her husband's side; for his shipmates, so that they might find him a worthy addition to their ranks; for Brand and his sneering compatriots, who wouldn't know true courage if it stared them in the face; but mostly for the shadowy figure standing alone on the quarter deck, hands clasped behind his back, watching him intently.

Monk edged forward. The wood was wet and his toes curled into the grain. He could feel his shipmates' worry like the thick, charged air before a storm. He needed a roll that would fling him hard and fast. The first one came. He took a step and slipped, catching himself as the entire deck gasped. He believed he could do this, though he had lied when he said he'd done it before. Never had he done it from such a height, or in the dark, or with such a pitching, angry sea beneath him.

The next roll was too small. Collingswood called, "Make your move, boy."

"Silence," Granite ordered.

Monk took a deep breath. The ship rode high, high, high, tipping past its peak. And he leapt, swinging into the roll, letting the ship's movement to right itself bring him in a delayed arc toward the dark, shiny rock. Higher and higher he rose, until he was nearly over the surface, but not quite. Could he fly far enough to land? He kicked and let go, all in one movement, closing his eyes and saying a desperate prayer.

He landed with a crash that smashed his knee and emptied his lungs, and instantly scrabbled for purchase. He hadn't made the top. He'd made the edge and was slipping down the slimy moss. He found an outcropping and seized it, slicing his hand on the sharp rock.

But he held.

A wave plunged over him, pulling him and the rope nearly into the sea. He pumped his legs and found a toehold, gasping for breath. He had a sense of shouting from the ship, but his only thought was to make it to the top before the next wave hit.

He brought his foot up, but could find no place for it. Terrified, he pulled with all his might, banging his barked knee against the rock, hoping the outcropping would hold. The next wave hit only his legs. He ventured a hand free, reaching above the edge for something to hold. He found a seam and wedged two fingers. Slowly, with all his strength, he pulled himself onto the flat of the rock. He rolled on his back and waved a length of the rope in the air. A cheer rose over the seething sea.

Granite had traveled the pulley chair first, though even at this distance Monk had heard Brand argue he wanted no one but his own men going over, and now Brand, Spears and Collingswood conferred, each holding a lantern to view the map they'd unrolled in the center of their tight circle. Granite, Mrs. Brand and her daughter, the last two of whom had been transported to the islet over Granite's fervent objection, stood apart—apart from the men and apart from each another. Granite stared out to sea, impatience on his face. Mrs. Brand looked sad. The little girl, tired of being held, played with a doll at her mother's feet.

Everyone, it seemed, had forgotten Monk, who had scaled the small peak that rose above the rock's flat surface, like a fat finger above a fist. The entire area upon which one could stand was no more than twenty by twenty, and where Monk lay in the dark, listening, he could see almost all of it. For the first time, he had a clear view of the map, though in the darkness and flickering lights, all he could see was a blue region, a tan region and a solid black line dividing the two. The land portrayed was unrecognizable to Monk, who could add geography to navigation, mathematics, knot making and carpentry to the vast inventory of skills he was certain he would never be master of.

"The entrance is supposed to be in the cave," Collingswood said, speaking in a low voice.

"What cave?" Brand hissed.

"The seam. There. Don't you see it?"

Monk had seen it before they arrived. A narrow, vertical opening in the peak beneath him. The space it opened into could hold Monk, but he doubted it would hold very many adults.

"That's not a cave, man," Collingswood said into the roar of the sea. "That's a slit. That could barely hold a—"

"Lower your voice! The old woman said we had to be in the cave."

"I am not going in that thing."

"Have you any interest in seeing your home again? Or would you care to stay in this godforsaken time forever?"

Collingswood huffed.

"See if you can fit," Brand said.

Collingswood gave Brand a scornful look and inserted himself, shoulder first, into the opening. "Aye. Now what?"

Brand crouched and held up the lantern. "How much space is there?"

"Almost none. I can barely move."

"Shove over."

Brand edged himself in. "Spears, now you," came his muffled voice a moment later.

Monk couldn't imagine what the men thought they would do once they made their way inside. He could see the mixture of disgust and wonderment on Granite's face as he watched this Merry-Andrew show from the far end of the ledge.

After a good deal of grunting and groaning, Spears worked his way in as well. Almost as soon as he disappeared from Monk's view, the rock started to hum and tiny green sparks like lightning bugs began to appear in a tight, neat dome that circled the peak. Monk gasped. He'd never seen such a thing before.

"Out!" Brand shouted in a panic.

Spears burst from the seam, tearing his britches, and Brand and Collingswood stumbled over him in their hurry to exit. Instantly, the violent humming stopped. With a pounding heart, Monk looked at Granite. His face hadn't changed, nor had Mrs. Brand's. It was as if they hadn't seen the sparks or heard the rumbling.

Collingswood struggled to his feet. "This is the place," he whispered.

"Is it?" Brand said with a sneer. "I couldn't have guessed."

"Mr. Brand," Granite called. "How much longer? The weather is turning."

"Ten minutes, no more," Brand answered, then in a lower voice said, "We shall travel in turns. My wife, child and I, and then you two."

"No," Collingswood said fiercely. "No. I was the one who found the old woman. If anything, I should go first."

"You fools," Spears spat. "We have no guarantee this will work more than once. Hell, we have no guarantee it will work at all."

"The old woman—"

"Bugger the old woman! I for one won't believe any of it until we're home. Let me step into the twentieth century and find my Ford changed into a chauffeured limousine. That's when I'll believe it."

"Nothing will change until this map is transported away from 1684. Then it will be as if it never existed."

"You're right," Brand said. "Let's get the hell out. Darling," he called, "come."

Mrs. Brand lifted the girl to her arms and crossed the uneven space uncertainly. Brand directed her into the seam and followed her inside. The peak began its terrible rumbling again, and Monk clutched the ground. Spears stepped forward next, but no matter how he tried— shoulder first, arm or leg—he could not seem to get the smallest portion of himself into the entrance.

"There's room," Brand said angrily.

"I cannot enter."

Brand stepped out. The rumbling stopped.

"It's no good. 'Twill only hold three," Spears said.

Mrs. Brand emerged, white-faced. "Alfred, what was—"

"Quiet." Brand glared at Granite. "Say nothing, my dear. Return to the edge until I call you."

Mrs. Brand carried the girl to the peak's base and set her down again. Monk saw Granite's pained look in Mrs. Brand's direction.

"What are we going to do?" Collingswood demanded.

"I know what we're going to do," Spears said, addressing Brand. "We're going to leave your wife."

"No."

"Why not?" Collingswood asked. "The captain will surely see to her. If it works, you can come back for her another time."

"I said no."

"She was not part of the agreement," Spears said. "Just because you chose to take a wife here—"

"Quiet," Brand said, cheeks flushed. "We're not leaving anybody here who knows about this place or the map."

"There's no room," Collingswood said. "And I'm not staying. You're a fool. She's bad luck."

"Shut your mouth."

Spears smacked his thigh and barked a quick, foul laugh. "Now I understand. Don't you see, Colly? He won't leave her because he's afraid of what she might do. With *him*." He jerked his thumb toward Granite.

"Shut up."

"If you can't control your wife, that's your problem, but she's not taking *my* place."

Monk saw the glint of steel in the lantern light as Brand removed something from his cloak. The air exploded with a white-hot bang that lit the night for one terrifying instant—long enough to see the shock on Spears's face before he crumpled to the ground, map still in hand.

Granite jumped to action, but Brand swung round, pointing a second pistol at him. "Stay where you are. This is none of your business. Keep to yourself, and you and your crew may leave safely."

"Alfred, for God's sake!" cried Mrs. Brand in horror. "What have you done?"

"Hold your tongue, woman."

The little girl began to cry. Granite's eyes met Monk's. The look on his face urged caution and preparedness.

Brand swung the pistol back to Collingswood. "Anything you'd like to say?"

The man held up his hands. "No."

"Then get the map." Brand turned the barrel again toward Granite.

Collingswood reached for the paper in Spears's hand and rolled it quickly. When he handed it to Brand he whispered, "What about him?" He inclined his head toward Granite.

Monk felt the hairs on his neck stiffen.

"What do you mean?" Brand asked, so low nobody but Monk could hear.

"I mean, if we mean to keep the map safe, no one must ever be able to find this cave. You said so yourself."

"The crew—"

"The crew will never make it out of here without him. He's the only capable seaman on board. If we kill him, our secret is safe."

Monk's stomach tightened into a sickening knot. He had to get to Granite and let him know he was in danger. He began to belly-crawl down the far side of the peak, hoping to alert Granite with a signal when he got to the bottom without the men noticing. He reached backward with his foot and lost his hold, sliding six feet and hitting his backside on an outstretched rock with a comical plop. He stifled a groan, though the landing had rattled his teeth. He made an urgent gesture in Granite's direction.

"Mama, Mama."

The little girl was smiling now, pointing at Monk. Mrs. Brand stepped forward, blocking the men's view of both her daughter and Granite, who turned seaward and edged casually toward Monk.

"What?" Granite mouthed.

"They lied. They're planning going to kill you."

Granite turned away. Monk wasn't even sure he'd heard. He didn't know what else to do. He peered around the side to where Brand was placing the spent pistol in his cloak.

"Now," Brand said to his wife. " 'Tis time."

"It won't *work*," Collingswood said, this time loud enough for all to hear. He pulled his own pistol out. "The cave won't fit four. One of us has to stay."

The little girl, busily playing, said "Night, night" and patted the doll.

Brand looked at his daughter and then his wife. The

second pistol wavered in his hand. "Come here," he repeated to his wife.

She bent to gather her daughter.

"Not her," Brand said. "You."

Mrs. Brand made a terrified, choking noise. "Alfred, what are you saying?"

Granite met Monk's eye and cut his gaze first to the sea and then to the ship. He made the subtle motion of a fish with his hand, and Monk understood. He peered into the darkness, nodding. It was a terrible risk, but they had no other choice.

"Come," Brand said.

"Gather your child as tight as you can," Granite said under his breath to Mrs. Brand as he passed.

Shaking, Mrs. Brand lifted her daughter into her arms.

Brand ran toward his wife and tore the child away. Then he grabbed his wife and yanked.

Granite charged and swung. He connected with Brand's jaw and pulled Mrs. Brand back to him. The pistol spun toward the seam. Collingswood dived for it.

"Now!" Granite yelled, and Monk grabbed the girl. Granite shoved Mrs. Brand hard and jumped, and Monk flew out after them, headfirst, clutching the child, whose cry exploded in his ear.

He hit the water, as hard as rock, and the cold battered his lungs.

Hold the girl. Hold the girl.

He crushed her to his side, kicking hard to bring himself upward. Nothing in his life had ever seemed so important or so hard. It was like he was swimming in molasses, and there was nothing but heavy, smothering cold.

A lighter dark hovered above him. He pumped harder and harder. At last he popped above the surface, gulping air like it was grog. The girl cried. She lived!

A shot lit the night, sizzling past his ear before the water swallowed it in a gurgle. He jerked to the side, and Brand called, "You will pay for this, Captain! I will hunt you till my dying day, and you will pay!"

The night was pitch. Monk had a vague sense of the ship in the distance but nothing more. He saw nothing and could hear only the roar of the sea and the girl's terrified cries. He tucked her tightly under his arm and began to swim.

CHAPTER ONE

Once upon a time there was a beautiful mapmaker. She made maps for kings and travelers and landowners. She loved her work because making maps made her dream of the world outside her shop. Many men courted her, but none won her hand, for they loved her for her beauty, not her maps.
— The Tale of the Beautiful Mapmaker

BRAND O'MALLEY MAP COMPANY BOARDROOM,
PITTSBURGH, PRESENT DAY

"What is it men see in maps?" Joss O'Malley asked fondly as she watched her friend's four-year-old son, Peter, staring intently at a framed antique map from his not-quite-steady perch on the top of the credenza.

Diane Daltrey, the former chief financial officer of Brand O'Malley Map Company and Peter's mom, lifted her eyes for a moment from the quarterly cash flow statement over which she was poring. "Key to the past?"

Joss thought of her own fascination. "Hints of the unknown?"

"Does this have a Skull Island?" Peter said enthusiastically, scanning the hand-colored paper. "I want to fight Hook to the death!" He growled and thrust his light saber in the direction of the conference table. Marty, the map tech, who had just unfolded himself from plugging in two laptop projectors, ducked to avoid being skewered.

"Or perhaps something slightly less poetic. Speaking of which"—Di let her fingers come to rest on the calculator—"things aren't looking so good here."

"I know we're a little strapped for cash," Joss said, biting a nail, "but that's not so bad, right?"

"Right. How important is money?"

"I'm heading up to see Rogan. I need a number."

"*Another* loan?"

"It's not a loan exactly."

"Honey," Di said, "when a man's already agreed to the price for the company and you're going back to ask for more, that's either a loan or insanity. Peter, please take the highlighter out of your mouth. Your little brother was playing with it."

Peter, who had jumped off the credenza, sighed and, with a Day-Glo green pout, handed the marker to his toddler brother, coincidentally named Todd.

Joss frowned. "Should we—"

"Not poisonous," Diane said without looking up. "Well, not too poisonous."

Marty extracted the projector's power cord from the grip of the third Daltrey brother, a baby in a portable car seat at Diane's feet.

"Do you know if this next one's a boy, too?" Joss gestured to the Epcot Center–sized ball under Diane's sweater.

"I told my obstetrician I'd kill him if it was."

"I wasn't great at college biology, but I'm pretty sure he's not the one who decides."

Peter tugged Marty's pant leg. "Did you know if you suck enough highlighter your pee turns green?"

Marty pursed his lips thoughtfully. "Actually, I didn't know that."

"It's true. Green works best."

Di flipped the page of the report and, without looking up from the paper, deftly dropped a Tory Burch–clad foot on the leash attached to the two-year-old's ankle, bringing him to a dead halt just out of reach of the stapler on the table.

Joss, who had long ago decided running a barely surviving company was nothing compared to raising three boys under the age of five, said, "I really appreciate you coming in."

"Oh, please. If I didn't get out of the house sometimes, I'd go nuts."

"I can see where trips like this would be pretty relaxing."

"I'm almost ready," Marty said to Joss.

"Go ahead. Di can work the numbers while I take a look."

He flipped a switch and one of the projectors filled the far wall with a huge gray map of straight and curving streets, some blue, some yellow, some white, each with its own name printed in tiny Helvetica caps.

"Cool." Peter let the saber fall to his side.

"City?" Joss asked Marty. If she'd had more time, she'd be able to figure it out on her own. One of the benefits of owning one of the world's largest printed map companies was that every city felt like home.

"Philly."

"Ah. City of Brotherly Love."

Marty grimaced. "Yeah, well, unless brotherly love includes free use of intellectual property, we got a problem. Here's the map from our favorite competitor, Duncan Limited."

Marty clicked the On button on the adjoining projector. A second map, light blue instead of gray, and with a Garamond typeface, was projected directly over the first. It, too, was a map of Philly, and when he adjusted the width, height and area of the display, the streets lined up exactly with the first. Not a problem in itself, Joss thought. Street maps, after all, were supposed to give you a nearly accurate representation of the area in question, and even a competitor like Duncan Limited could be counted on to represent the area correctly. The problem occurred when a competitor didn't bother to do the survey work to identify the streets themselves, and there was one sure way to find that out.

Joss typed a few commands into her laptop. "I just checked our database. We have three trap streets in Philly."

"Yep," Monty said. "Cranberry Lane, Hastings Drive and Compass Rose Alley."

Compass Rose Alley. Joss smiled. That was so her mother. "And?"

"And"—he walked to the wall and touched different places on the Duncan Limited map—"we have Cranberry Lane, Hastings Drive and Compass Rose Alley."

They were called trap streets for a reason, Joss thought. You couldn't find them anywhere in Philly—not the real Philly, at least. They existed only on maps produced by Brand O'Malley, and they were put there to catch the plagiarist mapmakers of the world, who found it easier to copy someone else's maps than survey their own.

"Call our attorneys," Joss said.

Di held up a hand. "You can't afford an attorney—unless it's a pro bono one."

Joss sucked her lip and gave her friend a beseeching look.

Di rolled her eyes. "I'll talk to David." David, her husband, was a lawyer.

Rogan's admin stuck her head in the door. "Mr. Reynolds will be ready for you exactly at five."

If only I'm ready for him, Joss thought. She gave Di a look.

"I'm close. I'll have it by the time we're up there."

Joss grabbed Luke, the baby, and Todd-ler. Di tucked the report under her arm and kept her fingers running furiously over the calculator. Peter trailed behind, protecting the rear from pirates and Sith lords. If Joss couldn't make payroll, she'd have to lay people off. Di had been the first to go six months earlier, raising her hand to save the jobs of others. Now Joss paid for Di's time by the hour and used her only when she could afford to. Joss remembered a time when the world had seemed effortless to her. She'd lift a finger and a maid or driver or chef would rush to do her bidding. Now she worked ten-hour days, six-day weeks, to keep the company afloat. Had the world really been that easy, or was that just the sentimental nostalgia that all people had about their childhoods?

They reached the elevator, and Joss put down the car seat so she could lift Peter high enough to press the Up button.

She prayed Rogan would be amenable. He'd been looking only to buy her father's company, Brand Industries, and the name of her mother's—Brand O'Malley, the most famous name in maps—for use on his GPS devices, but he was a great guy and he'd understood Joss's desire to keep her twenty-three-person business, her only inheritance from her mother, running and under her control.

What Rogan paid for Brand Industries, though more than he should have, would still barely cover the debt her father had run up before his death three months earlier, so Joss would see no money from that, nor from his personal fortune, which he had thrown into his failing company's coffers in an attempt to save face among his peers in the business world. And her mother's much smaller company, which had been more practically run while her mother was alive but neglected under her father's subsequent guardianship, had spent the last few years teetering on the edge of insolvency.

Joss felt like her life since her mother's death, not long after Joss's eighth birthday, had been laid out strictly to ensure she'd be able to assume control of the mapmaking company when she was old enough. Despite being a lover of literature, she'd applied to and gotten into a math and science high school so she could study geography. In college, she'd pursued a dual major of business and geography while she worked full-time at Brand O'Malley, learning the ropes from the very able managers there. At twenty, even before she'd graduated, she'd accepted in practice what she'd already had in theory—the top executive role—and for the past three years, as the sales of paper maps dropped like a lead printing press, she'd been doing everything she could to keep these fine, hardworking people—and herself—employed.

The memories of yachts, stretch limos and happy times over salmon *en croûte* at midnight were long gone, having followed her mother, the family money and, finally, her father out of her life. And while losing the wealth had taught the very important lesson that she didn't need money to be happy, she wouldn't have minded, just once, being able to make payroll without getting on her hands and knees and praying to the lords of cash flow that the money would arrive.

"So, how are you going to effect this miraculous largesse?" Di asked.

"The loan, you mean?"

"Yes."

"Rogan owes me a favor."

"A fifty-thousand-dollar favor?"

"The number's *fifty* thousand?" Joss said, distressed.

"The number's at least fifty thousand. I'm still checking."

"Crap."

"Crap," Todd-ler repeated happily.

"Oops." Joss shot Di an apologetic look.

Di wiped something that looked like chocolate pudding off her arm. "Least of my worries."

The elevator arrived. Joss swung the car seat inside,

leaned down again to grab Peter and said hello to one of the Brand Industries salesmen who was inside.

"Forty-eight," she said, and pointed out the correct button. Peter poked it and leapt to the floor, pointing the saber with a sneer at his image in the elevator's mirrored walls. His mother, lost in her calculations, pressed a sheet of paper against the wall and made a notation. Todd-ler started to chew a piece of Joss's hair.

"Say," the salesman said to Joss, "I understand congratulations are in order. Next week, is it?"

Joss gazed down at the diamond sparking languidly on her finger, so large as to almost be worthy of a pirate's treasure chest. "Yep. No point in waiting. When it's right, it's right."

"Yes, and you'll need to hurry with your office," Di said to the man. "The caterer needs the space to set up the tables."

The salesman's brows shot up, and Joss waved away his worry. "I'm not having my reception in your office. Diane thinks that just because I'm getting married in the Founders Room upstairs, it's an all-business wedding."

"It's the conference room for the Sales Department," Di said curtly.

"It's a gorgeous space."

"Now, should we all wear business suits," Di asked, "or is that just you?"

Joss sighed. "It's not a business suit. It's a skirt."

Di gave her a look.

"Okay, a business skirt—but it's Chanel!"

Joss knew Di didn't understand why she was, as Di liked to say, running her wedding "like the fourth-quarter employee recognition event." Joss couldn't explain. Everything in her life since she could remember had been done for expediency. It just didn't feel right to have anything except a small ceremony, in her favorite space at her dad's company—well, her dad's former company— followed by a quiet dinner in the dining room of the William Penn Hotel, where her mother had taken her for tea each Christmas when she was a little girl.

Di rolled her eyes. "I'm certain Coco didn't have it in mind for a bride."

Joss exhaled. It was going to be a long week. Tomorrow was her bachelorette party. Thursday was the party her soon-to-be mother-in-law was throwing for the large number of friends and relatives who couldn't be accommodated at the ceremony. Friday Joss left for the Academic Supply Show in Las Vegas. She'd fly back on Monday, just in time for Tuesday's wedding. Other than the ceremony itself, her mother-in-law was taking care of everything, which suited Joss perfectly. All the better for Joss to focus on the far more concerning issue of making payroll.

The elevator stopped at 36 and the salesman got off. Peter punctuated the exit with a saber flourish. "Will I get to see your wedding?" he asked. "Mommy says I can only come if I dress like the mail delivery guy."

"Your mommy's hilarious. And yes, you know I couldn't get married without you, pal. I'm counting on you to give me away."

She returned her thoughts to the problem at hand. *Fifty big ones. At least fifty big ones.*

"I think I'm going to have to resort to something more

than a favor for fifty thousand." Joss gazed at herself in the mirror and unbuttoned the top button of her blouse. "I'm going to have to try a little more—"

She found herself gazing into Peter's curious eyes.

"A little more what, Aunt Joss?"

Di gave her an interested sidelong glance; Todd-ler thrust his fingers into her bra.

"A little more hard work, Peter. That's what being a grown-up is all about." She rewarded Di with a tiny tongue stick-out and loosened Todd-ler's grip on the tender flesh.

"Exactly how *hard* is this work going to be?" Di asked.

"Jeez Louise, I'm hardly going to—" Peter's gaze shot right to Joss's face. *What is it with kids these days?* "I'm not going to work so hard I'll regret it."

"Good to hear," Di said. "Girls who work that hard can get a reputation."

Peter's gaze narrowed and slid between his mother and Joss.

"But let's face it," Joss said, "I'll do whatever it takes." She thought of Marty and his diabetes and the security guard with her kid on dialysis.

The jesting smile left Di's face, replaced with a brow raise. "Really?"

"Really. It's not like I haven't gotten hints he'd be amenable."

"I know, but . . . really?"

"It seems a small price, if you know what I mean."

"You're not going to . . ." Di gave her a look to fill in the missing word.

"Oh, for heaven's sake, no. I'm going to need far less artillery than that."

The door opened on 48, and they trooped out. Part of the deal for the Brand O'Malley name was these offices would go to Rogan's company when the papers were signed next month. He'd already taken over the chairman's office. Some of the people there, though, still worked for her.

"Howdy, Joss."

"Afternoon," she said to LaWren, the security guard. "How's Darryl?"

"Doin' good," she said. "We've got him on home dialysis now."

"Oh, that's great. Did he like the DVD I sent?"

"*Prisoner of Azkaban*? Oh yeah."

"Loved the Marauder's Map. We got to get ourselves into *that* business, eh?"

LaWren laughed.

Rogan's admin, Pat, a prim, thin-lipped woman who had been with Brand Industries since the dawn of time, had always reminded Joss of Miss Gulch, the mean neighbor who took Toto from Dorothy. Pat, however, scared Joss even more than her cinematic counterpart.

Pat frowned at the bedraggled group and saved a particularly sharp look for Joss. "It's after five."

"I can't help but notice Rogan is not actually in his office, so I'm thinking my lateness isn't going to be a problem."

"He'll be here soon. The video conference with the Sydney office went long. But it's better if you're here when he arrives."

Of course it is.

Joss gestured the group inside.

"Will the children—"

"Yes. Part of the analytics team."

Di sunk into the long couch, still working on the numbers, and Joss gazed out at the gorgeous view that used to be hers, especially the regally old-fashioned Gulf Tower with its brightly lit stepped crown modeled on the Mausoleum at Halicarnassus. Even more kitschy was the quaint weather beacon on top, which glowed red for clear weather and blue for precipitation, and blinked to signal a coming change. Winter in Pittsburgh was not always fun, but when one could view it against a twilight sky with the Gulf Tower beacon shining red, it all seemed worthwhile.

Peter jumped immediately into Rogan's chair and began to play with the phone.

"Er, maybe not, pal." Joss put Todd and the baby onto the thick Aubusson rug and straightened.

Peter collapsed with a disheartened sigh into the cushioned leather.

"Say, what's up with the Band-Aid?" Joss asked, trying to cheer him. She'd just noticed the Spider-Man bandage wrapped around his finger.

"Confection, Mom says."

Joss looked at Di.

"Infection," Di corrected. "You're wearing a Band-Aid because you cut your finger playing Teenage Mutant Ninja Turtles in the koi pond, and it swelled up big and red. Remember?"

"Oh yeah." He smiled a dreamy, dimpled smile. "Really cool pus."

Joss heard Rogan's voice in the corridor. "Oops."

Di nodded. "I've got it. One more second."

Rogan strode in, an impossibly handsome man with soft blond waves and piercing blue eyes that cut to the bones of any business deal. He grinned when he saw the extent of his welcoming party.

"Hey," he said to Peter, and nodded at Di. "Good to see you. Are we—"

"Nope." Di struggled to her feet. "We're on our way out." She handed the cash flow statement to Joss, swept Todd and the car seat into her arms and signaled to Peter to follow. Then she gave Joss a quick peck. "I'll see you tomorrow, eh?"

"But, the number . . ."

Di gazed pointedly at the report in Joss's hand, where Joss spotted a hastily scribbled note.

"C'mon, troops," Di said. "Let's pull out." She made a rallying motion with her hand and gave Joss a small wave. "Don't work too hard."

CHAPTER TWO

Joss glanced at the cash flow statement. *$63K,* the scribble read. *This may be the time to go all the way.*

Oh, fudge.

"Hey," Rogan said cheerily. "What's up?"

"I'm here with a request."

"Oh." He nodded, replacing the smile with a more guarded look, and made his way to the desk.

She stared at the weather beacon, gathering her courage. The red glow began to pulse. *A change is coming, that's for sure.* "I need another loan."

"Oh, Joss." The words bloomed with disappointment, and he sunk into the chair.

"I—I know it's a lot to ask."

"How much?"

"But we have a big order from the California school system coming in next month, which is usually one of our biggest of the year, and I know we'll be okay after that."

He gazed at the keyboard in front of him, more, she thought, out of embarrassment for her than anything else. He'd insisted she stay on to run the map company, and Joss wondered if he regretted his decision. "How much?" he asked.

She took a breath. "Sixty-three thousand."

He leaned forward, elbows on desk, fingers laced, and ran his thumbs back and forth across his lips, considering.

"I wonder," he said softly, "if you should think about closing."

"No," she said firmly. "We'll be fine once this quarter is over."

"I know you want to honor your mother, but I really think there's a way through Brand Industries' acquisition of the Brand O'Malley name that—"

"No. Please. The company stays open. I'm willing to discuss how."

He sighed. "I don't think I can do this. With all due respect, it's a bad bet, and I couldn't sell the board on it. Too hard."

Joss met his eyes and smiled. Pleading was not sexy. Being confident and direct with a business-person-to-business-person frankness—*that* was sexy.

"I'd like you to think about it." She'd made it a point this morning to put on her sexiest bra. It was a demi in beige and blue that lifted her breasts up like two scoops of French vanilla ice cream and ended just before her nipples began. Rogan was a very old-fashioned guy—the big surprise when she'd first met him. A little flash of ice cream. Perhaps a peek at some unskirted thigh. He'd be toast. The board would be hard, but let's face it, he'd be harder.

That was about the one advantage women had in the business world. Men didn't always think with their frontal lobes. Anyone who'd ever dated a man knew it.

And when the thought process did its little dance out the frontal lobes and over to the basal ganglia, it left a trail of mush in its wake.

She put the cash flow statement and her phone on the edge of Rogan's desk, stood up and leaned over to examine his desk clock. Waaay over. It was an ugly, ornate thing he's said his old girlfriend, Daphne, had gotten him. It managed to be both gaudily antique and tethered by a power cord—the worst of both worlds. She could feel herself shaking.

She had never done this before. It wasn't her operating style. But if this was all it took to keep the company afloat, in the overall scheme of things, it wasn't too much to ask. Business was business. Some people had the marbles. Some people wanted the marbles. Unless you could think of a way to swipe some marbles for yourself, you wouldn't get to play.

She could hear the *tick tick tick,* and even though she wasn't looking, she could feel his gaze reach all the way to her navel. The tenor of the room changed, as did the cadence of his breathing.

"I think," she said, giving him a smile, "you can convince them."

He had the good sense to blush. Rather a charming thing, if you thought about it. The little spots of color on his cheeks were the first step in the mush process.

"I-I could probably try to convince them."

Could you, now? Joss examined the clock for another long moment, then unbent and dropped in her seat.

"But . . ."

"But?" She blinked sweetly.

"But," he said, leaning forward in earnest, "it seems to me that for sixty-three thousand dollars I could expect a little more."

"What?"

"Open your blouse."

He said it in the same tone as if he'd said, "Hand me the scissors," or "Let's review the Ryneman numbers." Joss had to replay it in her head to ensure she'd heard it right.

"I-I—"

"I'd be risking my reputation," he said convivially. "Why shouldn't you risk yours?"

Risk and reward. The seesaw of business. There was a certain primitive poetry to it. At this point her task was to find the balance point. Her father, while never the best of role models, had schooled her well on this. "It's not personal," he'd said. "It's a game. And unless you can remove your emotion from the battle, you're never going to win." Of course, removing emotion was one thing. Removing one's blouse was quite another.

When she shifted, the diamond on her finger glinted and she nearly said no, but then she spotted her mother's beloved map—the one that had started it all—on the wall where it had hung for twenty years. Her mother had worked so hard for so long to get Brand O'Malley off the ground. She'd poured her heart and then her health into it, and had endured a marriage that appeared, at least to Joss, to be far from ideal. Joss loved maps, and she'd worked hard to master the business behind them. She could almost hear her mother's sigh of happiness whenever she ran her fingers over a newly printed one. Was her mother's dream for this company going to die with

Joss? No effing way. Time to put her business acumen to work.

She lifted her trembling hand and loosened the buttons.

"And open, please," he said.

"Your admin is sitting outside."

He pressed a button on his phone. "Pat?"

"Yes, Mr. Reynolds?"

"Close the door, will you. I don't want to be disturbed."

Joss sat frozen while Pat stepped into the office behind her, no doubt thinking the meeting was about liabilities and outcomes, which, come to think of it, wasn't far from the truth. Pat closed the door. Rogan leaned back in his chair.

Joss had at least imagined this possibility. It would have been foolish to entertain this strategy without having done so. But she'd been so certain Rogan would stop at a certain, albeit not purely innocent, level of flirtation.

She spread the silk.

His irises widened. It was a biological effect he couldn't hide no matter how skilled he was—or perhaps one might say *one* of the biological effects. The trick was going to be teasing that effect as far as it would go under her control without triggering a biological apocalypse. She was reminded of the men about to set off the first experimental atomic explosion in 1945 who were "pretty certain" it wouldn't destroy the earth's entire atmosphere.

She wondered about Rogan's next move. She also wondered if anyone in the Gulf Tower had binoculars.

He gave her a crooked smile and said, "Are you trying to seduce me?"

"No, actually. I'm trying to meet payroll."

"It's a pretty effective strategy."

"I would hope so."

Her cell vibrated. The sound of a text. She cut her gaze to the display. It was from Di. R U DOING IT?

Rogan pointed to the clasp between her breasts a tiny pearl dangled from. "Does that little thingy there open it?"

"It does."

"Would you mind . . . ?"

More than life itself. But this was the balance point. "I wouldn't," she said, leaning slightly forward, "but it seems to me that's something you'd rather do yourself."

He made a dry, choking noise.

"And all it takes," she said, "is a quick call to Charlie." Charlie was the president of the Brand Industries board. "Just to let him know the plan."

This was it. If he talked to Charlie, he'd be committed. Rogan licked his lips.

"May I?" He gestured to the clasp with an earnest look in his eye. "Just a touch?"

Bless his mother. He'd been raised to be polite. He'd once told Joss he'd attended etiquette classes throughout grade school. She pulled her chair closer to the desk and nodded.

He brought his hand to the metalwork, slipping his forefinger under the clasp and letting his thumb brush the swaying pearl. He tugged slightly, measuring the tension.

"Oh, Lord," he whispered.

The electricity in his touch surprised her. She breathed in the sandalwood on his skin.

"Charlie," she reminded him, though the way her voice faltered, she wondered if he understood.

"Right." He picked up his cell and pressed a couple buttons. Then his eyebrows went up and he hit the keyboard quickly. "Oops. Wrong number." He made a nervous laugh.

Joss was glad to see he was nervous, too. This wasn't exactly a stroll through the Nordstrom handbag department for her.

He tried the call again and held up a relieved finger. "Ringing."

She nodded and looked into the twilight. The weather beacon flash had changed to something else—a tiny shower of sparks. She wondered if the building manager knew he had a problem.

Rogan leaned forward. "Charlie— Oh." He put his hand over the receiver. "Voice mail."

She pursed her lips.

"Charlie, it's Rogan," he said. "I, ah, need to run a quick Brand O'Malley situation by you. I know the acquisition price has been agreed on, but a few things have come up. There's a request on the table for sixty-three more in the form of a thirty-day loan. Give me your thoughts." He hit the End button and put the phone down.

She crossed her arms, carefully pulling the flaps of her blouse closed. "We've got a problem."

"What?" The first hint of desperation broke in his voice. "I did it."

"You forgot something. Your support." Without Rogan's enthusiastic blessing of the plan, all Charlie had to do was say no. She began to button.

"Wait."

She stopped.

"The thing is, it's hard to be a cheerleader for something I don't fully support."

"Oh dear. I wouldn't want anything to be hard for you."

She came around the table, seated herself on the desk and leaned back on her palms. The flaps slipped farther apart.

He closed his eyes. Evidently, he'd heard of the "remove emotion" trick, too. "Does the deal include touch?"

She knew he didn't mean the acquisition. "Um . . ." She swallowed. This was certainly more than she'd bargained for. She could see an employee of some nameless law firm or accountant's office gazing abstractedly out a Gulf Tower window. "Can you be more specific?"

He pursed his lips, considering. "Palms, fingers, cheek and lips."

Oh. My. God.

"Palms, yes," she said at last. "The rest, no."

"Just palms, huh?" His cell started to vibrate, and he looked at the display. "It's Charlie. I have to tell you, I'm not feeling very enthusiastic."

The phone buzzed, paused and buzzed again. He lifted his shoulders in a question.

"Palms and cheek," she offered.

The third buzz and then the fourth.

"Fine," she said. "Palms, cheek and a single kiss."

"Nip," he corrected, and picked up the phone. "Charlie. Hi. You got my message?" He gestured for her to open her blouse. "It might inspire me," he whispered. "Yeah.

It's a short-term thing. Thirty days, paid in full. How do I feel?" He lifted a brow in Joss's direction, waiting, and with a private growl, she reopened the flaps of fabric. "Well, sales are improving. There've been a couple very nice peaks today." He gave her a broad smile. "And there's a big order coming in—a very big one, in fact. So, overall, I'm feeling pretty good about it."

Bingo.

While he wrapped up the conversation, Joss picked up her phone and thumbed a reply to Di. *Not at all. Just a little lingerie action. Whew!*

Rogan laid down his cell.

"Nice work," Joss said. "But the only 'big order' coming in is the one from the California school system, my friend."

"We'll see." He unfolded himself from the chair.

She braced herself.

He drew a finger from her belly to her sternum and flicked the pearl.

She gasped. It was as if all the current in the room were being driven through that single digit.

"I would love to get you out of all this," he said.

She snorted.

He brushed the silk off her shoulders. It slipped like a breath of air down her bare skin. He brought his hands to the clasp and unlocked it. The fabric, released from its binding, spread slowly, and he traced the soft rise below.

She inhaled sharply and fought to distract herself by admiring his patience. He seemed to understand the enhanced value of a delayed reward. Unhappily for him, it would be the key to her victory.

"Oh, baby," he said. "Have I ever told you how much I enjoy looking at your breasts?"

"Classy. Does that work on all the g—"

He pushed the wire and lace aside, and Joss's ability to speak vanished.

Remove the emotion.

"They're magnificent," he said.

"Thank you."

He stood up, opened her knees and inserted himself carefully between them. His suit was the finest Italian wool, but even Armani couldn't have planned for the tailoring challenge Rogan was suddenly facing.

Slowly, he brought his palms over the tips of her nipples. Back and forth, he moved. Just the barest touch. A ball of heat rose between her legs. *Biology,* she told herself. *Just biology.*

He tucked her hands behind her again, palms on the desk. Her breasts poked skyward. He brought his face to a nipple, and rubbed his bristled cheek across it. *This,* she thought nervously, *is how you lose the earth's atmosphere.*

He inched his hips closer, and when he took a nipple in his teeth, she arched automatically. If she weren't careful, that big order would be coming in exactly as he planned.

The weather beacon was throwing a multihued shower now, like the Northern Lights, or that scene in *The Natural.* It was the strangest damn thing. Of course, this wasn't exactly the most normal of nights, she thought as Rogan made a final lap. She considered his easy blond waves. *How many women have found themselves in this position with you, Golden Boy?*

"I want more," he said.

"I'm getting that impression. There's only one problem." She unwrapped her leg and locked it carefully across its mate. "We've finished the deal. Which isn't to say we might not play again sometime." Though she sincerely hoped not. Not this game, at least. She reached for her bra.

"Hold on. Let's think this through."

Think? She almost laughed. "Deal's done, Rogan."

"Please. Listen. You're spread out on my desk like this and still out of reach?" He lowered his voice. "I'm going to die if I don't have you. Right here. Right now."

"Is that the man who's acquiring my company talking?" She lowered herself to an elbow and regarded him closely. "Or my fiancé?"

His eyes shifted left and right. He knew he had stumbled into a trap, even if he couldn't quite see it.

"I-I put that ring on your finger."

"Indeed you did." She held it up to the light, letting all three glorious, white-hot carats sparkle. "Do you suppose they make nipple rings to match?"

He whimpered. "I just think that buys me an all-access pass."

"It does. But not until our wedding, my love. It's only another week. Think about it. Brandy, some nice wide bed in some exotic location you haven't yet revealed. No water."

"Exotic, yes," he said, still transfixed "Water, no."

"Definitely no water. Maybe a mountain in Switzerland or the Taj Mahal or Sydney—"

"I'm pretty sure there's water with that last one."

"—or Sydney inland. Nowhere near the ocean, because you'd rather have me treading the sheets than scared out of my wits."

"I take it snorkeling in Saint Bart's is out?"

"And it's not like you've been suffering," she went on. "You've gotten everywhere you wanted to go backstage—you've drunk the champagne, eaten the M&M's and hung out with the roadies. But if you want to get in the dressing room and party with the rock star, you're gonna have to wait."

"But I thought it was just a lark. You know, 'It's been such a whirlwind courtship, wouldn't it be fun if we waited to consummate it till our wedding night? It's only six weeks from now'—that sort of thing?"

"And?"

"I'm just so ready." He laced his fingers as if in supplication. "And so hard."

"This is business, Reynolds. Forget the personal side. Stick to the deal."

"Deal. Right." With obvious effort, he lowered himself into the chair.

She picked herself up and reclasped the bra. She hoped she still had a blazer in her office closet, because her nipples were going to be stiff for a week. Next problem to solve: ensuring the California order came in. That and shoes for the ceremony. She'd head to Sales next.

"I'm off." She hopped onto the floor, jarring the tender flesh.

He stood when she did. "Oh. One thing."

"What?" Cripes, she could probably press the elevator button with one of these things.

He took a step and accidentally kicked something across the room. It was Peter's light saber.

"Uh-oh," he said. "Yours?"

"Peter's, I think. I'll get it back to him." She smiled. She didn't need a light saber. Only a demi-bra and low morals.

He retrieved the weapon and leaned it against the wall.

"What I was saying was, I'm assuming the odds are pretty high you'll be able to pay back the loan, right?"

"Well . . . sure. I mean, what are you asking?" She wished she could put off thinking about next month's problems until next month, especially after what she'd just done to resolve this month's.

"What are the odds—I mean, realistically—that you will, A, have the money to pay this back, and B, not need more?"

She grabbed the cash flow statement. "High." The business world ran on lies. Ask anyone on Wall Street.

Rogan slouched against the desk, hands in his pockets, and gave her a gentle smile. "That's good. Because next month, the deal won't be quite the same."

Something in his tone made the hairs on her neck jump to attention. "Meaning what?"

"Meaning that if you come to me next month and for any reason can't pay back that sixty-three grand, the terms are going to become somewhat less attractive."

"How somewhat?"

He leaned toward her ear and described, in detail, the changes. Two items involved his Maserati. One, a speakerphone. And a fourth, Joss thought, wide-eyed, an act so technically challenging as to be impossible without guy wires and a spotter. So much for the etiquette lessons.

"But," he said cordially, "I would be willing to forgive the loan."

She exhaled relieved. "Of course you would. You're my fiancé."

He gave her an uncompromising look.

"But—"

"Business, Joss. Forget the personal side."

"C'mon. I mean, if I were in a little jam . . ."

The side of his mouth rose on the last word.

"Rogan."

He tapped a finger on the speakerphone absently. "As I said, I'm willing to forgive it. Completely. No loan. Nothing that hits the balance sheet at all. A gift. My own personal contribution to Brand O'Malley. And I'll make it a hundred—a hundred and a quarter—to cover anything else you may have forgotten. I mean, I was planning to give you a wedding present anyhow, and I know you well enough to know you'd rather have cash flow than a bracelet to match that ring."

A hundred and twenty-five thousand dollars. She let herself imagine for an instant what it would feel like to have the burden of meeting payroll for a few months lifted from her shoulders. She could almost feel the muscles in her back unkinking.

"Sounds too good to be true."

"It depends how you define 'good.'" He tossed a look in the direction of his couch.

Oh.

This is where the rubber hits the road, she thought. A real rubber. She tried to look at the situation objectively. A hundred and twenty-five thousand to clear the company's debt in exchange for something she was going to enjoy anyway. She also considered the trouble, sexual and otherwise, she'd be in a month from now if she couldn't pay back Brand Industries. She gazed at the speakerphone and thought about the front seat of his Maserati. Her father used to say, "A good manager makes decisions quickly. If they're right, so much the better."

"Terms?" she asked.

He chuckled. "Twenty minutes. Whatever I want."

A hundred and a quarter for twenty minutes. That was a lot of money, even if the prize was her. "You really think I'm going to be worth it?"

"A steal at twice the price."

She smiled. Gotta love that.

"And no speakerphone?"

"No speakerphone."

She shifted her weight. Her plan to wait to have traditional intercourse with him, that supposed jewel in the crown of all sexual joinings, had been a lark, just as he'd said. A special approach for the man she meant to be her husband. They were engaged. Hell, she'd even moved into his place. They'd done everything else imaginable and had no end of fun doing it. Nonetheless, there was a part of her that wished they could wait. It was only another week. But the realities of salaries, dialysis, diabetes and cash flow, not to mention her own driving curiosity about Rogan's prowess in that last unconquered area of delight, tipped the scales.

She took a deep breath. "I accept."

He reached for his belt buckle.

Despite the logic of the decision, sweat broke out on her palms. "You sure you wanna to do this?"

"Yes." He led her toward the couch.

"Only a week more."

"No."

"You've waited this long. What's a week more?"

"About seventeen cold showers." He gave her a long, deep kiss.

With a brush of a finger, the blouse fell off her shoulders and he unclasped the bra. He brought his mouth low and suckled. Her breath caught. He had an amazing tongue. When he lifted his head to admire his work, the air stiffened her flesh. He winced with desire.

"Twenty minutes? Good Lord, I hope I can last two," he said, and his words lit a lightbulb in her head. She could preserve their wedding night *and* satisfy his desire. What did Mick Jagger say? "You can't always get what you want?" Poor Rogan; at least he'd get what he needed.

She unbuckled his belt and reached for his fly. His pants dropped to the floor, followed by his shorts and his fiancée.

"Let me check that order," she said.

He groaned. "No."

"There might be a problem, of course, but if I give you a hand with it . . ."

"No, please. No hand— Oh, God!" His eyes fluttered shut.

"Are you sure Pat's going to obey your 'no interruptions' request?"

"Please don't mention Pat now."

She pressed herself against him and let her hand find

the right rhythm. It was like hypnotizing a chicken, only without drawing a line. The trick would be keeping any thinking he'd be doing down in the hormone-laden brain stem and out of that logical, reasoning cerebral cortex. He needed to stay hypnotized, happy and dumb.

Somewhere on his desk, a speaker squawked to life. "Mr. Reynolds?"

Crap with a capital K*!*

"Y-yes, Pat?"

Brain stem, here I come! She brought her mouth to where her hand had been.

"I'm sorry to disturb you," Pat said, "but Marketing called. Do you remember the Mitchell acquisition?"

"Um . . . um . . . vaguely." He had his palms over his eyes, pressing hard, like he was fighting a brain freeze.

"Midsize asset? Closely held?"

"Closely held." His hands moved haltingly from his head to Joss's hair as he fought to clear the fog.

"Marketing wants to know if you want to use a push-pull on this one."

"Oh, God, yes."

"Yes?"

"No. I mean yes. I mean I don't know yet."

"Oh, and Vince thinks we should have received a one-time benefit to GAAP income of seventy-eight million after the acquisition because the previous accrual exceeded our current estimate of liability. Is that right and should I let Finance know?"

At this point, Rogan had about as much chance of being able to answer that as he did of landing a space shuttle. His response was a dry gurgle.

"Mr. Reynolds?"

"Can you"—he sucked in a lungful of air—"handle it?"

"No problem," Joss said, and added a brisk trombone motion.

Rogan grabbed the wall for support. "No, don't handle it!"

"Don't handle it, sir?" Pat said. "Or handle it? I'm confused."

"Uh . . . uh . . ."

"I've got the report right here. I could show you—"

"*No!* Just . . . take . . . to . . . Finance . . . report . . . GAAP . . . handle." The effort was clearly overwhelming. He looked like he might begin to cry.

"You want me to handle it with Finance?" Pat said, clearly befuddled.

"Yes, please!"

"Do you mind if I just head home from there?"

"No. No. *Go.*"

Joss, who had no real musical ability, found herself moving easily from trombone to harmonica.

Pat said, "You're all taken care of?"

He let out a long, strangled cry that ended in an affirmative squeak.

Pat clicked off.

"No, no, no," he croaked, but he was clawing at the air like a lobster in a tank. "Not like this."

"Li' wha'?" Joss gazed up innocently.

He scrunched his face and curled his arms, as if he were summoning the spirit of the Hulk or perhaps pulling himself inside out face-first. With a grunt worthy of a lumberjack, he pushed her shoulders back and freed himself.

"Tchhhhhhhhhhhhhk-k-k." He gasped.

Oh, God, the cerebral cortex has risen from the dead! She was in big trouble.

He swung in a circle, dazed, making him look a little bit like a Geiger counter having a run-in with high-grade uranium.

She considered making a dash for it and hiding out until Tuesday, but it would only delay the inevitable; and, in any case, she didn't see her bra or blouse anymore, which would make for an awkward interlude on the elevator.

He swept her off the floor and into his arms. "Desk," he demanded hoarsely.

Your own fault, sister, she thought, clinging tightly as he hobbled wildly across the room. Supercharge him like that, and who knows what's going to strike his fancy. She was lucky she wasn't going to be smooshed against his window, performing an unorthodox game of office charades for the accountants across the across.

Rogan dropped her in front of the monitor. She shifted her hips to get them off what had to be either a torturer's mace or Brand Industries' famed Innovation Star award. This was going to be a pretty innovative initiative.

Somewhere, maybe next to the cash flow statement, wherever that was, her phone vibrated with an incoming text. Rogan didn't seem to be inclined to let her get it. He lifted her legs and repositioned her closer to him, knocking a stack of annual reports and the clock to the floor with a crash.

"Condom," she commanded.

"Not likely." Reaching around her skirt, he found her zipper and undid it. The skirt went the way of the reports. Only a thin pair of panties stood between her and the red zone.

He gazed at his handiwork. "Oh my God. This is the most awe-inspiring sight. Like Angkor Wat and Megan Fox rolled into one." He grabbed his iPhone.

"What are you doing?"

"Nothing." He held the phone at arm's length and pointed it at her.

"Rogan." She flung her arms across her chest.

"Just checking my call log. I think I might have missed something."

"You know how I feel about photos."

"You're right." He lowered the phone, contrite. "I shouldn't expect you to be as adventurous as Daphne. It's unfair to you and unfair to her."

"Daphne did this?" Daphne had breasts the size of Strawberry Whoppers and a chin that receded so far, it had to follow her in a cab.

"Everyone's different, of course. I respect your boundaries."

Joss hoisted herself up on her elbows, twisted one hip toward him and thrust her shoulders back. "Did she look like this?"

"Jesus." His mouth fell so far open, it looked like he was prepping for a root canal.

"That's it," she declared after he had come to and snapped. "And no transmissions."

"Well, maybe just the one. Small but, oh, so powerful." He reached for the panties.

Every touch reminded Joss how long she'd waited for this and how much she wanted it. "If we do this now, how can I be sure you'll still be interested on our wedding night?"

"Make it good."

A commotion rose on the other side of the door, and Joss immediately recognized the voice.

"Peter!" Diane shouted. "Don't open that without—"

The door banged open. "Aunt Joss *is* still here. There's her shirt."

"—knocking."

Joss did a barrel roll and dove under the desk. Rogan, attempting both to protect Joss and cover himself, took a step and caught his pants-hobbled feet in the cord for the clock, which he managed to kick into the wall, where it exploded into a constellation of gears and wood. Then he spun in a circle and landed flat on his back, shirttails over his face, with a thud that rocked the room.

Peter, unfazed, said, "I told you I left my saber here, Mommy. And look. I think Uncle Rogan needs a Band-Aid, too."

CHAPTER THREE

One day, an old man came to the shop of the beautiful mapmaker. He did not try to court her. He was in love with a widow in the town. He had brought many baskets of gold with him so that he could convince the widow to marry him. The mapmaker told him love cannot be bought. She said he needed to make the widow love him for himself. If he couldn't, money wouldn't matter. The old man didn't believe her. He told her he would hide his gold to keep it safe until he was ready for it, and he wanted her to make a map so that he would not forget where he'd hidden it.

—The Tale of the Beautiful Mapmaker

That was certainly a close one.

Joss giggled. *But it all turned out in the end, just like it did for the heroines in fairy tales—well, slightly adult fairy tales.* She buttoned her collar higher and hurried through the brisk November night across the crosswalk at Grant and Seventh, feeling the joyous warmth of lasciviousness on her cheeks. Rogan hadn't gotten what he wanted, nor even exactly what he needed, but she could rectify that tonight with something from her bag of tricks, and he had agreed—

reluctantly—to wait until their wedding night for the rest.

She needed to grab a bite before heading back for a slog through next year's product plans. Rogan was off to dinner with the owner of another potential acquisition. She hoped whoever it was had taken a negotiation class.

She had taken only a few steps south when she remembered the weather beacon. She was just about to turn back toward Seventh when a trail of sparks, like the final embers of fireworks, rained down over her head. Unlike fireworks, however, there was no heat or sizzle, and they were every color of the rainbow. When they hit the ground, they bounced like jacks, skittering over the sidewalk and street, scattering their tiny specks of luminescence.

Craning her head in both directions, Joss looked to see if anyone else was seeing this, but none of the other evening commuters seemed to care or even notice. One spark hit her, and she jumped, but it didn't hurt or burn. It sort of hummed, like a vibrating raindrop.

This is weird. She wondered if it was a chemical leak of some sort, but it was just so . . . pretty.

The majority of the sparks seemed to be falling farther down Grant. Curious, she followed them, and as she passed a narrow alleyway that angled off the main street, hardly wide enough to hold a car, she saw the sparks were at least twice as thick there.

She gazed down the two-block-long passageway. She'd never really paid it much attention before. It ran from the old Bell of Pennsylvania building past a handful of ancient buildings that faced the alley, ending at a church. The alley was deserted but lit, and the lights of the buildings spilled onto the pavement. As soon as she turned, the sounds of traffic faded. There was a quaint simplicity to the passageway—the lack of cars, she supposed, although the old buildings on it and the openwork metal spire that rose above it like a silent guardian gave it a sort of urban Currier & Ives feel.

The humming grew louder. Not electric. Beelike. A happy, inviting hum.

She reached William Penn Place, the first street the alley intersected, and the sparks and humming stopped. She could see them behind her, where she'd already walked, and farther on, where the alley picked up again across the road.

Even more curious, she crossed William Penn and continued. As soon as she stepped into the alley again, the sparks rained down, only so thick it was as bright as a spring afternoon. Then she noticed the sparks weren't falling to the ground here. They were accumulating like snow on a huge domelike thing that curved over the buildings along this block. Only the dome couldn't be seen, or, rather, it could be seen, but only because the sparks piled on top of it outlined its shape, which otherwise would have been invisible to her.

Her curiosity turned to stunned amazement. This was beyond out of the ordinary. This was—

All at once, the dome stretched like an enormous lens, turning her view of the building behind it, a little shop with a sign that read TOM JAMES, TAILOR, into something you'd see in a fun house mirror. Then, as fast as the dome had stretched, it snapped back, and Joss jumped, her heart thumping.

The thing seemed to be breathing—or seething. She didn't know which.

The sparks fell faster and glowed brighter. There was the smell of something—the ocean?—in the air. She looked at the building within the dome's confines.

Redbrick and black-shuttered with a peaked-roof, the three-storey shop was definitely from another time. It looked like it should be the home of Arthur Clennam or Scrooge or some other Dickens character. She'd heard Di talk about it before. It was one of the oldest buildings in Pittsburgh. It looked totally out of place in the middle of a downtown full of skyscrapers.

She took a step closer and then another, as close as she dared to the dome's edge. At the third step, the road jerked under her feet, and her head—or was it her whole body?—started to spin. She saw snatches of things she didn't understand—a stormy sea, a captain on an ancient sailing ship, a woman with her back to Joss poring over a map and even Joss herself, just a moment earlier, standing at the head of alley, before she'd entered.

Terrified, she struggled to find her footing, but just as she found a steady surface the world exploded into crushing supernova of light and noise, and she was flung backward.

The next thing she sensed, though barely, was her head smacking the cold street and the noise that hammered at her ears in the middle of this spinning, swirling storm. A pair of strong arms lifted her. She fought them, but they were unconquerable. They pulled her out of the swirling chaos, and a voice, deep and steady, said, "Spirit. I like that. A bit knocked about, but you'll be fine." With those words in her head and those arms around her, she stopped the fight and let the thickness fall over her.

CHAPTER FOUR

PITTSBURGH, PRESENT DAY

"Is she a spy?" Fiona, ever ready for a scrap, stumbled to her feet amid the fading sparks and reached for her dagger. "Belkin and his foolish assurances. Of course, there are going to be others after the map."

Hugh Hawksmoor, who was shaking off his own confusion from the jarring arrival in the future, examined the slim, fine-boned young woman in his arms with her simple wool coat, unadorned gray skirts and clean but modest bodice. He pushed a lock of chestnut hair from her face. "For God's sake, Fiona. She looks like a parson's wife. I hardly think we need to worry." Nonetheless, there was something intriguing about the spots of color on those aristocratic cheeks and the scent of plum and cloves on her flushed skin. At what had she been laboring? he wondered.

A horn tooted, and Hugh turned to see not a man with an instrument but metal conveyances with no horses racing to and fro on the cross street below. But before Hugh had time to digest this, Nathaniel called, "Look, it's a shop of some sort." He stood at the closest doorway, pointing to the GOING OUT OF BUSINESS sign in the dusty window of the redbrick building. "Abandoned, by the look of it." He met Hugh's eye. After a decade in his captain's service, Nathaniel Fallon knew his thoughts well. Hugh nodded, and Nathaniel lifted his beefy leg and kicked open the door.

"Leave her." Fiona resheathed her weapon.

Hugh carried the dazed woman from under the covered walkway and leaned her carefully against an alley wall. "I realize you are funding this expedition," he said, unfolding himself with a growl, "but I handle strategy and logistics. If there are commands to be given, 'tis my job, not yours. That's the deal we made."

Fiona buried her look of pique in a forced smile and gathered her skirts. "There may be a time when your thinking will not be so clear, my friend. We both have something at stake in this place, you know."

He damned his foolishness for sharing the story of his brother with her. That's what comes of too much brandy and loneliness. He prayed his crew would be able to maintain their station off the islet without being chased away or captured by a French ship. If he, Nathaniel and Fiona returned and there was no ship, they would die.

Nathaniel stuck his head out of the door. "By God, it's a tailor shop." He gestured for them to follow him inside. Hugh lifted his eyes beyond the rooftop, beyond the spire, to the monoliths of iron and brick rising ten times higher than a mainmast over his head. It was enough to make a man dizzy, though he remembered all too well Belkin's warning. "Stay focused," he'd said. "If you lose yourself in the changes the future has wrought, you'll turn in circles until you drop."

He pulled his attention away from the barreling vehicles on the road below, the cacophony of unrecognizable noises and especially the alluring young woman resting peacefully in the corner, and followed his companions through the door.

"This is the passage Brand used to return, then," Fiona said.

"I told you it was. There was never a doubt." Hugh drew back the curtains and looked out. By the time they'd satisfied their initial objective of ensuring that the shop was both abandoned and able to be secured, the woman with the intriguing cheekbones was gone. He wondered what if anything she would make of her near brush with the side effects of time travel. A few more steps and she might have found herself transported back to his time and to that unfriendly islet.

"We know there may be more men—"

"Brand is the only important one," Hugh said. "If we find him, we find the map."

Fiona gave him a look, which he ignored, turning his gaze back to the street.

"For now, let's concentrate on our immediate next steps, shall we? We need to find out what we can about Alfred Brand—his business, his life, his habits and, most important, his whereabouts."

She said, " 'Twould be good to know if we've landed in the right time to find him."

Nathaniel, who had been examining the space behind the establishment's little counter, unpinned a calendar from the side of a cabinet and held it for the other two to see.

Hugh gazed at the curious combination of the days of the month and a picture. The picture was odd: a woman in an ornate cream dress—a bride, it seemed—with a cascade of flowers in her hands, standing on the steps of a church, holding the hand of a somberly dressed man. But the far more important information the calendar held was the year. If the calendar was current, and, given its relatively pristine state, there was no reason not to believe it was, they were in the year of Alfred Brand's fifty-eighth birthday.

Hugh felt the black fist of loss like a wallop to his gut. There had been a chance, albeit a small one, that they would land before Brand had made his scurrilous trip to England, a trip that destroyed the lives of so many people. If they had landed before the two hundred and eleventh day of Brand's thirty-fourth year, Hugh might have had the opportunity to save his brother. Now he would have to settle for killing his brother's murderer.

The familiar choking anger rose in his chest, but he kept his face impassive. Vengeance was a bitter pill. "We also need a place to sleep, clothes and money. Since there are rooms upstairs, it looks like we can bed down here."

"And I can make clothes," said Nathaniel.

Fiona and Hugh turned in surprise.

"I wasn't always a ship's master," Nathaniel said, uncomfortable at their sudden interest. "I was a sheetmaker's mate for three years on a ship with a captain with a taste for women. I can make anything—and there's a drawer full of patterns back there."

"I think I speak for Miss McPherson as well when I say, to our very great surprise, we find we are set on that front. Fiona, will you—"

Her hand emerged from her pocket. It was filled with small gold ingots.

"Right. According to Belkin, a visit to something referred to as a 'pawn shop' will win us the currency of the day we need to continue."

"I'll hit the street. I'm sure one of these nice futurists will help me."

If men of the future were anything like the men of 1706, Hugh was certain she'd have no trouble getting all the assistance she could handle. "Er, you may want to consider your skirts. The woman outside seemed to wearing hers as high as her knees."

Fiona grabbed a pair of scissors from the jar, made a large horizontal cut in her skirt and chemise, then tore both across with a jerk. Hugh's eyebrows went up, and even old married Nathaniel, immune to beautiful women for as long as Hugh had known him, watched with interest as Fiona and her shapely calves made their way out the door and into the evening light.

"I know I've asked you this before," Nathaniel said when the door closed, "but do you really believe her story: that her family's future was stolen by Brand? I wonder at her motive."

Hugh checked the field of vision through the window in the adjoining room. He wondered just how close Brand was, and whether he had any way of knowing they'd arrived. He wished they had more weapons than the three pistols they'd been able to carry. "Did you believe that godforsaken rock would lead us here?"

"Upon my word, no. But rocks don't have ways of making men do their bidding."

It no longer surprised Hugh that Nathaniel observed more than he let on. "Aye, I believe her. And her motives are clear as day."

"Indeed." Nathaniel gave Hugh a dry look. "If only all motives were equally as penetrable."

Hugh ignored this, and they began the necessary process of securing the shop for what might transpire.

CHAPTER FIVE

"I will not make you just one map," the mapmaker told the old man who had hidden his treasure. "That wouldn't be safe. You must hide the way to your treasure by dividing the directions among three maps. Three is always safer than one." The man agreed and said he would come back in a fortnight for the maps. But a fortnight came and went and he did not return, then one year, then two. After a while, the mapmaker forgot about the old man.

—The Tale of the Beautiful Mapmaker

Rogan daubed alcohol on the back of Joss's head.

"Ouch! I'm telling you, something very strange was happening there." She was sitting on the toilet in his master bath. The bathroom still looked like it belonged to a bachelor even though she'd been living there for more than a month. There were a lot of changes she wanted to make, but work had been so busy, she just hadn't had the time. God, he looked good in pajama bottoms.

"What, exactly? You told me about the sparks."

"Did you see them?" Her head was so muzzy, it felt

like a freshman-year hangover, but the only alcohol she'd had so far tonight had gone on her scalp.

"No. Everything looked fine when I left." He put the top back on the alcohol and reached for the gauze strips.

"I'm not wearing a bandage."

He held up his hands. "There's no arguing with a bride-to-be. Did you see anything else?"

"Yes. No. I mean, I feel like there was a man there who helped me." What she didn't want to add was that the man was dressed like Russell Crowe in that old-time sailing movie and that he seemed to have emerged from an invisible dome that swelled and receded like a bullfrog's throat. Rogan would surely insist she head to the closest hospital for a CAT scan. There was more to that tailor shop than met the eye.

"A man?" Rogan put the bandages back in the medicine cabinet. She could see the muscles in his jaw flex. "What did he look like?"

"Dunno, exactly." She cut her gaze sideways. "He wore a sort of . . . navy thing."

"Did he say anything to you?"

She'd gotten only the barest of impressions. Tall, broad-shouldered and smelling of sandalwood—sort of like Patrick Dempsey, but with one of those wonderful, rumbly British accents.

"Joss?"

"What? No. Nothing of interest." *"Spirit,"* he'd said. *"I like that."* The memory made her grin.

"Well, let me know if you see him again, okay?"

She frowned. "You think he was following me?" That didn't make any sense.

"I just don't want anyone bothering you. So you'll tell me, right?"

"Sure." She shrugged.

"I think we'll have to chalk the bump up to a loose brick or something. You're lucky all you got was a little bang." His eyes glittered, and he leaned down to kiss her forehead, then look into her eyes. "Big bangs can be so debilitating."

He took her hand and led her toward the bedroom.

"And you're sure you don't mind waiting?" she asked as she got into bed.

"Waiting?" He hopped in beside her and stretched out along her length.

"You know. Until Tuesday."

"Ah, the proverbial wedding night." He grinned. "I thought I had you convinced this afternoon."

"Darn close. Thank God for little boys."

He gazed at her, eyes like shimmering blue lakes. There was so much about him that reminded her of the good parts of her father—generosity, sense of humor, ambition. But unlike her father, there was no hint of cruelty. And he didn't mind her silly waiting game for that final act of intimacy. Waiting had been her mother's wish for her, or at least that's what Joss had told herself. Her mother had loved to make up stories and tell them to Joss, and one of Joss's favorites was about a beautiful mapmaker and her little daughter, which undoubtedly explained why it was her favorite. The little girl is happy until her father disappears and her mother falls ill. As her mother lies dying, she tells the young girl to be wary of the men who will come to court her, that she must save herself for the handsome knight who will offer her all he possesses—his help and his heart. Which is why, Joss knew, she had seen Rogan as some sort of gift from beyond the grave from her mother, and why, despite the odds, she was still technically a virgin at twenty-three.

But technically was enough. What girl didn't look forward to a knight? Waiting seemed the least she could do—especially once he'd actually arrived.

It still felt weird for her to live in his home—hers now, too. But combining households had allowed her to put her condo up for sale, which would bring another influx of cash to Brand O'Malley.

"I feel like I waited a lifetime to meet you," he said gently. "Why would a few more days make any difference? In fact"—he drew a long, slow thumb over her breast—"I think we should refrain from doing anything in the next week that would compromise my ability to deliver, well, shall we say Tchaikovsky and the Fourth of July."

"'Tchaikovsky and the Fourth of July?' You know, Mr. Reynolds, you've excited my anticipation to such an extent that anything short of Mount Saint Helens is going to be a bit of a disappointment."

"Then pack your asbestos nightgown. Tuesday's going to be a cataclysmic night."

CHAPTER SIX

Hugh looked at the Olympian iron and glass structure that towered over him at the crest of the alley. He'd never seen the likes of it, even in the greatest palaces of the Ottoman Empire. This was surely a place of great magic. Fearing for his ability to stay focused, he turned instead to gaze down the sloping alley and let the morning sun warm his face. Passersby took little notice of him. That was good. It meant the outfit Nathaniel had made fit the times.

The aroma of bacon and toast from a nearby public house wafted between the buildings, and for an instant he was transported back to the cottage in Wych Cross twenty-two years ago—well, twenty-two years ago in his own time—with Maggie at the hearth and his brother at the head of the table, laughing and talking. And just as quickly the scene in his head turned to the table a year later, when he'd found the cottage empty and his brother sprawled in a pool of his own blood, dead of a pistol wound. Hugh's hand went automatically to the chased gold in his pocket, feeling its power like a charge. Hugh would never forget the shock of the discovery, nor the realization, crippling to a child of eleven, that he was totally alone. And the slow white-hot burn began again. For twenty-one years he had carried the poison-laced brew in his heart. For twenty-one years he had laid the path for vengeance, one stone at a time, until he found himself standing here, in this alley. He would not rest until he had destroyed Alfred Brand and everything the man held dear.

He pulled the timepiece from his pocket and opened it. *His blood for yours,* read the inscription he'd chosen so carefully. *A brother's promise.* He remembered every detail clearly—the smell of coffee in the jeweler's shop when he opened the door, the weight of the gold from his first prize as a captain in his pocket, the feel of the velvet over which the various choices had been laid and the horrified look on the jeweler's face as Hugh spelled out the words he wanted engraved there.

Joss stood cautiously at the top of the narrow road, the hanger holding her wedding skirt in one hand and her cell phone set to video in the other, and peeked down the alley. No sparks. No dome. And the Gulf Tower weather beacon was shining a serene blue. She slipped the cell back in her pocket and stepped off the sidewalk, leaving the throngs of down- and wool-bundled workers on Grant Street to begin her descent. As she crossed William Penn Place, she spotted the door of the tailor shop opening. She paused. A man stepped outside. It was the man from yesterday. She would have recognized the shoulders anywhere. Only today he had ditched the old-time navy clothes and was wearing finely cut pants, a vest and an ocean blue shirt. He turned to look up the street, and she found herself making a 90-degree turn to disappear out of sight on William Penn.

Oh, for God's sake.

But it wasn't fear, exactly. It was . . . She searched her brain for the root cause, and an image of Carter Fee, her fifth-grade desk partner, popped into her head.

Omigod, I have a crush on him!

That was just ridiculous, all evidence of heat on her cheeks to the contrary. She was an engaged woman—practically a married woman. She did not have crushes on men she'd barely met. Heck, she didn't really have crushes at all. The last one she remembered was Carter, and it had upset her so much she'd punched him in the shoulder anytime he did so much as look at her.

She peeked around the corner.

The man stood with his back to her, his head tilted as if checking the wind. He was well dressed, but there was a certain untamed wildness to the dark curls flapping at his collar and the way he held his shoulders open and at the ready, as if he were a marauding Viking ready to charge.

A blond woman with cheeks like Cameron Diaz and legs to match stepped out and walked to his side. She wore a pair of formfitting navy sailor pants—very on trend—and leaned in when she spoke. He listened intently, and they both swept the alley with careful looks. They seemed an odd pair to be running a tailor shop. Joss couldn't quite put her finger on why. Perhaps because they were both attractive—not that attractive people didn't run tailor shops, of course—but attractiveness combined with an air of being hyperalert made Joss think they were doing something illegal or having an affair or both.

* * *

The click of Fiona's heels behind him roused Hugh from his dark reverie.

"Have you eaten?" she asked, leaning in so close he could smell the scent of her hair. "You've been up half the night."

"I'll eat later. We need more on Brand. The company isn't enough."

Brand hadn't ventured far from his escape hole. After a few careful questions of a local militia man this morning, they were directed to something called the Carnegie Library, where they'd learned Brand Industries was located in the tallest building in the town, the iron and glass one that towered over the head of the alley like a Moorish man-o'-war. Hugh had spent a good part of the morning walking the building's perimeter and observing what he could.

"I can take that," Fiona said. "A nice publican down the street offered me whatever help I needed last night."

Hugh made a private cough and returned his gaze to the sky.

"At least we know where the passage is," she said, "and that it can be traveled safely."

"Where *one* of the passages is," he corrected. "There's more than one." The men who had returned from the past via that small cave on the islet had not traveled to the past the same way. Of course, Fiona would not be aware of that.

"I suppose you're right. We only know of two travelers, Phillip Belkin and Alfred Brand—well, five now if you count you, me and Nathaniel—but there must be more. And they couldn't have all come by way of the islet."

Hugh knew there was at least one more traveler, a man named Collingswood. There would have been a seventh as well, a man named Spears, if he hadn't been shot and killed. But he held his tongue.

"Where would Brand keep the map?"

Hugh had been pondering that himself. And despite what he'd told Nathaniel, he did try to maintain a careful level of skepticism when it came to Fiona. He believed her story, backed by the man called Phillip Belkin, that not only had her family's fortunes been reversed by Brand's theft of the map but history itself had been rewritten because of it. Nonetheless, there was a blind passion to her quest that made him uneasy, and he knew only too well how dangerous blind passion could be.

He looked around to see if anyone was watching, then bent his head. "A locked room is my guess," he said in a lowered voice. "The building is secured by an officer of some sort, though it seems he serves as a mere checkpoint. Brand Industries is located on floors thirty-six through fifty-eight." He shook his head, amazed at his own words. Fifty-eight floors! Who could imagine such a marvel? "There are additional guards up there. That's the place we need to search."

"Perhaps he destroyed the map," she said. "Wouldn't that have been wise?"

"It's possible, but I'm hoping Brand is worried enough about what would happen to the reversal he'd created in our time by taking the map to leave well enough alone. The last thing he would want is to undo all his hard work."

"So you think Brand knows of another passage?"

"Aye." He turned to Nathaniel, who was making his way toward them, bleary-eyed, biting a stray thread out of the length of yellow silk in his hands he called a "tie."

"He must. If he traveled from his time here to our time through the time passageway that ends on the islet, he would have died of exposure or thirst. Why, there couldn't be above a handful of ships a year that pass it."

"So there's another passage here, the one that allowed Brand to travel *to* 1682?" Nathaniel said.

"Aye. Remember, Brand first landed in 1682. He found and courted his wife. They had a child. He stole the map, which changed everything from the year 1684 on. Then he returned to his own time and discovered everything had changed there as well."

"Aye. He'd made himself a rich man." Fiona spat.

"And it took you more than twenty years, until 1706, to figure out what he'd done, with the help of Belkin."

Nathaniel nodded. "And that's when she hired you?"

"Aye," Hugh said. "So we have to assume that there is another passageway. It may not be here. It may be in some other town. But the fact Brand lived here both before and after traveling back in time suggests the other passage might be nearby as well."

"Did he stumble on it, do you think, or did he run into a traveler from whom the secret was prized, as Fiona did?" Nathaniel asked.

"Actually, he found *exactly* the same man Fiona did—Phillip Belkin. At least, that's what Belkin told us. This was when Brand was in England after he acquired the map. He told Belkin he couldn't go back to Pittsburgh the same way he came. Why? We don't know, though Belkin's guess was that the passageway Brand used to get to the past was too dangerous to attempt a return trip. Belkin says Brand was hunting for another way back to his own time. Belkin told him about the islet. Brand hired a captain with a ship, and you know the rest. How Brand first got to England from Pittsburgh, though, is uncertain. We'll probably never know for sure." He held up a hand as Nathaniel looped the tie around his neck. "I can do this."

"It's not like a stock," Nathaniel said. "More like a noose, at least according to the directions I found with the pattern. There," he said, tightening the silk at Hugh's neck. "You are wearing something called a 'half-Windsor knot.'"

"Good Lord," Hugh said, maneuvering his finger along the narrow space between the fabric and his Adam's apple. "It *is* like a noose. Is it meant to be a punishment of some sort?"

"Every picture I've found seems to show men wearing one. So, no, not unless the lot of them are criminals."

"Wouldn't surprise me in the least." Hugh stretched his neck in either direction. "Nathaniel, you've done an excellent job with the food and clothes, as have you, Fiona, with the money and shoes." He eyed the lethal-looking pattens she sported, with heels as high as a loaf of bread. "But we need a little more on Brand. See what more you can find out about his schedule and work habits."

Fiona nodded.

"And, Nathaniel, hit the cot. You've been up all night sewing. We'll need you fresh for later. I'm going to figure out the habits of the tower dwellers. There's got to be a way in. What is it, Fiona?" He saw her eyes flicker up the alleyway.

"I thought I saw a flash of something. Probably just a bird. Let's head in. I'm getting cold."

* * *

When they went back inside the shop, Joss padded the rest of the way down the alley. She was just nearing the entrance when a weird throb went through her and she stopped.

She froze. Remnants of yesterday's inexplicable events? No sparks had appeared, but she'd felt the same odd lurching in her gut—like the urgent pound-pound-pound of a boat speeding through the waves. With some trepidation, she stepped back to see if it would happen again. The street shook like it was under artillery fire, and flashes of images went through her mind's eye. She jumped back to safety. She was not imagining it. Where she had seen the sparks accumulate on the invisible dome the day before, there was still a force of some kind.

A pedestrian chatting on his cell approached her. She pulled out her phone, as if she were checking for messages, to watch him pass. Ten feet before he reached her, she saw his face contract for an instant, as if he'd been bitten by a mosquito. He kept walking, though, and when he was just a few steps past her, he flinched again. He turned around, confused, but saw nothing and continued on his way.

She wasn't the only one who was feeling this.

She put her hand out carefully, wondering if she could find the perimeter of this odd, invisible dome. And, indeed, a few inches beyond her she found a wall of moving air. She inched forward. There was a faint humming that increased the closer she brought her head, ramping quickly to a stronger screech. She closed her eyes and brought her face into it.

Immediately, the images returned. Vivid and confusing, one replaced another in the tiniest fraction of a second—a huge rocky mount against a raging sea, a baby crying, an ancient pistol firing in the dark and Joss herself from the evening before, at the head of the alley, walking through a shower of sparks to—

"Can I help you?"

Joss leapt about a foot. It was the blond woman, regarding her closely. She must have slipped outside without Joss seeing. The woman was even more gorgeous up close, with gold cat eyes, long legs and a body that could stop a *Superman* preview at Comic-Con. She had a British accent, too, though not nearly as warm as Tom James's. More Sienna Miller than Maggie Smith.

"I was, um, listening. I thought I heard a wolf howling. Strangest thing."

"A wolf? Here?" The woman put her hands on her hips. With her spike heels, her eyes were about a foot over Joss's head.

Joss chuckled nervously. "I guess it was just me. Say, I was wondering if I could see Mr. James. I'm having a certain tailoring issue with my skirt." She shook the hanger as if presenting evidence.

The woman's gaze went from the hanger to Joss's hips with an expression that suggested taking the skirt *in* wasn't going to be the fix.

"He's not here, and we don't do that sort of work anymore. New owners."

Joss considered. Pushing too hard would raise a flag—and a place that could toss up an invisible dome was not exactly one to be trifled with. On the other hand, she really didn't care for Sienna's attitude.

"I see. Well, you don't mind if I pick up the blazer and slacks I left here, do you?" she said, summoning an instant lie.

The woman rocked on her Space Needle heels. She didn't believe Joss any more than Joss had believed her.

"The stock is gone," the woman said. "I apologize. Everything was gone when we bought the business. Did the former owner not leave you a forwarding address?"

"No. But that's okay. I'll just grab a cop," Joss said, carefully emphasizing the last word. "A lot of times they know the emergency numbers to call for this sort of thing."

"A cop?"

"Yeah, you know"—Joss pointed a finger and cocked her thumb—"bang-bang?"

The woman's eyes flared, and she reached for something at her back.

The door opened so hard the knob made contact with the brick. Tom James or whatever his name was gave the woman a meaningful look. *"Fiona,"* he said sharply. "That will be enough."

Fiona, eh? That was the name of a double-crossing whore if she'd ever heard one. The woman probably cheated at checkers, too. Joss gave her a smile.

Fiona's hand returned to her hip and she flounced off.

"What can I do for you?"

Joss looked up into James's face. He was a good four inches taller than Rogan and ruggedly handsome, where Rogan's looks were Wall Street-by-way-of-Andover classic. Specks of green, gray and sky blue swam in James's eyes like a northern sea, and he regarded her with what could only be described as careful interest.

"I-I—" She held up the hanger, feeling her breath catch. "A skirt. I have a skirt."

He looked at the garment, his scarred brow lifting in an arch. "A brushed brocade. I saw something like this in Malay once. Very handsome. Would you like to come in?" He tilted his head toward the shop.

The interior was spotless and precisely laid out, two square rooms separated by an entry hall in which an ancient counter stood. There were baskets of notions along its length, and a brass cash register that might have made change for Woodrow Wilson. To her right, bolts of cloth lined the walls: wools in browns, blacks and grays; cottons in whites, pinks and blues; silks in myriad patterns and a rainbow of colors. To her left, in the room that was barely visible behind a half-drawn curtain, she spotted a short raised platform in front of a large half circle of mirrors. It was a fitting room, and yet nothing suggested that any in-process work was going on here. Somewhere in the back of the house, a man and a woman—Fiona, by the sound of it—conversed.

"Now, what can I do for you?" James asked.

If he recognized her, he didn't show it.

"I, ah . . . I think I might have fallen out there." She gestured toward the alley.

"What? Just now?" He frowned.

"No, last night."

"Oh. But you are well?"

"Well, yes, but—"

" 'Tis lucky." He neatened the bits and pieces on the counter.

This was irritating. "Yes. Yes, it is, but—"

"Why, my uncle slipped in the rain in Covent Garden after a spot of winkles and buttermilk. Never walked again."

She blinked. "It wasn't like that."

"I'm glad to hear it." He extracted a measuring tape from the shelf behind him. "A lady can't be too careful—or my uncle, come to think of it."

Okay, now it was a point of pride. He'd held her in his arms. No man should forget that. And no man should be reluctant to claim the honor.

"But it wasn't so much the fall that interested me," she said, "as the rescuer."

The tape slipped but he caught it. "Rescuer?"

Okay, she hadn't dated a lot in college. She'd been too busy trying to keep her head above the water with her studies and on-the-job training. But she hadn't been a hermit. She knew full well that when she'd switched herself into "connect" mode, she'd gotten results. A free drink, help from the smart guy in accounting, a flat-tire change. Surely she couldn't have lost all of that after two years of being buried in cash flow statements.

"Yes," she said. "Someone helped me. I really, *really* wanted to thank him." She might be rusty at the calibration, but she knew the amount of suggestion she'd put into those last two words should have been enough to score her an immediate confession if not a case of Veuve Clicquot and the keys to his condo. She waited for the flood of explanation.

"I'm sure he knows you're grateful. People are intuitive that way—especially rescuers."

Jeez, this guy was tighter than a pair of Ricky Martin's pants. She took a look around. No sparkles, no fireworks, no sealed buckets of cocaine. Nothing to suggest nefarious activity at all unless you counted the fact that a least three people were working at a tailor shop that looked like it hadn't had a customer since sometime last summer.

The crush's embers were dying in this acknowledgment-less vacuum. Unless she was willing to say, "Look, pal, if you think I'd ever forget those forearms of yours, you're insane," there didn't seem to be anything more she could do. He wanted to keep his secret, and even the possibility of being the object of Joss O'Malley's crush was not enough to change his mind. Irksome, indeed, but it didn't give her a lot of choices. She ducked her head toward the door. "Well, thanks, I guess."

He made a polite noise. "The skirt?"

"The skirt? Oh! The skirt. Right." Now she was stuck. She certainly didn't want to leave her wedding skirt with this ring of weird, nonworking tailors, even if their leader had eyes like a geothermal lake and smelled of a brisk ocean breeze.

Think, Joss, think. You need a reason why you brought the skirt in but now want to take it home. You need a reason and it's . . . it's . . . She could barely come up with a sound with those glittering eyes upon her, let alone a good lie.

"I-I—"

"Aye?"

Was he mocking her? *Oh, crap.* There was no way out. "I need to get it hemmed," she said, peeved with her lack of ingenuity. "You do hem, don't you?"

"Of course. We're a tailor shop." He took the skirt and

examined it. "How many inches do you want to have it taken up?"

No inches. The skirt was perfect, absolutely perfect. In the old days, before her father had drained the family wealth trying to shore up his company, it might have been a couture dress from a Paris designer with a trip on the corporate jet for every fitting. But her friend Richard had found this for her in his Eons vintage clothing shop and had hand sewn a lining into it that had come, he said, from the same bolt of fabric that supplied Audrey Hepburn in *Roman Holiday.* Of course, Richard was a huge Audrey Hepburn fan and had been known to exaggerate when it came to his favorite heroine, but the point was, with the skirt, her mother's gorgeous Dior blouse and a bouquet of gardenias, Joss would be an elegant shell pink execu-bride, rocking both the spirit of her mom and the world's most elegant actress, and what could augur a better future than that?

"A tenth of an inch," she said. Oh, God, what had she done? The nonworking tailors would take her skirt. She'd never get it back. She'd be standing in the Founders Room wearing a pair of Old Navy cargo pants.

"A *tenth* of an inch?" he repeated.

"Yes."

His brows went up. "I . . . I'm sure we can do it, but—"

"But you really can't," she said, grabbing it back. "I understand. It's short notice."

"It is?"

"Yes. The wedding's in less than a week—next Tuesday, to be exact—and there's the bachelorette party tomorrow and a party for the family at the History Center on Thursday. Way too much for me to think that I'd even have time to pick it up, let alone that you'd have time to do it."

He retrieved the skirt gently. "We can do it. But I wonder if you should consider a different color? Pales, I believe, should be reserved for the bride."

She pressed her lips together. "I *am* the bride."

Something shifted in his eyes. Was it surprise? Disappointment? *Don't be ridiculous.* But there was no denying the change.

"*You* are the bride?" His eyes trailed down to her hand.

For once the ring felt like an embarrassment. She shoved her hand casually in her pocket. "I am."

"Many felicitations." He made a quaint, old-fashioned bow. "A wedding skirt, then . . ." His attention went from the garment to a calendar on the wall showing a bride and groom, then back to the garment. He scratched his jawbone, obviously confused. All at once a look of horror came over his face. "I beg your pardon. Is this an undergarment of some sort?"

"No, it's *not* an undergarment," she said, annoyed. The skirt had cost her three hundred dollars. New, it would have been twice that.

"This is the dress, then? In its entirety?"

"Yes."

His concern grew.

"There's a top, too," she added.

He laughed, and for the first time Joss caught an unveiled glimpse of the man from the night before.

"Aye"—the green in his multicolored eyes turned light and frothy—"I had imagined there might be."

His tone made Joss wonder whether he also imagined the lack of a top, and bubbles of adolescent helium flooded her veins.

"My hesitation," he said, "is with the outfit as a whole."

Oh boy. She hoped he wasn't another one of those mutton-sleeved, Little Bo Peep wedding dress pushers— or, worse, a fan of architectural, this-will-be-out-of-date-before-you-finish-the-honeymoon–type gowns. "Oh?"

"I see you elsewise. Are you perhaps familiar with the goddess Nike?"

Nike? Where was this conversation going? She cocked her head and made the curvy symbol with her finger. "Like 'Swoosh'?"

He hesitated. " 'Swoosh'?"

"You know, the little . . ." She pointed to her feet, but no spark of recognition appeared in his eyes. Maybe they didn't have Nike in England? "Never mind. What about her?"

"Nike, the goddess, is oft depicted with wings spread in flight. She is the goddess of battle and victory. Aphrodite is more beautiful, but to a discerning eye, Nike is far more engaging, for she has the flush of exertion on her skin."

His eyes met hers, and the helium bubbles rose to a simmer.

"I was fortunate to be given the opportunity to visit the home of the Earl of Hartlet," he said. "My family was not wealthy and such an excursion was rare indeed. The earl had a beautiful hall of sculpture. One in particular caught my eye. I am not a connoisseur of the arts, having neither the time nor fortune to be so, but I am a man, and the image of that work has lingered with me."

He drew a pad and pencil from below the shelf and began to sketch.

"Her feet and arms were missing, which gives her a bit of the appearance of a prisoner, but—oh!—what a prisoner. Her head is high, and her eyes, determined. She is captured at the moment of flight, lifting like an angel from the earth. She wears a dress—a chiton, I believe it is called—that falls in graceful waves from her shoulders."

His able pencil strokes showed a woman in a Grecian gown, one leg behind the other as if she were running, the movement rendered in streams of fabric that sailed into the imagined wind behind her.

"And here," he went on, drawing a cross-body slash from each shoulder to the opposite side of the waist, "was the harness by which the fabric was held."

Joss stared, entranced. It was both feminine and vaguely warrior-like. "Wow."

"That," he said, meeting her eyes, "is how I see you."

"Me?" It seemed a wildly seductive thing to say, but there wasn't a trace of irony on his face. It was just an honest compliment.

"Have I offended you?"

"No," she said. "Not at all. It's just—I don't know—that seems sort of not like me."

"Truly?" He sounded surprised. "I have only met you, of course, but there is a certain vitality that is unmistakable. Does not a generous portion of courage come with it?"

"I . . ."

"Come. Let me show you."

"Here? You have a gown?"

He laughed. "Aye, I suppose you could call it that."

CHAPTER SEVEN

Meanwhile, men continued to try to win the hand of the beautiful mapmaker. One day a dark, handsome man came into her shop. He didn't want to court her. He admired her maps. He asked her about the places she drew. He looked at copies of the maps she'd drawn and made her tell the stories of the men who had asked for them to be made. He wanted to take her to places beyond her shop. He told her he came from a land far away.

—The Tale of the Beautiful Mapmaker

The man led Joss into the fitting room, removed her coat and nudged her onto the raised platform. The light was soft and flattering, and, unlike the unforgiving mirrors in most department store dressing rooms, the mirrors here, flecked with age, seemed to reflect back an almost idealized version of herself. Joss could imagine a lot of people plunging into something they shouldn't have in this room.

He gazed at the bolts of fabric. "I know I saw something . . ."

After some sorting, he said, "Here," and withdrew half a dozen rolls of silk. Two were in jewel tones, another in black, two in white and one in a shimmery taupe. He held the white out for her inspection. The fabric slipped through her fingers like petals.

"Beautiful." Her eyes went immediately to the taupe. It was the color of café au lait, opulent and rich. Moreover, since black was out for a wedding and white was too sweet for Joss's tastes, taupe was the only choice simple and elegant enough to suit her tastes.

"I like this one," she said.

He drew out a length of fabric. "May I?"

She nodded, and he draped the expanse over her shoulder. She inhaled. It was beautiful, like something a Hollywood siren of the thirties would wear. She pictured Carole Lombard on Clark Gable's arm.

"Nice," she said.

He was gazing thoughtfully at her reflection in the mirror. "I should like to see the white."

She shifted. "I'm not sure."

"'Tis a classical conceit," he said. "Purity, of course—always appropriate in a bride—but also strength."

He let the taupe fall, and maybe it was the way the silk ran over her skin, but she felt as if she'd been stripped bare. Her blouse and skirt could have been made of air. Her mouth dried. Suddenly, this seemed like a slightly dangerous activity for ten in the morning.

"I'm a little thirsty."

He smiled. "Let me see what we can find."

"What in God's name are you doing?" Fiona demanded.

"Keep your voice down," Hugh said as he searched

the stores Nathaniel had gathered the night before. He was enjoying his sartorial liaison with the spirited young woman—the cheek of that canty "I should like to thank the rescuer" still glowed in his head—and he wanted nothing to disturb it. "I am passing the time, nothing more. The woman's to be married in a costermonger's apron, for God's sake. I am trying to persuade her to wear something else."

"She's a spy."

"If she is, I'll resign my commission. She lacks the sangfroid to be an operative of any sort, let alone Alfred Brand's. She's curious about our arrival yesterday. Nothing more. Wasn't there a bottle of hock here?"

Nathaniel, who had been pouring the last of it into a mug, looked sheepish. "Sorry, sir."

"You're taking an unnecessary chance," Fiona said.

Hugh swept the mug into his fist and ran a sleeve over the rim. "Isn't it time for you to follow up with that publican friend of yours?"

Fiona sniffed and made her way down the back stairs. When Hugh heard the door slam, he said to Nathaniel, "What are your skills when it comes to the gowns of Greek goddesses?"

James placed the mug in her hand, and Joss smiled. The ceramic was cool to the touch, just what she needed to counter the heat rising from where he'd brushed her skin. She took a deep gulp and nearly choked.

"It's wine!"

His brows knitted. "Aye?"

It was also room temperature, and she felt the dry, fruity warmth slither all the way to her toes. "I guess I'm just not used to having wine before lunch."

"I can get you something else."

She looked at the bolt of white silk he was gathering. "No, it's fine." She swigged another mouthful. So much for working, she thought, then gasped. "What time is it?" She jerked her phone out of her pocket and checked the screen: *10:27. Hell's bells!* The operations team would be walking into the main conference room right now to give her the updated production schedule. She needed to let her operations guy, Louis, know she was going to have to push the meeting back.

She tapped the screen to pull up her list of contacts. "Sorry," she said to James. "I have to make a quick call."

He looked at the phone as if it had grown a tail and was emitting smoke.

"What? You've never seen one of these?" She held up her much beloved iPhone.

He shook his head.

Jeez, what kind of non-tailor academy did he go to?

"Oh, it's really cool." She held it out for him to see. "See, I pull up the list here, and then just tap the screen to bring up the Bs. I choose my person . . ." Her thumb worked the screen deftly. "Then I can either call or text or even e-mail." She hit Louis's mobile number.

"E-mail?" His brows knitted.

"I'm stuck in another meeting," she said when Louis answered, and did a little shrug in the direction of her companion. "Do you mind if we push it back until eleven . . . um, thirty?"

"No prob."

"Thanks. See you then." She hit End Call. "Not so good if they figure out the boss is playing hooky."

James nodded, clearly still in awe over the hardware. Joss returned the phone to her pocket. *Must be a Sprint customer.*

"Boss?" James said.

"Yeah, Louis works for me."

"You are his superior?"

"Well, you wouldn't say that if you saw me trying to optimize the production schedules, but, yes, technically."

He considered this, then nodded.

"Have you been in this location long?" she asked. As long as they were chewing the fat here, she might as well try to hit some of the high points on her agenda.

He removed a cuff link and began rolling up a sleeve. "No. Not very."

"Seems like kind of an unusual location—the alley, I mean." His forearm was tan and ropy, like a construction worker's, with a fringe of glinting copper. Definitely carrying arms.

He unrolled the white fabric and laid it on the counter. "It's close to where we need to be."

Which could mean almost anything.

"Tell me about your fiancé," he said. "Would he like you in this?"

"Cripes, I think he'd like me in anything." Or out of anything, for that matter, she thought. Bringing Rogan into this conversation made her uneasy.

"Have you known him long?" James folded the silk methodically, end over end.

"Hardly at all. We met three months ago, around the time my dad got sick. We had dinner together, and it was nice, but it was when I saw him standing at the hospital the next morning, waiting to go in with me, that I knew he was the one. What about you? Where are you from? I can tell it's not Pittsburgh."

He smiled. "A place called Wych Cross, not far from Eastbourne. My brother was a bookkeeper there. He raised me until I was eleven. After that I went to live with a distant cousin."

She shook her head. "I don't know it."

"It's in Ashdown Forest, a beautiful place."

"Ashdown Forest?" she said, straightening. "Winnie-the-Pooh's forest?"

She thought of that map of the Hundred Acre Wood, the first map she'd fallen in love with. She knew for many people maps were about finding something or getting somewhere, but for Joss, the best sorts of maps were the ones that drew you into a world all their own.

But it seemed James had no more knowledge of Pooh than he did of iPhones. He showed no signs of comprehension.

She said, "I cannot believe you grew up in Ashdown Forest and don't know *Winnie-the-Pooh*. It's a children's book about a boy, Christopher Robin, and the little teddy bear he loves. Christopher Robin is a very proper English schoolboy—well, apart from living in a forest, I suppose—and takes care of the animals there like Kanga and her baby, Roo, Eeyore, the donkey, and Pooh. Oh, it's wonderful. But the map of their forest!" She put her hand over her heart. "They live in the Hundred Acre Wood, which the author

based on the visits he made with his children to Ashdown
Forest. And the book's illustrator, Ernest H. Shepard, created this absolutely magical map of the forest that appears
at the front and back of every book, which invites you into
wonderful places like the 'Sandy Pit Where Roo Plays' and
the 'Pooh Trap for Heffalumps' and my favorite, 'Eeyore's
Gloomy Place (Rather Boggy and Sad).'" Joss spoke the
names in her best British accent, which admittedly wasn't
very good. "Oh, it just couldn't be more beautiful. It was
the first map I ever loved."

The corner of his mouth rose. "You fall in love with
maps?"

"Oh, God, over and over. *Treasure Island, The Swiss
Family Robinson,* Lewis and Clark, Christopher Columbus, the London Tube. They all seem to tell a story. I even
had a notebook where I kept all my map observations. I
was like Harriet the Spy, poring over my book of secrets."

The smile disappeared. "A *spy* book?"

She waved away the question. "Ah, it's a girl thing. The
point is I've got it pretty bad for maps. Which is a good
thing, I guess, since that's what I do for a living."

His brows rose. "Indeed?"

"Oh yeah, it's the biggest barely-making-it map company in the world. It used to be bigger, before this"—she
tapped the phone in her pocket—"pretty much eliminated the need for paper maps."

He considered this, expressionless. "Well, I regret I do
not know your bear. But I can tell you Ashdown Forest is
a lovely place to be a boy. It was the happiest time of my
life. I was quite sad when I had to leave."

"I'm sorry. That must have been very hard." Joss

thought of the day her mother collapsed and died, and how everything seemed to change in a blink of an eye. She knew what it was like to have one's world swept away, to feel rootless and terrified, like a mouse dodging the waves on a storm-tossed beach.

He gave her a small smile and gestured to the fabric. "Shall we try the white?"

"Yeah. Why not?"

She waited for him to drape the silk over her shoulder, but instead he picked up a pair of scissors and cut.

"Oh no!" she cried. "I hate to see you ruin it."

He laughed. "We shan't have ruined it."

When he finished, he held the ends as one would hold a towel for a toddler getting out of the bathtub. She took another gulp of wine and put the mug on a nearby table. Inhaling, she lifted her arms, and he drew the fabric around her. His hands were capable and quick, and the silvery scars that crisscrossed them seemed to suggest a life of action.

"Oh, it's like a toga," she said.

"Not quite. A toga is a man's garment. The chiton is unequivocally feminine. Hold this." He indicated the two end flaps of the fabric, which, having been wrapped around her body, under her right arm, now met over her left shoulder. She grabbed the ends, and he attached the flaps to each other with a pin a few inches from the corners of the fabric. Joss could smell the tang of a sea breeze on his skin.

"You can let go," he said.

She released the fabric, and it fell in a curved wave across her body, curling around her right hip and up to her shoulder. The fabric hung open on her left side except where it had been pinned over her shoulder. She gestured to the wide expanse of right chest showing, which, if the chiton was all he was suggesting she wear, was going to make for a memorable ceremony. "I'm assuming we're not done here."

He laughed, and the sound filled the room like the notes of a bassoon. "There were goddesses who wore it with a breast showing—at least, I've seen it so in paintings. I take it you'd prefer your Nike to be, er, somewhat less intent on distraction."

"Yes, please."

"You may be abandoning a winning battle strategy."

"A risk I shall have to take—although I suppose Rogan would like it."

James looked at her, curious.

"My fiancé."

"Ah." He grasped the fabric hanging under her right breast, did the same with some under her right shoulder blade, then pinned that at her shoulder, creating a sort-of loose, open sleeve for her right arm. "How's that?"

She looked at herself in the mirrors. The silk hung in fitted waves that followed her curves without clinging, and even in this rough assemblage, the beginnings of the gown he had sketched shone through.

"There's something missing." He dug through a large basket in the corner, rattling cases of pins and buttons in the process. He extracted a spool of white ribbon and examined it. "Not quite." He dug some more. With a flourish, he pulled a length of twisted gold rope, about a half inch in diameter, from the collection. "*This,*" he said triumphantly.

He looped the rope around her waist, crossed the ends in the front of the gown, crossed them in the opposite direction in the back, then tied the ends.

"And there," he said, pleased, "is our goddess."

Joss gasped. All she needed was a golden apple or the reins of a chariot. The effect was stunning. Not only did she feel beautiful, she felt powerful and worldly and slim and tall. If they could conjure magic from a bolt of fabric and eight feet of twisted satin cord, what else might those hands be able to do?

"Lift your hair," he said.

He had stopped looking in the mirror and was now gazing directly at her. There was something in the way he had said it that made the bubbles reach a hard boil. That's when she got scared.

She hopped off the platform and began pulling at the makeshift dress. "I-I . . . have to go."

CHAPTER EIGHT

"Stop."

The hand on Joss's arm was no longer the hand of a rescuer. It was the hand of a man intent on having his way. A shiver went through her.

"I have to go," she said.

"Why did you come here?" James's eyes shone a heated aqua.

"To see about my skirt."

"I don't believe you."

His words surprised her, and she could feel the warmth fly across her cheeks. She pulled her arm loose and began to unpin the chiton. "I'm sorry to hear that."

"Why did you come here? Speak the truth."

She didn't like that he saw through her. People did not talk to her that way. She pulled off the silk and dropped it on a table. He moved between her and the room's exit.

"I *am* speaking the truth."

He chuckled. "I wouldn't have expected you to scruple so. Say it."

She wished she had Peter's light saber, though she

supposed the look in her eyes right now was almost as daunting.

He lifted his chin in challenge. "*Say* it."

"Fine. There's something going on here. I don't know if you're a tailor or not, but there's something going on here that's just plain weird."

"Weird?"

"Sparks, explosions, invisible domes that shiver and shake?"

"And you came here to find out?"

"Yes."

"I think this is what you came to find out." He pulled her to him and buried her mouth with his. The kiss was neither romantic nor halting. It demanded an answer, which she damned herself for giving. A charge exploded in her belly. His mouth was hard and practiced, and she returned his hunger with her own, spurred by the iron arms at her back and the scent of a storm-laden sea that hung on his clothes and skin.

"Let me go. This is wrong."

He caught her wrists and backed her against the wall, lifting her hands above her. "Nothing that feels like this can be wrong." He kissed her again, and she struggled to free herself from his grip. She was exposed, unable to hide her feelings in a fortress of cool indifference. He held her until she stopped moving. Then he let go, and her hands found their way into the thick, dark curls on his head. She urged him closer, intensely aware of the power of his massive body and the overwhelming current that was running between them.

He paused, breathing heavily. "I want you. Now."

She gasped as he lifted her onto a sturdy low table and lifted her skirt.

"I can't," she said.

His fingers found her bud and rolled it open. Fire crackled in her veins.

"Can't?" he said. "Or shouldn't? There's a difference."

She was wet. More than ready, and he could see it on her face. Her thighs ached for joining, and she said nothing as he stripped her of her panties.

He flung his coat on the floor and loosened his trousers, letting the shirttails fall on either side of his granite length. The flushed skin there shone like polished wax, and he was as wide and long as a pillar candle.

He caught her knees and lifted them, pushing her onto her palms. With a wild noise, he spread her legs.

Every cell in her body demanded she submit to the fire, but she knew she must not. "Please, no. I'm engaged."

"I don't want to marry you. I want to plow you." He tore off his shirt, and after two exploratory presses he gave a thrust hard enough to bury himself inside her.

His eyes widened, as did hers. He beat his hips against her, and she writhed, trying to harness the stormy pleasure.

"You came for this," he whispered.

"No."

"Say it."

"No. No. *No.*"

"No, you don't like the ops plan, or no, you don't want a fill-up?"

Joss jerked from her fantasy. Everyone in the darkened conference room was looking at her. Louis, her ops man-

ager, who had refilled his own cup, was holding the cof-
feepot over hers.

"I mean, it *is* empty."

"No, no," she said, flushing and waving him on. "Coffee's fine."

"But the plan's a problem?" he said, cautious.

Christ, she'd barely heard the plan. What was wrong
with her? Why would a tailor or whatever he was have such
an impact on her? It was the chiton, and the way his eyes
had sparkled when she'd talked about maps. She reminded
herself to stick to the facts. Just because he'd watched her
walk all the way up the alley when she left didn't mean he
was about to bang her senseless on a tabletop, now, did it?
She looked around quickly. She hadn't said that out loud,
too, had she?

"No," she said, "the plan is, um, good."

"Is it what you were imagining?"

She shot him a look and immediately regretted it. He
hadn't meant her fantasy.

"I mean, if you're not sure," he said, "the team would
be happy to hit the drawing board again—"

"No, no, no. The plan is . . . well, what can anyone
really say about a plan like that? I have the utmost confidence that you guys can make it work."

He nodded hesitantly. "All right, then. We'll make it
happen."

*And you wonder why your company is teetering on the
edge of insolvency?*

CHAPTER NINE

*The dark, handsome man won the hand of the mapmaker
and they married. They had a beautiful daughter, and they
gave her everything she could want—toys, dolls and even a
magical place guarded by a pair of lions. She lived like a
princess. Everything was perfect until the dark, handsome
man began to want more. "But we have so much," said the
mapmaker, who needed nothing more than her little princess
daughter and her handsome husband and her lovely maps.*

— The Tale of the Beautiful Mapmaker

This time he heard Fiona's footsteps, though he fervently wished he could have been left to the quiet of his thoughts. The woman with the love of maps had a fire in her that intrigued him. He had enjoyed their discussion and could still feel the softness of her skin on his fingers and see the engaging sway of her hips as she'd climbed the path to the high street. He touched the ball of white silk. Aye, he would very much like to see that chiton on her. In truth, he would very much like to see it off her as well. He'd known enough to be wary, but the fact that she'd openly mentioned maps to him had reduced his concern.

It would take a canny spy indeed to be that purposefully provocative.

"What did she want?" Fiona demanded.

"Nothing. An adjustment to her garment." He lifted the silk and began to fold it.

"Nathaniel says you were dressing her."

"Nathaniel would do well to concentrate on his own assignments."

Fiona watched him. "I don't like her."

Hugh said nothing.

"I think she was watching for us. I think she knows."

"You're wrong. She's curious about a shower of sparks that knocked her senseless, as any intelligent woman would be."

Fiona snorted. "You know nothing will stop me from reversing the wrong that's been done to my family."

"I'm well aware of the assignment."

"She had best not return."

"She will, however. And I shall handle it." He gazed at the brocade skirt on the odd twisted-metal contraption for hanging and allowed himself a private smile of anticipation. He wished, however, the skirt were not to be a wedding garment.

Fiona, evidently growing tired of this game, changed the subject.

"I have news," she said. "It concerns Brand."

"Aye?"

"The publican did something called a 'search' for me."

"And?"

"Brand's dead."

Hugh swayed. He thought he might be sick. His life

had been ordered by this imagined meeting with Brand. Every step in his career had been taken to bring him to this place. Every skill he'd pursued—pugilism, tracking, fencing, pistols—had been chosen for its value in his mission. For the second time in his life, his reason for living had been snatched away. "Are you certain?"

"Aye. He died three months ago. After a brief struggle with cancer." She pulled a piece of paper from her pocket and read. "'A descendant of the wealthy Brand family, Alfred Brand steered Brand Industries in the direction of computer electronic parts in 1980s. The company, which had struggled in the last few years, was burdened with debt and sold just before his death. He is survived by a daughter.'"

Josephine. She's alive.

"What else? What about his fortune?"

"It says he drained the family fortune in recent years to save the company. In fact, it says he was about to file for personal bankruptcy when he died."

"What about the company? He wouldn't have let the secret die with him. Someone has to know. Someone has to have been charged with protecting the map. It was the key to the Brand family fortune and 'twill be the key to anyone who hopes to continue to harness that power into the future."

"The daughter," Fiona said.

"Not the daughter," he said sharply, thinking of that innocent dark-haired child. "Someone else. What else does your paper say?"

She ran her finger down the words. "'The company was purchased by Brand's handpicked successor, CEO wunderkind Rogan Reynolds, and a team of investors.'"

"*Rogan* Reynolds?" He endured a stab so real he could almost feel the edge of the blade.

"Aye. Why?"

He smacked the counter with his fist. "Bloody hell, she *is* a spy."

CHAPTER TEN

"Another martini, please," Joss said.

"Oh, I don't know," Di warned as old Sam, the long-time bartender at the William Penn Hotel bar, reached for the gin. "It's your second. Don't you have to stay on your toes for business? You never know when a map crisis is going to precipitate."

"Funny." Joss nibbled at the remaining olive, thinking about the morning's visit to the tailor shop. "You know, I can loosen up when I want to."

"Right. Look at your bachelorette party: you, one pregnant woman drinking club soda and a teething baby. Just doesn't get more rowdy than that."

"You know I don't like big parties. Never have." Well, at least since her father's company started going bust and everything in her life became so cost focused. She wiggled her napkin at Luke in his car seat on the bar. He gazed at her with wide, unblinking eyes, oblivious to the fountains of saliva pouring down his fist into the crevasses of his neck.

"You don't like big parties because you never had time for big parties," Di said. "You're the only person I know who attended college orientation week with their corporate attorney."

"We were being sued. It was a great chance to learn how things like that work."

"You need to have more fun. We need to have a stripper or something. Isn't that what Rogan's having at his party tonight? Maybe one of these nice gentlemen at the bar here will remove his clothes for us."

Sam, who looked as if he were sporting a small beanbag chair under his uniform tuxedo shirt, moved the car seat enough to put down Joss's martini and wiped his hands on his apron. "Anything else I can do for you?"

The vision of Sam in a sequined G-string popped into Joss's head. "No. Thank you."

"Word to the wise," Di said as Sam walked away. "Grab fun while you can. You never know when it's going to evaporate. The closest I've gotten to sex in the last four months is when David wiped baby vomit off my crotch."

"I was actually having a little fun this morning," Joss said, smiling into her drink. There was something about a crush that made you want to talk about it, even when you knew you probably shouldn't.

"Oh, really?"

"Have you ever used the tailor in that alley across the street from our offices?"

"Your idea of fun is going to a tailor? Wow, we really do have a lot of work to do here."

"It wasn't the going to the tailor." Joss flushed. "It was the tailor himself."

Di looked at Joss over her glasses. "Murray, the white-haired tailor from the shtetl in Warsaw?"

"Uh, no. Must have been the son. His name was Tom. Tom James." Her James certainly hadn't sounded like the son of a Murray from Warsaw.

"For heaven's sake, they're not really named James," Di said. "That's just a name Murray picked. Sounded upper-crust, I guess. Or maybe he thought it fit the look of the building. It's one of the oldest buildings in downtown Pittsburgh, you know. But, in any case, I'm not sure how you had fun there. I mean, apart from the obvious fact it's a tailor shop, it's been closed since July when Murray retired to Punta Gorda."

"It . . ." Joss was getting confused. First the sparks, then the dome and now his name clearly wasn't James. She cast a nervous glance in Di's direction. They were close friends—the closest—but she still didn't think she could share the really weird aspects of this encounter with her. She decided she'd stick with the crush. The martinis were definitely helping there. It was the only part she felt on firm footing about anyhow. "Okay, look. There was this guy there. I guess I just assumed his name was James. Thirtyish. British. Really cute, like Patrick Dempsey cute. And he was kind of flirting."

Di put down her glass, and Joss felt the intensity of her gaze. So go the risks and rewards of sharing crush info. "I told him I was engaged."

"Of course you did. And?"

Joss smiled. "He didn't stop."

Di flung up her hand for a high five.

"It's not like flirting is some amazing new experience," Joss said, meeting her slap. "I am engaged to a pretty sexy guy."

"Yeah, but that was, like, business flirting."

"*Business* flirting?"

"I mean, I know you met in a coffee shop then went out to dinner and it was love at first sight, and then your father meets him and they really hit it off. But c'mon, what are the odds of you falling in love with a guy with a GPS company that could bail out your father's business and then extend a helping hand to yours? Don't get me wrong. I'm not suggesting either you or Rogan did it for that reason. I'm suggesting you're so genetically tied into keeping the Brand O'Malley Map Company afloat that sniffing out a guy like that was programmed into your DNA. Your chromosomes were probably rubbing their hands together and laying out a merger strategy the instant you met him. I guess I'm just glad the guy with the biggest GPS company in the world didn't look like Murray—and, by the way, he really does have a big GPS. What the hell were you two doing in that office? Poor Peter's still asking questions."

They both giggled. The martini was starting to hit Joss hard.

"Yeah, thanks for that," Joss said in mock irritation.

"I texted you! You didn't respond! How was I to know I'd be walking into an episode of *The Real World*?"

"No, I mean it. Thank you. I wanted to wait until our wedding night. Rogan had me against the ropes."

"I don't know. It didn't look like you were putting up a particularly aggressive defense to me."

"Ha. You know how I feel, and it's just a few more days."

"Honestly, Joss. No one should end up with the first

guy she's slept with. They're like the first pancake off the griddle when you're making Sunday breakfast. You know what those are like. What about this Murray stand-in with the English accent?"

"I hope you're not suggesting I sleep with him."

"No, I am definitely not suggesting that. But a kiss . . . A little light petting . . ." She lifted her palms and shrugged her shoulders as if she were Murray. "Please. Everyone needs a Mr. Mistake. That's how you know the guy you're with is the right one. Honestly, if I hadn't slept with Glenn, how would I have known David was going to be such a good father?"

"I'm not following."

"Glenn was huge, if you know what I mean." She grabbed the base of her glass and gave Joss a significant look. Joss thought of that pillar candle. "Would a man like that have made a good father?"

"Good point."

Sam reappeared and nodded toward the club soda. "Ya want another?"

"No. Thank you," Di said. "I found it to be large but unfulfilling." Then she added under her breath to Joss, "And the moral is, how would I have known that without playing the field a little?"

"That's the moral, is it? Okay, that explains Glenn. What about Brad, Andy and that Brazilian with the recumbent bike?"

"You're missing the point. David is perfect. He mops up vomit. He's happy to watch the kids because it means he can put on the Three Stooges. And he's generous enough not to have a penis that could double as a garden gnome."

Several patrons turned their heads.

"Gee, and you said this wasn't going to be a good bachelorette party." Joss swirled the olive in her martini, thinking back on the morning visit. "He told me I looked like a goddess. Nike."

"Really?"

"And he made me a chiton."

"A *kite*-en?"

"I know, I'd never heard of one either. It's a goddess's dress. He wants me to wear it for the wedding. Or, rather, he wants to make me a real one to wear for the wedding."

Di shook her head. "That's got to be a one-of-a-kind pickup line."

"Oh, you should have seen it. All he did was cut out a piece of fabric, drape it over me—"

"He was *dressing* you?" Di squeaked the barstool so hard, Luke dropped his fist and started to cry.

"Well, I mean, just some fabric. Then he tied a piece of gold rope across my chest—"

"Now we're talking."

"—and I was totally transformed. I've never seen anything like it before. I looked elegant and confident. It was . . . really nice."

"You were in his shop, and he was dressing you. How did this amazing event transpire?"

Joss's face turned hot. "Well, that's the funny thing."

"Oh, *that's* the funny thing?" Di pulled an ice cube from her glass and ran it over Luke's gums.

"Yeah, I was there to get my skirt hemmed. And he found out it was going to be my wedding skirt and said he saw me in something entirely different."

"God, please tell me this means we can get you out of that funeral home greeter outfit?"

"He took me in the fitting room and started making this toga thing on me—but it's not a toga because they're only for men—and he said I looked like a goddess." Joss pretended she needed another napkin so that Di didn't see the sparkle in her eyes. "And the amazing part is, I did. Like Athena or Britannia or something."

"Britannia," Di said significantly, "has a breast bared." Luke sucked the cube, spit up a little and went back to his fist.

"Yeah, that topic came up."

The arch of Di's brow went higher than St. Louis's.

"*Stop,*" Joss said. "Nothing happened."

"Except for the dress!"

"No. I told him I couldn't do it."

"Why?"

"You know . . . There's not enough time."

"So, don't wear it next week. You can still let him fit you." Di put a finger on her lip. "Hmm. I wonder how well *he* would fit you?"

"*Di!*"

Di looked at her watch. "Do you suppose this mysterious British-Jewish tailor-goddess maker has evening hours?"

"No, no, no."

"Come on!" Di grabbed Luke's car seat handle and swung him off the bar. "This is a bachelorette party. I don't want Luke to be the only one getting breast action tonight."

*   *   *

They padded down the alleyway, giggling, with Joss shooshing Di and Di tugging Joss's arm to pull her along.

"I feel like I'm in ninth grade."

"Good," Di said, "because I'm sure you spent ninth grade acting like an old lady."

A light was on in the tailor shop.

"He's there!" Di cried.

"Oh, let's not do this. I feel embarrassed."

"It looks like a house. Do you think he sleeps up there? Do you think he takes women up there?"

"There's this woman who works with him," Joss said. "Blond."

"Ugh. But he's definitely not sleeping with her."

"How can you be sure?"

"Sex with your coworker in a tailor shop? Lacks imagination. I think it's the clients he beds, when this blond chick is gone for the night. I see him!" she cried. "Patrick Dempsey is definitely in the building. He *is* cute."

James was seated at a desk, arranging items in front of him, and Joss felt an instant wave of disabling shyness. "Let's just look."

"C'mon. Your whole life has been about just looking. Time for a test drive."

"Di, please."

"I'll tell you what: let's sneak around the back and see what kind of car he has."

"Maybe this isn't such a good idea."

But Di had already started jogging down the side of the building, jostling young Luke nearly out of his Moo Cow cap. Joss followed her as far as the corner, casting nervous glances over her shoulder to ensure James hadn't moved from his seat.

"Sports car or SUV, do you think?" Di called. "God, it had better not be a Prius. Nothing says 'I'm hung like a Greenpeace organizer' like a Prius."

Joss wrung her hands nervously. The martinis must have been doubles. She hadn't felt this weavy in ages.

"I'm taking bets!"

"For heaven's sake, keep your voice down." Joss stole a glance at the upstairs windows. *Would he really take women up there?* She wondered if having sex inside the dome would be different from having it anywhere else. She had a vision of white silk sheets, gold rope and a slow, careful rhythm.

Her eyes traveled to the downstairs window and the desk was empty.

"Nothing," Di called, a voice in the darkness. "No car at all."

Joss jumped a foot. James was standing beside her.

"Di," Joss called, panicked.

"Damn," Di continued. "I was hoping for a big red sports car, you know, maybe with a license plate that read I LENGTHEN or SEW BIG."

"*Di!*"

"Good evening," James said with a bemused look. "Would you like to come in?"

"I couldn't believe it when Joss told me you'd made her such a beautiful dress," Di said.

She was sitting on a chair in the fitting room, with

Luke sleeping at her feet, while James stood, slouched against the doorframe, and watched Joss try not to pace. Joss could feel his smile and was working hard to hide hers. She prayed she hadn't made herself into the biggest idiot this side of Ashdown Forest.

"Joss, is it?" he said. "I hadn't remembered to ask your name."

"Joss O'Malley, yes." She extended her hand. "And yours?"

"Hugh," he said, shaking it. "Hugh Hawksmoor."

His hand was twice the size of hers. It felt warm and steady, and a flash of her earlier fantasy returned to her hard enough to make her toes tingle. The front door opened, and in a moment the blonde entered the fitting room. Di looked her over, caught Joss's eye and shook her head confidently. The blonde smiled but the emotion did not reach her eyes. "You've returned," she said to Joss.

"Yes, we were walking and, um, sort of ended up in this direction." The smile was off-putting in itself but even more so after the reception the woman had given her this morning. Joss noted she was all in black now, and Hugh, who had retained his charcoal trousers, now wore a loose-fitting black shirt over them. She found herself gazing wistfully at the shirttails.

"Is your fiancé here?" The blonde looked around curiously. "Hugh mentioned you are engaged to be married." The final words had been delivered with an unmistakable emphasis.

Hugh cleared his throat. "Fiona, this is Joss and her acquaintance . . . ?" He turned to Di.

"Diane Daltrey," she said.

For a moment, the room erupted in the sounds of forced cordiality.

"We're so sorry to interrupt here," Joss said. "We should be heading out."

"Not at all," Hugh said. "I was just looking over the books. 'Tis nothing that can't wait until tomorrow."

"Do you have anything to drink?" asked Di, who was clearly determined to stay. "I'm parched."

"I think we have a pot of coffee upstairs."

"Gosh, wine would be nice. Especially for Joss," she added in a camouflaging cough.

"Wine, then?" Hugh met Joss's eyes.

She nodded reluctantly, and he excused himself.

"Tell me about the lucky fellow," Fiona said to Joss. "I believe Hugh said his name was Rogan."

"Rogan Reynolds, yeah. He's great."

"It's Joss's bachelorette night," Di said.

Fiona's interest sharpened. "Oh?"

"The wedding's in a week—right after a benefits meeting. We're hoping to stir up a little fun before then. Joss's idea of fun is a surprise plant visit. I'm trying to kick that up a notch."

"I see." Fiona nodded.

"We're sort of in the market for a Mr. Mistake."

"*Di,*" Joss squawked.

"C'mon," Di said. "Every woman needs one. At least one. One last guy before she takes the plunge. The man who'll remind her how horrible men are in comparison to her husband; you know, the sort with all his best points between here and here." She gestured to her stomach and thighs.

"For God's sake, Di!"

"So if you know of anyone . . ."

Hugh entered with a tray of cups and a corked bottle under his arm.

Fiona nodded tightly. "I'm afraid I might."

Snagging a cup and handing it to Joss, Di said to Hugh, "I for one would love to see Joss in that dress. She's told me so much about it."

Hugh gave Joss an even look. "That would be the bride's call."

She flushed. Half of her wanted to kill Di, but the other half wanted to keep the adolescent excitement of the crush going. "Sure. I suppose."

"Oh, look." Diane nudged the car seat enough to wake Luke. "I'm afraid the baby's hungry. Is there a quiet place I could make myself comfortable?" She gave Fiona a helpless look, and Joss rolled her eyes. Di was the most *non*-helpless person she knew and frighteningly unperturbed to nurse Luke anywhere. In fact, she'd nearly caused several cars to veer off the road last time she'd sat outside at Starbucks.

In a moment, the fitting room was empty save Joss and Hugh. He seemed different. A little cooler, a little more direct. A little more, she had to admit, like the man in her daydream.

"Who'd have thought I'd be having wine with you twice today?" she said with a nervous laugh.

"Who indeed?" He unfolded the piece of silk. "This time will you wear it as the goddess herself would?"

She shifted. She knew what he meant. Without the distorting influence of clothes. However, the fitting room offered no separate changing area. The way she saw it, she had two choices. She could say yes, ask where the ladies' room was and look like an idiot. Or she could say yes, bite the bullet and look like someone who had maybe done it once or twice before.

She drained her glass.

Yes or no?

She thought of the dress, that gorgeous, empowering gown. The woman who wore that dress was the sort of woman who just put it on. Dammit, if she was going to have fun, this was the time. *Game on, dress. I'm doing it.*

"Yes, of course." She took a deep breath and stepped onto the platform.

The room was darkly lit, and the soft lights were pointing at her. The mirrors surrounded her in a half circle. Hugh drew the curtain across the entrance and gave her a long look. Why did this feel like a private strip show?

But that was ridiculous. There was a woman breast-feeding upstairs—or at least pretending to. No, the right metaphor here would be a doctor's office. He was a professional. His assistant would be wandering in and out to see if he needed help. And if Joss had any hope of wearing the dress someday, she would have to have it fitted properly.

Right. Easy as a colonoscopy.

She reached for the tie of her dress.

It would probably be easier if he turned his head, she thought. Actually, it would probably easier if he were supervising this by phone from somewhere in the vicinity of Cleveland, but that was not meant to be.

His gaze was not prurient, but it was direct, and she found herself fumbling with the inside button. Diane von

Furstenberg had probably not been thinking of the ease of disrobing for one's tailor when she'd designed her famous wrap dress.

"You said you work with maps."

"I do, yes." She freed the button and considered her lingerie. A beige bra with black lace seemed almost passable. But the low-cut cheeky panties were something else entirely. A business-like beige opaque in front, the panties were jaw-droppingly sheer on the other side and flounced with sheer ruffles. And if that weren't enough, a tiny skull and crossbones made of shimmering black beads adorned the center of the elastic on the back. It was perhaps the most distinctive pair of panties she owned, and as Rogan liked to say, they definitely screamed, "Let the treasure hunt begin!" All in all, probably not what she would have picked for a visit to the doctor's office or the tailor.

"You mentioned your fiancé, Rogan, earlier. Is he Rogan Reynolds?"

"Yes," she said, flustered.

"Rogan's an unusual name. I read something about him today, and I wondered."

"That's him."

"Do you work for Brand Industries as well?" he asked, tumbling the pins in his palm.

The question wasn't surprising. A lot of people thought her mother's company was part of Alfred Brand's empire. Her mother had been, Joss thought sadly, but not the company.

"No, actually. A lot of people think that. We do share office space with them in the USX Tower."

He held out his hand for her dress.

She slipped it off her shoulders and handed it to him.

At this point the only strategy was to play it cool. She knew she looked okay in lingerie—better than okay, really, especially wearing it with three-inch black pumps; nonetheless, she wished that her ass wasn't being reflected like two large ruffled spotlights about a thousand times over in the mirrors behind her. On the other hand, that probably kept his eyes off the nipples straining through the lace of her bra.

"There must be a lot of old maps there." He handed her the chiton, repinned at the shoulders.

"Yes." She lifted her arms and hurried the fabric over her head. "A pretty extensive collection, actually."

The chiton was open on one side where the two flaps met, but overall, she was more covered than not.

She looked in the mirror. The gown was striking—even more so now with the waves of fabric falling against her. He grasped the flaps and held them just behind her waist, demonstrating what the gown might look like after it had been fitted properly. The place where his hand brushed her skin burned.

"Only the simplest adornments," he said.

"I'm going to carry sunflowers."

"Quite fitting." He smiled. "Look at the back."

She turned, and he followed. The fabric hung down far enough in back to show the tanned plane of her back, intersected by the narrow band of her bra.

"Just the gown, I should think." His gaze went from the line of the bra to her eyes.

"I-I—"

But she, too, wanted to see the dress without the marring effect of lingerie. She wanted to feel the fabric against her like a second skin. And if she were totally honest, she wanted to feel the weight of his gaze on her as she did it. Whether it was the martinis or Di's nagging, before she married Rogan she wanted to have one tiny adventure that she could look back on and smile about.

Feeling like she was about to make the first leap in a skydiving class, she maneuvered a hand to the clasp of her bra in the back.

"May I?"

He found the clasp and her breasts fell loose. She slipped the bra off her arms and for an instant he had an unfettered view, then she pulled it free.

There, she thought. *I've had my adventure. I'm done.*

If it affected him in any way, he didn't show it. He took the bra without even looking at it and waited.

She gulped. Did he expect the *panties*, too? This was more than skydiving. This was skydiving naked with an instructor you barely knew. She flushed, deeply conflicted, but it seemed to be worse to do nothing. She snagged the panties, slipped them off and let them drop.

Only the thinnest silk stood between Hugh and her, and when she moved, the long waves of fabric slid over her skin, caressing it.

"Come," he said. "I need to do the fitting." He held out a hand and led her off the platform. Then he knelt, slipping off each shoe, a reversal of Cinderella that sent a sizzling trail of sparks up her spine.

"I see you in sandals—something touched with gold, aye?"

Nodding, she tried not to think about being naked. She tried not to think about the fact that from his position, there was almost nothing that couldn't be seen or imagined. But most of all, she tried not to think that in some small number of moments she would have to return the dress and redon the panties and the bra without the comforting camouflage of five yards of raw silk behind which to hide.

He worked quickly, pinning the fabric along the open flap: at her thigh, at her hip, at the rise of her breast. The silk clung to every curve, even the small rise of her belly, which she normally hated but tonight looked exactly right.

When he unbent, he was quite close, so close she could see the pulse at this throat and smell the fresh breeze scent of his skin. The air between them hummed with promise.

"Lift your hair."

It was the command he'd made that morning, the one that had sent her running. Was it a test—a test to see if they'd passed that point? Or was he flaunting the fact he knew they already had?

She lifted her arms and twisted her hair into a loose knot. He was right. It looked stunning, and the approval on his face took her breath away.

He was so close, she wondered if he'd kiss her. More important, she wondered if she'd kiss him back. A daydream was not real life.

"I want to make this dress for you." His eyes glowed green as he took in his work.

"You can't," she said softly. "There isn't enough time."

"If I make it, will you wear it?"

She thought of that skirt and she thought of Nike, with her striking strength and ethereal beauty. "Yes." It was barely a whisper.

"Will you come back tomorrow for a final fitting?"

"When?"

"Six o'clock," he said. "Just before we close."

She crossed her arms, unsteady. She wished she had more experience in the gray areas of seduction, to know what, if anything, he was suggesting. She knew, hard and fast, she would do nothing to hurt Rogan. But she'd never tarried at the edge of danger with the boys she'd dated. They'd either been dating or they hadn't. There had been no question.

He saw the unease on her face.

"I have no intention of drawing you into something that would hurt you," he said carefully. "But I want to see you in this dress, and I want to see you again before you marry."

Well, if she wanted direct, there it was. And the truth was she had enjoyed this little bit of harmless derring-do. It sent a wonderful frisson through her that was just the distraction she needed on this stressful road to the ceremony. Perhaps Di was right: she had missed too much in life.

"Then yes," she said. "Thank you."

She heard Di's voice on the stairs and stepped away.

The women entered, laughing, Fiona holding Luke against her shoulder.

Di did a 360 of the room without breaking stride. When her gaze came to the bra on the table, she started. With a happy clap she said, "Well, I see we've made some progress here. I'm impressed. C'mon. Let's see it."

With her hands in the air, Joss turned in a circle, and the women made reassuring oohs and ahs. "There's still supposed to be some gold rope that crisscrosses my chest"—she shot Di a threatening look—"but you get the general impression."

"Oh, I definitely get the general impression," Di said. "Will you wear it for the ceremony?"

Hugh's eyes flickered to Joss's, and she felt the pleasure of shared agreement effervesce in her blood. "Yes."

Di exhaled. "Thank the Lord."

Hugh's mouth broke out into a small smile. "I believe I can second that. Fiona, will you help Joss out of the gown?" And with a quick bow he exited the room.

CHAPTER ELEVEN

One day the old man who had hidden his treasure returned to the beautiful mapmaker's shop. Many years had passed since she had seen him. She said, "I was afraid you'd forgotten." He said, "I had not forgotten, but the woman agreed to be my wife because she loved me. I did not need the money to buy her hand. We live in a little house beside the river, and I've never been happier. I want you to have the gold because you gave me such good advice."

—The Tale of the Beautiful Mapmaker

With the women's voices rising and falling beyond the closed curtain in the fitting room, Hugh shifted the coats in the entry, and found Joss's handbag.

She was a spy, he thought, and one he had invited within his own well-guarded perimeter. He cursed himself for missing what would have been obvious to anyone—anyone, that is, who hadn't been guided by an organ far less dependable than his brain.

He would have liked to say that organ had been his heart—and he had certainly found himself irresistibly drawn to her passion for maps as well as her determined curiosity about him—but he was afraid the true culprit resided somewhat south of that beating mass.

That dress. Those breasts. The fire in those eyes . . .

Idiot. She was here to betray him and still he could not tear her from his thoughts.

She'd said she was engaged to Rogan Reynolds, and the large diamond on her hand certainly seemed to testify to that, but whether she was or not hardly mattered. She was in Reynolds's employ, and if her reward for that collaboration was monetary or something more primitive, Hugh would ensure that she paid a price for her part in it.

He opened the clasp on her bag and dug through the hidden bits and pieces of a woman's life. With any other woman, he would have died before committing such a transgression. It was ungentlemanly, and his cheeks warmed despite the knowledge it was necessary.

He pushed aside the ring of keys, the change purse and the sleek, heavy rectangle, thinner than a deck of cards, with which she'd made that audible connection with her colleague. Had he more time, he would have certainly pored over the last, but the primary object of his attention was flatter and stiff, almost like a single playing card, displaying a portrait of its owner, that had been used like a key by the people entering and leaving the inner reaches of the building she called the USX Tower.

There it was. He slipped the item into his pocket and would have closed the bag and placed it back under her coat except for a small liquid-filled bottle that caught his eye. The voices beyond the curtain showed no signs of slowing. He removed the cap and lifted the bottle to his nose. It was her. That scent of plums and jasmine. He closed his eyes and immediately the long stretch of back and the way she'd let his eyes glide over her filled his head.

Whether she was a spy or not, he would have liked Fiona and the friend to have disappeared. He would have liked to watch Joss pull that dress over her head. And he would very much have liked to lift her onto the work-table, pressed her hands behind her and watch that small, round mouth move as he plumbed her.

He wished he could say it was for revenge, but he knew better.

That, he thought, is the trouble with allowing one's heart to be breached. In that direction, there is only pain. For now, he must remain single-minded. Brand was gone, and he couldn't kill him to avenge that horrible death so many years ago. But he could destroy Brand's reputation—his business, his legacy, whatever he held dear. If Joss was hiding the map, and if Reynolds or Joss were privy to the reasons it must be kept hidden, Hugh would destroy them, too.

He slipped the bottle and card in his pocket, feeling them clink against his timepiece, then placed the bag under her coat and went outside into the wind-tossed night, hoping the stench of thievery would not linger on him long.

Fiona slipped her head out the door and squinted into the dark alley. He could be no more than a cipher to her. "Are you there?" she whispered.

"Aye."

"They're done. Do you have it?"

"Aye."

The door closed, and again he was alone. He withdrew farther into the night. He did not wish to see Joss again, given what he was about to do.

From the safety of the darkened cross street, he watched, unseen, as Joss tumbled out with the baby chair in her hand, followed by her friend and the baby. Fiona, hostess to the last, held the door open and looked down the alley.

"Ooh, it's a windy one," Fiona said. "Bundle up, ladies. 'Twas a pleasure to meet you, Master Luke." She squeezed the lad's hand. Hugh wondered for an instant if Fiona had ever wanted a child. He knew little about her. He had taken no time to learn.

"Is Hugh around?" Joss asked hesitantly, and he felt a warmth he would not have expected. "I wanted to say good night."

"I believe he's busy with something upstairs."

"Oh."

"C'mon, kiddo," Diane said to her. "Another time."

Fiona waved and closed the door.

Diane leaned low, struggling to find her balance as she lowered the baby into the little chair.

Joss took the chair and both women wobbled a bit as they began their ascent of the alley, Joss because of the weight of the child and her friend because of the weight of her belly. Every instinct called on him to ensure their safe passage, but he resisted. He had a job to do that he could not do with Joss on his arm.

He was just about to turn to head down the adjoining

street when a pair of men walked into the alley. The hair on his neck bristled.

The men presented no imminent danger. He'd seen enough unsavories to know whether one needed to put up one's guard. Nonetheless, he didn't care for the way they stopped as the women passed.

Joss stumbled but caught herself. She'd had much to drink, he knew, and was wearing those ridiculously high pattens.

"Evening, sweetness," one of the men said.

Hugh stepped into the light, unfolding his shoulders like the mainsails on a man-o'-war. "Joss."

She turned, and the men hurried away.

In a few strides, he was at the women's side. "Where are you going?"

"I'm catching a cab a block over," Diane said. "Joss is walking me there."

"Let me escort you." He took the little chair and offered Diane an arm. He found himself almost afraid to add to the powerful cataract of emotion Joss had stirred when he touched her earlier, though he could feel her presence next to him as keenly as if he held her in his arms. And this night he needed to keep his mind clear.

"You don't have a coat," Joss said.

"I'll be fine. I've endured worse." There might still be a way to salvage his plans for the evening once he'd deposited them safely at their destinations.

They turned down William Penn, past a low brick building called the Allegheny HYP Club and the stately silver tower beside it with its odd-shaped windows. What had happened in three hundred years that spawned the need for so many buildings rising straight in the air? It was as if the busiest part of London had outgrown itself and swelled halfway to the heavens. How did the engineers and masons build such monuments? Did the occupants of the towers feel the thrill he imagined, gazing down at the people on the streets? He'd ridden the moving box up the gut of the USX Tower, half in fear, half in wonderment, and though he'd caught only a glimpse of the view from the landing on which he'd stopped, it had given him the same thrill he felt at the top of a mast.

"There's one." Diane lifted her hand and a yellow carriage roared up the street and stopped before them. The horses had disappeared, Hugh thought, replaced by growling metal beasts.

He handed Diane in. As she thanked him for the help, he passed the baby chair to her. The driver was a young man of indeterminate origin.

"Will she be safe?" he said to Joss.

"Yes, of course."

He closed the door uncertainly. The world had changed so much. The cab drove away. He looked at Joss.

"Where can I take you?"

He expected to be given a street corner or some other feint.

"I need to get back to work."

He froze. Her card was in his pocket. She would not be able to get in. What's more, with her in her office, he could not chance his expedition. Had she seen something earlier? Did she know what he'd done? Was she laughing at him right now?

Accepting the loss of another day in his mission and a

growing frustration with his inability to control his emotions, he bowed and followed her toward Grant Street.

"A woman should not work so hard," he said, though the sentiment seemed vaguely ridiculous, given the situation.

"Story of my life. I do it for my mother."

"Why does she require such an effort?"

"She doesn't. I mean, not actively. She died when I was eight. But she loved maps. She . . . well, she and my father did not have a very happy marriage. I don't think she really got to do the things she wanted to in life, so I try to do things I think would please her. Half the things I have to guess at, of course, because I didn't really know her as a grown-up. Oh, Christ." She swiped at the tear forming in her eye. "But I feel her out there, approving, so I think it's working."

He gazed at her closely. Was she toying with him, preying on a prior knowledge of the situation with his brother? Despite the sense this might be a trap, Hugh felt the overpowering rise of empathy and tried to, but could not, hold his tongue.

"I, too, know what it is to be duty-bound, to feel the memory of another as both a weight and a wind."

Her eyes grew clear, and in that instant he knew that about this at least she was not lying.

"That's exactly the way it feels. Who is it for you?"

His throat tightened. "My brother."

"I'm so sorry. Older or younger?"

"Older."

They reached Grant and waited for the traffic to stop.

"You can drop me here," she said. "I'll be fine."

"As you wish."

"My mother died suddenly. It was awful. I never got to say good-bye."

He recognized the gentle prompt in the silence that followed. He even wanted to say it, but was mortally afraid he could not.

The carriages raced up and down the street. He could see the glow of the street lamp glinting in her hair.

"My brother was murdered."

She stopped dead. "Oh, Hugh." She laid a hand on his wrist.

He bit back so hard on the thickness rising in his throat, he thought he might choke. He opened his mouth to deflect her concern, but no words came.

A tear striped her cheek. "How did you live with the knowledge?"

That was the question. In seven words she had struck at the core of his being. If she lifted a dagger now to drive it through his heart, he could not have stopped her.

"One carries on," he said at last. "I think of him every day."

"And I of my mother."

The carriages stopped and that odd sign in the shape of a human figure lit. He had learned from observation that it signaled to those on foot it was safe to cross, but she did not move. Instead she squeezed his arm.

"It's like we're trapped," she said.

"Leg irons of joy and pain."

"I do wonder if that's what either of them would have wanted."

He could not speak.

She let go of him, and he felt unmoored. The crossing figure began its urgent blinking.

"I should go," she said.

He nodded, and she hurried into the street. Halfway across she stopped. "What was your brother's name?"

He hesitated. What difference could it make? She probably already knew. "Bart."

"Bart." She smiled. "I'll think of him, too."

He didn't know how long he'd stood there, tempest-tossed and adrift, but when Nathaniel said his name, he realized he was shivering.

"I was starting to get concerned," Nathaniel said. "Fiona was watching from the window. She saw you meet up with the women."

"Were you afraid one might attack?" he asked with a wry smile.

Nathaniel handed him his coat. "That isn't what I was concerned about."

Nathaniel, Hugh knew, saw more than he said. He slipped into the heavy wool and inclined his head in the direction of the tower. "She works there."

"I know."

"No, I mean there. About two-thirds of the way up. See that light? That's the map company. I found her name on a posted list today while I was scouting."

"Are you not supposed to be there instead of her?"

"Aye. But what could I do when she said she was returning to work? I have the card that serves as a key. I don't know how she got in."

"Perhaps they recognize her, and that's enough."

"Perhaps." He turned, and together they began to walk down the alleyway. "Nathaniel, you knew my brother."

"You know I did, Monk."

Hugh felt a touch of nostalgia. It had been many years since anyone had called him that. There were few left who even knew him by the name his shipmates had given him for his monkeylike propensity to swing through the sheets and lines. Of course, Nathaniel had served for many years under Bart before joining Hugh's crew when Hugh made his captaincy. Nathaniel was one of the sailors who'd come to help Hugh when Bart was murdered. Hugh's fingers went automatically to the timepiece, feeling the engraved words, as familiar to him as the scars on his hands. Only this time he felt the perfume bottle as well. "Would you say you knew him well?"

"As well as any man, I suppose. Not many were able to pierce that reserve."

Hugh thought of one who did, the only mother he'd ever known, and the happy time they'd shared as a family before Alfred Brand destroyed everything. "Do you think he'd be glad for what I'm doing?"

Nathaniel gazed into the lambent night. "Well, I've never had a brother murdered, so I don't know that I'm a fair judge, but I can say this: you have been a faithful attendant to his memory. But I don't know that he would have wanted an attendant, only a brother."

They stopped at William Penn, and Hugh turned back to look up the rise, the twinkle of scattered lights in the tower as arresting as those in the sky.

"I think," Hugh said, "if Rogan has been invested with Brand's secrets, Joss doesn't know. I think her engagement to Rogan is her only connection to all of this."

Nathaniel made a regretful noise.

"What?" Hugh demanded. "What do you know?"

Nathaniel unfolded a piece of paper and handed it to his friend. "This is what I found while I was out. It's a list of directors of Brand's company. Joss O'Malley is on the board."

CHAPTER TWELVE

Joss was sipping her morning chai tea when a shadow fell across the binder of contracts she'd been reviewing.

Rogan, looking like something out of a George Romero movie, stood in her office doorway.

"You're blocking my sun, pal."

"No sun. Please, no sun." Like a medium contacting the dead, Rogan massaged his temple and made a long, quiet moan. "Ibuprofen," he croaked.

He was wearing the same shirt and pants he'd been wearing the day before. It would be fair to say he wasn't up to his usual high standards of grooming. In fact, it would be fair to say he looked like shit, but Joss, out of the inexplicable affection she had for her party-loving fiancé, held her tongue.

"I couldn't help but notice you weren't home when I left this morning." She opened her desk drawer and rummaged for the painkillers.

He sighed. "It was a long night."

"*Hm.* You know the rule. Strip club with the boys, condoms for a year."

"Ouch." He winced.

"And blood tests quarterly."

"That's harsh."

"Is it?" she asked. "Or is it really smart?"

He cleared his throat as LaWren, the guard, walked by. "Trust me," he said. "You have nothing to worry about. Those women couldn't hold a candle to you."

"It's the candle holding I'm concerned about." She opened the bottle.

"Now, Joss, you know that would be unethical *and* illegal." He gave his chin a prim lift. "I shudder to imagine it."

"Yeah, you shudder, all right. You don't seem to mind when I'm doing it."

"My father advised me to close my eyes and think of England."

"A remarkable act of courage."

"Thank you."

She opened the bottle and spilled two pills into his hand. He popped them like Tic Tacs and grabbed her mug to wash them down.

"Christ," he said with a grimace, "that is the worst coffee I've ever tasted. How was your little get-together?"

"Would you believe I stripped for a guy I barely know?"

He snorted, and his hands flew to his head. "Oh, Joss, stop! Don't make me laugh."

"Actually, I did—sort of. I went to a tailor. I've decided to wear something different Tuesday."

"Different from what?" His eyes twinkled.

She got up to retrieve another binder. "Okay, I know guys don't pay attention to things like that, but it may make a difference to you to know I'll be wearing a sort of Greek goddess thing instead of the skirt and blouse."

"Oh, thank God. I was afraid I'd be having sex dreams about Carol Brady."

She gave him a full-body bump, and he laughed again.

"Any more cracks like that," she said, "and I'll be forced to give you the complete rundown of the bachelorette party, which included, but was not limited to, club soda at the Tap Room, breast-feeding at the tailor's and running, giggling, through the streets with the car seat."

"Stop!" he cried, bent from the laughter.

"Capped, of course, by me returning to the office to do the end-of-month report. Oh yeah, we know how to tear things up."

"Poor Joss." He touched her hand affectionately. "Your father said you were the only kid with gray hair he ever knew."

For good reason, she thought, and then immediately wished she hadn't. Yes, her father had been a complete asshole to her mother. She remembered that clearly. And yes, he'd been brutal to his business partners, a fact that had come back to haunt him later when he needed help. But there were also good things about him. He'd brought her to business meetings when she was little. She remembered sitting on his lap while he rattled out instructions, his deep voice rumbling through the room.

One of the things she loved about Rogan was that he'd befriended her father. In fact, she was sure that had a lot to do with why she'd fallen in love with him. A chance conversation in line at a coffee shop had led to a long dinner. She'd told him about her father's illness and the hospital visits that had become a regular part of her routine. The next morning, at the door to the hospital's visitors' entrance, she'd found him waiting, flowers and magazines in hand. They'd visited her father together. It was only then that she'd discovered he, too, was a corporate magnate. And since she'd chosen to use her mother's name at eighteen, it was also only then that Rogan had discovered the father she'd been talking about was Alfred Brand of Brand Industries. Unsurprisingly, the men hit it off instantly, and soon Rogan had taken over the morning shift. In another month, Rogan had agreed to buy her father's failing company and infuse it with new capital. A month after that, her father was dead, and she and Rogan were engaged.

She looked at the ring. Why, when she looked at the beautiful diamond and thought about what it stood for, did she feel a nagging hint of ambivalence? Rogan was great. She knew being married to him would be wonderful. She guessed it was because there would always be that specter of her parents' marriage hovering out there in her mind.

"Say, my key to the rare map room still works, doesn't it?" She returned to her seat and dropped the binder on her desk. "I mean, I know you're putting in new security, but the changeover isn't until next week, right?"

"It still works. Why?"

"I don't know. I was thinking about my mom, and I thought I might take an hour and go through the old stuff again. I know she loved it. It makes me feel like she's near."

"Sounds great. You could use a little break. Oh, and about the party tonight—"

"I haven't forgotten. Aunt Cathy: hard of hearing but won't admit it. Uncle Jared: don't mention politics. Cousin Brad: the only one who doesn't know his wife is sleeping with his business partner. See, I pay attention."

Rogan smiled. His mother had invited half of Pittsburgh for cocktails tonight at a private room in the nearby Heinz History Center.

"I have to duck out of here at six to get Brad at the airport," he reminded her.

"That's fine. I'll meet you at the party a little before seven thirty."

"Perfect."

She gave him a lopsided smile. "Let the roller-coaster ride begin, eh?"

"Indeed."

"Oh, wait, I forgot."

"What?"

"I must have left my card key at your place. I had to sign in downstairs. Can I get yours, just for today?"

He reached for his wallet. "It's going to make getting to the men's room a little trickier."

"Give me a call. I'll be happy to escort you."

CHAPTER THIRTEEN

The beautiful mapmaker was happy to have helped the old man. She didn't want the gold, for she, too, was as happy as could be, but she didn't want to offend him, so she thanked him and left the gold where he'd hidden it. Later, she told her dark, handsome husband the romantic story, but her husband only wanted to hear about the gold. She didn't tell him the old man had given it to her. Instead she told him the old man had thrown it in the river. Her husband said the old man was a fool.

—The Tale of the Beautiful Mapmaker

The sound of a distant phone ringing broke her concentration. Five fifty? Holy crap! A low-fat peach yogurt and a Byzantine nondisclosure agreement from the Uruguayan Office of Survey and Measurements were not exactly likely to win the prize for the most absorbing combination, yet somehow she'd missed her five-thirty deadline.

She grabbed her bag and ran. She didn't want to be late for the fitting, though she told herself that was because she had a hectic schedule that night, not because she wanted to see Hugh. The blouse she'd picked for the cocktail party, a Jaipur-inspired print, looked great, and, perhaps more important, today's lingerie didn't present such a picture of insouciant unrespectability. Nonetheless, they were quite fine. She smiled.

"Have a great dinner," LaWren called, lifting her gaze from the multiscreened guard desk when Joss passed. "And find that card."

Joss made her way out of the building and opened her umbrella. Rain had fallen softly and steadily all day, though it was supposed to clear up soon. She hurried down the alley, slowing only when she saw that the lights in the tailor shop were still on. With a curious sigh, she slipped through the weird, buzzing skin of the invisible dome and opened the door of the shop.

Fiona, who was standing behind the counter, smiled and said hello.

"Is he in there?" Joss shook out her umbrella and pointed to the other side of the curtain.

"Hugh, do you mean?"

Who else? "Yes."

"Oh, I'm sorry. Hugh's been delayed. He asked if you'd wait. He shouldn't be longer than half an hour."

Joss considered. That was going to make the fitting tight. Nonetheless, she didn't want to miss it, or him.

She took a seat in the fitting room, pulled out her cell and began to answer some of the late-afternoon e-mail.

Hugh stole a glance at the woman with the metal studs in her brow and ambled across the lobby of the USX

Tower. Two days of reconnaissance had made one thing eminently clear: few people in this busy, crowded world paid attention to anything. He was wearing a dark pair of trousers and a dark shirt, but he suspected he could have walked through the place in his full captain's kit and no one would have batted an eye. His chosen time reflected a compromise between the anonymous rush of five o'clock, when hundreds of workers streamed out of the moving boxes into the streets and he could slip upstream without drawing attention, and the reassuring emptiness of seven o'clock, when he could make his way through the offices upstairs with little notice.

He brought the piece of wood to his ear and began to talk and nod. He'd had Nathaniel fashion a little deck-of-cards rectangle like Joss's that afternoon. It had none of the magic of the decks of cards that seemed to be in use by half the visible population at any given time. Nonetheless, it would allow him to linger unnoticed for long periods of time by the tollgate that had been set up in front of the entrance to each collection of moving boxes.

The event he awaited had happened twice that morning and three times that afternoon, so he knew if he was patient, he would likely be rewarded.

He was in luck. In less than a quarter hour, a woman with an armload of books and satchels, wearing a pair of those impractical shoes, took an unattended step and tumbled to the slick floor, scattering her belongings in every direction.

The guard ran to her side. Hugh hurdled smoothly over the gate, slipped into the group heading into the moving box and, following the process that seemed to be laid out for riders, said, "Forty-six, please."

He wondered if Joss was disappointed he was late.

Joss hit Send, looked at the time and sighed: 6:25. Their time together would be sadly compressed.

Fiona stuck her head in. "I apologize. Hugh just let me know he'd like to meet you at the tavern at the William Penn Hotel for a glass of wine, if you're willing."

It would have to be a damned quick one. She needed to be back on Grant on her way to the History Center by seven fifteen. She gathered her umbrella and bag. "Should we reschedule the fitting?"

"You needn't worry. The dress is actually finished. Hugh has it with him. If there are any modifications necessary, which I doubt, you can bring it back tomorrow. How's that?" She gave Joss a good-service smile. "I think you'll like it. It's beautiful."

Joss was halfway to the William Penn Hotel when her phone rang.

"Joss?" It was LaWren.

"What's up?"

"I think I found your card."

"Really? Where?"

"Do you happen to know a really cute guy, about six two, with a scar through his eyebrow?"

Omigod! Hugh had found the card, though why he was dropping it off at her office instead of giving it to her at the fitting, Joss couldn't guess. "Yes, I do," she said happily.

"Okay, well, he's breaking into your office right now. Is that a problem?"

Joss felt her blood chill for an instant before a bottle rocket shot to the top of her head, exploded in a dizzying fireball of heat and rained down in flaming embers of shame.

"What exactly to you mean?"

"I mean the monitor flipped to your office hallway. The guy entered his card and opened the door. Since I knew you'd lost your card I checked the system to see whose card that was. Every once in a while two cards are given the same code, but it's pretty rare. Anyhow, I checked to see who it was, so we could have that fixed—and, of course, so you could kick his ass for going into your office—but the system said it was you. It's your card."

Joss felt ill, physically ill. She'd been tricked, and she'd fallen for it—hard. Her brain was running in six directions, a hundred miles an hour. He hadn't wanted a fitting, a last chance to see her before she'd married. He'd wanted a known time for her to be out of her office.

Oh, God, oh, God. And still her feet were taking her toward the hotel bar, hoping but not believing that he'd be sitting there, holding the dress, and this would all be a big mistake.

"Joss?"

"Yeah, I'm here." She could barely think over the horrified buzzing in her brain. He must have taken the key from her purse the previous evening. "What's he doing? Can you see?"

"Sure, I can see everything. The security company was in last week and upgraded everything. There's a camera

right in your office. Didn't you see it? It's in the ceiling?
Looks like a smoke detector?"

She frowned. "No." *Why wouldn't Rogan have mentioned doing that?*

"He's looking through your files."

She thought of what she had in her office. Contracts,
new product plans, some personnel stuff. Was he a thief?
Or a corporate spy? She was trying to think straight, but
all she could hear was: "I want to make this dress for you.
Come back tomorrow. Right before we close," and all she
could see was the look on his face as he pinned the silk up
that long, gaping chasm.

Bastard.

"He's looking at the picture on your desk."

"What?" It was a shot of her and Rogan at a party. Di
had snapped it without their knowledge. Joss was laughing at something he'd said, and he was rubbing her hand
with his thumb as his eyes twinkled in delight.

"Oh, he's opening your file cabinet!" LaWren cried.
"Do you want me to call nine-one-one?"

Oh, God, more people knowing she's been suckered?
"No. Let's see what he does." She began to jog back toward the office.

"He's looking at a map."

"Which one?"

"I can't . . . Hold on. It's big."

"Is it the one of Uruguay?" So much for the nondisclosure.

"Jeez, I don't know. Why don't you look?"

Then Joss remembered: the security cameras fed a protected company website. Occasionally, just for fun, she'd pull up the page and amuse herself with the amazing things people do when they forget you're watching.

"Hang on." She stopped and pulled her phone away from her ear. Then she typed the URL into the tiny screen, followed by her ID and password. In a moment, she watched a reasonable facsimile of her office pop into view.

The transmission was jerky and incredibly small, but there was no way the man was anybody but Hugh. She could feel the cold rain hitting her ankles.

"Joss?"

She heard the tiny squawk coming from her phone and hit the Speaker button. "Yeah, I'm here."

"Do you see the map?"

"Yep." It wasn't the map from Uruguay. It was an antique map. The one she had mounted on her wall. It was of France, from around 1700. She'd bought it at an auction because she'd loved its intricate compass rose. "Wait," she said suddenly, "I've lost the picture. I'm looking at the lobby instead."

"Sorry," LaWren said. "I'll lock it for you. There. Do you see it again?"

"Yes. Got it." What was he looking at? He seemed to be examining the edge of the map, as if looking for an artist's signature. Then he stepped away and moved out of camera range. "Where's he going?"

"Let me check." Joss heard LaWren punch a button. "Got 'im. He's in the contact room."

The contact room was a long stretch of glassed-in hallway with a few chairs and some magazines. It was where visitors were sometimes placed to await their host. Joss saw the image appear on her screen.

In the brighter light of the contact room, Joss could see Hugh was dressed in black from head to toe, and she realized it was the same outfit he'd been wearing the evening before. She wondered if he'd been planning to break in then. She wondered if that's why he had walked with her. She thought of his murdered brother and felt her face grow hot with embarrassment. She had cried—cried!— and now she barely believed he had a brother, let alone one who had been murdered.

"So, who is he?"

"Pardon?" Joss said, shaking off the humiliating thoughts.

"You said you knew him. Who is he?"

"He's . . ." What would she say? What would she tell Rogan when he asked about her new wedding dress? Her mind went in quick, tight circles around an impossible track. There was nothing else she could say. "He's a tailor. . . . My tailor."

"Oh, Joss, did he find the key in something of yours he was working on?"

"Yes." Essentially. She felt a hot anger begin to stir in her gut. It was one thing to embarrass her—something he'd done thoroughly and completely. If there were an Olympic medal for betrayal, he'd win the gold. But it was another to embarrass her in front of her people. And while she hadn't mentioned the dress, how long would it be until the gossips could add that detail? *Poor Joss. Tricked by her wedding dress maker into giving up her security key. I hear he told her she'd look like a Greek goddess. And now she doesn't even get the dress.*

She felt her hand balling into a fist around the handle of her umbrella.

Hugh was contemplating the breadth of the office floor through the thick glass wall, evidently planning his next step. He pressed his hands together and began making his way toward the offices at the opposite side of the building.

"Can you block the doors?" Joss said suddenly.

"What?"

"Block them. Can you block them with a code or something?" There were two security doors, one at each end.

"I can't block them, but you need a key card to get them open."

"He's got a key card. Mine, remember?"

"Not if I deactivate it."

The sound of a keyboard clacking came over the speaker.

"Done," LaWren said triumphantly.

Hugh held the card in front of the reader. Joss couldn't see it, but she knew what appeared. A little red light with a tiny, dismissive *click*.

Ha!

He stepped back, confused, then looked around.

It sucks, huh, to think one thing is happening then discover it's something entirely different?

"What about the PA?" Joss asked. The public address system was used only for important announcements—"The holiday party begins in fifteen minutes"—or true emergencies: "The north bank of elevators have lost their power."

"I got it."

Joss heard the static *pop* of the speaker being turned on.

"What about targeting it?"

"Just to the contact room?"

"Yep."

"That I believe we can do. Your father put that in after he got tired of hearing about cars in the Brand Industries parking spaces with their lights on."

Hugh was trying the other door now. Sadly for him, that didn't work either.

"All right. Tell him he's about to be arrested. Tell him the police have been called."

The feed Joss was looking at didn't include any audio, but she didn't need it. Hugh jumped about a foot at the sound of LaWren's voice, then pounded the wall in disappointment. *Perfect.*

"Now, do you want me to call the police?" LaWren asked.

"Can he hear you?"

"No. I got my finger on the button."

"Good. I don't want him to know it's me. No, I don't want you to call the police. They'd just arrest him. I've got a better idea. Ask him if he has any weapons on him."

LaWren complied. Joss could see Hugh shake his head on the screen. "Tell him you don't believe him. Tell him to turn around, then lift up his pant legs."

Hugh's head spun back and forth. He was trying to determine where the camera was. When he lifted his gaze to the ceiling, he was looking straight at Joss. She almost jerked the phone away.

With a visible sigh, Hugh turned, his hands held loosely in the air. When he'd made a full circle, he raised each pant leg to mid-calf. Other than a pair of dark socks and shoes, there was nothing of interest.

"He's clean," LaWren said.

"It's hard to tell sometimes. Tell him to take off his shirt."

Joss felt the slight pause. "His shirt?" LaWren said.

"Yes."

She gave the command.

Hugh unbuttoned his cuffs, jerked the shirttails loose and pulled his shirt over his head.

His chest was broad and taut, with a light dusting of copper hair that ran from his sternum past his belly. He looked like someone who spent all day doing work far harder than lifting a bolt of silk to the cutting table. And though the resolution on Joss's screen was something akin to gazing at the *Mona Lisa* from outside the ladies' room two galleries away, she could see a particularly ugly scar running across the thickest part of his arm.

"Man," LaWren said. "Sure beats the thieves we got on the South Side."

"Tell him to turn," Joss said.

"Turn, please," LaWren said.

When he did, they both gasped. The scar on his arm was nothing compared to the web of silvery lines on his back.

"My God," Joss said.

"He's a *tailor*?"

"No, obviously not. He's at least a thief. I don't know what else." The picture was quite stunning, Joss had to admit, especially with nothing left but a pair of close-fitting trousers, though that seemed to only make her angrier. "Can you see? Is anyone else still working?"

"George on forty-seven. Chris on forty-seven. And Mary on forty-six— Wait, no, she's got her coat on. She's heading for the elevator."

"That's good."

"Well, I'm not too worried. I'm mean, he's stuck where he is, and it's pretty clear he doesn't have any weapons on him. That is," LaWren said, lowering her voice, "unless you count—"

"I don't."

Joss considered her options. At this point, he'd gotten nothing of value. He knew he was caught. The key would never work again. But there was still the matter of a deeply bruised ego.

"LaWren, I'm not done here."

"Oh boy. I was afraid you were going to say that."

"I want his pants."

"You know he's gonna balk."

"You're attributing a pretty high level of fastidiousness to a guy who just went through my drawers."

Joss could feel the unspoken witticism in the silence that followed, and another bolt of heat shot to her face. "You know what I meant." *Christ, he's embarrassing me without even trying now. Well, two can play at that.* "Pants."

LaWren sighed and opened the mike. "Would you mind removing your pants, sir?"

"Sir?" Joss squawked. "Now he's a sir?"

"I thought I'd give him a little break. He's going to be standing there in nothing but his shorts in a min— *Whoa.*"

Joss jerked the phone closer. Hugh had kicked off his shoes and was unbuckling his belt. There was something hypnotizing about the way he handled the leather, briskly and without ceremony, before unzipping his fly. His boxers were blue with yellow stripes, like a banker's shirt, only that waist and those thighs were nothing like Joss had ever seen at her neighborhood branch. He dropped the trousers to the side, threw his shoulders back and gave the camera a withering look. The rest of him was decidedly *un*withered.

"Wow."

Joss had to agree, though she'd have cut her tongue out with tailor shears before admitting it.

He said something. Joss couldn't hear. "What did he say? What did he say?"

"He asked who's detaining him. He's got one of those sexy British accents. 'May I have the pleasure of knowing who is detaining me?'" She imitated him in a deep voice. "You know, all PBS."

"Oh yeah. He's a real Regency hero. Tell him to piss off."

"Can I make it like a question, so I can hear him answer?"

"No."

LaWren complied, then made a worried noise. "He looks *mad*."

He did, and Joss was glad there was a glass wall, forty-six storeys and an iPhone between them.

She'd almost decided he'd had enough, then her eyes fell on the gold sandals she was wearing—in November!—the sandals she'd run to three stores over lunch to find. "I want the rest."

"Joss!"

"Look, he was supposed to be my Mr. Mistake."

"Boy, you got your wish, sister."

"No, I mean before my wedding. Not to sleep with. To flirt with. To have a *thing* with. My last *thing*."

"If that's your last thing, I think you should rethink the rules of engagement."

"Would it make any difference to you to know that he conned me into trying on a dress by telling me I looked like a Greek goddess, watched me strip naked, made an appointment for tonight so that he could see me 'one last time' before I got married, then stole my key card and left me waiting in his shop while he came here?"

LaWren clicked the mike. "Drop your shorts, asshole. There's a map missing, and we're not stopping until it's found."

Hugh's face turned six shades of purple.

"Off with 'em, pal. This isn't my only gig tonight."

He threaded his thumbs along the waistband and dropped the fabric to the floor.

LaWren exhaled first. "Are you seeing what I'm seeing?"

"Yikes." It was riveting.

"No map there."

"Nope."

"Not unless it's rolled up pretty tight."

"Yep."

"What are those things on each side of his stomach? They look like little cliffs."

"Hell if I know. Never seen 'em before."

"I like cliffs," LaWren said. "Very scenic."

"Anyhow, you can see why I wouldn't want to tell the police."

"I can see why you wouldn't want to tell Rogan."

"The guy's an asshole *par excellence*."

"You got that right." LaWren blew out a puff of air. "I think we should have him turn around. I mean, that map could be anywhere, right?"

"Suit yourself."

"My sweet Lord," LaWren said an instant after she gave the command. "That's a rear end you can take home to meet the family."

Joss dragged her eyes away from the screen. "I think we may have done what we needed to do here."

"We have. Definitely."

Neither woman spoke.

"Well, certainly now," Joss said.

"Right." Another two beats passed. "I'm not seeing an exit strategy here," LaWren said.

"Well, let's think. We know he doesn't have a map."

"Yeah, that's pretty clear."

"And we know I don't want to call the police."

"Yep," LaWren said.

"So, why not just unlock the doors . . . and run?"

"Oh, the fourth-grade strategy?"

"Yes."

"I'm liking it."

The rain had stopped. Joss closed the umbrella. "Tell him you'll be watching until the elevator door closes. And tell him not to do anything funny, or we'll call the police."

"I don't suppose 'anything funny' includes getting dressed?"

"No, I'm afraid not."

"Shoot."

"Only if necessary."

Joss hovered out of sight on the far end of the outdoor concourse. She told herself she wanted to be sure he'd left the building, but she knew the real reason she was waiting and she hated herself for it.

He emerged from the doors in long, purposeful strides that spoke of a life where there'd been little room for diversions, though, of course, she reminded herself, he'd made room for a diversion with her when it had suited his purpose. She waited until he cleared the outside steps before heading into the building. She signed in and stopped to see LaWren, who gave her a hug, told her she deserved a much better Mr. Mistake and offered to make her a copy of the security tape.

Joss declined and made her way to Rogan's office, stopping at the vending machine for a bottle of water. He had a private bathroom. She was going to dump her tote, refresh her makeup and zip down to the History Center.

She tore the annoying plastic seal off the top of the bottle, popped the valve and squirted some water into her mouth. Of course, Rogan said everything about bottled water was annoying, but where else were you going to find chilled refreshment that doubled as a watering can? She squeezed a healthy dose into the fern in the hallway.

Sighing, she pushed open the door and put down the bottle. Then a force like a freight train hit her, and she was slammed into the wall, arm pulled taut behind her, with an overpowering weight holding her in place.

"Frightened?"

It was Hugh.

Her heart was pounding and the wall was cold. She must have dropped her bag, because she didn't feel it on her shoulder anymore. It was clear in the blink of an eye that with the office emptied out she was terrifyingly alone. "Yes."

"Don't be." He put his face quite close to her ear. "I won't hurt you, but we're going to stay where the eye can't see us. Do you understand?"

"The eye?" He wasn't making sense, which was scaring her even more.

He pointed to the camera on the ceiling. "Is it listening now?"

"Yes."

"You're lying."

"Am I?"

"You would have screamed already." And as if to emphasize his point, he loosened his grip and waited. "I want you to take me to the map room, the one you told me about."

"Why?"

He didn't answer, just nudged her legs open with his foot and patted her down. When he got too close to her breasts, she drove her elbow into his side.

He gasped, sighed and turned her to face him. "I told you I wouldn't hurt you. I would appreciate the same consideration."

"I'll be the judge of what hurts and what doesn't." He was still so close, she couldn't free herself. She could feel his thighs flex as he moved.

"I want to go to the map room and I'll not ask again."

"It's locked." She spotted the bottle of water. It was almost within reach. "The key's in the desk."

He swung his head for an instant to take in the lay of the room. "Pray, then, go to the desk and get it. However, if you make any gestures that suggest you're in trouble, I will drag you out of this room, and I can assure you, you will not care for what happens after that."

There was enough grit in his voice to make her believe him.

"On the count of three, aye? One, two—"

She grabbed the bottle and swung with all her might. It hit him hard, and he was stunned but still on his feet. She dove for the door and had a hand on the frame when her feet went out from under her. She hit the carpet with a crash, and he pinned her wrists to the floor.

"Dammit! You work for Brand! Don't deny it." He was breathing like a bull, and his knees dug hard into her sides.

"I can't breathe."

He eased his weight a degree. "Do you deny it?"

Over the years Joss had encountered scores of people angry with her father. She was just sorry that Hugh turned out to be nothing more than another person with an ax to grind. "Why would I deny it?"

"Why would you deny it?" he cried, disbelieving. "Perhaps because he's one of the most singularly selfish and evil men I've ever had the unhappiness to meet!"

"Do you think you're the first person to tell me that? He was a hard man. Learn to live with it. I did. What do you want? Money?"

"Don't insult me."

The fire in his eyes turned white-hot—a proud, determined white-hot—and Joss saw her comment had hurt him. She also realized that if he hadn't taken a swung at her now, he wasn't going to.

"I want the key to the map room." He let go of her wrists and released his knees.

Rogan's key would open it and that was in her back pocket, but she'd be damned if she'd just hand it over. "It's in my desk."

She wriggled a few inches, and he caught her. "You're a liar." With swift precision, he checked her blouse, bra and velvet jacket, then flipped her on her side and found the key card in the back pocket of her tuxedo pants.

He pulled her to sitting and held the card in front of her. She slapped him.

He ran his hand over the mark she'd left, looking surprisingly abashed. He did have a weak spot: manners.

"Let's go." He lifted her to her feet. "The quicker we get this done, the quicker you can get to your little party."

She brushed herself off and began to move toward the door.

"Ah ah ah." He caught her. "I think you'll have to make contact with the guard first. Tell her, if you would, that you believe you saw someone in the building near your desk, and ask her if she'd be good enough to make a quick check." He settled his bulk against the door. "Don't do anything foolhardy."

At this point, Joss simply wanted to get this over with. She pulled the phone from her bag and dialed. "Hi. Yeah, it's me."

"Changed your mind about the copy of the tape?" LaWren asked.

"No, that's not why I'm calling. I actually . . ."

Hugh gave her a stern look.

". . . saw someone outside my office."

"The guy with the luscious rear?"

"Ah, no. Not him at all. Someone else."

Something caught Hugh's eye. He went to the corner of the office and knelt down.

"Someone else? His ass as fine?"

"Actually, it's not bad. But the point is, I guess, the guy I saw is nobody I recognize. Do you think you could take a quick look around?"

Hugh tugged something loose. In his hand was the demi-bra from her escapade with Rogan on Monday. She barely heard LaWren's reply. There was nothing to be gained from responding to the question on Hugh's face. Pride battled pride deep in her soul. Should she hold her tongue and feel the shame of having him think she'd thrown in her lot with a guy who cheated on his fiancée, or speak the truth and feel the shame of her rather incautious behavior. The line went dead. She punched End and said, "It's mine."

He shook his head, placed it gently on the couch and made a theatrical gesture toward the door.

CHAPTER FOURTEEN

Her back quivered with anger as she walked. Of course, given the fact she worked for Brand, Hugh had little sympathy to spare, especially after the indignity he'd just endured. Nonetheless, he allowed himself to imagine how the moonlight might move over that slim expanse as she reached for a decanter of wine on the bedroom floor or arched in pleasure as he stroked her.

Her admission that the undergarment was hers had been a blow. Foolish though it had been, he had nurtured a hope that the partnership between her and Reynolds was just business, that the ring and her tales of a wedding had only been parts of a play acted out for his benefit. But there was no denying the significance of that bit of wire and silk. Had she taken Rogan to bed right there on the chaise? Hugh thought of her rocking slowly over his hips, in full view of an unshaded window, damning the eyes of anyone bold enough to look upon their joining.

But he had more to concern himself with than daydreams. What he needed was the map upon which had been written the letter of agreement, the letter describing the two pieces of land to be traded with the signature of the two landowners at the bottom. However Alfred Brand had reached the past, he had arrived with one objective: to stop the transfer of a parcel of land from his many-times great-grandfather to Fiona's grandfather. The land had been part of an exchange, a piece with a much-needed stream for the Brands in trade for more arable land for Fiona's farming family. A year after the transfer, Fiona's grandfather had found one of the richest seams of tin in the kingdom on the land that had once belonged to the Brands.

Alfred Brand had arrived in the world of his many-times great-grandfather three years before the transfer, and, except for a short diversion to court and marry Maggie Brand, had focused single-mindedly and often underhandedly on finding his relation and stopping the transfer. But even with his careful planning, Brand had nearly been too late. The deed of intent had been filed by the time Brand had finally put his hands on the map. Without the signed map, however, the deed of intent was worthless. Then, to ensure the men didn't go on with the transaction anyway, Alfred Brand paid someone to swear out a warrant for the arrest of Fiona's grandfather for treason. His lands were confiscated by the Crown. The moment Brand stepped from that islet through the narrow cave entrance and returned to Pittsburgh with the map in his hand, it was as if the map had never existed. Brand, who had left his time a man of modest means, returned to a world in which his family had been wealthy for centuries.

Hugh had seen the map once before, on the islet, when he was a child. If he could find the map and return it to the past, Hugh could restore what had been taken from Fiona and her family, but more important, he could reverse three hundred years of Brand family wealth and prosperity. Brand might be dead, but a man treasured his name above all, did he not? Brand Industries was his legacy. Hugh would destroy that and whatever else remained of the man in a single blow.

Joss stopped at a nondescript door. She held out her hand. Reluctantly, Hugh placed the card in it. As she waved it in front of the lock, Hugh spotted a framed certificate on the wall titled the "The Brand Philosophy." It was a description of the ideals Alfred Brand expected his workers to embrace, both florid and, if the first few sentences were any proof, hypocritical. Hugh gazed with disgust at Brand's signature at the bottom, done in a script as ornate and self-important as that of any French emperor.

The door clicked and they entered. The room was narrow, lined with chests that held wide, shallow drawers. Under softly lit lamps stood a slanted worktable upon which sat a magnifying glass of some sort as well as white gloves and small biscuit-shaped weights. There were no windows. The eye, he noted, was positioned over the door.

He let door click behind them and leaned against it. "Find a map and sit at the desk," he commanded.

"Which one?"

"Any one. You need to look like you're working."

With a sigh, she opened a nearby drawer, selected the top map and settled in at the worktable. He figured the first chest of drawers was out of view of the eye and decided he would begin his search there.

"Good. Now, keep your head down and look the part," he said. "I'll let you know when I need your help."

She picked up the magnifying glass and searched the map on the table before her. "How did you get back in to our offices?"

"I held the door for a woman carrying a mop and pushing a large bucket."

Josh laughed. "So good to know being polite still gets you somewhere these days. And how did you know I'd go to Rogan's office?"

"I didn't."

Great. I just walked into it, Joss thought. "You know, I might be able to help if you let me know what map you're looking for."

"You've helped quite enough." He opened the first drawer and pulled out the entire contents—six maps, separated with sheets of pristine white paper—then flipped through them, scanning the fronts and the backs. None of these maps was like what he'd seen at all. In fact, they appeared to be of areas in the Orient. He returned the maps and considered with a grimace the number of drawers he would have to search.

"Honestly, I can help," she said.

"Keep your head down. It mustn't look like you're talking to someone."

She returned to the glass and positioned herself with her back to the eye. "Tell me what you're looking for. The maps are arranged by source and time period."

"England," he said with some reluctance. He did not care to let her even that far into his confidence.

Her brow went up. Did she know about the stolen

map or not? He was finding it extremely difficult to read her.

"We have a number of English maps," she said. "My mother was English, you see. If you care to be more exact, I can narrow the search further."

What connection her mother had to the maps here, he did not know. "East Fenwick," he said after considering his prospects. Something flickered behind her eyes.

"The maps would be in those drawers." She pointed to a cabinet a few yards from where she sat.

"Bring them to me."

"I'd appreciate it if you wore gloves."

He nodded. "As you wish."

She snagged the gloves as she stood, stuffing them into the same pocket he had so recently explored. A certain entrancing confidence radiated from her like perfume, but the addition of male trousers, which revealed her body in a way no woman would ever dare in his time, pushed the effect from interesting to frankly provocative.

She bent to open the lowest drawer and pulled out a handful of maps, taking care to hold them by the paper separators. She walked by the desk and placed them on the chest in front of him. "There are four drawers of southern England." She placed the gloves on top of the maps.

"They're tight," he said, slipping one on his hand.

She bit her lip. "Better let me do it then."

She slipped the gloves on easily and leafed through the pages, pausing to let him review each one over her shoulder.

"Why do you possess such a large number of maps?" he asked, wondering if Brand had indulged in reversals of fate in other times as well.

"I told you, we sell maps."

"Alfred Brand had a map company?" Hugh was amazed. The irony overwhelmed him.

"This is not a part of Brand Industries," she said hotly.

Again he sensed an underlying resentment. What *was* the connection between her and Brand?

"'Tis a cover of some sort; then? Your own idea?"

"It's not a cover. It's a real company. Mine."

He looked at this slip of a girl, hardly more than twenty. "You run this?"

She shifted. "I try. It's something I do to try to honor my mother."

No. The flicker in her eyes gave the lie to this fabulous tale. "You'll pardon me if I don't believe it—the company, the maps or the dead mother."

She stood up, furious, and jerked his arm hard enough to turn him. Before him hung a small but beautifully illuminated map of Surrey. Beneath the frame hung a plaque that read:

IN HONORED MEMORY OF MY MOTHER,
WHO INSPIRED US WITH HER DEDICATION AND SPIRIT.
WE WILL NEVER FORGET YOUR LOVE OF MAPS.
—JOSS O'MALLEY

When he turned back to Joss, her eyes were wet.

"Do you believe me now?" she said, and wheeled back to the chest of drawers.

He felt a rush of shame that took him back to the days when his brother would have boxed his ears for such an impertinence. What had he become?

"I-I regret my words about your mother. They were

most ungentlemanly. You honored me with your confidence, and I betrayed it."

She made no sound.

"I feared your words were a way to get me to open up about my brother. For that, I am quite ashamed."

Her shoulders relaxed a little. She brushed a wrist past her nose, sniffing, and toyed with the magnifying glass.

So the mother was true. He looked again at the inscription. He wondered if the daughter was capable of inspiring as much feeling as the mother. The little he'd seen so far suggested the answer was aye.

And then he noticed a detail drawn over Redhill Brook on the Surrey map. "Hang on. What's this?"

She turned, reluctant, and looked where he was pointing.

"Sheep. They're meant to indicate pastureland. Sheep for pasture. Upside-down Ws for hills."

"But I know that stretch of land. That's marsh. Nothing but mud and weeds. Completely unusable."

"Perhaps it *was* pastureland"—she checked the year of printing—"in 1701."

He shook his head. "No, I can assure you. That piece of land has been marsh since time immemorial."

She shrugged, an unapologetic curve rising at the corner of her mouth. "Surely you didn't think maps tell the truth?"

"Aye. Indeed, I did."

She laughed. After his misstep, the sound was as sweet to him as the soughing of wind through t'gallants.

"Disabuse yourself of that notion," she said. "Maps don't tell the truth. Maps tell the story the mapmaker wanted to be told. Look at this." She pointed to a map of the world on the opposite wall. "This is a Mercator projection map. It's convenient and mostly accurate for those of us who live between the Tropic of Cancer and the Tropic of Capricorn, but look at Greenland. It's one-eighth the size of South America in square miles, but you'd never know it from that map. Nonetheless, the Mercator projection is a damned convenient way for eighty percent of us to view the world."

"But how would it help anyone to believe a piece of land is pasture when it's marsh," he said, returning to the rendering of Surrey.

"Perhaps the mapmaker owned that stretch of land. Or the person who commissioned the map. And perhaps that person was eager to sell the land to some unsuspecting farmer. What would make the land appear more valuable—little sheep capering over the terrain or a bunch of cattails and horseflies?"

He was stunned. "But maps are supposed to be accurate—as accurate as possible. Why, I use navigational maps and sometimes contribute to them. The men who make those maps pride themselves on the level of accuracy they provide."

She laid the white paper over the topmost map on the chest and picked up the stack. "Let me ask you a question. Do you fish? Or hunt?"

He narrowed his eyes. Did tailors fish or hunt? "Aye, I fish. Occasionally."

"Do you have a favorite place?"

"There are maps which show where the shoals and banks are located, which are usually the best source of fish."

"I didn't mean the maps. I meant you. Do you have a favorite place?"

He thought of the inlet off Brest, where he could almost always count on a score or more of tuna, enough to feed his crew for a week. "Aye."

"And did you tell your mapmaker friends about it, so they could put it on their maps?"

"Well, no. These are personal things. Each man has his own places."

She laughed. "So you see, the maps your friends make lie in a different way, though it is through no fault of their own. The maps your friends make leave out relevant and perhaps critical information."

"But that's—"

"How maps can mislead. They put sheep in; they leave fish out. There are two questions you need to ask yourself about any map: Who made it, and what story were they trying to tell?"

Maps can also distort when they disappear, he thought, but pushed the notion aside so he could admire the gleam of passion in her eyes. "Brand must have loved this room."

"No, actually. He had little regard for maps."

He gazed at her full-faced. There was no hint of dissembling anywhere in that open visage. What would induce her to say what she'd just said unless she truly had no knowledge of the theft? "Indeed?"

"He considered nothing of much interest unless it made money, and the money the maps made was beneath his notice."

That disinterest had stung her. Hugh wondered why.

She went to the next drawer and pulled out another set. "Are you a sailor?"

He started. "Pardon?"

"You said you fish. You use navigational maps. Are you a sailor?"

"Not much of one," he said cautiously. "My brother was."

"Was he really a sailor? I mean, you said he was a bookkeeper, but then again, you also said you were a tailor."

He heard the pique in her voice and felt another wave of shame. "There are things I have to do," he said stiffly. "I apologize if you feel you've been misused."

She snorted.

"I wasn't lying about the chiton. You looked lovely in it. Truly." He saw the faint gooseberry stain that worked its way up her cheeks. "In truth," he said huskily, "making your acquaintance has been quite satisfying, and despite what's happened, I should very much like to—"

"Go to hell."

The heat of her words surprised him. No, there would be no easy peace between them, and it had been foolish of him to try to broker one. He gave her a cold, unapologetic look.

She dropped the maps on the chest. "You're an asshole."

"Oh?" he said carefully. "No '*par excellence*'?"

He watched the realization wash over her. It had been only a snippet of conversation, but he'd recognized her voice when it joined the other coming from the ceiling. He had no doubt she'd been the instigator of the commands.

He had never faced down a woman who'd forced him out of his clothes before. It was an interesting feeling, he had to admit, and more than a little satisfying. He was beginning to discover the twenty-first century offered more than noise, height and blather.

"I-I—"

"I shall take your silence as an apology."

She made no response, though a number of emotions stirred on her face.

"That is," he said with new interest, "unless it indicates something more?"

The volcanic rumbling she labored to stifle was, in itself, payment for the injury.

"'Tis no matter." He made a low bow. "I am satisfied with the apology."

She turned on her heel and dropped into her chair. "You have a lot of nerve thinking *I'd* apologize after what you did to me."

"Gloves?" he inquired.

She flung them at him.

He sighed and retrieved them from the floor. With effort he managed to fit the tips of a finger and thumb in and used these to page through the maps.

"Here. This one," he said upon reaching the third. It was a map of London—not the map he sought, but he recognized the lettering and highly stylized marginalia. Fiona had shown him a map done by the same mapmaker when she'd first purchased his participation in this adventure. And, more important, it was just like the one he'd seen on the islet. Who could have guessed that he'd be hired, twenty years later, to find the very same map?

"This is the mapmaker, but 'tis not the map. Come. Look at it."

Joss walked over, fury oozing from every vein.

"Do you recognize the mapmaker?"

She gave him a long look. "Of course I do. It's my mother. Though I wonder what it's doing here with the antique ones."

He blinked. "Your mother? That's impossible. 'Tis a map from the eighteenth century."

"It appears that way, doesn't it? But it's not. That was my mother's gift, you see. She could make maps like they did in the old days. Aged paper, quills, hand-mixed ink. But it is the beauty of her designs that make them so wonderful. Look at the cartouche."

He was still lost in trying to sort out how a modern map could look so like the ones he had seen before. "Cartouche?"

"This piece here." She pointed to the fantastical shield-shaped inset in the lower right corner. Decorating the cartouche were two Scottish Blackface sheep, one of those medieval towers called a pele that one stumbled upon occasionally in the countryside, a hawk, a bare-toothed hunting dog and a wild boar.

"Is a cartouche like a legend? Legends I know. Even nautical maps have those."

"No," she said curtly. "A cartouche is different. It holds the title of the map, and it can also tell you for whom the map was made, the name of the mapmaker and even the purpose of the map. It is a story in itself, almost all told through symbols. 'Start with the cartouche,' my mother used to say. 'It's where the story is hidden.'"

"And in this case? What story does it tell you about this map of London?"

"I don't know."

"Joss," he said.

"I don't. My mother was a very good storyteller, though she rarely shared the stories behind her maps. I know a few things—not as many as I'd like. She stopped making maps before I was born. I suppose she was too busy working. But I know the meaning of this." She tapped the wild boar. "That's on the crest of the O'Malleys. It's the symbol my mother used for herself."

The hair on Hugh's neck rose. "O'Malley? Is that not the name of the map company?"

"Brand O'Malley, yes."

"Was O'Malley a partner of Alfred Brand?"

She laughed a short, bitter laugh. "I suppose you could say that. My mother is Margaret O'Malley, and she was married to Alfred Brand."

Hugh felt the ferocious spin of a maelstrom, worse than even the one sailors fear off the coast of Scotland. Joss was the daughter of Alfred Brand, the man he had sworn to destroy. And she was also the daughter of Maggie Brand, the only mother he had ever known and the one woman he would protect, even at the cost of his life.

CHAPTER FIFTEEN

One day, the dark, handsome man decided to see if he could find the gold the old man had thrown in the river. He said he would follow the river as far as it took him. The mapmaker was sad for her husband. She knew once a man fell in love with gold, there was no way to stop him.

—The Tale of the Beautiful Mapmaker

"How did we miss this?" Hugh demanded sharply.

"It says Brand had one daughter—Josephine." Fiona waved the paper the publican had given her. Nathaniel smoked his pipe silently at the tailor shop's small counter.

Hugh growled. "Joss *is* Josephine."

"Joss, Josephine. What difference does it make?"

Nathaniel blew out two quick rings and met Hugh's eyes with a look of careful concern. Hugh had not told Fiona everything about his brother's murder. She knew Bart had been a bookkeeper, but she was not aware Bart had been a much-decorated captain in the Royal Navy and the reason Hugh himself had gone to sea as a boy after the death of their parents. Nor was she aware that the islet to which she'd hired Hugh to take her was an islet he'd visited once before, on a fateful stormy night, when he was ten. But Hugh knew that neither of those facts was the reason for Nathaniel's present concern. Nathaniel had witnessed enough of Hugh's feelings for Joss to see the emerging stress points in the vessel of this mission.

"She is still the daughter of Alfred Brand," Fiona said, "which makes our objective here all that much clearer."

"We are here for the map and the map alone."

"That's a lie and you know it. I don't care what we agreed. The man who gave me your name said you'd been asking questions about Brand. He said there was a fire in you he'd seen in no other. Did you think I didn't know you intended to murder Brand? Did you not think that's why I hired you?"

Hugh gazed at her, speechless at this revelation. What other missteps had he made? "What if I had intended it? Brand is dead."

"But his daughter is not."

"We are not going to harm her."

"Who are you to set the limits of my vengeance?"

He crossed the room with such fury, she backed against the wall, and he brought his nose almost to hers. "Damn you! You know nothing about the limits of vengeance. Brand murdered my brother. Murdered him in cold blood. And if I find myself willing to stay the hand of vengeance with this girl, then you will, too. 'Tis my ship, and without it you will spend all of eternity on that accursed rock, clutching a map that will never be filed with the Lord Keeper. Do you understand?"

It took a moment before the anger in him subsided enough to see her surprise. And then he realized what he'd said.

"Your brother . . . ?"

"Aye."

"Oh, Hugh."

He held up a hand to stop her, too agitated to speak, and clutched the timepiece in his pocket. *His blood for yours. A brother's promise.*

"Hugh, don't you see? Finding that map is more important than ever. Joss Brand possesses it. You said so."

"I said she possesses a map that looks like the map of Edinburgh you have in your cabin on the ship. You've seen it yourself." He gestured to the London map done by Maggie Brand he'd taken from the map room, much to Joss O'Malley's dismay. He did not wish for Fiona to know the connection Joss's mother had to him and his brother—he was still trying to come to grips with it himself—so he had said nothing to her about the identity of the mapmaker. " 'Tis not the map you seek. 'Tis of London, not East Fenwick."

"There are other maps there!"

"We looked at them all."

"I know you believe that room represents all she possesses, but, Hugh . . ."

He didn't respond. Fiona picked up the London map. " 'Tis exactly like the one of Edinburgh. . . . With the same scroll at the bottom right."

" 'Tis a cartouche," he said. "It tells the story of the map—or, rather, it tells the story the mapmaker wants to tell of the map, though sometimes, it seems, the story is only for the amusement of the mapmaker."

"It is most amazingly detailed," Nathaniel said, breaking his silence. "A menagerie of animals of which Noah could be proud. What are these?" He pointed to an unusual series of vertical, horizontal and angled dashes that were woven through the designs along the border.

"I don't know," Hugh said. "A background design of some sort, I suppose."

"'Tis odd that it's printed in a bolder ink than anything else. If it were meant to be a background design, wouldn't it be in a lighter shade?"

"Wait," Fiona said. "What's this?" She had flipped the sheet over. "It's a note—but not in English."

Hugh took the map and examined it. The words were in a backward-slanted script, but it did not look like Arabic, and some of the words went right off the page, as if the person writing hadn't seen the end of the paper.

Nathaniel, who had been looking at the words as well, broke into a smile and tapped him on the shoulder. "Leonardo," he said.

Hugh shook his head. *Of course.* He held the paper up to the mirror on the wall. Immediately, the words popped to life.

"I think," Nathaniel said, "the writer used the map for a blotting paper, perhaps unintentionally."

Hugh looked closer. Only parts of the note were visible. "'. . . she has hidden it, though I cannot think where . . .'; '. . . perhaps it doesn't matter. After all, we have come this far . . .'; '. . . I grow impatient with her silence in this as in all things . . .' and '. . . the map that set things to right must never be found. . . .'"

"Is it in Brand's hand?" Nathaniel asked.

Hugh thought of that ornate *A* in *Alfred,* as large as a

walnut on the framed statement, and the *A* in *After all* on the paper in front of him. He nodded reluctantly.

"'. . . she has hidden it,' he writes!" Fiona pointed excitely. "*She!* Don't you see? Joss must know where the map is. Her father said so himself."

"She is not the woman of whom he speaks."

"What other woman could it be?" Fiona's eyes narrowed. "What do you know of Brand you haven't told me?"

Nathaniel tapped his pipe.

Hugh sighed. "Brand's wife was an accomplished mapmaker."

"What are you saying? That a woman from the world in which we stand now made maps that traveled all the way back to the eighteenth century?"

"Perhaps she wasn't a woman from this time." Hugh thought of the woman he'd first met on his brother's ship, forced to endure the most miserable of husbands. Hugh had never thought about it in these terms, but it was true that, personalities and Brand's clumsy accent aside, there had been a sense of something odd or ill-fitting about Brand that one never got from Maggie. Was it possible she'd been a woman from Hugh's own time, not, as he had always believed, a traveler from the future who had been an unwitting companion on her husband's nefarious journey? Had Brand been in England long enough to woo and marry an eighteenth-century woman—and to father a year-old child by the time Hugh met him?

Nathaniel said, "If I may ask, Fiona, what did Phillip Belkin, the man who knew your grandfather, tell you about the East Fenwick map?"

"He said my grandfather commissioned the map

showing the new property lines, then delivered that map and the deed of intent to his neighbor, James Brand, the other party in the transaction, who was to deliver it to the Lord Keeper of the Great Seal to execute the transfer. And the transfer was executed—until Brand found a way to go back in time to stop it."

Nathaniel's eyes cut to Hugh's for an instant before he spoke again. "I can understand how you believe Alfred Brand changed events, m'um—we have seen the unexecuted deed of intent, Brand was clearly a man of wealth, and he certainly used the passage to travel to the past—but how can you be certain the transfer you say Brand reversed ever took place. By your own explanation, once Brand changed events, everything changed for everyone. How could you know? How could *anyone* know?"

Oh, Nathaniel, what intelligence you hide in that sailor's thoughtful stare. Hell, it had taken Hugh two retellings, one with figures representing the key characters in their current and former lives drawn on paper, before he'd thought to ask the question.

Fiona narrowed her eyes. Nathaniel coughed and bent low to retrieve the stub of a pencil from the floor.

"It was Belkin. I, of course, knew nothing of what could have been—what *should* have been. But Belkin told me stories, stories of when my family, the McPherson family, was wealthy. When my grandfather was a great man in the village. Belkin's cousin worked my grandfather's land. Belkin knew the people in our neighborhood—when my grandfather had wealth and after Alfred Brand took it away. And Belkin thought what Brand had done was terrible."

Nathaniel stayed his course. "But," he said, shaking his head, "how did Belkin know? The same question applies. Begging your pardon, m'um, but being a late addition to this adventure, I may not have all the pieces down properly."

"He knew," said Fiona, "because Phillip Belkin was in another time when it happened, like we are now." And to Nathaniel's raised brow she added, "That's right. When you are out of your born time when events change, you remember the before *and* the after. Otherwise, like the rest of us, you don't. Belkin's the one who convinced me I could do this, who told me where the passage was."

"And that brought you directly to Captain Hawksmoor and his ship?"

Fiona must have sensed something more in his question, for her answer was fast and fierce. "Aye, I found Hugh. My grandfather rots in debtor's prison, and my father works in the Brand family tin mine, where he's lost an arm and nearly his life. I think I have a right to be impatient."

"I think everyone understands why this is important to you," Hugh said. "I have a different question. Belkin says your grandfather commissioned a map, in the time when he thought there would be a transfer. Do we know anything about the mapmaker from whom he commissioned it?"

Realization dawned on Fiona's face. "Aye. He said my grandfather told him it was a mapmaker in London, off the Strand—the oddest mapmaking shop he'd ever seen."

Hugh looked at Nathaniel, and Fiona looked at Hugh. "What does it mean?" she asked.

"Nothing, probably. Brand might have met his bride in the process of trying to figure out how he could stop his forebear from trading the land. I wonder if she knew

what he was planning when she fell in love with him."
Hugh felt certain she'd known by the time Hugh had
met her. Her discomfort with her husband's activities had
been obvious. "I think we're forgetting one thing here."

"What?"

"Rogan Reynolds. What does he know?"

"He was here today," Nathaniel said.

Hugh's head swung around. "What!"

"Aye, not long after the girl left. He said Joss invited
him to see the dress. He asked a number of questions: how
long we'd been here, your background as a tailor. And
when he left, he walked around the building—twice."

"He knows," Hugh said as a cold certainty snapped
through his bones. "He knows we're here after the map."

"Or," Fiona said with a smile, "he's afraid you're charming his woman out of more than her wedding skirt."

That was a possibility, of course. Hugh didn't know
what, if anything, Joss had told Reynolds about the goings-
on in the shop. Until this instant, he hadn't been sure if
Reynolds had succeeded Brand as protector of the map,
and while he still wasn't absolutely certain—a walk around
a building was not proof, after all—he knew from this
point forward they would have to take every precaution.
For Reynolds, possession of the map meant possession of
wealth beyond any honest man's imagining. Even in its dismal financial state, Brand Industries was a vast empire that,
with a little luck and good management, could be rebuilt
into a king's fortune. Men had killed for far less.

"I think it's a code." Fiona was gazing at the map.

"What?"

"The dashes in the cartouche. I've seen codes that are

made up of symbols instead of letters. If the note from Brand says she has hidden 'it' and the 'it' is the map, then this might be a code indicating where it's hidden."

Hugh looked at the cartouche again. He had to admit, the odd pattern did give the marks the look of a cipher. "What good does it do, though? Maggie Brand is dead. The key to the code might have died with her."

"Unless there's someone who knows how to interpret her codes," Fiona said.

Joss. "She told me she knew but little of her mother's maps."

"And I'm sure you haven't considered the possibility that she's lying."

"She wasn't." How was he so sure? Or did he just want to believe?

Fiona snorted. "Stop protecting her. She's a Brand. Did she or did she not grow up in great wealth while you grew up without a brother and I grew up penniless?"

He didn't answer. The answer was aye, and Fiona knew it.

"Then she bears the guilt," Fiona said. "Get her. Bring her back through time with us. She can look at this map and the one in my cabin on the ship. Trust me. She'll tell us what she knows."

"By my word, Fiona, you will not hurt her."

Nathaniel said, "She can't be held accountable for the family into which she was born."

"Like hell she can't," Fiona said. "And, Hugh, I think you'd better ask yourself if you're willing to do what you came here to do." She left, slamming the door behind her.

CHAPTER SIXTEEN

Joss moved quickly across Smallman Street to the History Center, cursing. Not just because she was late for the party. Not just because she'd nearly twisted her ankle in the high heels she was wearing. But because Hugh had foiled her company's security, stolen her mother's map, and, worst of all, had caught Joss taking what she'd thought had been anonymous revenge on him via the security cam. No, scratch that. The worst part had been the faintest suggestion of a twinkle in his eye that seemed to imply the revenge had been more reward than punishment.

Grrr.

She had no idea if or when she'd see him again. He'd left the offices as unexpectedly as he'd arrived. And now she'd have to explain to Rogan why she wouldn't be wearing the new gown she'd just told him about that morning.

Another thing niggled at her from the map room. She'd told Hugh she'd been surprised to find one of her mother's maps there. But that was a lie. She'd seen her mother's maps there before. What was strange, however, was that one remarkably similar to the one Hugh had taken, a map of Manchester that usually hung framed on the wall in the map room, was missing.

Ah, well, perhaps Building Services had moved it temporarily when the room was repainted. She'd follow up with them tomorrow.

She slipped through the door of the History Center and called, "Reynolds Party!" to the guard as she ran toward the elevator.

When she entered the party room, Rogan spotted her instantly and gave her a warm wave. He was standing with three well-dressed older ladies. One was his grandmother, Joss knew, and the other two must be his great-aunts. He was the dutiful young relative, bending to hear them. When Rogan's mother joined the circle, Rogan bowed out. He intercepted Joss at the long bar, where she was ordering an extra large Cabernet, and gave her a kiss.

"You look great," he said. "How was the fitting?"

"Disappointing. They can't finish the dress in time."

"Oh no. Will I still get to see it?"

Joss downed a generous swig of wine and avoided the question. "Did your mom notice I was late? Am I in trouble?"

"You are not. I have been the convivial host, chatting up the out-of-towners and prepping them for my bride's arrival. Come," he said. "Let me show you off."

CHAPTER SEVENTEEN

The mapmaker gave her dark, handsome husband the three maps she'd made for the old man, but she did not tell her husband where the gold was. Instead she told him a riddle. "The maps are the same. Three to one. Follow the path of the maps. Words can hide so much."

—The Tale of the Beautiful Mapmaker

"Why would Reynolds come here?" Hugh asked Nathaniel, the sound of Fiona slamming the door still ringing in his ears.

"I don't know. 'Tis possible the girl invited him to the fitting, you know."

Hugh chewed the inside of his mouth. If she had, it would mean she hadn't wanted to be alone with Hugh, and he was loath to admit that bothered him. He had been so certain there had been a spark between them.

"I am astonished the girl is Brand's daughter," Nathaniel said gently. "Is she, then, the girl you saved?"

Hugh thought of that terror-filled night and how he'd feared for the half-drowned child in his arms when they were fished out of the sea, more dead than alive. "Aye."

"Does she know?"

"No. I don't want her to know."

"You haven't told her her mother cared for you? That she made a home for your brother, Joss and you for over a year?"

"How does one tell a woman of the twenty-first century that her mother fell in love with one's eighteenth-century brother and that her blackguard father would have chosen to abandon her on an islet in the North Atlantic rather than leave his wife behind? How does one even begin a conversation like that?"

"'Tis her right to know, Monk."

Hugh remembered those first few days after the rescue. His brother Bart—Granite to his crew—had moved Maggie Brand and her daughter to the captain's cabin while he, Bart, joined Hugh in the general crew's quarters. Hugh wasn't sure when the plan was formulated, but by the time they were a day's sail from Portsmouth, he knew Maggie and Josephine would be coming to live with them in his brother's small house in Fareham. But when they pulled into the harbor, there among the faces on the dock was Alfred Brand's. How he had returned to the past, Hugh did not know. It could not have been through the passage that ended at that rocky islet, for there he would have surely perished.

In the blink of an eye everything changed. Bart had the four of them smuggled off the ship to a distant inn. He resigned his commission, had his agent sell his house, and found them a small cottage in a village at the edge of Ashdown Forest, where Bart had found work as a clerk in a mill. Despite the loss of everything familiar, the four of them settled down into the most joy-filled, carefree time of Hugh's young life, a time that ended all too soon with the discovery of Bart's bloodied body in the cottage and the disappearance of Maggie and little Jo from his life.

His blood for yours.

"Tell me, Nathaniel, who would want to know the destruction one's father has wrought?"

Nathaniel sucked on his pipe thoughtfully. Hugh could feel his gaze. "And in the end," Nathaniel said, "you discovered Brand didn't kill them after all."

That had been Hugh's worst fear, that after Brand had murdered Bart, he did the same to Maggie and little Jo. The not knowing had been torture, for Hugh's young mind had imagined scenes of such horror that many nights he could not sleep at all. And now, twenty years later, to have found the mother gone and the daughter engaged to the man likely to have been invested with Brand's dying secrets—it was almost too much to bear.

"No, he didn't," Hugh said with a sigh, "though I doubt he'll find his way into heaven because of it."

"Interesting, I think, that Joss found you after all this time, and that you were drawn to her."

Now that Hugh knew, he couldn't help but pick up the echoes of Maggie in her face—that sapphire gaze, those queenly cheekbones, the faint flush of peony on the skin—though he could see the unforgiving profile of Alfred Brand there as well. How could he have missed it? And now he had dragged her into this dangerous adventure. He didn't know what Reynolds knew or suspected. If Joss was a coconspirator with Reynolds, Hugh had potentially endangered the mission he and Fiona shared. If

Joss was not a coconspirator, Hugh was afraid—deeply afraid—he had implicated Joss in Reynolds's mind. He knew men would go to great lengths to protect the secrets maps revealed. In the time of that great sailor, Christopher Columbus, Ferdinand and Isabella had set a penalty of death for anyone foolish enough to be found with a copy of their kingdom's most valuable treasure, the map that held the secrets of the New World. He prayed Joss had not told Reynolds of the visit she and Hugh had made to the map room. It was far safer if Reynolds believed Hugh was a suitor.

"I have to find her," Hugh said. "I have to warn her."

"And what of the map?"

"She doesn't know anything," Hugh said, voice rising.

"But she may, Hugh." Nathaniel held up his hands. "She may. 'Twas her mother's map. And her father was a very powerful man."

Hugh slumped. "You're right. 'Tis the oddest thing, Nathaniel. I had no idea Maggie was a mapmaker. She never touched paper or pen the year I spent with her."

"She was in love. Talk to Joss. She may hold the secret to the map's location."

Hugh shook his head firmly. "No. I just can't believe she would share in Alfred Brand's secret."

"'Tis not beyond the realm of possibility, you know, that your affection for the girl as well as for her mother is blinding you to the possibility."

"Are you arguing Fiona's case now?"

"This touches more people than Fiona. I suspect there are enough lives that have been ruined by Brand's venal act in the last three hundred years to fill the City of London."

"I care nothing for that. I need to avenge my brother."

"You cannot bring him back, Hugh. But you can do what he would have done. Bring the girl to the ship. Let her look at Fiona's map."

Hugh tried, but he could see no other way. "She will not go willingly."

Nathaniel shook his head. "No."

"Dammit, if I bring her to the ship, it will be under my protection. I will not allow her to be hurt."

"I know you'll do what needs to be done."

CHAPTER EIGHTEEN

Joss's feet had just reached what she called the Elmer point of the evening: that is, the point where one's feet throb like Elmer Fudd's thumb after he accidentally hits it with a hammer. She decided she would slip over to the coatroom to kick off her shoes and extracted herself politely from the never-ending stream of Uncle Jared's jokes, leaving only frail, old Great-Aunt Cathy, who smiled despite Joss's near certainty she couldn't understand what her nephew was saying. Joss was almost to the door when Di grabbed her.

"Hey, we've barely gotten to talk. Let me buy you a drink."

"God, let me get out of these shoes first. They are *killing* me."

"But, oh, what a way to go. I love the leopard print. And are those roses on top? I haven't been able to wear shoes with a heel in five years."

"To be honest, they're a lot better when I'm lying down than standing up."

"Speaking of that," Di said, leaning in closer, "how's our friend, the tailor? Did you go back?"

"Yes. Don't ask."

"Well, if your cheeks right now are any indication, something interesting happened."

"Oh, something interesting happened, all right, but not what you'd imagine."

Di grinned. "I don't know. I can imagine a lot."

"He wanted a map."

"What? That's not the sort of boundaries I thought you'd be playing with. Maybe I need to buy you two drinks."

"Sounds heavenly. Let me get out of these shoes and I'll meet you. Hope nobody minds my bare feet."

"I'm hitting the ladies' room for I think the ninth time tonight. My table's over there in the corner, the one with the bucket of ice for my feet."

"Classy."

"Say, I've got a pair of those little roll-up ballet flats in my coat pocket if you're interested. Nights like this, my feet usually blow up to the size of Volkswagen Bugs. But tonight, for some reason, they're '61 Caddies, so even the flats are of no use to me now."

Joss looked down to see fuzzy flip-flops peeking out from the bottom of her friend's pants. "You're the bomb. See you in a flash."

Joss found Di's coat and snagged the flats. Then she slipped her feet out of their sleek torture chambers. Letting out a deeply satisfying vulgarity, she straightened, rubbed her back and found Hugh standing beside her.

"Oh my *God*! What are you doing here? Is there an indignity left I haven't suffered today?"

"I'd like to talk to you."

"Oh, now you'd like to talk to me." She slipped the soft black suede on. "Do I have to give you my Social Security number? Or tell you how much I weigh? Will you be uploading the video of you charming me out of my clothes to HowIScamWomen.com?"

"At least I used charm."

She repeated the earlier vulgarity, adding a robust "you" at the end, and turned on her now comfortable heel.

"Wait," he said.

She let out a long huff and stopped.

"It's about the dress."

Not the dress again. She was starting to hate the hold the dress had on her. It was wrapped up in one big ego-building, ego-busting tangle, like a string of dusty Christmas lights when you didn't know if they'd light up or electrocute you.

"What about it?"

"It's done. I'd like you to come back to the shop. I'd still like to have my hour with you."

She shook her head like a dog with water in his ears. "Are you *effing* kidding me? You want me to come to your shop—now, after you deliberately deceived me, after you stole my key and broke into my office, after you took my mother's map—when I know you're not really a tailor?"

"What I'd like to do," he said, "is put you into that dress, kiss you once and drink to the sad fact that after tonight we will never see each other again."

Despite everything, she felt her knees start to wobble. She'd never known a man to be quite so honest. Besides, there was just something about the colors in those eyes—

"Honest"? Is that what you just said? Jesus, do you hear yourself? This guy couldn't be honest if you put a gun to his head.

"The only place I'm going to be in an hour is in bed with my fiancé."

The muscles in his face contracted. "As you wish. Is Reynolds in there?" He inclined his head toward the crowd.

"Of course he is."

"Might you honor me with an introduction?"

"Sure. Right after I publish my secret diary on Facebook."

"I take it that's a no."

"I think you'd better leave."

"I'm not leaving until you say you'll come with me."

"Then I hope you enjoy talking to the coats."

She strode back into the party room.

Happily, Hugh thought, the celebrants appeared to be both large enough in number and lubricated enough with alcohol to be oblivious to the fact there was a stranger in their midst. He tucked himself into a corner and waited. He'd spotted Rogan sitting at the bar almost as soon as Hugh had entered the room. Hugh would probably have recognized him from the portrait he had seen, but there is a certain charged look that passes between lovers that is unmistakable, even across the length of a party floor, and Reynolds's gaze had found Joss at once. The look had lasted only an instant, but the instant couldn't have been more overtly possessive if he'd pressed her against the wall and made love to her in full view of the room. Hugh winced.

It stung Hugh deeply, and he was already in no mood to grant Reynolds quarter. Which is why he ordered a whisky and took a seat next to the man of the hour.

Reynolds, who was sipping what looked to be a whisky himself, held out a hand. "Rogan Reynolds." His communicator, one just like Joss's, was sitting on the bar.

Hugh shook it. "Hugh Ashdown."

"You a friend of the bride's?"

The barkeep put Hugh's whisky down, and he downed it in a gulp. "Aye. I know her through her mother."

"Ah." Reynolds inclined his head toward the loudest section of merrymakers. "It's a madhouse, isn't it?"

"Indeed."

An older man tapped Reynolds on the back.

"Pardon me for a moment," Reynolds said to Hugh, and turned.

While Reynolds exchanged pleasantries with the man, Hugh slipped the communicator into his shirt pocket. Then he signaled the barkeep for another round. Joss was in the corner with her friend, Diane. So long as he kept his head bowed, she was unlikely to spot him. He admired the line of her long, graceful neck as she spoke.

"Sweet old guy," Reynolds said, turning back. "Can you believe he's almost eighty?"

"In truth? 'Tis amazing what good living can do for a man."

Now a younger couple awaited their turn. Reynolds shrugged his shoulders sheepishly. "Groom's work. It never ends," he said, and turned his attention once again.

Hugh slipped off the stool. With a quick look to ensure Joss wasn't watching, he walked toward the quieter hallway. When he was out of sight, he removed the communicator from his pocket. He retraced in his mind the steps Joss had taken when she employed this tool. It took him a few tries, but he managed to get the thing to light up, revealing a set of controls that bore pictures—a sun, a clock, a musical note, a set of gears. What could it all mean? Then he spotted the word "Photos" under a painting of a sunflower.

"Photos," he repeated aloud. He knew it came from the Greek word meaning "light." The sunflower looked so real, set against a blue sky, and he remembered Joss mentioning she was to carry a bouquet of sunflowers at her wedding. He reached to touch the picture and the screen changed again. CAMERA ROLL, it said. Another word from the Greek, he thought, remembering the lessons he had endured. "English lawmakers sit in a bicameral assembly," Bart had instructed, "from the Latin *camera,* which means 'chamber.'"

He touched the words again, and this time the device truly surprised him. A portrait of Joss unclothed appeared, and his heart clenched so forcefully, it almost brought tears to his eyes. She was beautiful, of course, and the round, firm breasts held his attention for a considerable length of time; but in the end, his desire was overcome by a burning anger not only that Reynolds would possess such a thing but that he would be foolish enough to leave it unguarded on this box.

Hugh fiddled with the device, repeating what Joss had

done, until he found what she had called the "contact list." Then he pressed "Joss O'Malley."

He watched her from the hallway as she held up a finger to Di and stepped away to open her tiny bag. She looked at her communicator for an instant and then he heard her voice coming right out of the thing in the palm of his hand.

"Rogan, where are you?"

He brought the device closer to his mouth. "Rogan is at the bar. Come outside for a moment. I want to talk to you."

She craned her head left and right, and Hugh stepped out of sight.

"No."

"I would advise you to reconsider."

"How did you get his phone?"

A phone, was it? Hugh didn't answer. He tucked the phone back into his shirt pocket, feeling the tiny squawk of her voice against his chest. Then he ducked through the crowd and returned to his seat next to Rogan, who welcomed him back with a smile.

"You'll never guess what happened to me," Hugh said.

"I *know* what happened to you," Joss said, feeling her irritation rise. "I was there, remember?"

But Hugh didn't answer—or, rather, he didn't answer *her*. He seemed to be answering someone, though.

"I run a tailor shop," came Hugh's faraway voice. "Interesting line of work, of course, if you don't mind a never-ending parade of women in their undergarments."

She heard the rumble of male laughter.

"What the hell are you doing?" she said. "Who are you talking to?"

"And this woman comes in. Extraordinarily handsome. Fair skin, a high, well-placed bosom, hips to rival those of Botticelli's Venus."

"The real deal, huh?" said another voice, and Joss nearly jumped out of her skin. The other voice was Rogan's! She looked wildly around the room.

"The real deal. Aye. Well put. Naturally, I didn't hesitate when she insisted I do the fitting right there."

"Naturally."

What the hell was he doing? Surely he wasn't about to tell Rogan about her?

"And the woman has on the most alluring bits of underclothes," Hugh continued, "the sort of things that would have shamed Cleopatra."

She spied him at last. He was at the bar, spinning his yarn to a rapt Rogan. She started running toward them.

"I know the look," Rogan said. "Devastating."

"Indeed. And the woman wants to try on the dress unfettered, if you follow."

Holy hell! She dodged Great-Aunt Cathy and nearly tripped over a stray flower girl.

"And?" Rogan said.

"And I'm hardly going to argue with her, am I? Off come the underclothes, as easy as kiss-my-hand, and suddenly there's nothing between us but an unconcerned smile and heels as high as church spires."

"A religious pose, then?" Rogan laughed.

Run, Joss, run!

"I'm a silk man, you see. And, oh, those wisps. Transparent ruffles, like the wings of a dragonfly, and the most amazing black—"

She clapped a hand on Hugh's shoulder, hard enough to make him choke, or at least that's what she hoped. "Have a minute? Mary's outside."

"Mary?"

"You know, from that place? She wants to catch up."

"Well, I—"

"I promise we won't be long."

Hugh smiled. "For you, anything." He stood, downed his whisky and nodded to Rogan. "Another time?"

"I'm sure of it."

Hugh followed Joss obediently into a long, windowed hallway that led back to the main part of the museum. "That was harder than it needed to be," he said.

She whipped the phone out of his pocket. "You asshole!"

"Back to that, are we? I told you I needed to talk to you."

"Talk, buddy. You've got two minutes."

"Did you invite Rogan to the fitting tonight?"

"*That's* what you wanted to talk to me about? No, I didn't invite him to the fitting. It wasn't exactly something I wanted him to be there for, and in any case, the dress is supposed to be secret from the groom until the ceremony."

Something changed behind those gray eyes. When he spoke again, the playfulness in his voice was gone.

"Did you tell him about the map room?"

"No. Jesus. This isn't exactly the place for deep confessions. I've barely had time to say hello since I arrived."

"Tell me the truth, Joss."

"I'm telling you the truth."

"Listen to me. I'm sorry for the things I did, but I need you to promise that you won't mention anything about the maps to him—anything."

"Why?"

"Promise me," he said with urgency.

"Hugh . . ."

"Please."

"Yes. Fine. I promise."

"Thank you. Now I'm going to tell you something you shan't care to hear."

"I'm astonished."

"It's important. Come." He took her by the hand and led her down the hallway, near a door that led to an outside balcony.

"What?" she demanded when he stopped.

"I lied when I said I wanted to do the fitting. I'm here on a mission. I must right a great wrong that was done to many people."

"Gosh," she said. "You make breaking and entering sound so noble."

He ignored this. "This mission must be my focus. But I did not lie when I said I wanted an hour with you."

She felt her cheeks warm and wanted to kick herself.

He pressed his advantage. "When I saw you in that dress—"

Joss signaled Hugh to stop. A former colleague of Rogan's had entered the hallway, chatting with his wife. After they passed, another guest stumbled out of the party. This was nowhere to talk. She inclined her head toward the balcony.

*   *   *

Di slipped out of the bathroom and made an irritated growl. Three stalls and three women who apparently needed more time to pull up their panty hose and zip their skirts than Di had needed to complete grad school. Christ, if it took that long to pee when she was going twenty-seven times a day, she'd have to strip naked and take up residence in the bathtub.

She started for the table, expecting Joss to have returned from her call, but she wasn't there. So Di slipped onto a barstool beside Rogan. "I hope you don't mind me stealing Joss for a while. We're doing a girl thing."

He lifted a brow. "I sort of like girl things. Maybe I could watch."

"Forget about it, Prince Charming. We're talking dresses, shoes, cramps—you know."

"Speaking of that, what ever happened with that tailor? Did Joss go for the fitting?"

"Did you ask *her*?"

"No, I didn't. Not yet."

"Then I can't reveal anything," Di said. "Dresses are supposed to be secret, you know."

"She didn't tell you anything?"

"I believe she said the tailor's a fan of maps, if that makes any difference."

"Maps?" Rogan spilled his drink. "How's that?"

"Who knows? A lot of people like 'em. Thank God, right? I mean, I know Joss is hoping the company is coming out of its slump."

"Right. Will you excuse me? I see someone I should probably catch up with."

"No problem. If you see Joss, tell her I'm waiting."

* * *

The night breeze turned Joss's skin to gooseflesh, and Hugh immediately took off his coat and held it out to her.

She shook her head and led him away from the windows. The balcony was narrow, and when they turned the corner, Pittsburgh's North Shore lay like a starry bulging blanket across the hills beyond the river.

Hugh inhaled. "Look at the bridges."

He was right. They were beautiful: the sleek, wide bridge that carried the never-ending traffic from downtown to the North Hills and the stately old Sixteenth Street Bridge, with its gleaming yellow arches and fantastical orbs and seahorses bursting from the spotlight-lit pylons at each end. It belonged, she thought, on one of her mother's cartouches.

And there were more bridges, almost as far upriver as the eye could see.

She said, "The City of Bridges, you know."

"How do they build such things?" His face had the enchanted look of a child.

"See the yellow one," she said. "That's my favorite. Those are armillary spheres on the top—I know because I did a book report on it in fifth grade. It's like something out of a story, really."

He gazed into the night. "We call them astrolabes, but, aye, I see what you mean."

"We call them astrolabes"? "Who are you?"

He chuckled. "'Tis a question I've asked myself more than once. Will you please take my coat?"

She was shivering now, but before she could demur, he slipped it over her shoulders.

The wool was warm and carried his subtle scent. She nodded her thanks reluctantly.

"I built a bridge once," he said. "A small one. Across a river we needed to ford outside Copenhagen. And it was only temporary, but it was a fancy piece of engineering, no matter the size."

"So, you're a tailor who fishes, sails, pursues missions and builds bridges."

A curve rose at the corner of his mouth. "Seems unlikely, does it not?"

"In the extreme."

"Would it surprise you to discover I am not a tailor?"

"It would surprise me to discover you *were* a tailor—though I did like that dress," she added with a touch of longing.

"The dress. Aye. When I saw you in that dress . . ." His finger worked the button on his cuff in a surprising show of diffidence. "When I saw you in that dress, it made me wish I *was* a tailor. No, that's not the whole truth. It made me wish I had met you before you needed to choose a wedding gown."

Joss's blood began to buzz. His eyes had turned the softest green-gray, like a sea just before dawn, and she had to remind herself her fiancé was only a few yards away.

"I want you to know," he said, "none of what happened there between us was a lie."

What *had* happened there? She thought about that bubbling effervescence and how nice it had felt. She wondered why certain things happened the way they did.

The wind shifted, and he moved to block her from it with his body. When he caught her arm to bring her closer to his sheltering bulk, she tilted her chin instinctively and he found her mouth. For a long, slow moment, they kissed, and Joss felt the crackling heat that comes from venturing too close to the edge of an inferno.

"I-I can't do this." She pulled away in a fit of jangling nerves.

"And I shouldn't have tested you. Especially now."

" 'Especially now?' "

He turned to face her. His eyes hardened to the color of battleships. "Your father did a thing that you must help remedy."

If was as if he had doused her with cold water. "So you said." She wiped her mouth.

" 'Tis a matter of necessity. You have no choice."

"What does *that* mean?"

"It means," he said with an unwavering gaze, "you must come with me now. If you give me your word, I will allow you to make your excuses to your fiancé."

"You'll *allow* me?" Was he insane?

"You will be gone a day, no more."

"No one 'allows' me to do anything."

"In this case, I'm afraid you have no choice." He made a casual movement, and Joss realized that when he'd blocked the wind, he also blocked the door.

"I'm getting married Tuesday. And I'm supposed to be leaving for a trade show."

"I will have you back by this time tomorrow."

"No."

"Joss, there is no refusal. You will accompany me. One way or another."

There was something about his unemotional certainty that sent a chill through her.

She saw one chance. With a sigh, she nodded reluctantly and made her way past him toward the door. "Wait," she said, and pointed to the railing. "My purse." He took a step to collect it, and Joss bolted. She flung the door open but her foot caught on the step. He grabbed her and spun her around, tucking her arm up behind her back.

"You gave me your word. You're about as trustworthy as your father."

"I didn't give you my word," she said fiercely. "I never said anything."

"You're a Brand. Would it have made any difference?"

"*Yes.* I am not my father. My word means as much to me as yours does to you."

He stopped and pulled her into the light of the moon. "Then give it to me now."

He dared her with his eyes, those damning gray eyes.

"I give you my word."

"Your word on what?"

"I give you my word I won't try to escape."

"And you will abide by my direction for the next twenty-four hours? In return, I will warrant your safe return as promised."

Had she any choice? "Yes."

He evaluated her face carefully, then, with a grunt, released her arm. "There." He pointed to another doorway, one marked FIRE EXIT ONLY. It was propped open with a brick. She stepped into the stairwell, and he followed her down the steps. Despite the kiss, she was far from certain she was safe with him. There was an undercurrent of danger that seemed to ooze from every pore of his. She also wondered what possible excuse she could use to keep Rogan and everyone else from having a complete meltdown when they found out she was missing.

When they reached the outside, he said, "There are some maps you must examine."

"Oh, joy. And how will that take twenty-four hours?"

"They are not close."

"How close is not close?" she asked.

"Far."

Her cell phone buzzed. She pulled it out of her pocket. It was a text from Di: WHERE R U?

He took the phone from her hand. "R? U? Is this a code?"

"Yes. I know it's a tough one to crack."

"'Diane Daltrey,'" he read. "Your friend?"

"Yes." She snatched the phone back.

"What will you tell her?"

"The only thing I can."

He watched her work the communicator again. Her fingers flew over the top, almost as if she were playing a tiny organ. But he watched her closely. The words she had written were CALL ME WHEN YOU'RE ALONE.

In a moment, the communicator played a song. "It's her." Joss ran her finger over it, then put it to her ear. "It's a long story," she said, "but I need your help."

He could hear the faint sound of a reply.

"I'm with him," she said, and the word passed between them like a secret.

He didn't know what Diane said next, but a clearly distressed Joss said, "I don't know. I just don't know." She turned her back to him, but he could hear nonetheless. "Listen, I need you to cover for me. Can you sneak out without anyone seeing you? If you can, then call Rogan once you're in your car and say I'm sick and spending the night with you. Oh, Christ, you can't call him! I have his phone. You'll have to figure it out. Maybe call the History Center and leave a message. Okay, can you do that?"

She listened for a moment.

"I don't know," she said. "I'm going to go directly to the airport tomorrow evening for the trade show, so whatever you choose for my illness, don't make it so bad that I'd miss that."

"Thank you," she said after another pause. "I owe you—big-time."

She pressed the button and slipped the communicator into her pocket. Her silence unnerved him. He could guess what she'd led her friend to believe. An unpleasant lie for a bride to sign her name to. In truth, he was no better than Rogan with that ungentlemanly portrait. Hugh had exposed Joss every bit as cruelly.

"I'm sorry you had to do that. Does she think . . . ?"

"It doesn't matter what she thinks," Joss said coolly. "I'll tell her the truth when we get back."

He doubted Joss would tell her *this* truth—the truth about what would happen once they reached the time passage.

When they passed Twelfth Street, Hugh turned to take

one last look at the narrow balcony where he and Joss had kissed. The space was dark, awash in the shadows of the night. Then the blond head of a man appeared and looked directly at him.

Hugh pulled Joss quickly across the street and out of view. He told himself he was imagining it. From that distance in the dark, they couldn't have been seen. But the sooner they reached the alleyway, the better.

"Do you see that?" She pointed toward a squat black bridge toward the north.

"Aye."

"That is where Meriwether Lewis pushed off with the boats he'd had made here in Pittsburgh for the expedition."

"Intriguing. Men don't usually push boats off bridges."

The quip had served its purpose. The set of her mouth loosened.

"I meant where the bridge now stands. The boats were called pirogues, I think."

"Another fifth-grade report?" He caught her hand and hurried her under the overpass that led to Eleventh Street.

"Eighth," she said. "From here he sailed to Saint Louis, where he and Clark began their official journey."

"Ah." Hugh hoped he nodded in what appeared to be an appreciative way, as he had not the least idea what she was talking about. He wondered if Rogan would follow them and if Fiona and Nathaniel had secured the doors of the tailor shop.

"Lewis and Clark?" she said, as if prompting him to understand. Evidently, his nod had not been appreciative enough.

"Aye. The expedition. Remarkable."

"You have no idea whom I'm talking about."

"I do."

"Do British schools not cover American history?"

"Is there such a thing?" He laughed, then caught himself, but it was too late.

She stopped. An odd mixture of fear and repulsion had come over her face. "Who are Lewis and Clark?"

He shifted. "I didn't study them."

"George Washington?"

He clenched his jaw.

"Benjamin Franklin? Abraham Lincoln? Henry David Thoreau?"

He didn't reply. He couldn't.

"Who are you?" she demanded.

"Keep moving. I doubt you will credit the truth."

"Try me."

"In time." He quickened their pace. They had just passed Tenth when she said in a low voice, "Oh, Christ, it's Louis."

"Joss!" the man called, and Hugh sped up, passing his companion as if the two of them were strangers. He assumed it was a man with whom she worked, and Hugh did not want her to be compromised by being seen with him.

Joss slowed to talk to the man, and Hugh turned the corner and stopped, keeping her just within his field of vision.

"She's inside," he could hear Louis say. "Do you have a minute to be introduced?"

"I-I—"

She met Hugh's eyes and he released her with a nod. He didn't like to let her go, even for a moment, but he didn't want to raise Louis's suspicions, either. As she slipped into a public house, he jogged to the opposite corner to watch.

Hugh paced, looking toward the windows, where he could see Joss, and up the cross street. The quiet of the street was making him nervous. He crossed back and walked toward Tenth. When he got to the corner, he ran into Reynolds.

"Good evening." A cold chill ran up Hugh's spine. He had a knife, but had not thought to bring a pistol.

"Evening."

There was a sheen of perspiration on the man's face. Hugh had seen it before, on men in their first battles, and he did not like the look of it. He wished he knew whether Reynolds had seen Joss go into the public house.

The man's hand went to his coat, and Hugh nearly fell upon him. But Reynolds did nothing more than bury his hand in a patch of green bulging from the pocket.

"Joss is ill," Reynolds said.

"I'm sorry to hear it. The excitement of matrimony mixed with an abundance of food and wine, no doubt." Hugh smiled with a bonhomie he did not feel. "Will you be at the ceremony?"

"No, I cannot. I will be out of the country. I shall have to give you my congratulations here." Hugh extended his hand.

Reynolds took it hesitantly. "Thank you."

"Take care of her. You're very lucky."

The hand returned to its lump of green. Hugh wondered if Reynolds had a pistol hidden there and felt sweat break out on his back. Reynolds appeared to be waiting— for what, Hugh was uncertain, but he hoped Joss did not choose this moment to appear.

"Good to see you," Hugh said. "Thank you for an enjoyable evening."

Reynolds nodded. Hugh waited until he started walking, then made his way up Tenth, stopping as soon as he rounded the corner. He listened for a beat or two, turned, then watched Rogan until he disappeared at the next street. Then Hugh flew back to the public house, nearly bowling Joss over as she stepped outside.

"What are you doing?"

"Quiet. Don't say a word. Stay in front of me." He directed her back toward Tenth, up to Liberty and, after he'd taken a look down the street, toward the lower entrance to the alleyway.

Hugh heard footsteps approaching quickly behind them. "Go to the shop," he said sharply and slowed as she went ahead. He stole a glance over his shoulder and got only a fleeting glimpse of a man a block away with a green stocking cap over his head.

Hugh began to jog to catch up with Joss, who was turning into the alley. *Hurry.*

He felt a flick, like the sting of a bee, on his shoulder. He burst into a run as searing pain shot down his arm. Another *pop,* and his feet tangled. He hit the stone walkway.

Joss turned. "Hugh!"

He tried to claw himself upward, but it was nearly impossible with only one working arm, and the man was striding purposefully closer.

"Go!" Hugh croaked, and pulled himself to his feet. *"Go!"*

But she ran toward him. She hadn't connected the man to Hugh's fall, and with each step she took, Hugh waited for a pistol shot to pierce the easy target of that pale silk.

He made it to his feet just as she reached him.

"Oh my God, you're bleeding!" She wrapped his good arm around her shoulder and gazed around wildly. "Who? Who?"

"Run," he said. "We must run."

Together they flew toward the narrow path.

"There!" he cried. "Across the way, in the alcove, under the vaulted ceiling!" He felt the vibrations as they drew near, sending currents through his already quaking legs. They ran through the perimeter, and the familiar charge nearly jerked him off his feet. He wondered if she'd be afraid. He wondered if she'd remember. With the ground shaking hard and sparks flying around them, he propelled her toward the shadows. The evening exploded with the power of a broadside, and he pulled her hand against him, his shoulder howling with pain, and held his breath.

CHAPTER NINETEEN

Her dark, handsome husband left, and the mapmaker missed him deeply, but in the years that followed she worked on her maps and raised her princess-daughter until she was as beautiful as the mapmaker herself. She taught her daughter to make maps, too, maps as beautiful as the ones she herself made.

—The Tale of the Beautiful Mapmaker

Joss heard the thump of a melon in the dark, and winced in pain as her skin tore against wet, cold rock. Hugh's arms fell limply away from her sides, and he began to buckle.

She grabbed him, but could only manage to ease his slide to the ground. Her heart was pounding, and she didn't know where she was or what they'd gone through. The ringing in her ears was deafening, and in the inky black beyond the immediate darkness around them she saw stars falling—no, they were sparks—and was stunned to hear the roar of ocean beyond.

They weren't in the alley. They weren't in Pittsburgh.

She stumbled over him awkwardly, trying to arrange herself so she could get ahold of his arms and drag him with her.

When she got through the narrow opening into the open air, icicles of spray beat at her relentlessly and the wind howled. She grabbed him and pulled him free of the opening. He made no noise, which terrified her. With his head and shoulders clear of the passage, she could examine his face in the flickering light of the sparks. Blood ran from his forehead into his ears and neck, and a far more alarming patch of crimson covered his chest.

"Hugh," she said, shaking him. "Hugh."

She ran her hands over his chest and shoulder. She couldn't see a wound in the dark and didn't know how he'd been hurt. Another shower of sparks illuminated the ugly dark hole. His skin was clammy, and her fingers went to his neck for a pulse. She felt nothing.

"Hugh!"

He made a low, almost inaudible grunt, and a rush of relief washed over her.

"I think you were shot. What happened?"

He mumbled something, but the wind's roar obliterated it. As her eyes adjusted to the dark, Joss could see they were on a rock over the sea. She pulled off the coat Hugh had given her and laid it over him.

The next instant a wave smacked her to the rock. The salt stung her nose. She was terrified of water. Choking, she struggled to her knees and crawled back to Hugh, who was snorting. She was soaked now and freezing, but she found the coat and brought the heavy wool across his chest. The water had cleared the blood from his face, but new rivulets snaked their way across his wet skin.

"Ship," he said hoarsely, and groaned again.

"What?"

"Ship. Do you see one?"

She stumbled to her feet. There was nothing but black beyond the dying sparks. She shouted, "Hello!" but her voice was lost in the wind. "Hello!" she shouted again, but received no response. She had the oddest flash of déjà vu, but it was gone as quickly as it had come.

"No ship," she said. "Where are we?" But his eyes were closed again, and her heart jumped into her throat. "Hugh? Hugh!"

His lids flickered open, then closed. "The other side. Try the other side."

She was afraid to leave him, afraid he'd be swept away by a wave. How had they gone from an alley in Pittsburgh to a rock in the sea? Her mind raced through a dozen options, but none of them made sense.

She spotted a metal spike near the base of the cave they'd emerged from. It had a circle at the top, almost like a large iron needle. She pulled it. It held. What its use was, she did not know, but it didn't matter. It would serve her purpose.

She reached for his belt.

After she'd loosened it and pulled it free, she threaded it through the opening in the spike and tightly around his ankle. As an anchor against the waves, it wouldn't hold forever and probably ought to have been used around his chest instead, but it would do for a moment.

By "the other side," she assumed he meant the other

side of the peaked cave that loomed over the small patch of rock on which they were situated.

She made her way across the vibrating rock. On her fourth step the same weird buzz she'd felt in the alley hit her, and the crazy slide show of images began again: Hugh falling, Fiona in her mile-high stilettos, Di with the baby seat on her arm and Rogan—no, not Rogan. It was a man the size and shape of her fiancé, but he wore a stocking cap and gazed at her from the end of the alley.

"Stop it," Hugh croaked.

She jumped. "What?"

"Keep moving. We need the ship. Try the other side."

She flattened herself against the cave's sloping side and used her foot to feel the way forward. When a wall of water sprayed upward, she jerked and nearly lost her hold. The back edge of the cave was directly over the water. The sight of it terrified her. She could not convince her feet to move. She clung to the freezing rock and felt like crying.

Then she thought of Hugh, and the blood on his shirt. He needed help—help she couldn't give.

With Herculean effort, she turned her head so that she was looking out to sea.

She tried to ignore the waves crashing at her feet and the noise of the wind, and scanned the place where the dark haze met light, which she assumed was the horizon. She heard something above the roar. Was it Hugh? Was he calling out for her? She strained to catch the sound, but whatever it was disappeared.

A flash of white appeared on the water, then disappeared. She tried to keep her eyes on the spot. Was it a ship? It appeared again, paired with another.

"Here!" she yelled. "Here!"

The patches grew larger. It was coming closer. It was a ship!

"We're here!" she screamed, but there was no return call. And the sails, though still moving, had stopped growing larger. The ship had turned. She could see the masts clearly now, though she couldn't imagine how a masted ship stayed upright on these waves. She was going to lose them.

"Here!"

What could she do? She had no matches, no wood— no way to build a fire. If she only had a lighter. Then it struck her.

She shoved her hand in her pocket, hoping the water hadn't shorted them out.

She pulled out her phone and Rogan's. She tried his first. It was dead. She threw it out to sea.

Please, please, please.

She pressed the button on hers. A light flickered and went out. She tried again. Nothing. She tried again. It turned on!

She moved the slider carefully with her thumb and delicately paged through her apps to find what she was looking for: a flashlight. She flicked it on, picked strobe and held it out to sea.

The light blinked its quick, urgent glow. "Help!" she cried. "We're here!"

She braced herself against the rock and waved the phone. She knew it was small, but maybe if she made broad strokes with her arm . . .

"Ahoy!" came a distant voice.

"Ahoy!" she shouted. "Ahoy!"

"Stay there! We're coming."

She edged back, an inch at a time, and when she had the rock firm under her feet again, she ran to Hugh. "They're coming!" she cried.

He didn't move.

CHAPTER TWENTY

Joss had insisted Hugh be transported first, and now she stood shivering in the cold, despite the blanket around her shoulders, watching the sailors attach his litter to the rigged pulley line. Cold and dizzy, she was dreading her own moment of transport and unnerved by the trousers and tailcoats the officers wore. She was deeply concerned about Hugh.

"Will he be all right?"

A lieutenant named Roark, a portly man with closely cut red hair who had followed the first sailor over to the island, gave her a steely look and said in an English accent very much like Hugh's, "I shouldn't worry too much. The ship's surgeon is a fine one. Trained in Paris." Despite Roark's words, however, there was a look of concern on his face.

"Where are we, exactly?" she asked.

It seemed a simple enough question—and far simpler than the next she would ask—but it was as if a veil had dropped over the lieutenant's ruddy face.

"The North Atlantic, m'um."

She was at sea, hundreds of miles from Pittsburgh. It was more than hard to fathom; it was impossible. "And w-when?"

He paused. "November eleventh."

"In what year?"

He shouted to the men who were unintentionally rocking Hugh's litter as they adjusted the pulley. "Damn you! 'Tis not a crate of cabbages you're transporting there, for the love of Hades." Then he gave her a careful look. "For that I'm afraid you'll have to wait to ask the captain."

The year's a secret? What was this?

"Then would you mind," she said, "telling me where I could find him."

Did she detect a smile on his face? "That, too, will have to wait. Come, let us get you safely lodged in your quarters."

There was an undercurrent in the words "safely lodged" that made her distinctly uneasy.

"I have a phone, you know," she said, indignant, and held it up.

Which was a mistake, for Roark lifted it from her hand. "That, I'm afraid, will have to be confiscated." He slipped it into his pocket.

While she alternately fumed and shivered, the rigged litter delivered Hugh to the ship and returned, not as a litter, but as a seat fashioned out of woven ropes. Still irritated, she refused Roark's offer of a hand as she threaded her legs into it. Closing her eyes, she tried to beat back her growing panic. If she let it, the fear would paralyze her. She gasped as the seat lifted into the air, swinging wildly in the wind. She wished Hugh was there to reassure her, then kicked herself for worrying about herself when she should have been worrying about him.

She could hear the waves breaking beneath her like the snapping jaws of alligators, and she closed her eyes and began to cry.

When she opened them again, she was over decking. An able-bodied seaman lifted her free, and she was handed into the custody of two men with guns.

CHAPTER TWENTY-ONE

*Then one day the mapmaker fell ill, and she knew she was
going to die.*

*"I have no money to leave you," she said to her princess-
daughter, "but you do not need to worry. Men will come
from far away to court you. But you must save yourself for
the knight who will share with you all he possesses—and I
do not mean gold. I mean his help and his heart. For that is
the man that will put everything to right. Beware all others."*

—The Tale of the Beautiful Mapmaker

At dawn, Roark tapped on her door and announced himself. She had been brought stew, bread and beer, and been
given a set of sailor's togs and a small hanging cot on which
to sleep, but she had not been allowed to leave her tiny
room. The ship hadn't moved since she'd boarded, which is
to say, the ship hadn't made forward progress, for it pitched
and rolled on the water like an out-of-control roller coaster
at an amusement park. The only unusual sounds she'd
heard had been several bloodcurdling cries that she hoped
had been Hugh's, as it might mean he wasn't dead.

Throughout the night, she had turned over various

scenarios that might explain their appearance in this remote place, though nothing had emerged from this exercise except a throbbing headache and the sickening sense that whatever mess she found herself in now was both serious and irreversible.

Needless to say, she had not eaten or slept, and as she went to the door, she had to struggle to keep from tripping over the rolled-up ends of her borrowed pants.

"I wonder why you'd bother knocking," she said, "since you hold the key."

Roark ignored this. "You sent for me?"

"No, I sent for the captain."

"The captain is otherwise engaged. How can I help?"

"How is Hugh?"

His lips pressed into a thin line. "You have an unusual interest in his health."

"I'm his friend."

"I'm afraid that remains to be seen."

"What's that supposed to mean?"

"It means that until the patient wakes, we have no idea what relation you are to him. Someone, after all, fired that pistol. If that is all, I must take my leave. We are quite busy on deck."

"It is not all. I demand to see the captain."

"I'm afraid you'll have to address your concerns to me, madam, for the time being."

"What are my rights here?"

He looked at her as if she had spoken this question in Finnish.

"My rights," she repeated. "Doesn't the Geneva Convention apply? May I send the captain a note?"

He sighed. "I am unfamiliar with Swiss law, but if you insist, I will deliver what you write. However, I cannot guarantee it will be read or acted upon."

He found a pencil and a dingy piece of brown paper in his coat—she was certain she smelled lard on it—and she dashed off a fiery screed, demanding, among other things, the return of her clothes, a report on the state of Hugh's health and access to her phone.

She stuffed it into Roark's hand and gave him the finger after he closed the door.

In a quarter of an hour, a closemouthed Roark reappeared.

"Follow me, please. And take care not to speak to any other crew members."

He led her down several sets of steps into the bowels of the ship. The tossing had lessened, which made walking considerably easier, but the passageway was narrow and dark and smelled like dirty, wet athletic socks.

A short, elderly man in a long black coat and little rectangular glasses who reminded her vaguely of Benjamin Franklin stood at an open doorway. "You may have a moment or two, no more."

She peered into the room expectantly and saw Hugh. She ran to his side, nearly knocking over a bedside stool. She wanted to throw her arms around him, but the care with which he had been tucked into his cot and the ashy pallor to his face made her stop. He was very still, and for a moment she thought he was asleep, but he opened his eyes and smiled.

"Joss." A single word, but it made her heart sing. His shoulder was bandaged and his arm had been wrapped with linen to hold it close to his side. There was linen around his head as well.

"Oh, Hugh. What happened? Are you going to be all right?"

"I was shot," he said. "But that's not why I passed out on the islet. I must have hit my head. Mr. Lytle, the surgeon, removed the ball. He says the wound is clean. He has given me laudanum."

He spoke slowly, and she thought of the awful screams in the night. How far from land were they that they'd attempt such a thing themselves?

"Was that man going to rob you?" she asked. "Is that why you were shot?"

He closed his eyes, and the muscle in his jaw flexed. "Probably. It's likely that your arrival scared him off. I expect I'm alive because of you."

She thought about what she'd seen in that alley. She'd been so intent on Hugh and that circle of blood, the rest was a blur. All she remembered were a few pedestrians—an older couple, a man in a green stocking cap—and Hugh yelling "Go!"

"I am given to understand you are displeased with your situation," he said.

"I am not displeased. I am furious. I'm being held as a prisoner. I don't know who the asshole is running this ship, but when we get back to land I'm going to slap him with a lawsuit so fast it'll make his head spin."

"His head is spinning already. I'm certain of it."

"Have we been drugged? That's the only explanation I can think of. This is a really old ship, like out of a movie or something. I'm not even sure it can make it back to land."

He licked his parched lips and gave her a steady look. "This ship can make it anywhere there's a draft of eighteen feet. She's the most able creature on the seas."

"Jesus, you sound like *you're* the captain of this thing." Then she spotted the dingy sheet of brown paper under a washcloth at his side and sunk slowly onto the stool. "Oh my God. You *are* the captain, aren't you?"

His chest rose and fell in what she assumed was a laugh.

"I have passed your rather indelicate recommendation for Roark's court-martial to our first lieutenant, by the way," he said. "I'm afraid he is reluctant to begin proceedings, however. Feels the accusation is unjust."

"Because Roark *is* the first lieutenant." She felt dizzy.

"Aye."

How could Hugh be a captain? How could they be at sea? What had happened inside that bizarre invisible dome?

"But in the alley—and here . . ." Dry-mouthed, she tried to bring something—anything—into an understandable focus in her head. "The world shook, and there were sparks and heat."

"You are not the first to characterize the effects of my embrace so, but you are the first to do so dressed as one of my men. 'Tis an interesting variation, I must say."

"Hugh." She had known something was out of sorts from the moment she'd seen the sparks falling from the Gulf Tower, but to have the world rebooted like this, everything she thought she'd known about him tossed out like a half-eaten quesadilla from Taco Bell . . . "You're not a tailor?"

"No. I told you I wasn't."

He had. But he had also told her so many other things that had proven to be untrue, she hadn't even believed him when he said he'd been lying. And still there was the troubling matter of the year.

Ask, a voice inside her said, but she was afraid of the answer.

"And this is your ship?"

"I am the captain, if that is what you ask. I am a captain in the English navy, and while my orders are to prowl the Atlantic for French ships, I have stretched the spirit of the orders almost to the breaking point in order to get us to where we stand right now."

Ask.

"As far as I know," she said voice shaking, "we are not at war with France."

"'Tis 1706, Joss. We are most certainly."

She felt the floor beneath her sway, and for once, it was not the ocean, the invisible dome or the feel of his arms around her. It was shock, pure and simple.

"It's not 1706," she said, unbelieving, though she knew it explained everything she had seen.

"Joss, listen to me. Our time here is short," he said. "Mr. Lytle, the surgeon, will return presently, and neither I nor you may speak of what's happened with him."

"What *has* happened?" There was dried blood on Hugh's forehead. She spotted a basin of water and dipped the washcloth in it.

"There is a time hole that leads from the islet in 1706 to Pittsburgh in your year. That is how Fiona, Nathaniel and I arrived, and how you and I left. Roark knows, but he's the only person on the ship who does."

She dabbed at his forehead, and he tried to pull away. "Let me," she said.

He submitted.

"I will instruct Lytle that you and Roark are the only people who are to attend me. I have seen men on laudanum and their secrets do not stay secrets long."

"Of course." Her head was spinning.

"And when you are not here, I ask that you find a map in Fiona's quarters. I don't know where it's hidden. 'Twas done by your mother and is very similar in design to the map I took from you, which Roark has. We are looking for clues about the whereabouts of a map of East Fenwick. 'Tis very important"—he took a labored breath and coughed—"that the map be found."

"Why?"

He hesitated. "It will right a great wrong."

"The one you say my father was involved in."

"Aye."

Mr. Lytle returned to the doorway. "I'm sorry, Miss O'Malley. You must go."

"Another moment," Hugh instructed.

"Captain—"

"So long as I possess my faculties, I will run this ship. Another moment."

The surgeon made a bow and left.

"I will tell Lytle my limitations on who may attend me when he returns. Roark will be taking the first watch." Hugh closed his eyes. He wanted to sleep, she could see that. She laid the cloth on the edge of the basin and turned reluctantly to go.

"Joss?"

"Yes."

"You can trust Roark. I give you my word. If anything were to happen . . ." His voice trailed off.

"Nothing will happen," she said.

"Nonetheless, he will know how to get you home."

Lytle had returned. Through the haze of a burgeoning fever and the effects of the laudanum, Hugh heard the scratch of the quill and opened his eyes.

"Mr. Lytle, I will allow only two people to serve as my attendants until I recover: Mr. Roark and Miss O'Malley. Do you understand?"

The man's brows lifted. "There are doses that will have to be given and bandages to be changed."

"Then teach Mr. Roark, aye?"

"As you wish. I will tell the surgeon's mate."

Hugh closed his eyes and returned his labored thoughts to Joss. It was a bad situation, he knew. Reynolds had revealed himself, if not to Joss, for Hugh was almost certain she hadn't spotted him, then at least unknowingly to Hugh. Every bone in Hugh's body ached to bring the villain to his knees. The attack showed how dangerous the situation was, and yet one fact could not be denied: the man had had a clear shot at Joss and had not taken it.

This above all things colored Hugh's thinking.

Joss loved Reynolds. Despite the kiss Joss and Hugh had shared at the party, which Hugh had credited only to the wine and excitement, Joss had given Hugh no indication her loyalty to Reynolds had changed. And Reynolds, when given the opportunity, had acted in a way that suggested his heart, too, was engaged. If Reynolds had acted in any other way, Hugh thought with considerable regret, he would have exposed him to Joss in a second. But Reynolds hadn't, and that had to be enough for Hugh. He must put his own feelings aside. The daughter of Maggie Brand would not suffer at his hands.

"You need to rest, Captain. I can see your color rising."

"I will."

The crinkling of paper awoke him several moments later.

"Allow me," Lytle said in the dark, extracting the note from under Hugh's arm. "I shall put it on the shelf here."

"Wait. Please. Will you read it again? Just the last paragraph?"

Lytle adjusted the lamp and brought the paper under the light. "'Finally, I would willingly forgo my other demands for the chance to see my companion. I am quite concerned for his health, and I find it is exceedingly cruel of you to force him to suffer in isolation, whatever his wounds might be. Until this is resolved, you are a captain unworthy of my respect. Joss O'Malley.'"

Despite the heated thickness in his head, Hugh settled back onto the pillow and smiled.

CHAPTER TWENTY-TWO

Joss was pleased to see that no guard awaited her when she exited Hugh's sickroom. She was less pleased to realize that a guard or two might have been useful in helping direct her back to her room.

It was 1706, if she could believe it. But why would he lie? And what else could explain the ancient ship, the historical costumes and the stink of athletic socks?

She picked up her pant legs, trying without much success to keep them above the water sloshing across the floor. "Ablest creature on the seas," eh? She made her way up one set of steps, past a knot of sailors who jumped to attention as she passed, to the place where she thought the next staircase was, only to find a small wire pen holding a cow, a goat, three pigs and a cat.

"Miss O'Malley?"

She turned. Roark was hurrying toward her, ducking under each beam as he passed. For an instant, she was afraid there was some bad news about Hugh, but the tentative smile on his face dispelled her concern.

"Would you accept my apologies, m'um?" he said.

"Mr. Lytle made it clear Captain Hawksmoor was not to be disturbed, and confinement is standard practice with an unknown. The captain was quite beside himself when he heard what I'd done."

"Certainly." She extended her hand and her pant leg dropped in the water. "I was probably a bit hasty myself. I believe my request for a court-martial can be withdrawn."

"Put on hold is all the captain has promised." He took her hand and bowed. "Thank you. I will endeavor to earn your continued allegiance. In fact," he said, clearing his throat uncomfortably, "those are my orders."

"Excellent. Perhaps you can start by pointing me toward Fiona's room."

"Miss McPherson, do you mean?"

"I guess. Tall, blond, legs that reach up to about my—"

"Aye, 'tis Miss McPherson," he said, and smiled nostalgically.

He led her up two flights of stairs to a passageway. At one end was a door flanked by two red-coated men with guns. It was not to this door but to one immediately to its left, however, that he took her.

"This is her room," he said, and in a louder voice added, "I certainly hope the transfer went smoothly." He unlocked the door and ushered Joss inside. "The men are under the impression the captain, Miss McPherson and old Nate were met by another ship after we left them on the rock—the same ship from which you and the captain recently returned."

"Ah." Always good to know the story if you were expected to lie through your teeth. She thought of the story about her own made-up illness Di was feeding Rogan as well as the story about a fling with Hugh she'd led Di to believe before that and felt a stab of guilt. She didn't usually lie, let alone juggle quite so many at one time.

Fiona's room was more spacious than hers but filled almost to capacity with a hanging cot, a trunk, a desk and a chair. There was a door to what she supposed to be a closet in the adjacent wall.

"I believe you are in want of this." Roark pulled her mother's map of London from his coat and handed it to her.

A young boy ran by the door, stopped, turned on his heel and stuck his head in the door. "Mr. Lytle's compliments, sir. You are wanted in the sick bay. Your watch."

Roark made his good-byes and agreed to let Joss know if anything changed.

Joss looked at the map. What part could a map of London play in righting a wrong done by her father? She closed her eyes and thought of her mother and the golden hair she wore tied up in a knot. She remembered the stories her mother had told—always so vivid and engaging—and how on the very best days, her mother would stop what she was doing, pull Joss into her lap and begin to spin some fantastical yarn. Joss thought of *The Tale of the Beautiful Mapmaker* and the handsome knight and felt a wave of nostalgia. Ah, Rogan, what a knight you seemed that day outside the hospital. . . .

She smiled, but the internal smile wasn't quite in line with the outside one, and she couldn't figure out why, apart from her worry for Hugh. Then she remembered the visions she'd seen on the islet. Why did that figure in the green stocking cap make her uneasy?

She sighed and looked around. Where would Fiona

put a map? Joss began with the usual places—the desk
and its single drawer, which yielded little but paper and
ink, and the trunk, which contained gowns and shoes.
Remembering detective novels she'd read, she even
checked the sides of the trunk and desk drawer for a false
panel. Nothing. And, in any case, why would Fiona have
to hide a map?

Joss checked the closet next, only to discover it wasn't a
closet at all. It was the door to a much larger room whose
far wall was lined with diamond-paned windows, through
which the disappearing wake was visible. She scanned the
low, wide cot, far larger than her own, and the long table
with its richly upholstered chairs, thinking, Cripes, for a
barely afloat ship from the 1700s, this is space fit for—

A captain.

She turned her head toward Fiona's neatly made bed
and then, through the door, back to the gently swinging
double-width cot.

Ah.

Good manners forbade her from entering—not to
mention the guards outside the door—though it did
not forbid her taking in everything she could from the
doorway. There was a chest of drawers in the corner,
and a desk beside it. Above the chest, an oval mirror
hung from the ceiling by a ribbon. She wondered if that
was where Hugh shaved. The desk was empty—the rolling of the seas made setting anything down an exercise
in futility, she supposed—but a dozen or so books were
roped into a bookshelf on the wall above it. The most
personal object in the room was a small, rough-hewn
box that sat just under the cot, the wood around its

brass lock burnished by regular use. She would have given up an order from the Chicago Public School system to look inside.

She heard a noise and turned to find a small wardrobe against the wall where she stood. The noise sounded again, and she realized the wardrobe door was not fully shut. When the ship tipped one way, it yawned open an inch or two, and when the ship tipped the other, it bumped closed. She watched, mesmerized as a glimpse of bleached linen came into view and disappeared. Underclothes? His nightshirt? Fiona's chemise?

Leaning in, she tried for a closer look, taking care to keep her toes proprietarily on her own side of the great divide. She thought she saw a hint of ruffle, though that didn't necessarily clarify the issue, as she knew a man in Hugh's time might reasonably be expected to wear a ruffled shirt, though she certainly hoped it eliminated underclothes as a possibility, at least for him.

She grabbed the door handle with one hand and the doorframe with the other and leaned in so far,. she was practically doing an iron cross.

"Miss O'Malley?"

She slipped and scrabbled to her feet as Roark, clearly taken aback, watched.

"Yes?" she demanded. "I was doing something for the captain."

"I'm sure he is appreciative. I have come about the captain."

"What? Is something wrong?"

"You know his requirements about attendants. He is resting comfortably, but things are a-hoo on deck. I'm afraid a French cutter has clipped the horizon. I am needed. Will you be able to go to him?"

"Yes. In just a moment. Mr. Roark, I hate to bother you, but I have a plane to—er, a very important appointment to make this evening. I have to return to the islet soon."

"We will do our best, Miss O'Malley. I'm afraid the French navy is not always as sensible of schedules as one would hope. Oh, and I meant to tell you the captain has had me move you to a different cabin. It is across the hall from this one—the one with a scorch mark on the door. Nothing to worry about. Just a bit of cannon fire."

Comforting.

"Thank you, Mr. Roark. I'll be down as quickly as I can. I have a little more to do here."

His gaze went uncertainly to the place where she'd been hanging. "Shall I call for a hook and line?"

"No," she said. "Thank you."

He took his leave, and Joss finished her search, emptying Fiona's cot of its mattress, shaking out the sheets and tapping the walls in search of a hidden storage area. Nothing. She plopped on the cot and looked at the chest. The room was a bust. In fact, she thought with some consternation, it looked like no one had ever set foot in the place. She could see the mop marks around the base of the trunk.

Mop marks around the base . . . ?

She jumped up, wrapped her arms around the sides and pulled the trunk forward.

A folded sheet came into view.

Bingo.

CHAPTER TWENTY-THREE

The beautiful mapmaker died, and many men came to court the daughter. But the princess-girl, now an able woman, waited for the knight who would share with her all he possessed—his help and his heart.

—The Tale of the Beautiful Mapmaker

She spread the thick vellum on Hugh's cot, watching his fitfully sleeping form before returning to the map.

The Edinburgh map was identical in style to other maps her mother had created. This, she supposed, could mean only one of two things: Fiona or some other time traveler had stolen one of her mother's maps and brought it to the past, or her mother based her mapmaking on some eighteenth-century artist's style. There was a third possibility, of course, but it was so far-fetched as to be beyond consideration.

She examined the work—the lush, hand-printed colors, the beautiful copperplate script. How clearly her mother's passion for her art had come through in the execution. Though Joss did not know when or even the reason why her mother had abandoned this calling in order to mass-produce maps, Joss had always associated the reason with the story of the heroine in *The Little Mermaid*—Hans Christian Andersen's dark, unsparing tale, not the sanitized Walt Disney version. Andersen's mermaid gives up her voice and tail in order to walk on land and be near the handsome prince, and every step she takes on her new feet feels as if she's walking on swords. Had Joss's dad been the handsome prince? She didn't know, but for all the joy her mother's hand-drawn maps brought Joss, they held an element of sadness as well.

But what could Hugh, or indeed anyone, find in a map of Edinburgh? Or, for that matter, in the map of London Hugh had taken from her company? She unfolded that one as well. What struck her immediately was the exact duplication of the cartouche: both had the Scottish Blackface sheep; both had the pele tower; both had the hawk, the hunting dog with teeth bared, and the wild boar; and both had an odd dashed background. Since each of her mother's maps usually had a cartouche made specifically for it, Joss was puzzled as to why two disparate maps would share not just similar but identical cartouches. What's more, she had the strongest sense the map that was missing from the map room—not the one Hugh had taken, but the one she thought Building Services might have moved—had the same cartouche. She hadn't looked at it—*really* looked at it—in years, but she certainly remembered there being sheep.

She moved the maps to the side and rested her head on her fist, gazing at them thoughtfully. She could feel the warmth of Hugh's body and the labored rise and fall of his chest. Maps, maps and more maps. What had her father done? What were Hugh and Fiona really looking for? And what, if anything, did her mother have to do with it?

She heard Hugh's voice and realized with a start that she'd been asleep. It took a moment to figure out she was at his side on a stool, not in his arms, especially as the dream she'd been having had been a long and subconsciously enhanced replay of that kiss on the balcony. Di had been right. There was something quite satisfying about having found her Mr. Mistake.

He shook the covers loose, and when she tried to straighten the sheet, he caught her by the arm.

"Duck!" he cried in a muffled rumble. "'Tis Reynolds!"

"No, no," she said, trying to soothe him. "You're dreaming."

He flopped to his side, breathing shallowly. She laid a hand on his temple. He was on fire. His cheeks were flushed, and a sheen of moisture glistened on his skin.

"Aye, the fever has begun," came the surgeon's voice behind her, and she jumped. She hadn't realized he was in the room.

"What can we do?" she asked.

"Wait. 'Twill grow worse before it grows better."

If it grows better. In 1706, they were two hundred years away from having antibiotics. She felt a new kick of fear for him—and for herself were she to lose him.

"On his phone. The scurrilous cad." Hugh thrashed at the sheets.

Joss stole a glance at Lytle. "I mean no disrespect, but I think you had better leave. Can you give him more laudanum?"

"I cannot. He is a large man, but I fear more would be tempting fate."

"May I have a fresh basin of water, then, and some towels?"

"I'll tell my boy." Mr. Lytle exited.

She touched Hugh's forehead, caressing that scar that ran through his brow. "It's all right. It's all right."

He calmed a bit. "She must not see," he whispered.

"Who, Hugh? Who?"

"Fiona. Need Fiona. Oh, why did Maggie leave?"

Joss pulled her hand back as if she'd been burned. *Maggie? My mother, Maggie?*

"Maggie who?"

"The blood! Oh, the blood!" he shrieked. "I'll kill him! I'll kill him with my own hands!"

Mr. Lytle returned, followed by a boy carrying a basin and towels. The boy handed them to Joss.

Hugh called out again, and Lytle frowned. "Keep him comfortable. If anything changes"—he shook his head uncertainly—"send for me."

For the better part of the afternoon, Joss kept Hugh as cool as she could, and his cries gave her much food for thought. She was heartened to see his discomfort ease, and he fell into a quieter sleep. As for the ship, it never slowed, and Joss prayed they were moving in a large circle that would deliver her soon to the islet.

Sometime later—she must have dozed—she was awakened by Mr. Roark, who carried a chop and a mug of beer.

"I don't think he'll eat." She gazed at Hugh's pallid complexion.

"It's for you," Roark said. "Take it to your cabin. Get some rest. Let me take a shift."

"But the French—"

"Are gone. Did you not know? Ran into the protective arms of *L'Achilles,* one of the French navy's largest ships. I called off the chase."

"*L'Achilles* is a rather poor name for a ship, don't you think?"

"Hardly matters when you carry forty-two guns. We are heading back to the islet. I am hoping to touch there in half a watch."

She must have frowned, for he added with a gentle smile, "Two hours."

Lytle arrived with the next dose of laudanum, and Joss got to her feet.

"Keep him cool," she said to Roark.

"When it comes to water, m'um, I am uncommonly handy."

Hugh jerked to a thickheaded wakefulness, burning like his limbs were afire.

A trickle of broth dribbled into his mouth. He lapped it weakly. He felt as if he were made of lead. It required the most daunting attention to swallow.

"You've been sleeping," Roark said. "How do you feel?"

"Awful." His voice was a hoarse whisper. "What have I said?"

"Oh, a number of things. You spoke of the young lady."

Hugh had a foggy memory of Joss reaching for him, caressing his head. Had it been a dream?

"I hope I did not—"

"You did not. You said nothing to embarrass yourself or her."

"And what else?"

"You spoke of a yellow bridge and something you called a 'skyscraper.'"

"Oh dear."

"You were on quite a tear," Roark said. "Called the skyscraper *hubris*. Then there was the usual—our points on the wind, the dismal state of the chains, calling for your best glass. You did comment upon my sailing once or twice."

"I hope not unhappily."

"If it had been, I would hardly repeat it."

"And that's all?" Hugh felt awash in snippets of dreams, like rats biting at his extremities. He wasn't sure what was real or imagined.

"Well, there was something about a villain named Reynolds—"

Hugh clapped an arm on Roark's sleeve. "What did I say? Was she here?"

"Do not fret yourself. She was not here. You accused Reynolds of the worst sort of mischief. I take it he's the one who . . ." He made a gesture toward Hugh's shoulder.

"She mustn't know."

"I shall not speak of it."

"No! Do you hear me? She must not know!"

"Aye, sir. You must rest. Your fever is getting worse."

A knock sounded. "Roark?" Joss called. "Is Hugh awake? May I come in?"

"Send her away!" Hugh cried. "Send her away! I don't want her here."

"Sir—"

"Not even for a moment. Only you. You or no one."

Roark sighed. "I shall be returning her to the islet within the hour. Are you certain you don't want to say good-bye before she goes?"

"No," Hugh said with a fevered certainty. "Get her off the ship."

CHAPTER TWENTY-FOUR

"I don't understand," Joss said, ignoring the men holding the water-crossing seat for her. "Why wouldn't he want to see me?"

"He's very feverish, m'um," Roark said. "Do not take it ill. I'm sure he does not know what he said."

"Then let me go to him."

"That wouldn't be a good idea. He's resting. Please. The seat is ready. I promise I will give him your report on the map when he is better."

Knowing her departure was imminent, she had written up her thoughts, though other than letting him know the cartouche on the Edinburgh map was identical to the cartouche on the one he'd taken from the map room, there wasn't much to tell. It would help, she thought, if she understood a little more about what Hugh was looking for and, more important, why. But lacking that knowledge, she could do no more than add her belief that the map missing from the map room shared the same cartouche as the other two. Then she sealed the note and gave it to Roark. She hoped it would help.

Roark had returned her phone, and she knew from checking it surreptitiously below that it was after five. Even if her arrival in Pittsburgh was as quick as their departure, she'd have to hightail it to the airport to make the flight to Vegas. Nonetheless, she felt very uneasy about leaving Hugh.

"Will he return?" she asked, tilting her head toward the islet and the twenty-first century beyond it.

Roark shrugged his shoulders. "I don't know the captain's plans."

Joss stepped into the rope seat reluctantly. One of the men tightened the knots around her legs and another the one across her lap.

The surgeon appeared on deck and caught Roark's eye. A signal of some sort passed between them.

"What is it?" she said.

"If you'll excuse me," Roark said, "there is an issue below. Mr. Vanderhaut, the ship's bosun, will oversee the transfer on this side and Mr. Ross is already on the islet to help you there. Make that a Spanish bowline, if you would, Mr. Vanderhaut. This is precious cargo."

"What is the issue?" she demanded. "Does it involve the captain? Is the captain all right?"

"Miss O'Malley, he is in good hands. Mr. Lytle will do everything he can."

Everything he can?

The chair jerked and suddenly Joss was aloft and moving fast. She squeezed her eyes shut automatically, trying not to let unbridled terror run rampant, but her curiosity was too great. She slitted her eyes and saw Roark's face pale as Lytle spoke to him in whispered tones.

"Take me back!" she cried to the bosun.

"You'll be fine," he boomed. "Look at the sky."

The sea churned beneath her, in a neat imitation of her gut as she saw Roark tear down the ship's stairs. "No, it's not the water! I want to see the captain!"

But Mr. Vanderhaut only waved.

When she was in sight of the islet, she repeated her demand. Ross, however, seemed far too busy working the pulleys to respond. When she was on steady ground—the adjective "safe" being out of the question on the windy, sea-swept rock—Ross began to release her from the seat.

"Don't know what sort of Merry-Andrew show these contacts of yours think they're running," the persnickety Scotsman muttered. "'Tis beyond comprehension that a ship would collect you from here rather than the safety of our deck. I hope for both your sakes you're worth the effort."

Not exactly a man likely to grant her a favor. "I want to go back."

"To the ship?" He hooted. "My orders are to ensure you're comfortable here, then leave as quickly as possible." He released the final rope and stood.

"Could you at least ask them how the captain is?"

He gazed out to the ship, moored a good quarter of a football field away. "I dinna have flags, lass."

"Is there any other way?"

He sighed and cleared his throat. "Hail!" he shouted.

The men on deck stopped, but the winds were strong.

"Hail! Report the captain's health!"

The men gazed at each other, confused, and Ross repeated his request.

There was a scuffling on deck, and Joss hoped that meant someone was consulting Roark or Lytle. Meanwhile, Ross was knotting himself into the seat. At last a flag went up, then another, then another. Three flags strung on a line.

"What does it mean?"

He pondered. "My signal reading is not as strong as it might be. The first is 'Status.' The second . . ." He squinted, rubbed his eye and looked again. "I believe that's the signal for 'Steady course.'"

"And the last?"

He tightened the last knot and gave the rope above his head a strong jerk. "'Stay clear.'"

Chapter Twenty-five

Joss landed in the alleyway with a crash, scattering some trash cans. She put a hand to her aching temple and crawled to her feet as a shower of sparks rained down on her head. She'd waited until Ross touched on deck and the rope had gone slack before making her way to the little cave, and it had been with a heavy heart that she'd watched as the men on the ship ran onto the yard-arms, ready to make sail as soon as Roark or one of his appointees spotted the telltale sparks that would mark her departure.

Almost a whole day had passed since she'd left. She'd left Di waiting for her and then lied to her in order to get her to lie to Rogan. She'd left Rogan in the midst of a party when she should have been at his side. And now she'd left Hugh when he might be very ill. If she wasn't careful, she was going to end up like her father, irreparably hurting the people she loved.

And now her teetering business was at risk. If she wasn't in Vegas and prepared for the meeting with that buyer tomorrow morning, she could kiss good-bye a sale that might pull the company from the brink.

She pulled out her phone. Thirteen messages. Great. She realized she'd left her wallet at the office, which meant she'd have to run to the USX Tower before grabbing a cab.

She broke into trot and dialed Di. Di answered in half a ring.

"Where are you?"

"I'm . . . back."

"And?"

The ground was still shaking, and Joss could tell she was about to pass through the dome. "And I had my adventure." Mountains of guilt lay piled on her shoulders. She hated lying to a friend. She hated lying about this.

"You slept with him?"

She stepped through the dome and the images flashed by. One, however, caught her eye, and she stopped.

"Joss?"

"What? No. We kissed." The snippets of conversations and faces went by faster and faster. Hugh, Fiona, her.

"You were gone all night and all day."

"We did a lot of talking." Hugh again, then sparks and two men—no, three men on the islet with their backs to her, with a woman and her child nearby. The men were conspiring. That was the only word for the low tones and shifting eyes and—

"The way you said that sounds serious," Di said. "Do you mean about the wedding? Are you thinking of calling off the wedding?"

"Yes—I mean, no." Now, why would she have said yes? "I don't know. No."

"That's a lot of answers."

"I don't know what I'm feeling." One of the men in the vision turned. She gasped and nearly dropped the phone. It was her father!

"Joss? What? What happened?"

"I-I have to call you back."

Unthinking, she slid the phone into her pocket and let the images fly by. Good God! It came again and again, interspliced into dozens of other pictures, but there he was. Her father! Was the woman her mother? Was the baby *her*? Had they traveled back in time? Had he known of the alley passage? And how did Joss even know what she was seeing was the truth and not just part of someone or something else's desires?

She jerked her head back to gain a moment to think, but the lure of the images was too strong. She saw her father again, this time in contemporary clothes. He walked past the alley on William Penn Place with her mother at his side. She cast a heartbreaking look down the little street as he urged her forward, oblivious to both the alley and the glance. Then Hugh replaced her father in the images, and Joss and her mother, and then Di appeared and the three of them were walking up the street after the ill-fated visit to his shop two nights ago!

If that part was true—and she knew it was—what did it mean for truth of the other parts?

The scene grew dark, and the images slowed and drenched themselves in sepia, their edges bending and curling like ancient daguerreotypes. Mr. Lytle appeared on the deck of Hugh's ship, and Roark's face paled again and he ran. Then a hazy figure appeared at the bottom of the alley, framed in shadows and holding a gun. Sparks flew, and the figure ran through them. She could see the empty eyes shaded by the stocking cap and the shoulders so like Rogan's.

Take off the cap. Take it off.

The head drew nearer, like a zoom to a close-up in a movie, and a hand reached for the bottom of the cap.

Joss jerked out of the dome, too afraid to look.

She didn't want to know. She didn't want to think it. It was ridiculous. The man who'd never done anything but treat her like a queen? Foolish vision. She cursed herself and started to run.

Rogan shooting Hugh? No. Why? For what purpose? She thought of those fevered ramblings and Roark's worried face. No one but a madman could have shot someone on a busy thoroughfare and then abandoned him in a pool of blood.

God, she shouldn't have left. She shouldn't have left here, and she certainly shouldn't have left Hugh. It seemed like the moment she decided to look for a Mr. Mistake, the world had come to pieces.

She exited the alley and stopped while a line of cars passed. She looked at her phone: 6:13. It was going to be tight making an eight-thirty flight. With an impatient huff, she pressed the Cross button and spotted a hand-lettered sign taped to the pole.

ARE YOU CURRENTLY TAKING PRESCRIPTION
ANTIBIOTICS? ADULT SUBJECTS, AGES 18–54, NEEDED
FOR RESEARCH STUDY ON SIDE EFFECTS
ONE HOUR. $75. CALL NOW.

She froze. The light turned. A woman passed by her and stepped into the street.

She could go back. She had to.

There was an early morning flight. Would she make it? It didn't matter. It didn't matter if she missed the flight or her wedding or the buyer. A man's life was at stake.

The light began to blink, warning her to cross before it was too late.

Instead she turned, pulled out her phone and pulled up the number of her dentist.

Chapter Twenty-six

She waited on the islet, clutching a bottle of antibiotics for the "toothache" that had miraculously struck her on Grant Street. Thank God her dentist had evening hours.

It was almost dawn. She'd waited all night in the cold and crashing surf at the edge of the cave, huddled in her now considerably dirty white spring trench coat. The flashlight on her phone had raised nothing more than the lonely call of a far-off seabird.

Surely the ship would appear again. If it didn't, she would return to the alley, but she refused to believe her sacrifice would be wasted. She would not make the dawn flight. She had tried Rogan's cell from her office, only to remember she'd thrown it into the sea. Then she'd tried his home and office phones, missing him at both places. She knew he thought she was heading from Di's place to Vegas, and had left a message saying she was sorry she'd missed him, that the stomach bug had been horrid and that she'd see him soon; but the fact that she missed connecting with him seemed somehow prophetic, and the messages he'd left on her phone, while concerned and warm, had an underlying hint of desperation to them that had made her shift uneasily as she listened.

She'd had a lot of time to think in the dark, sea-rocked night—about her mother, about her father, about Rogan and about Hugh. She had come to no conclusions. It would have been foolish, ahead of the facts, but she knew when she and Rogan met again, she would never look at him the same way. No matter what she learned or didn't, there would always be a doubt tucked into the back of her mind.

A gray-pink glow had begun in the east—what she knew now was the east. Soon she would be able to see the horizon.

Please come. For Hugh. Please return.

There was no reason for the ship to return to the island. But still, she hoped.

The glow grew brighter. The world—her world—teetered on the edge of a new beginning. Somewhere in Las Vegas, a man sat in a chair in a hotel restaurant, sipping his coffee and reading the *Wall Street Journal* as he waited for Joss. The list of people to whom she owed apologies was growing longer and longer.

She wasn't afraid, at least not for herself. Though if the wind picked up and waves reached the top of the islet, she would have to return. Then she would be afraid only for Hugh.

The first shining rays hit the sky and ran like liquid

silver over the water. She stood and chivied herself up the seam to the tiny vertical opening at its peak, from which she gazed westward, northward, eastward, and at last she saw it—a tiny spot of white far to the south, growing larger with each passing minute.

Joss removed the coat and waved it back and forth and back and forth in the air.

Chapter Twenty-seven

"Miss O'Malley, 'tis a surprise to see you again," Roark said gravely as she was lifted from the seat onto the ship's deck. "I'm sorry the news is not better."

"Take me to him."

"Mr. Lytle is with him."

"I thought he didn't want Mr. Lytle," she said under her breath. "In case he spoke."

Roark gave her a heart-wrenching look. "He hasn't spoken since midnight."

She was shocked at the change. Hugh's skin was deathly white, and he hardly breathed.

"Oh my God."

"He is very ill, m'um," Lytle said. "There is little more we can do but wait."

"Can he swallow?"

"I have been keeping him hydrated."

"I need him to take some pills. Can we grind them into water for him?"

"We can, but what sort of pills are they?"

"You'll have to trust me. They will help." *If anything will at this point,* she thought.

Lytle looked to Roark. Roark met Joss's eyes and gave Lytle a nod.

"This is very irregular," Lytle said, but made the concoction, a triple dose. Joss was not going to take any chances.

Both men held Hugh upright as Joss dribbled the liquid into his mouth, trying to keep the tears of fear from clouding her sight as she worked.

She stood at his side long enough to ensure he didn't throw it up, then asked for a bed, a clean set of clothes and requested to be awakened if anything happened.

Now there really isn't anything else to do but wait.

When she opened her eyes, after a sleep that seemed as long and deep as a winter hibernation, the sun was low in the sky.

No one has come for me. That has to be good. Or at least not very bad.

Nonetheless, she threw on the coat and ran to the sickroom.

Roark was seated outside with his head in his hands, and Joss's knees nearly buckled.

"What?"

His head jerked up and he waved away her immediate concern. "There is no change. I'm sorry. I was . . . I must have dozed off sitting here."

"No change?" She felt like crying.

"No change is . . . better than I expected."

"Let's give him more."

"More? Are you certain?"

She didn't know what a dangerous level would be. She knew that they used to give a single shot of antibiotics instead of a course of treatment with pills, something they still did in less-developed countries, so she didn't think overdosing was a risk, but she wasn't certain. She wasn't even sure this antibiotic was the sort that treated the kind of infection Hugh was suffering from, but it was all she had. "Yes."

Joss mixed more pills with water, and Roark lifted him again while she dribbled the concoction into Hugh's mouth. He seemed even more listless than before, and much of the liquid spilled down his chin.

"Come," Roark said when they had their patient resting again. "Let us eat."

She finished a slice of fish pie without tasting any of it and was clutching a mug of coffee when Lytle opened the door to the officers' mess.

He took off his glasses and rubbed his eyes, and Joss felt her stomach drop a foot.

"The fever has broken."

Joss was the first to the sickroom door. "He's awake," Lytle's boy said, and turned the handle.

"Oh, Hugh—" She stopped.

He was smiling weakly, and Fiona held his hand.

"Oh."

Joss was simultaneously relieved and immensely irritated, though she knew relief was the only feeling that mattered.

"I beg your pardon," said Roark, who had appeared behind her. "I forgot to mention that Nathaniel and Miss McPherson were dropped off by the other ship earlier this afternoon, while you were sleeping."

Hugh smiled. "Good to see you, Joss."

"He's still very weak," Fiona said.

Had there been a note of accusation in her words?

"Are you hungry?" Roark asked, grinning. "The cook is making plum pudding."

"There will be no plum pudding for my patient," cried Lytle. "Do you wish to kill him, now that we've raised him from the dead? Broth, perhaps. Nothing more."

"I must acquiesce to the surgeon," Hugh said, "but please see that the cook puts it on the menu again for tomorrow."

"We will see about that, sir. We will see about that. Now I want my sickroom to be emptied. You may return in the morning—one at a time, of course—if the patient continues to improve. Until then, be off."

"You will continue to give him the pills as I've directed?" Joss said.

"I will," said Lytle.

Joss exited, as did Roark, who patted her happily on the shoulder. Lytle followed with an empty basin in his hand, and the boy gave them all a good-bye nod and closed the door with a firm *click*.

CHAPTER TWENTY-EIGHT

Hugh shifted uncomfortably. He would have preferred that Joss stayed instead of Fiona. And he would have strongly preferred to avert the flash of fire he'd seen in Joss's eyes when she'd arrived, despite the fact that that flash had given him permission to hope. Now he was afraid his hope would slip away if he didn't act quickly.

"Get the boy," he said to Fiona.

"We need to talk."

"Get him."

Fiona huffed but got up. In a moment, the boy was by Hugh's side.

"Aye, sir?"

"Find Mr. Roark. He is to stop any further passages to the islet. It's too dangerous at present. Do you understand?"

The boy's eyes flickered toward the calm sea beyond the porthole, but his face remained unchanged. "Aye, sir," he said, and exited.

That boy has a future, Hugh thought.

Fiona gave Hugh a long look. "Would you like to tell me what happened?" She pointed to his shoulder.

"No" was the honest answer, but there seemed no way to avoid it. "I was shot."

"Aye, that is apparent. My interest lies in who did it."

"Who do you think?" His shoulder was ablaze with pain. *Please, God,* he thought, *don't let Fiona turn this into another argument.* There are certain women one should never take to one's bed, though other than an increase in fractiousness, Fiona's behavior toward him had not changed since that night and she never made reference to it again. Had she regretted it as much as he?

"I can think of two possible guilty parties."

"Don't be absurd. The girl knows nothing."

"She lives a life denied my ancestors," Fiona said, the anger as quick to flame as overdry gunpowder.

"Then she is guilty of being born into the wrong family. 'Tis all." That, and being affianced to the wrong man.

Fiona glared, but let the subject pass. "How do you know it was Reynolds? Did you see him?"

"The person who attacked me wore a green stocking cap over his face—"

"Then it could have been her."

"Allow me to finish. I was with Joss, and I had seen Reynolds only a few moments earlier with the same green o'erflowing his pocket."

"Does he know you know it was him?"

"I don't think so. He didn't see that I'd spotted the cap."

"Bloody bastard. Though there's no denying this is the proof we needed. He is—was—in league with Brand. He has the map. I say we go to his house, use whatever means necessary to convince him to surrender it, then leave him with you for the happy prospect of avenging your brother. The people who profited from that map will pay dearly for their greed."

Hugh winced. Fiona had a way of opening that wound as if she were wielding a cutlass. The shock of discovering Joss was Maggie Brand's daughter had left Hugh fighting a storm of conflicting feelings. He resented Joss's wealth as much as Fiona. Bart's income had been reduced to a tenth of what it had been after he took the clerk position and made a home for Hugh, Maggie and little Jo. But even that situation had been far better than the one following Bart's murder, when Hugh was sent to live with a cousin who had immediately apprenticed him to a blacksmith in a distant village to fend for himself. It was there, in the inferno of his employment, Hugh had hammered out plans to avenge Bart's death, and it had taken him twenty long years of arduous work to bring them to fruition.

So, aye, the courtly display of wealth at that party, the business empire, the fine clothes, the sense of entitlement that radiated from Joss like subtle perfume, grated on him. And, of course, that bloody diamond she wore was like a lightning rod for his resentment as well as for another emotion he was just discovering could be as potent.

The conundrum Joss presented was a hard one. He couldn't avenge himself on her father. And as a man who had loved Maggie Brand as a mother, Hugh could neither avenge himself on Maggie's daughter nor on the man Maggie's daughter believed would bring her happiness. If he believed for an instant Reynolds would hurt her, he wouldn't hesitate to destroy him. But he did not believe

Reynolds would. So now Hugh would have to sit back and allow the man who held Brand's nefarious secret—and who had just shown he was willing to kill to protect it—to possess the woman Hugh desired.

The anger that had been simmering in him for so long would explode soon in this infernal crucible. But who would be burned?

"No," Hugh said. "We will find the map and return it to the past so that we may reverse what's been done, but we won't lay a finger on Reynolds."

"*What?*"

"I shan't touch him, nor shall you."

Her cat eyes glowed with fire. "Did you know he's having a special security system put in? Did you know that he's already begun to turn the capital in Brand's company into untold riches for himself?" Her voice grew louder. "Did you know that an attendant who was with Brand as he lay dying said she overheard Brand and Reynolds talking and that Brand mentioned a 'sea captain' and that he called for a curate before he died, no doubt to ask for forgiveness for the sin of murdering your brother?"

Hugh felt like he'd been slapped, and it must have shown on his face.

"That's right," she said. "While you've been trotting around after the girl like some sort of pathetic lapdog, I have been gathering information. Reynolds knows, Hugh! He knows everything!"

Hugh's fingers ached with the desire to strangle the blackguard. His fingers ached and his heart suffered.

"When did he know? When was this supposed death-bed confession?"

"In September."

When had Joss and Reynolds fallen in love? Was it possible Reynolds had purposefully seduced her after he'd discovered her father's secret? It was all he could do to keep from ordering Fiona out of the room and calling for Joss immediately.

"Listen to me. Joss is ignorant of her father's wrongdoings. I will not allow her to be hurt in any way."

"I'm not asking you to hurt Joss," Fiona spat. "I'm asking you to do your duty."

"*I* will determine my duty," he said hotly. "Joss is innocent, and she loves Reynolds. I will not destroy her in that way."

Nathaniel appeared in the doorway with eyebrows raised, and Hugh knew he had overheard. Fiona jumped to her feet. "You're a fool," she said to Hugh, and pushed past him into the passageway.

"Perhaps. Do not say a word to her about Reynolds. If you do, our quest here will be over. The ship will return to England immediately, with you on it."

"I hope you do not live to regret this." She banged the door as she left.

Hugh didn't know which would be worse: living to see Reynolds hurt Joss or living to see him love her.

"Nathaniel," he said, "find the girl. Bring her here."

CHAPTER TWENTY-NINE

Joss finally found Roark on the lowest deck of the ship, examining a pile of chains with links the size of her bathroom mirror. "There you are," she said.

Roark snapped upright, banging his head on the low ceiling. "How can I help you, Miss O'Malley?"

"I need to be transported to the islet. I was told to speak to you." She was peering down at him from several steps up in order to avoid the water sloshing back and forth across the floor. She had fulfilled her obligations here. The adventure, as it were, was over. She'd abandoned her business, her fiancé and her friend. She probably needed the time-travel equivalent of a Concorde flight to a confessional booth, but she'd settle for a bumpy Royal Mail drop-off next to some garbage cans in Pittsburgh. *I bring the antibiotics and Fiona gets to do the bedside hand-holding?* It hadn't exactly been the fairy-tale ending she'd imagined, and she could feel her pique like an angry wasp buzzing inside her head.

"Aye, well, it cannot be attempted at present," Roark said, rubbing his head. "Perhaps tomorrow, when the conditions will be more favorable."

"What conditions?"

"Unfavorable ones."

"Such as?" The sea for once was calm.

He chewed his lip. "The gears on the taffrail have broken. 'Tis a most pressing situation."

"Oh." Gears on the taffrail? "Is that why you're down here?"

"Aye."

"Will it take long to fix? I mean, they are fixable, right?" The thought of spending a week on board this tub with Hugh and Fiòna playing bedroom hide-and-seek every night was not appetizing.

"They are fixable, but as always in these matters, the timing is uncertain."

"I see. Well, please let me know."

Roark, who hadn't bumped his head since his first month at sea, bowed, checked his crown for blood and wished the captain could settle his romantic problems on his own.

CHAPTER THIRTY

Joss crested the stairs onto the floor she now referred to as the Lido deck and made her way to her room.

When she stepped inside, Fiona shoved her into the wall.

"Where's my map?"

Joss shoved her back, hard enough to knock her into the desk. "Back off, sister. I can take your ratty-ass butt." She doubted she could, but she'd heard Di's son Peter say the line while playing Transformers and she'd been dying to use it ever since.

"Hugh could be dead because of you."

"Apparently, you haven't checked Google News lately. He's *alive* because of me."

"You and your precious fiancé."

Joss narrowed her eyes. "What *about* my fiancé?"

Something flickered behind those green eyes. "Nothing. Marry him. He'll be just like your father."

"You don't know my father."

"You are mistook, my friend. I know your father. One may know a man by the deeds he's done."

Joss had just about had it up to her eyeballs with the obtuse accusations and far less obtuse resentment. "What could he have possibly done to you?"

The fury glowed in Fiona's eyes like fire pits in hell. "Ask Hugh. If you dare."

Chapter Thirty-one

Joss nearly bowled over Nathaniel at the top of the stairs.

"Miss O'Malley." He beamed. "What a happy coincidence. I was just looking for you."

"Were you?"

"You are needed down below," he said. "Captain's orders, m'um."

"The captain's *orders*?" Perhaps a lifetime of wealth had affected her more than she cared to admit, but she did not appear on command.

Nathaniel shifted under her glare. "Aye."

"And if I refuse?"

Two sailors fixing holes on a spread of canvas beyond the landing stopped their work and looked up. Nathaniel, who had clearly never confronted such a possibility before, moved his lips wordlessly.

"Would I be thrown in the brig?" she asked.

"I-I cannot recommend refusing."

She flashed a look at the sailors, who immediately returned to their work. "Tell me, Nathaniel, when will the gears be repaired?"

"The gears, m'um?"

"On the taffrail?"

One of the sailors broke into a laugh.

"Two days without grog," Nathaniel barked in the man's direction, and added more patiently to Joss, "I am most sorry to report that taffrails lack gears of any sort, Miss O'Malley."

"No gears?"

"None. They are, well, the railings that surround the stern. Wood," he added, unnecessarily.

"I see." She felt her ears begin a slow burn. "Then perhaps the captain will be good enough to explain why Mr. Roark cites the state of the gears as the reason for keeping me from making my way to the islet."

"I feel certain he will find that most fulfilling," Nathaniel said, and breathed a loud sigh of relief as she clattered downstairs.

When she opened the sickroom door, Hugh was trying in vain to pull his twenty-first-century shirt over his bound arm. Pique deferred momentarily to horror. "What in God's name are you doing out of bed? You can barely stand!"

"I'm fine," he said, though sweat trickled freely down his temples. "I'm glad you're here. I need to speak to you. 'Tis a matter of some importance." He fought to get his shirt inside his trousers. She noticed his clothes had been brushed and pressed.

"Get back into bed. I insist."

"Ah, if I had a crown for every time a woman's said that to me. I need your help."

"And if I had a crown for every time you've said that . . . Is that why I've been summoned?"

He frowned for an instant. "What? Oh. No, I read the letter you left. Why didn't you tell me in the map room there was a map missing?"

"I didn't think it was relevant at the time. For the record, I do not respond to orders."

He stopped his awkward one-handed buttoning to give her an amused smile. "And yet, here you are."

Grrrrrrr. "I am not here because of your order. I do not respond to orders—yours or anyone else's."

" 'Tis hardly worth an unhappy word between us, I assure you, but everyone on this ship obeys my orders, you included. Should you care to test the proposition, I would be happy to oblige."

His steely-eyed gaze made her unwilling to continue the argument, let alone test the proposition. Even in his weakened state, he seemed entirely able to prove his thesis. She took a small step back. "What do you want?"

"Tell me about the missing map."

The map was no longer missing. One of the voice mails she had listened to in Pittsburgh was from Marty, the map tech. He'd looked it up in the assets register. Rogan had signed the map of Manchester out three days ago with the notation "Personal." There was no reason why he shouldn't take it. Though it had hung on the wall of the Brand O'Malley map room, it was a Brand Industries asset, and Rogan and his investors owned the company. She herself had brought more than one particularly beautiful map to her office or condo over the years. She refused to let herself believe Rogan's by-the-book borrowing was an issue, though added to the odd visions she'd had in the dome, it was unsettling.

"What about it?" she said.

"You say it has the same cartouche?"

"I *think* it has the same cartouche. I don't know. I haven't looked at it for a while."

"And where do you think it is?"

She hated that he had zeroed in on the one topic she wanted to avoid. "I think it might have been taken out on loan."

"By whom?" He gave her a look. "Reynolds?"

"Yes." She waited for a witty reply or an accusation, but he face remained emotionless.

"To his office?"

"No," she said, "I don't think so. At least, it wasn't there yesterday."

"Then his house?"

She hated to answer. "I guess. I don't know."

"When did the two of you begin courting?"

She narrowed her eyes. "August. Why?"

"I . . . I thought there might be a connection to something else. 'Tis of no import. Can you get me in there?"

"His house?

Hugh nodded.

"I can," she said. "I live there, too."

Chapter Thirty-two

Joss paced the familiar length of Grant Street, furious. She felt like she'd been led around like an ox with a nose ring since she met the man who trailed two steps behind her. She'd been tricked, stripped, manhandled, robbed and forced to lie. All that remained was being forced to walk the plank and doing his laundry. If this was sexual adventure, she'd stick with late nights at the office.

"You're unusually quiet, Joss."

She made an indeterminate noise and continued along the darkened sidewalk. Worse than the things he made her do, though, were the things he seemed to know, about her mother, about her father, about the maps—things he wouldn't share. She felt like a kid, too young to be let in on the secret. It made her feel frustrated and powerless.

He said, "I only ask because—"

"I hope you remembered to bring your pills."

"I did," he said. "And I thank you for your efforts on my behalf. Mr. Lytle says they may have saved my life."

"*May* have?" She snorted.

He caught her with his good arm. "Joss, please. I hope you do not think—"

She shook herself free. "I want you to answer some of my questions."

His face flickered. "I will answer what I can."

"How do you know my mother?"

The question seemed to shock him. "I-I—"

"Look, my mother died when I was eight. My memories of her are almost all good. Of course, I didn't know her as an adult. I wish I had. But when you act like you know something about her, but keep me in the dark, it's like you're holding back something that belongs to *me*. Maybe you don't understand that, but it hurts."

"I do understand, Joss. I told you I lost my brother when I was a boy."

"If that's not a lie."

"It's *not*."

"Fine. Okay. Then you know what I mean."

He shifted. She could see him considering. He said, "You're asking me to tell you things I'd prefer not to tell."

"You're asking me to violate a trust I have with the man I'm going to marry. I'd prefer not to do that, either."

He sighed. "Your mother and father were in the past."

She felt like she'd had the wind knocked out of her. Her parents? In the past? Were they denizens of the past, or had they visited it like she just did? And why did they go? And why didn't they ever mention it to her? "Did they come through the same place we did?"

"They returned that way. I don't know how they arrived."

There was more. He was holding something back.

Would he force her to chip this story out like bits of silver in a mine? "Why?"

Hugh plucked at his thumb. "Your father wanted a map."

A map. Just like Hugh. There was more he wasn't saying. She could see it in the hazy gray of his eyes. If he was going to treat her like a child, she was going to damn well act like one. "Why? Why did my father want a map?"

"You're asking me to guess his motive, Joss. I didn't know what he was thinking."

"You and your bloody companions have been acting like you've known it since this whole mess began. Tell me. Dammit, Hugh, tell me."

"He wanted to change the future."

She felt the impact of his words like a blow. "Don't be ridiculous," she said. "You can't change the future."

"Of course you can," Hugh said gently. "We do it every time we cross a street or help a friend or ignore a wrong. 'Tis the easiest thing in the world."

"But you're talking about something else, something bigger."

"Am I? The impact of a small change grows over time. Think of a sum of money accruing interest. A ha'penny now may look very different than the fortune of a sultan in a hundred years, but that does not mean it can't produce it."

Her father had wanted a map so that he could change the future. She felt dizzy thinking about it. It would certainly be in the range of her father's ambition. But her father had never shown any interest in maps. In fact, he'd seemed to belittle her mother's love for them.

"I take it he found it, then?" she said. "The map, I mean."

Hugh nodded grimly.

"Of course he did. He failed at very few things. And what did he change with the discovery of this map?"

"He prevented the transfer of a small parcel of land out of his family."

"When?" Her brain was whirring like one of Di's calculators.

"Sixteen eighty-five. Does 'Edgemore Cut' mean anything to you?"

She gazed at him with suspicion. "Sir James Brand, one of my forebears, lived on an estate called Edgemore. He's the one that made us rich."

Hugh nodded. "Do you know how?"

"Quite by accident, a laborer discovered a huge vein of tin on a piece of his land in England, and tin was almost as valuable as silver then, used in every sort of manufacturing."

"That's right."

She began to sway. She could see the workings of her father's brain, felt his objective like it was her own. "On a piece of his land whose transfer my father prevented."

"Aye. The map we seek redrew the border between two neighbors in East Fenwick who each sought something the other's land offered. The neighbors were James Brand and Fiona's grandfather, Jonathan McPherson. It was a fair trade, a good trade. It satisfied both men, and the vein was discovered on your forebear's land after it had been traded away."

She felt a wave of relief that left her breathless. "Then my father didn't stop the transfer."

"Your father did stop it. In the world the way it should

be, the transfer took place, and for several hundred years, until your father went back to change things, Fiona's family, the McPhersons, enjoyed the same wealth you enjoy now."

"No." Joss shook her head. What he said violated every principle she had ever understood about the world. "That's impossible to know."

"It's not if you lived it. I met someone like us—like you and me, Joss—who was lost in a different time for fifteen years. He had come from Fiona's grandfather's time and knew Fiona's grandfather. When you leave you take your memories with you, just as you did when you landed on the islet with me. The first time he tried to return, he landed in 1718 and saw that everything had changed for the McPhersons. The McPhersons didn't know it, but he did. The second time he tried to return, he landed in 1706 and told Fiona what he knew."

"But that was a long, long time ago."

"Not for Fiona. Not for her grandfather. He's not been knighted like your forebear, though the tin was found on land that was rightfully his. He rots in prison. Right now. In the time we traveled to. When I sail back to England, Fiona will go once again to the magistrate to beg for his release. He is very ill, Joss. And he will die there if we can't help. He will die there without having seen his family once in the last ten years."

"But the map . . ."

"If we find it, the map, along with the deed of intent that we already have, can be filed. It should have been filed in 1685, the year the transfer was intended to have—and did once—take place. But the best we can do is file it in the year that exists when we reach the islet, the year 1706. It must be accepted by the Lord Keeper of the Great Seal, a man named Sir William Cowper. I think your mother's maps may hold a clue. None of the three is the map of East Fenwick we seek, but together they may tell us something about where to look."

"Why do you think that?"

"Two reasons. The first is something your mother told me."

Her jaw dropped. "You knew my mother?"

"I did, Joss. She told me a tale about a woman who made maps."

It was more than she could believe. That story was the reason she'd held on to her virginity until now, though she'd never told anyone except Di and Rogan. The girl who lived like a princess waited for the knight who saved her. And the dark, handsome man who sought the map so he could find the gold—*he* was the sort of man from whom the girl had to guard herself against.

"My mother told me the same story."

Even in the dark, she could see the flush on Hugh's cheeks. Was it because he knew she'd just recognized him as the dark, handsome man? And how could he have known her mother?

He cleared his throat. "I can see you are surprised. I-I think your mother may have known the story of Fiona's grandfather and may have foreseen the day when the map would need to be found. I think she may have hidden clues. In her tale, the heroine says to the dark, handsome man, 'The maps are the same. Three to one. Follow the path of the maps. Words can hide so much.' Well, you said the cartouche can hold the legend. Do you see? 'The maps are the same.' The map of London I took from the map room and the map of Edinburgh you found in Fiona's room share the same cartouche. You think the third one, the one of Manchester that Reynolds borrowed, does as well. 'Three to one. Follow the path of the maps.' I think the three maps will lead us to the one."

Joss didn't know what to believe anymore. Had her mother foreseen this? She remembered how often her mother had told her the story. "You said there were two reasons for you to think the three maps will lead you to the one you seek. What's the other?"

His jaw flexed. "Your mother drew the East Fenwick map we seek. She was the mapmaker Jonathan McPherson and James Brand used."

"But that would mean . . ."

"That she came from the past. I think your father met her there and fell in love."

Her mother came from the past? Joss was dazed by this upending of everything she had known.

"How long were my parents in the past?"

"I don't know."

"And you think my father met her there?"

"It's possible. In fact, I think it's probable."

Then a sickening thought came into her head. "Do you think my mother—"

"No, Joss. I don't. I don't believe your mother had a part in the plan. I think she found out after the fact, and I believe she decided to do what she could to stop it." His eyes were clear green. He believed what he was saying, even if Joss hardly could.

"And if the three maps lead you to the one?"

He met her eyes. "Then the future will change. James Brand will be stripped of the land on which the vein is found. The vein will be discovered on land that is rightfully the McPhersons', and Fiona will be able to buy her grandfather out of prison."

"And the McPhersons will be wealthy."

"And the Brands will not."

"Just like that?"

He nodded. "Just like that."

She looked at him, shocked—shocked and angry. "Okay, first, I don't believe you. And second, even if I did believe you, why do you think I'd help you do something like that?"

"I think you do believe me, Joss. I think that's why you're so upset."

"But that doesn't mean I'll help."

"Your father was a bad man, Joss. He cheated thousands of people out of what was rightfully theirs. He did it without regard to anyone but himself."

His words stirred the cauldron of shame and guilt that she, as the heir of a wealthy and ruthless man like Alfred Brand, had always carried with her. It felt like such a betrayal of her father to feel the shame she did. She had been raised to love and respect her parents, and she had loved her father. Yet she'd known the sort of man he was, in business and toward her mother. Could she love the man and hate the deeds?

"That doesn't mean I'm willing to strip him of everything he held dear," she said.

He caught her again, this time far less gently. "He

didn't mind stripping others of what they held dear. He was brutal to your mother. I think she hated him, Joss, and I'd be very surprised if you didn't think so, too."

She struggled in his grasp. She wanted him to leave her mother out of this. Being hated was not enough evidence to convict her father of the crime Hugh described.

"You don't know what you're asking me to give up," she said, growing desperate.

"Perhaps I don't. I never had the advantages you've had. Few have."

"It's not the advantages. Dammit, it's the memories that come with them. I had a life. Full of holidays and jokes and arguments and birthdays. You're asking me to give all that up."

"Your father will still travel back in time. Your parents will still marry. Only this time we've made sure he won't find the map. You'll still have your life, but it will be different."

"No." She was terrified now. He was backing her into a corner.

"Joss, a man rots in prison because of your father. Right now. He will die without having seen his family. Can you live with that?"

She couldn't, but she wasn't ready to give up. Not quite yet. "Why do you hate him so much?"

"He lied, Joss. He bullied, and he cheated almost every man with whom he had dealings."

"He was no worse a manipulator than you. What reasons do *you* have for coming here? What parts aren't you telling me?"

The wild anger in his eyes told her she'd hit home.

"Your mother hated him for his crime," he said. "I believe she did whatever she could to undo it. You bear the stain of his crime, whether you want to or not. You must undo it. And if the bald theft of hundreds of people's rightful futures is not enough to interest you in atonement, perhaps this will be: your father murdered a man in cold blood who tried to stop him, while I watched—and I have excellent reason to believe that man was not your father's only victim."

She slapped Hugh.

He stepped back out of reflex more than surprise. The accusation, however, never left his face.

Furious over what he'd driven her to and what more he still expected, and unable to begin to comprehend the heinous charges he'd just laid at her father's feet, Joss muscled past him and set out for Rogan's house. She would do it, had known in her heart she had no other choice. She didn't need Hugh to tell her what her duty was. She'd grown up knowing her duty, and somewhere deep inside she'd always known that someday, somehow, she'd be called upon to make amends for her father's sins.

When she heard Hugh's measured footsteps behind her, she was glad he had the good grace to keep his distance. She had no intention of sharing her tears with anyone.

CHAPTER THIRTY-THREE

He watched her slim, aristocratic back, damning him with its rigidity as she turned down Fourth. He had perhaps been overly hard on her, but he had precious little time to convince her. Reynolds had already tried to kill him once, and Hugh couldn't count on his luck a second time.

He tried concentrating on the pain in his shoulder to keep his mind off what might happen when Joss saw Rogan. He'd gleaned from what little she'd said as they made their way to the islet that she hadn't seen Rogan on her foray back to Pittsburgh to collect the medicine. Thus, this would be her first meeting with him since the attack. He knew she hadn't recognized Reynolds that night; nonetheless, he wondered if trusting his instinct that Reynolds would not hurt her was too great a gamble.

She stopped in front of a massive three-storey house with a columned portico and gleaming red double doors. It was easily ten times the size of the house Hugh had shared with his brother and Maggie. It reminded him of the London home of a moneylender he'd had to visit once when his first lieutenant got himself into trouble in a card game.

Apart from a single light in what appeared to be the drawing room, there were no signs of anyone being at home. The moon had just risen, which meant it was near ten.

"Is he there?" Hugh felt a wave of shame when he saw the remnants of tears in her eyes, which she hastily wiped away.

With a frosty look, she pulled out her phone, pressed the console and held it up to her ear. After a moment, she pressed the console again and slipped it into her pocket.

"No," she said. "And it's a good thing he's not. I'm supposed to be in Vegas. I'm not sure what excuse I'd use to be home sooner."

He considered asking where her fiancé might be this late at night, but decided against it. "And you have the key?"

"Yes."

"How is the house secured?"

"I told you, I have a key."

"Once you go in," he said. "In case I need to follow."

He had tried to say it as casually as possible, but he saw the way her face changed. She reached in her bag and pulled out her key. "I'll leave the door unlocked. Is there something I need to be concerned about?"

He struggled to hold his expression in check. He wanted to warn her without directly implicating Reynolds. "You saw what happened to me, did you not?"

"Whoever did that wouldn't hurt *me*, would they?"

Lord, he hoped not. "I have no reason to believe it. Nonetheless, it never hurts to be on your guard."

"I'm going to ask you something, and I want you to be honest with me."

"If I can."

"Is there any reason, any reason at all, for me to be afraid of Rogan?"

It pained him to see how much asking that simple question had cost her. It would be so easy to say aye and take her in his arms. But he knew in his heart Reynolds wouldn't hurt her.

He shook his head. "No."

Relief streamed into her face. "Why don't you come in with me?"

"I need to keep watch out here." In truth, he felt things would be worse for her if there was any record of him being in the house with her, and he remembered clearly how the eye in her office had allowed her to see him. For all he knew, Reynolds had the same sort of device here. He also wanted to watch in case Reynolds returned while she was inside.

Her hands shook as she inserted the key into the lock. "If you're trying to scare me, it's working."

He longed to give her shoulder a reassuring squeeze, but he knew the gesture would not be appreciated. "I don't mean to scare you, but I do mean to make you conscious of your safety. If you feel or sense anything unusual, I want you to trust your instincts."

It was the most he could say. He hoped it would be enough.

She unlocked the door and went in but stopped, as if a new thought had come to her. "You know," she said, turning, "even if you're right about my father changing the past, which I don't believe, all that would do is start the loop over. The McPhersons will be rich until the time my father first goes back, and it will all change again."

"It won't, Joss. Your father stumbled into the past through a hole we haven't identified. Somehow, perhaps with the unintentional help of your mother, he got the map upon which the transfer depended and returned to the future with it, which instantly changed all the years in between. Later, he met a man who knew of your father because he was a time traveler himself. It was Phillip Belkin, the same man who eventually contacted Fiona. Your father had drunk too much and didn't hold his tongue about how he'd come into his wealth. Soon Belkin had the map in his hands and pulled a gun on your father. Your father promised him a huge sum to give it back, which he did—and your father knocked him on the head and shoved him into a time passage. Belkin came to in a raging river and barely survived."

"Where is this other time passage?"

"We don't know." Hugh rubbed his neck. He wondered if she believed him. He wondered if anyone could believe anything so preposterous.

"Fiona has offered to give him a share of her family's fortune when it's returned," he said, picking up where he'd left off. "And unlike your father, she's actually made a down payment on that promise. So the loop will not start over. Your father will go back to the past, marry your mother, conceive you and take the map to Pittsburgh, but when he relives the incident with Belkin, Belkin will not be so foolish. He will pocket the map and return it to Fiona, ignoring your father's generous offer. That will reverse the changes Brand wrought forever. Fiona, Nathaniel and I won't have to go hunting for it. I'll never return to Pittsburgh. And you and I will never meet."

What Hugh hadn't included in his explanation was that the incident with Belkin and the gun happened after Brand had returned to the past a second time, in order to kill Bart.

She looked at him as if he'd just pulled a gun on her himself. "Just like that, the life I lived will be erased? I'll still live, but everything I know will be different?"

There was no way to make it sound any better or easier than it was. "Aye."

Joss closed the door without saying another word. Hugh felt the click of the latch like the slash of a blade and took his place among the shadows.

Joss listened to the whir of the ancient boiler in the basement as it worked to heat the house's interior. Built in the early nineteenth century, the house was one of the largest and grandest residences in the heart of downtown. The first time Rogan had brought her here, she asked if he thought he should call a repairman, and Rogan laughed. He said he found the noise charming.

Rogan.

How differently she felt about him now than she had a mere twenty-four hours ago. She wanted to blame Hugh for planting the seeds of doubt in her mind, but she knew he wasn't entirely to blame.

She didn't know what she thought anymore. How much of the doubt she felt came from the snippets of visions? How much came from the truth she'd discovered on that balcony at the History Center—that she'd enjoyed another man's kiss, even if the other man was the loathsome Hugh Hawksmoor? For the first time in her life, she'd lost confidence in her chosen path.

She'd always understood her path, always followed it. Joss had run the house after her mother's death because her father needed his home life not to be a distraction. Joss had worked hard to ensure the map company survived because that's what her mother would have wanted. She had fallen in love with Rogan because he loved her father and could save her mother's company, and because somewhere in the back of her mind Joss had heard the line from her mother's tale: "And the girl knew the knight was the man she would marry because, among all her many suitors, he was the only one who had offered to help her put things to right."

She dried her eyes and tried to clear her head. If the map was here it was most likely in the den on the second floor. She started up the stairs.

Hugh ducked into the shadows across the street, every sense in him straining to anticipate what might happen next and be prepared to act. A light came on in a window on the upper floor. His heart began to beat faster. He waited—one moment, then two. The fact that there had been no screams or calls or noise of any kind reduced his worry. He wished he could be there with her.

Someone turned onto Fourth. Hugh watched from his hiding place until the man's face came into view. It was not Reynolds. He breathed a sigh of relief.

When he turned back, the light was out. What did it mean? Had she found the map? He listened for the sound of the door opening. Nothing came. His eyes returned to the upper floor.

Where was she? How could he endure this terrible wait?

The sound of the water being turned on nearly made her jump out of her skin. Rogan *was* here. He was in the master suite on the top floor. He liked to read the *Economist* in the tub. He should have been expecting her usual end-of-the-day call from Vegas. She wondered why he hadn't picked up when she rang.

She turned off the light and stood in the doorway of the den, where she hadn't found the map, uncertain about ascending. *You're being ridiculous,* she thought. *It's Rogan, for God's sake.* Nonetheless, she paused a full minute before continuing up the stairs.

The water was still running when she entered the bedroom. The door to the bathroom was shut, and his clothes were on the floor. His phone was on the bedside table. He must have forgotten to take it in with him. He had been working in bed. His laptop was open and running. His wallet and pen were on the bed next to it.

She knew where she wanted to look next—in Rogan's tiny study off the bedroom, a room he usually kept locked because it contained the safe and a number of confidential files. She ran to the door to try it and was lucky. It was open. The ancient desk, polished and holding nothing but a blotter and a charger for his phone, stood beside a low wooden file cabinet. And there it was, just above the file cabinet—the map of Manchester, the third of the trio. Though he'd signed it out, the sight of it here, in his locked study, was enough to stop her in her tracks.

It was hung on a spot on the wall that had formerly been blank. The frame in which it had been displayed in the map room had been plain and black. The frame it was in now was ornate, intricately carved wood and at least three times as thick as the former one.

The only lamp turned on, the one between the bed and the bath, cast a small circle of veiled light. She could see the cartouche, but not clearly. There was another lamp on the file cabinet. She reached up and lit it with a faint *click*.

The file cabinet was fairly deep, however, and the map was hung high enough to make examining it from where she stood difficult. She cleared a path on top of the file cabinet, pushing two heavy Chinese lion-dog bookends closer to the lamp and a tray that held paper clips in the other direction. Then she kicked off her shoes. She hoisted herself up on top of the cabinet and twisted herself around so that she faced the map. She wanted to pull it off the wall so she could lay it flat to look at it. She grabbed the lower corners and discovered, to her surprise, that they were bolted to the wall. Then she saw the wire extending from the frame at the far edge and fastened at regular intervals down the wall.

Jesus Christ, it's set with an alarm!

She ignored for a moment what this said about Rogan and decided to do her examining while it was on the wall. She was finally close enough to the cartouche to see it. In most aspects, it was like the other two, with the same design and odd dashes. But there were several extremely fine lines of Latin around the outside, drawn in a different ink. She'd taken four years of Latin in high school, and she caught a few of the words, but she needed to get closer. She brought a foot underneath her and braced it against the dog bookends to leverage herself into a slightly higher position. She stretched and stretched. She needed just a couple more inches—

Hugh saw the light flicker and go out and heard the faint sound of glass breaking, and his heart jumped into his throat.

In six steps he was across the street and up the steps to the door. He flung the door open and raced up the stairs, half conscious of the sound of water, fighting the pain in his shoulder and terrified for Joss. Halfway to the third floor, he heard the water stop and the word "Joss?" He froze. The voice was Reynolds's.

He held his breath, waiting for her answer.

"Oh, crap, sorry," she said. "I was trying to surprise you."

"What the hell's going on out there? Are you okay?"

"Um—"

The slight pause reignited his anxiety. He kicked off his shoes and flew up the remaining steps, two at a time.

She was waiting for him when he entered, a finger up to her lips. Then she pointed to a room off the bedroom. She formed a word with her mouth: *Rogan.*

On the floor in the room behind her were a few decorative pieces. Had she and Reynolds had a fight? A lamp lay broken on the cabinet top, and the map was on the wall.

"I'm fine," she called, apparently to Reynolds, though she looked at Hugh. "I knocked some books off the bedside table." She picked up the pieces and put them next to the lamp.

"What are you doing home from Vegas?" Reynolds called back to her.

"I ended up not going until this morning. Then, my connection in Charlotte kept getting delayed. When they finally canceled it, I decided to head home. I moved the meeting to tomorrow afternoon."

"That sucks."

"Tell me about it." She looked at Hugh and shrugged.

He went to her wordlessly and leaned in to her ear. The faint floral scent she gave off was mixed with fear. "Are you all right?" he whispered.

"Join me in the bath," Reynolds said. "I'll make you feel better."

She nodded to Hugh, but he noticed her hands were quaking.

"Give me a minute," she called. "I'm going to look for a snack."

Hugh could see her pulse in the hollow of her throat. "Is that the map?" he asked.

She nodded again.

"Can we take it?"

Her head gave a little shake. "The frame's locked to the wall," she said, barely forming the words. "I was trying to lift it off. That's what happened."

"How are you feeling?" Reynolds called from the bathroom. "I talked to Di. That sounded like a miserable stomach bug."

Hugh murmured, "Is there anything unusual on it?" He knew there wasn't much time.

"Oh, Jesus, I was puking my guts out!" she shouted. She looked around the room, darted to the bed and came back with a pen, whispering, "Yes. Words. But they're in Latin. There are a lot." Her breath tickled his ear.

"Latin? I don't read it."

"I do, a little."

He gazed around for paper, but saw none. He held up his palms in a question. She tried the desk drawers but they were locked. He could hear the sounds of washing. Soon, Reynolds would be reaching the end of his bath.

Joss's eyes flicked from the bathroom door to Hugh. She handed him the pen, a light, slim black thing, then turned away and pulled off her shirt.

Hugh didn't know which struck him most, her courage or that fine porcelain back. She looked at him over her shoulder and pointed to the area of skin above her shoulder blade.

Hugh shook his head. "He'll see it."

"No. I'll put on a nightgown. Hurry, there's a lot. I'll translate."

Hugh gazed at the pen uncertainly, then tugged at it. It separated into two pieces: a top and a body. Would it write on flesh?

She turned and nestled against him, putting her mouth near his ear. "I'll do the best I can. I'm not great. Write what I say." Hugh tried not to let his eyes linger on the wanton slips of ethereal fabric covering her breasts.

"My mother's beside herself about you," Reynolds said. "Do you think it's too late to call?"

"Yeah, probably. I'll ring her in the morning."

She leaned over the file cabinet and began to translate in a hushed voice. Hugh wrote.

"'Laocoön followed by a wide—no, large—crowd. Very large.'"

Hugh was amazed at the rapidity with which the point made its way over her skin. When he got too close to the band of satin, she pulled away and brought her fingers to the clasp at the center of her back and unhooked it. She pulled the straps free and let the whole thing drop to the floor. He swallowed dryly.

"'Ran from the fort.'" She ran her finger along the words. "'And cried—shouted—O unhappy citizens, what fury have you?'' Oh my God!"

Hugh jerked, realizing her exclamation was not a part of the translation. "What?"

"This is from the *Aeneid*. It's the Trojan Horse." She ran her finger along the lines around the cartouche until see reached the end. "See? 'Trust not their presents nor admit the horse.' Dr. Hulick would kill me if I'd forgotten this."

"Is anything different?"

She looked at each line carefully. "I'm not sure exactly. I don't think so. It looks like the standard text."

He heard the gurgle of a drain being unplugged and the rush of water that followed. She froze.

"Go," she said, panicked. "We have enough."

He handed her the pen, and she scrabbled at the closure on her breeks. He padded to the top of the stairs to the sounds of Reynolds toweling off in the bath. Hugh hurried down the steps, and his last vision of Joss was as she dropped the breeks to the floor, lifted a cotton nightgown over her head and let it fall over her naked body.

CHAPTER THIRTY-FOUR

The whole thing had happened so fast, Hugh thought, it had taken on the form of a dream in his fever-weary brain. Had she been afraid as he left her? Had Reynolds's voice carried the false casualness of a man who intended his fiancée harm? Would she bed him? Had Hugh forced her into a situation in which she was left no other choice? Or would she find the assurance she needed in her lover's arms? Above all else, Hugh prayed she would not discover the truth about Rogan.

He paced the night shadows across from the silent house, holding his aching shoulder and thinking about the Trojan Horse. He knew the story well enough. It had been one of Maggie's favorites, after all. And his brother had always loved Virgil's tales of the sailing Aeneas. But what could the story of that cunning stratagem tell him about the lost map? Had Brand hidden it in a horse? Or did Reynolds represent the Greeks, who were not to be trusted?

He held his arm tight against his side and waited for something—anything—to happen that would give him a reason to fly up the stairs again and carry her away.

But none came. And when the moon reached its zenith, he dug the pills out of his pocket, swallowed two as Joss had instructed and settled onto the cold ground to wait for morning.

CHAPTER THIRTY-FIVE

Joss emerged into the cool Sunday morning air of Fourth Street feeling as if she were leaving a life behind. Rogan had been perfectly wonderful, but she'd felt like she was lying in bed next to a stranger. So much had changed in the last two days, it was if she'd been set adrift in some vast ocean and forced not only to find her way but to depend on instincts she didn't even know she had.

Which is why she'd wakened him at five to tell him she wanted to delay the wedding.

He'd been shocked, and had tried to coax a reason out of her, but he had to settle for a tearful "I don't know. It just doesn't feel right." And he *had* settled for it, telling her he'd put her up at the William Penn Hotel until she decided what she wanted to do. So she'd dressed, bade him a regretful good-bye and started out to find what the next few days would bring.

The translation, or at least the start of it, was still on her back. She'd taken care to keep that side of her out of Rogan's view all night and now found herself eager to find Hugh—more eager than she would have expected—to figure out what, if anything, the excerpt from the *Aeneid* meant.

The idea that helping Hugh find the missing map would lead to an earth-shattering change for her did not scare her anymore. Sometime in the night, she'd found peace with the notion that she'd be setting to right the wrongs of her father. It was something she had always wanted to do, and life, at last, had brought her the opportunity to do it.

The only part that hurt—the only part—was the idea that somehow she'd been wrong about Rogan. She thought back to that chance meeting in the diner. The man she'd met there, the man who met her outside the hospital the next morning—that man could not be capable of violence against another. Of that she was as certain as she was about anything she had ever known. Something had changed. She didn't know what.

She wasn't willing to let go of Rogan, but she wasn't willing to move forward with him, either. She didn't know what she wanted. But something told her that helping to right the wrongs of the past would give her some answers about the future.

She lifted her lapels against the wind. For the first time, she set off for the day not knowing where the carefully mapped path of her life was leading. It was both terrifying and exhilarating.

Despite a careful scan of the street, she found no signs of Hugh. It was foolish to let this worry her, she thought. He hadn't said he'd meet her here. Hell, they'd barely had time to say anything. Nonetheless, she'd spent the night thinking he had stayed close. She had to admit she'd taken some comfort in this fact. She remembered the feeling of his hands on her back as he wrote, and a charge went through her.

Her phone rang. It was Di.

"Jeez, isn't it a little early?" Joss said. "How did things go in Vegas?"

"Yes, but women in their thirty-sixth week never sleep, and things went great. I saved your sorry ass. The deal's a go."

"Yay! You're wonderful. I knew I could count on you. Thank you for being able to go at the last minute."

Di had been the last call Joss made before she returned to the alley a day and a half ago with the pills in her pocket.

"Omigod, I was thrilled. Two nights away from the kids? I would have happily paid *you*. And you know David's mother: she was glad to help out—as long as I promised I was coming back, that is. The only trick was sneaking onto the plane. Say, do you think if I have the baby here I can parlay it into some windfall—you know, like offer to name it Steve Wynn or Bellagio or something?"

"I thought Peter was counting on Storm Trooper."

"For a middle name. And nothing says, 'I'm a force to be reckoned with' like Bellagio Storm Trooper. But speaking of your sorry ass, how sorry *is* your ass today?"

Joss knew this was going to be a tough conversation. "Pretty sorry, actually, but not for the reason you'd expect."

"Uh-oh."

"I, um, delayed the wedding."

"What?"

"Look, nothing's happened with Hugh." *Make that: Nothing's happened with Hugh I could possibly explain, even to myself.* "I just think I'm not ready."

"Joss, c'mon. What happened? You disappeared for two days. Were you with Hugh?"

"Yes." Joss found herself examining the heads of the pedestrians in front of her, hoping she'd spot Hugh's dark hair and instantly recognizable shoulders. She also found herself checking out the sidewalks as she walked, looking for pools of blood.

"And?"

"I told you, nothing happened."

"Joss, you do not spend two days with a man and then cancel your wedding if nothing happened. Something *had* to have happened."

She thought about Di's words. She wished she'd had more experience with men. Rogan was it, except for a couple casual boyfriends in college.

"Listen to me, Joss. Are you going to see Hugh today?"

"Yes." She sure hoped she would.

"Find out."

"What do you mean?"

"I mean, find out what your feelings are. For Rogan's sake. For your own. If you'd been married ten years, I'd say you were bored. But, Joss, to feel this way when you've been dating only three months . . . Something's up. You have to find out."

"Mr. Mistake, huh?"

"No, Joss. Mr. Save-You-From-Mr.-Mistake. Find out."

Hugh counted to thirty after Joss had passed him on Fourth, then emerged from the shadows. Rogan had not hurt her, but that didn't mean he wouldn't follow her, and the last thing Hugh wanted was for Rogan to find his fiancée with the man he wanted to kill. Hugh waited until she'd reached the end of the block and was just about to step into the street when he saw Reynolds exit the house. Wealth, happiness, power—every aspect of the man's carriage inflamed Hugh's hunger for revenge, and he felt his hand once again closing over the timepiece in his pocket. Hugh returned to his hiding place, but Rogan headed quickly east on Fourth, not west as Joss had. Hugh considered his options, then began to make his way in the direction of the rising sun.

Joss exited the coffee shop, listening to Di describe the terms necessary to close the deal in Las Vegas, when she spotted Rogan walking down Grant, away from his office and the USX Tower.

Joss paused, a sickening sort of feeling rising in her gut. He couldn't possibly be heading toward Hugh and the tailor shop, could he? His path seemed to be taking him right toward the alley.

She covered the phone. "Rogan?"

He turned, and when he saw her he stopped, concerned.

Joss put the phone back up to her ear. "I need to call you back."

Hugh saw Reynolds turn. Then he spotted Joss. She ran up to her fiancé and touched his arm. The gesture sent a jab of pain through Hugh's heart, and he realized that after last night's shared intrigue, he'd assumed her feelings for Reynolds had changed. It had been a foolish assumption, clouded by hope rather than informed by facts. There had just been something about the way she closed the door to the house that morning that made Hugh think she'd closed the door on Reynolds as well.

Joss's interaction with Reynolds appeared cordial, if restrained. Each seemed to be watching the area around them to ensure no passerby could overhear. A moment later Joss pulled Reynolds away from the people walking past, as if what she had to say were for his ears only. She tilted her head toward the alley. He shook his head. She nodded more forcibly. The conversation appeared to be ending. He touched her sleeve and let his hand drift down to hers. She squeezed it, and when he leaned in to kiss her, Hugh had to turn away.

It was exactly as it should be, he reminded himself. They were affianced. She'd never led him to believe anything else.

When he turned back, Joss was crossing Grant in the direction of the USX Tower, and Reynolds was watching her. Hugh didn't know which hurt him more—the way Reynolds looked at Joss as if his world were tied up in every step she took, or the way he himself watched Reynolds, praying that one day he might feel the same connection to Joss.

She disappeared into the tower, and Hugh expected Reynolds to continue his walk along Grant. But Reynolds stuffed his hands into his pockets and sauntered down the alley. Hugh trotted to the corner and watched until he reached the tailor shop. Reynolds looked both ways, tried the door of the shop, then lifted his foot and broke the lock.

Hugh felt as if he'd been kicked himself. Rogan's act did not surprise him, but coming on the heels of that short, intimate conversation, it forced Hugh to ask himself exactly what secret Joss had just whispered in her fiancé's ear.

CHAPTER THIRTY-SIX

Joss stepped off the elevator feeling like a jerk. When she'd spotted Rogan heading across the street toward the alley, and all she could think of was the vision she'd had at the edge of the dome. She'd called to him, expecting, well, she wasn't sure what, and all he'd done was look happy to see her and say that he understood if she was confused and that he'd wait for her as long as it took. With a wave of guilt big enough to surf on, she'd thanked him and sent him on his way, toward a meeting on the other side of town.

That's where lying to your boyfriend gets you.

She waved to the weekend guard when the doors opened, started down the empty halls of Brand O'Malley and punched up Di's number again.

"Yep, sorry. Where were we?"

"What happened?"

"Oh . . . Rogan."

"Is he mad?"

"No, he's perfectly supportive. God, I feel awful."

"But it's better you take the time now to figure this out rather than later. Believe me."

"I guess."

"Happily, I will get to lighten your awfulness as I lie here, dropping fresh strawberries into my mouth and reveling in the fact that there is absolutely no one in this king-size bed with me. The guy in Vegas wants to look at the inventory to see if they can move any of the old stuff. Was that old scanning project ever restarted?"

Joss stopped. She had totally forgotten about the scanning project. It was one her mother had started right before she fell ill, a catalog of company assets. Her father had insisted she pull the plug on it in a series of cost-cutting moves, and now it sat unfinished, on some ancient hard drive somewhere, waiting for a time when Brand O'Malley had the funds and/or interest to start it up again.

"No," Joss said, her mind going in a thousand directions. "You'll have to get someone to pull what they need, one at a time, from the warehouse. Say, can I call you back?"

"Again? Is it Rogan?"

"No."

"Hugh?"

"Maybe both. Unlike your bed, mine seems a little *too* full."

CHAPTER THIRTY-SEVEN

Joss jogged down the steps outside the USX Tower, feeling something odd in the air. She hitched her orange tote over her shoulder, lifting her gaze automatically to the beacon at the top of the Gulf Tower. No falling sparks. Not today. Nor, she thought, looking around at the sparsely populated plaza outside the building, any sign of Hugh. Her anxiety, tempered by the concentration the task upstairs had required, now began to grow unchecked. She had something she wanted to show him, thinking of the paper rolled up in the tube in her tote, but mostly, she just wanted to make sure he was alive and breathing.

She debated whether she should head to the tailor shop or back to the house, where she'd last seen him, and decided the house was the more likely candidate, which immediately made her flush, bringing to mind Rogan and the unjust suspicions that had made their last conversation so awkward. She supposed there would be a fair number of awkward conversations before she figured things out.

She trotted across Grant and walked south. She'd gotten nearly to Fourth when the back of her neck prickled.

She turned around, but the sidewalk was empty. She went a few more steps and swung around again. Hugh stepped behind a bus shelter, but he knew he'd been spotted and he stepped out. Her relief at seeing him was lessened by the obscure irritation she felt at him hiding while she worried, and by the odd, guarded look on his face.

She waited as he jogged across Grant's wide, empty lanes.

"Were you following me?" she said. "I was looking for you."

"Aye. I have reason to believe someone might wish you harm."

It was a lie. She had no doubt. His manner was almost cold—completely different from that of the man who'd run up the stairs to save her the night before.

"I'm fine," she said. "Though I feel bad we had to do what we did behind Rogan's back."

"I'm certain you do." The gray in his eyes was as hard as iron and the scar in his brow seemed to pulse red. "Why were you looking for me?"

"I-I wanted to see if you were well, for one thing."

He began to walk. "Tired—but well enough, aye."

Another lie, she thought as she followed. He looked like hell. She decided not to ask if he was taking his pills.

"Is that all?" he asked.

"Well, I—" She stopped herself. If that's the way he was going to be, he could stuff the tube she had for him right up his annoying British backside. "Yep, that was it."

"What about the Trojan Horse?

"What about it?"

"Did you look at the excerpt? Was it the same?"

"Yes," she said hotly. "It was the same. What you wrote and what I remember seeing matches the text exactly."

He gazed briefly into the distance, digesting this. "And what do you think it means?"

"I guess it means we should watch out for Greeks bearing gifts."

He growled but said nothing.

She turned down Fourth and he followed her in silence. When she reached Smithfield, she found a construction crew blocking the sidewalk. Joss remembered they were preparing a building here for demolition. One man worked a jackhammer, another a torch. When the jackhammer started again, and she crossed to the far side with Hugh on her heels.

"Where are you going?" he asked over the sound.

It seemed more like an accusation than a question. "Back to the house."

"Not the tailor shop?"

"No. Why?" It wasn't even in this direction. Joss reached the great lions that guard the grand façade of Dollar Bank, one of Pittsburgh's oldest banks.

"The dark, handsome man and the mapmaker had a beautiful daughter, and they gave her everything she could want—toys, dolls and even a magical place guarded by a pair of lions."

The looming Corinthian columns and massive polished brass doors gave the building the look of a Greek temple. Supporting the pediment were a pair of beautiful, naked women—caryatids, she remembered from college art class—who, like Joss, accepted their fate with unblinking stoicism.

"Someone broke the lock on the shop," Hugh said. "Tore the place apart."

She felt her anxiety grow. "Was it the same person who tried to shoot you?"

"He didn't try, Joss. He succeeded. And aye, it's a possibility."

There was something in his tone. Something unpleasant and exploratory. Then it hit her, and she wheeled around. "You think I had something to do with it."

His face didn't change. "Did you?"

"How could *I* be involved?" she cried. "I'm the one who's sacrificed everything to help."

"'*Sacrificed everything*'?" He snorted. "What have *you* sacrificed? Your business? Your home? The family fortune that brought you your every desire? So far, you have sacrificed nothing. The only thing you've lost is a map, and I took that myself."

"I nearly sacrificed my relationship with Rogan." With Hugh like this, she had no desire to share the news of her now delayed wedding with him.

"How?" he demanded, and the jackhammers stopped before he lowered his voice. "Did you not take him to your bed last night?"

A few passersby turned, and she led him back from the busiest part of the sidewalk. "Christ, you have some effing nerve. I didn't, as you so quaintly say, 'take him to my bed,' though by all rights I should have—he is my fiancé, you know, not that that's ever seemed to matter to you."

"I was not the only person on the balcony at that party." The sparks from the torch were visible behind him like some dark angel's halo.

"I was drunk."

"You might have been, but that doesn't change what was in that kiss."

"Oh, Jesus. Don't make something out of it that wasn't there. It was a reflex."

His nostrils widened. "What, pray, is your meaning?"

"My meaning is that the tingle you get when you kiss is the equivalent of coughing when your throat tickles. It means *nothing*."

"Reflex, is it? Like this?"

He drew a finger across her breastbone, and she gasped. "Yes," she hissed.

"Or this?" He kissed the place where he had touched, and she bent her head back without thinking.

"Yes." This was a dangerous game.

He inserted his bulk like a shield between her and the workers and teased a nipple. "And this?"

His boldness shocked her, and the warmth he fanned in her was like a drug. When the jackhammer pulsed to life amid the falling sparks, she imagined it as him, between her thighs. "Yes," she lied. "Any man can do it."

"Reynolds?"

"Of course Reynolds."

His hand fell away, and he cradled it as if he'd been wounded, which only churned her whirlpool of emotions higher. She could defend herself from his carnality; his vulnerability was more challenging. For a long moment he said nothing, and the sidewalk-jarring sounds of the work crew again filled the silence between them.

"What reflex was it, then," he asked, his face emptied of hardness, "that brought you to the islet with those pills?"

She made a small noise. The memory of the fear she'd had for him came back with a wallop, and he pulled her softly into his arms. She hated that his height made her feel safe. She hated that his quest made her feel like she might one day deserve the advantages she'd been given. But most of all she hated that the way his heart beat as he held her made her want to forget everything she knew about Rogan. It was a betrayal and a damned ugly one. Treason raged in her and so did guilt. Her blissful, easy happiness had been destroyed because of Hugh, and she hated him—*hated* him—at this moment for making it happen.

"Tell me you didn't betray me, Joss," he said into her hair. "Tell me you had nothing to do with the break-in."

Betray *him*? There was only one person she'd betrayed, and that was Rogan—because of *him*. She shoved Hugh away. "You miserable prick."

Something in his eyes changed. She could almost hear a snap, like the sound of an I-beam as a building collapses, and the vibrations at their feet easily could have been the aftershock.

"'*Miserable*' is the last word to describe it," he said with cold fire, "and if you had the courage to discover the extent of your reflexes, milady, you might find out."

He brought his mouth down on hers in a bruising insult of a kiss. She struggled against the desire, but when he backed her against the lion's plinth, she gave way, and—with a boom that nearly deafened her—so did the ground beneath them.

CHAPTER THIRTY-EIGHT

Joss was catapulted into cold, rushing water that sucked the wind out of her and flung her instantly out of Hugh's arms. The dark water covered her head like a grave, and every move she made seemed to carry her lower. Lungs screaming for air, she clawed at the water but found no purchase. She was moving fast, but didn't know where. With a painful *clunk,* her body hit something solid, and the force threw her for an instant over the water's surface, long enough to scream, "Hugh!" before liquid filled her nose and mouth. One rock smashed her foot and another her shoulder. She was tumbling down a hill of water.

Flailing helplessly, she tried to find her way upward but couldn't. She was sinking. She could feel the weight of her clothes dragging her down. Terror jerked her limbs like a marionette's. She kicked and pumped as she was thrown side to side. She had to breathe, had to.

She heard Hugh's muffled voice. "Joss!" he screamed, and she reached but couldn't find him.

Her elbow bumped something, and she grabbed with all her might. It was an arm. Hugh's. She got a handful of his hair and a death grasp around his neck. But instead of helping, he was fighting to free himself. He broke her hold and pulled away.

She surfaced and snorted a gulp of air. The next instant her head smashed against something, and she tasted blood. She was falling, falling . . .

Something jerked her hard. An arm around her throat was choking her. No strength to struggle.

All at once her face was in the air. The arm wasn't choking her. It was towing her, guiding her. The water was still hurtling them somewhere, but she could breathe. They were in a river, and it was raining, a torrential downpour that turned the sky black. She would never be warm again.

Hugh reached for a branch overhanging the water and caught it, but it tore from its roots. The river raced on, clipping stones and bouncing them off ledges.

"Bloody hell!" he cried. "It's the Tarr Steps!"

The words meant nothing to her, but she could feel Hugh's panic and hers rose accordingly.

"Can you grab it?" he asked her.

"What?"

"There's a bridge ahead. Can you catch it and hold on?"

"I don't know. I'll try." She wanted to cry.

He careened off another stone with his legs and for an instant she saw the bridge. It wasn't like any bridge she had ever seen. It barely rose above the water. In fact, water was spraying over it. And it was made of long, flat stones perched on more than a dozen stone piers. No rails. No wood.

They would hit in a matter of seconds. She could see the only choice was to go between the piers or be smashed against one, but going between would require her face to be underwater, and she knew she couldn't do that willingly.

Hugh relaxed his grip and turned her so she was beside him, not behind.

"Take that one! There!"

The water raced faster and the noise rose in a roar. Joss spotted an overhanging branch and grabbed it. Hugh clung to a pier. They were apart now, which terrified Joss. She pulled herself slowly out of the water, the weight of her clothes almost impossible to overcome. She got a knee on the shore and used the branch to pull herself upright.

"Joss!"

Something bumped her as she stood, and she fell back in the water, hitting her head hard.

In an instant, her body disappeared under the bridge.

"Joss!" It was that awful night on the islet again, and he felt the same paralyzing responsibility.

A log had slammed against two piers between him and the shore. If he could get to it, he could use it to get to land, but that meant letting go and, even for an instant, that didn't seem possible.

He drew himself along the stones laid across the piers. Could he hold them while he kicked across? He moved slowly, turning sideways so the force of the current could pass on either side.

A little more. A little more.

He caught the log and wrapped his arms around it. Kicking hard, he made his way down its slippery surface to shore and crawled, shivering, onto the bank. With a wrenching groan, he pulled himself to his feet and raced around the bridge. His heart nearly stopped. Joss was facedown in the water ten feet from shore, her body limp, and she was held in place only by an overhanging branch that had snagged her clothing.

He ran along the water's edge, looking for something he could use to grab her. Finding nothing, he edged his way to the branches, found the one holding her and pulled slowly.

He managed to move her slightly. He was terrified she'd slip free and go downstream, though he was far more afraid it wouldn't matter because she was already dead. At last, she was close enough for him to catch her sleeve and he pulled her to shore.

He put his ear near her mouth. She wasn't breathing. He banged her chest with his fist. Once. Twice. Water trailed out of her mouth. He did it again. More water.

"Joss!" he cried, as if she were asleep instead of not breathing.

One more time, he brought his fist down.

She coughed.

"Joss, Joss," he said, shaking her shoulders. "Joss."

She turned on her side to cough up more water, and he collapsed with relief. He pulled her into his arms and held her tight. He nearly cried. So much had been taken from him. He couldn't lose her, too.

"I hate the water," she said.

"I know."

He released her reluctantly and put a hand to her temple, where an open gash bled freely.

"Thank God you're all right," he said.

She looked at the crimson on his fingers. "You have a pretty broad notion of 'all right.'"

She was shivering, and he pulled off his wet coat and put it on her. It was wet but he knew it would warm her. The rain was still sheeting down, and it was cold. He knew exposure was a real risk. They needed to do something and do it quickly.

He scanned the fields and road beyond the river for signs of civilization.

"Any thoughts on next steps?" she asked, rubbing her head.

"Aye. Watch out for the lions."

"I take it we found the other passageway, the one used by the man with the gun."

"That seems likely. So now we know of two. One in the alley that leads to the islet, and one behind the lion statue that leads here." He watched the water gnash its furious path under the bridge. "The passageways seem to be put in places that make their use rather self-limiting."

A glimpse of orange caught his eye. "What is that?"

She turned. "Oh my God! It's my tote." He jumped to his feet and rescued the thing from where it had lodged in a tangle of vines.

"What is it?" he asked, but before she could answer, a noise pulled his attention from her.

"What? What do you hear?"

It was carriage wheels, and he ran to where he hoped he could intercept the vehicle.

* * *

A carriage, then, she thought. *Well, that narrows the year down to somewhere between, say, 1400 and the nineteenth century.* She wrapped the coat more tightly around her. No need to expose mid-millennial mores to any more flesh than absolutely required.

The carriage had stopped and she could see Hugh gesturing to a clearly uncertain driver. She couldn't imagine what story would explain a drenched man in twenty-first-century trousers with a bullet hole in his shoulder and a bleeding woman wearing trousers. Nonetheless, she hoped whatever he said worked. She couldn't feel her fingers or her feet, and she knew that was a bad sign.

Hugh trotted back. "Come. Let me carry you. He'll take us to Dulverton."

She grabbed the tote and let him lift her. It was as if she weighed nothing. "Then we are in . . . ?"

"Exmoor," he said. "In 1706."

CHAPTER THIRTY-NINE

Joss thanked the servant for helping her into the gown of her host's dead wife, said she would be down to breakfast in a few moments and closed the bedroom door with a *click*. This was her first solitary moment in the light of day since they'd arrived, and she needed to find out if the precious contents of her case had survived.

The generous and apparently lonely owner of the carriage had insisted they spend the night at his estate and had provided blankets, bandages, food, wine and fire in large supply. He was a widower and utterly charmed by Hugh's story that he had absconded with Joss and had been on his way to Gretna Green to marry her when their horse had stumbled and fallen on Tarr Steps—charmed enough, at least, to agree not to insist on sending a message to Joss's parents or the local magistrate.

Of course, Hugh's story had meant they were deposited for the night at opposite ends of the house, with two footmen and a locked conservatory between them, for which Joss was grateful, given her strongly conflicting feelings about her traveling companion. She was thankful he had saved her, but she had not forgotten the bitter ending to the events in front of Dollar Bank, nor that tomorrow was to have been her wedding day. She looked guiltily at her hand. Rogan's diamond still sparkled there. It had not been swept away in the freezing river, and she thought perhaps that was more fate than chance.

She removed the tote from under the bed. Her hands shook as she unsealed the plastic tube. Would everything be ruined so that, guilt-free, she could say to Hugh his quest would go unfulfilled, or would the maps she'd so carefully gathered at work a day ago have survived?

She slipped her hand in. The paper was dry. She removed the sheets carefully and unrolled them on the bed. First, the map of London that Hugh had taken from the map room. Next, the map of Edinburgh that Joss had found under Fiona's chest on the ship. Third, a full-size color copy of the Manchester map she'd found yesterday in the electronic archives, matching the map they'd seen in Rogan's study in all aspects except one: there was no hand-lettered excerpt from the *Aeneid* on it, though she had found the excerpt online and slipped a printout of that in the tube, too.

And last, but certainly not least, another surprising find in the Brand O'Malley archives: a full-color photocopy on a sheet of perfectly preserved parchment of a map of two small properties in East Fenwick, Sussex, with their borders redrawn to allow one owner to enjoy more arable land and the other access to a stream in the Sussex hills.

* * *

Joss gazed at Hugh in his fitful sleep, his head propped awkwardly into the corner of the carriage as they hurried toward Portsmouth. Despite the pills, he was still weak, and the adventure in the river had not helped him any. It had taken half a day and a trip to the market town of Taunton for Hugh to negotiate an advance of funds against his naval salary, funds they had used to rent this carriage and would need again to purchase passage aboard a ship bound for the North Atlantic. That was Hugh's stated destination, though she wondered if his objective might change if she told him about the map in her tube.

She had not brought herself to tell him about the map of East Fenwick, and she wrestled with her reluctance. Surely he was right: that people whose futures had been taken deserved to have it restored. Yet, if what he told her was true, none of them except Fiona had any idea what they had lost. Of course, if what he said was true, no one in the Brand family would realize it when their centuries of fortune and ease were stripped away, either—no one, that is, except Joss, who, being currently lodged in another time, would feel the loss upon her return most painfully and for the rest of her life.

And while Joss had no doubt she could live with privation, it would be the rendering as false all the memories that had come with her life—her father showing her how to ride the ski lift outside their Aspen home, playing princess with her friends in the back of the family limousine, sitting on her mother's lap for a surprise visit to New York or Disney World or Paris—that would make the loss painful.

Balancing that was the notion of an old man in a

prison somewhere in England who hadn't seen his family in ten years. She felt an unexpected lash of guilt knowing that the power to reverse his fate sat literally and figuratively in the palm of her hand.

She reached for the tube and it slipped, hitting the floor with a bang. Hugh opened his eyes.

"What is that?" he asked, rubbing his eyes. "You've been clutching it since Pittsburgh."

"It's nothing. My notes. I managed to save the map you took and the one of Fiona's."

"Did you?" He sat up. "Why did you not tell me earlier?"

"We've been a little busy."

"Shall we open them? There may be something even yet you haven't noticed."

Tell him about the copies, Joss. Tell him.

She remembered the feel of his hands upon her that night as she translated the Latin, and in his gaze relived both the spark of conspiratorial adventure and the undeniable desire she'd felt as she bared herself to him. That was twice she'd skirted the line of propriety, twice she'd betrayed Rogan, and still he—Hugh—had had the audacity to ask her if she'd had something to do with the tailor shop break-in. Self-centered man.

She knew she'd been playing with fire. She needed to make a choice. She held up the diamond that had survived so much and looked at it. *Is there a reason you're still here?*

She looked up and Hugh looked away. He had caught her examining the ring.

"How long will it take?" she asked, flushing. "To Portsmouth?"

"A day, if you do not mind riding all night."

She did not. Contemplating the alternative, in fact, made her stomach churn. Given the telltale zippers and tailoring of their twenty-first-century clothing, they had taken care to dispose of them as soon as they could outside their host's house, and Hugh now wore a suit that had once belonged many years ago to their host's son. It was, according to Hugh, in a "decidedly old-fashioned cut," though she had to admit the plum velvet and bleached linen gave him an elegance that surprised her. The pale primrose color of the low-cut silk she wore contrasted well with the blue in her eyes, and she had twice found Hugh staring at her since she'd descended at breakfast.

He'd told her they would go to Portsmouth, where they could buy passage under assumed names on a merchant ship to the North Atlantic, hoping they might cross paths with Mr. Roark. Though Hugh had many naval captains among his acquaintance, he could hardly appear before them to ask for passage looking as if he had abandoned his ship.

"Will they be worried?" she asked. "Mr. Roark and Nathaniel, I mean."

The corner of his mouth rose slightly. Had he noticed her omission of Fiona?

"Worried?" He chuckled, as if the word weren't in an English sailor's vocabulary. "They will wait there until I return or until they're down to five days' worth of supplies."

"How long will that take?"

"Three months. Longer if they cut down to half rations."

"Then your hurry is for . . . ?"

"For you, Joss. I am quite sensible of the timing of your wedding."

The warmth on her cheeks turned to heat. He thought their unexpected voyage past Tarr Steps had ruined her chances of attending the ceremony. Little did he know that if her plans lay in ruins, she had only herself to blame. She thought of those hard arms and that furious kiss by Dollar Bank. "I'll explain my absence somehow."

"A runaway bride?" he offered without the hint of a smile.

"Full of regret." She met his gaze.

"You could blame me." His eyes were unreadable.

She knew it would hurt Rogan more if he believed she hated him than if he thought she'd slept with another man. "I'll think of something."

For a long moment, the clanging of the wheels was the only noise in the carriage.

"Thank you for saving me," she said at last. "I was absolutely paralyzed. I've been terrified of water since I was a little girl. Never learned to swim."

He looked out the window as if he were gazing back into another time. "You're welcome. I would have been unhappy to lose you. I'm afraid I've come to feel responsible for you."

She felt a flutter in heart, and the sound beneath the wheels changed. The carriage was crossing a bridge.

"I was thinking of something you said to me," she said.

He stiffened. She was sure there were parts of the last few days neither of them wished to remember.

"You said something about steps when we were in the river," she added.

His shoulders relaxed. "Tarr Steps, aye. 'Tis the name of that stone bridge."

"You recognized where we were?"

His gaze returned to the window. "I have seen the place before, though from an admittedly more comfortable perspective. My parents—and I, I suppose, though I do not remember it—lived in Williton for a time before they died and my brother took me into the service with him."

"If you do not remember it, how do you know Tarr Steps?"

His finger began to work the seam of his pants. "I came here with my brother once a long time ago."

"To visit relatives?"

"To bury him. He lies in the churchyard at Crowcombe."

"Crowcombe?" she cried, for she had seen that very name on the inn in the town they had just passed. "We were just there. Shouldn't we stop?"

"No," he said, paling, "I do not think—"

"But when was the last time you were here?"

"Then," he said carefully.

"Oh, Hugh, you were a boy. You must stop."

"'Tis not a happy memory for me, Joss."

She thought of her own mother's ashes being scattered over the waters beyond Nova Scotia, a place Joss had imagined at the time was as far from Pittsburgh as her mother thought she could convince her father to take her remains. With no grave to be the focus of her mourning, Joss's sadness had spread to fill every place she'd ever occupied. "Think of what it would mean to him . . . and to you."

He looked at her and after a long pause made a noise that she took as assent, though the sorrow in his eyes made her wonder.

"Driver," he called uncertainly. "Turn around."

He gazed at the distinctive round stones of the church and the noble, squat bell tower as he climbed the path. The hillside that rose above it clung to the last withered vestiges of summer, and the grave markers lay scattered there like ancient flowers, in varying colors and states of repair.

He knew the sight of the hastily engraved stone would wrench his heart, and he ascended the hill reluctantly. The only things left for him to sell that day twenty years ago had been his brother's medals, which he'd dug out of the box Bart had helped him make. He'd been too shamed to tell the silversmith he was selling them to pay for the headstone of the man who had earned them, even though it might have brought him a few shillings more. He remembered the long ride from Wych Cross, his home with Maggie, Bart and little Jo, to Crowcombe, lying in the wagon beside the casket and marker, hungry and alone, gazing up at the stars, wondering how he would ever pay for his return.

And now here he was, two decades later, coming here without having swung the sword of justice on his brother's behalf.

He reached the end of the path and let his eyes trail over the meager stone.

CAPTAIN BARTHOLOMEW HAWKSMOOR
EXCEPTIONAL HERO IN THE CAUSE OF HIS COUNTRY
BORN 1655, DIED 1685
NEVER TO BE FORGOTTEN

Bart had not been given the obsequies of an officer. He had left the navy a year earlier to hide his new family from Brand and broken all ties with the service as well as his seafaring acquaintances. So Hugh had made the words on the stone as fitting as his eleven-year-old imagination would allow. He had been the only person apart from the curate who stood in this churchyard when the casket was laid in the ground.

He touched the cold stone. Granite for Granite, he thought, remembering that long-ago nickname. He dropped to a knee, wincing at the pain in his shoulder.

Oh, Bart.

His eyes began to sting, and as always he seized upon the thought of Alfred Brand to defend against the on-slaught he feared would follow. The sorrow was no match for the anger, which had been carefully honed over time, made sharper with each passing year, until it stood like a chevaux-de-frise, capable of fending off even the most daunting attack.

He felt the tension harden his shoulders and descend like steel over his chest. He closed his eyes, cutting the fuel upon which the sadness feasted.

She was watching him from her perch in the church-yard, and he damned her for it—and for bringing him here—she the daughter of the man who had slaughtered his brother like a Christmas pig. He could still smell the fetid blood and hear the buzz of flies and his own harrowing sobs.

He thrust himself to his feet, his chest girdled in pain.

I have failed you, Bart. In the worst way possible. But Maggie's daughter lives. You must see I cannot hurt her. I saved her that day. And even if she.weds the man who profits from Brand's terrible crime, you must see my hands are tied.

The steel tightened around his chest until each breath was like the plunge of a dagger.

He hated that she lived, hated that she warmed Reynolds's bed, hated that she had her mother's eyes, hated that her existence kept him from holding Bart's knife to Reynolds's throat and making him confess the extent of his crimes.

But she would not keep him from reversing Brand's ill-gotten fortune. If Joss had found such unbounded happiness with Reynolds, their love could bloody well survive the absence of wealth. Hugh would find that map, get it to the Lord Keeper and ensure Brand Industries was wiped from the face of history forever.

He marched down the rise and past a startled Joss. "Get in the carriage," he said. "We've dallied here enough."

CHAPTER FORTY

She felt his silence like a blow and wondered what she had done to offend him. The carriage hurtled along the road at an alarming rate—Hugh had ordered the driver to make up the lost time—and she clung to her seat for support.

"Where are the maps?" he demanded. "Take them out."

She bristled at the tone. "I don't think we'll be able to do much with them here." She could barely hold herself upright.

"Nonetheless." He flicked his wrist as if he were Emperor Commodus in *Gladiator*.

"You do realize I'm not a servant. I have been helping you mostly of my own accord."

He held out his hand. "The maps. Please."

The "Please" fell considerably short of polite. "Perhaps it would be easier just to manhandle them out of my possession, like you did with the key to the map room?"

His hand remained in place, though the look in his eyes suggested they could easily reach that eventuality.

With a sigh, she collected the tube from the floor. She removed the London map, Fiona's Edinburgh map and, with a begrudging jerk, the color photocopy of the Manchester map. She capped the tube, careful not to reveal the archival copy of the East Fenwick map, reminding herself she owed Hugh nothing.

His eyes widened when he saw the Manchester one. "But how . . . ?"

"There are things called computers. They can store copies. It turns out someone—not me—made one a long time ago. I printed them when I was in the office yesterday, before I ran into you on the street."

He looked at the case, then at her. "You didn't tell me."

The accusation was clear. She had known for at least a day and had not shared it with him.

She could hear the blood rushing in her ears. She'd expected him to be grateful, but he was playing the betrayal card again.

"No," she admitted. "I didn't."

She expected a harangue but didn't get it. She would have preferred a harangue, she thought, to the look of hurt surprise he wore. He took the maps from her hand and spread them on his lap, burying his gaze in the paper. "There's no excerpt from the *Aeneid*."

"No. The excerpt must have been added after this copy was made. I don't know why."

"But the cartouche is the same?"

"Yes, almost exactly, which was very unlike my mother. But you can see it's all there, just like in the other two: the sheep, the tower, the wild boar that's the symbol of the O'Malley family, the hunting dog with bared teeth, the hawk—" She gasped. "The hawk. Hugh Hawksmoor. That's you." The boar gazed happily into the sky at the circling hawk. Joss felt her world shift. It was as if everything she had ever known about her mother had been turned on its head. "Was my mother in love with you?"

"Not me. At least not the way you think." His finger traced the wheeling hawk. "If the boar is your mother, then the hawk is my brother."

"Your brother . . . who was murdered?"

"Aye." He did not raise his eyes from the map.

"But how . . . ? How did they . . . ?"

"They met on my brother's ship. He, too, was a navy captain—a far better one than me. He was thirty then and your mother about two and twenty. Your father was brutal to her. I told you that. My brother was not."

"You were there." The realization shocked Joss, but it shouldn't have. Hugh had hinted that he'd known her parents.

He nodded. "And so were you."

Joss felt a dizzying wave pass over her. "*I* was there?"

"Your father was in the past for several years. He met your mother there. I don't know how, but her mapmaking had something to do with it. He wooed her, won her and married her. And given the fact you were a tiny child of one or two as we sailed for the islet—"

"*I* was with you? With my father? With the East Fenwick map?"

"Aye, Joss. And your mother and my brother. You were born there, I think."

She was astounded. She wasn't just an accessory after

the fact to this time travel. She had been there, witnessing the whole thing. And Hugh as well!

"How old were you?"

"I am thirty now."

And she was twenty-two, which meant . . .

"You were ten!" she cried. "It was right before your poor brother was murdered."

Hugh felt the conflagration rage within him—the fiery anger over his brother, the suffocating guilt of not being able to avenge him and the cooler, steadier flame that burned in his heart for Joss. But at the moment it was the steadier flame that gave him pain. However *he* might have acted, he had come to believe that Joss was incapable of deceit. She had fought him every step of the way—which was only honorable and right—but she had fought him openly. That she had hidden the map pained him more than he could say.

"I . . . Aye, it was near that very time." He stared at the map, unseeing.

He also grieved for Joss; to hear such a story about her parents and to discover so much had been hidden from her for so long would be painful. Indeed, he could feel her shock even if he did not wish to meet her eyes. But she had chided him for hiding information about her mother, and he was determined to respect her wishes.

"You will pardon my distraction," he said. "My brother is very much in my mind at present."

She stared at Hugh's profile, confused. His brother had loved her mother. Had they made love? Had her mother been an adulterer? Had her father known or suspected? And had Hugh thought the relationship between his brother and her mother a good thing or bad? She knew Bart had been Hugh's guardian and that after Bart was dead, Hugh's life took a turn for the worse—how could it not for a parentless young boy? And unlike her mother, Bart hadn't just died, he'd been murdered.

A terrible fear uncoiled in her.

"Did my mother leave my father for your brother?"

Hugh stole a glance at her and returned to the map with a long, quiet sigh. "Aye."

Her lungs stopped. In one long, horrible second she saw everything exactly as it must have happened. Her father had murdered Bart. She was certain of it, absolutely certain. It explained Hugh's anger and her mother's enduring sadness—a sadness Joss had worked so hard and so unsuccessfully to lift. And Joss loved her father, even knowing what she knew, but it broke her heart to think that his unrelenting need for power and control could have led him to such an act. She couldn't deny it, couldn't say it wasn't in his character, and while she wished it weren't true—though that was like wishing the sun wasn't in the sky—she wished she had known the truth a long time ago, so she could have helped him atone for what he had done.

She wrapped her arms around her sides and began to mourn the father she had never known.

Hugh studied the map, though he barely saw what he looked at. He could feel the pain in her silence. How horrible it must be to discover your mother had left your father.

"Look at the border here." He pointed to the cartouche's edge, hoping to distract her. "It has the same markings, though the dashes and lines and Vs and arcs seem to occur in different places, do you see?"

Her shadow fell across the map and a trembling finger traced the place he indicated. Then a large drop hit the paper and spattered in a circle.

She was crying!

His looked at her and his heart nearly broke. "Joss, what is it?"

"My father," she said in a choked voice, while two more tears striped her cheeks. "He murdered your brother, didn't he?"

Hugh pulled her into his arms, heedless of the maps, and her body hitched as he held her. He had no right to keep the truth from her, though he wished he was not the one who would have to say the words.

"Aye. I'm sorry, Joss."

"Sorry for *me*?" Her muffled voice rose from his chest. "Oh, Hugh, I'm so sorry for *you*."

He pulled a handkerchief from his coat and put it in her hands.

"How did it happen?" she asked.

"'Twas a long time ago." He patted her back, unwilling to deepen her despair.

"Tell me," she said. "Please."

"I came home from a day playing in the fields and found his body lying in the dining room. Shot."

"Oh, Hugh."

"I knew when I walked up something was wrong. The cottage seemed empty, lifeless—and 'twas never like that when you and Maggie were there."

She pulled back, cheeks wet, to look at him, amazed. "We *lived* with you?"

"You did. In Ashdown Forest. 'Twas the happiest year of my life. I loved Maggie as a mother. And I loved you, too."

She fell back against him, and he hugged her as if she might disappear.

"I knew he must have taken you back with him." He did not add that at first he'd feared they might both be dead. "I knew you were sad to leave me because you left a book Maggie had made for you. 'Twas one you loved to hear. When she was too busy to read it to you, I did. You made me tell you once it was my favorite, though it wasn't—I loved the tales from *The Odyssey* she told—but 'twas the only way to make you stop asking. You left it under my pillow. I found it that night.

"*The Tale of the Beautiful Mapmaker?*"

Hugh nodded.

"I have the barest memory of that book." She touched her heart, incredulous.

"I only know it was your father," Hugh went on, anticipating the obvious next question and hoping to save her from having to ask it, "because I was there on the islet when he returned to Pittsburgh the first time, map in hand." Hugh would die before he would tell her Brand had been willing to abandon his daughter in order to ensure his wife would return with him to Pittsburgh. "Your mother said she was staying with Bart, that your father could take his map and make a life for himself without her and you. She would not be a part of it." That was as close to the truth as he would get, and it was close enough. "Your father told Bart he would come back and find him and kill him."

She lay perfectly still against his chest. "But it could have been someone else?"

"Aye," he lied. "It could have been."

"But it wasn't."

She began to cry again. He held her like this for a mile or more. It was a moment he could never have imagined—comforting the daughter of his brother's murderer and wishing for the first time the awful act had never happened, not for his own happiness, but to save someone else's. It was as if he could breathe again after a long time underwater. He opened his lungs and savored the sweet, fresh air.

She sat up and wiped her face. "Thank you for telling me. I'm sure it must have been awful."

He took her hand. "'Tis awful for both of us. I wish it had been otherwise."

All at once she started. "Hugh, if this map will change what occurred, will your brother be alive?"

How he hated to answer this question, for both their sakes. "No," he said, shaking his head sadly. "The map will change everything from 1706 onward. My brother was killed in 1685."

"Oh, Hugh, I'm sorry. Did you think that perhaps it might?"

"Aye. Once."

She squeezed his hand, then blew her nose and attempted to regain her composure. "I have something for you." She found the case where it had fallen and uncapped the lid. Wordlessly, she withdrew another wide sheet of paper and unrolled it.

His heart began to pound. It was the map of East Fenwick, the one that would restore each parcel of land to the rightful families. "You found it."

"No. That's not it."

"What do you mean? It says '1684.' It shows the two parcels in question. I saw this map in your father's hands on board my brother's ship. This is most certainly the one." He remembered the repellent greed on the men's faces—like that of rats feasting on a scrap of garbage.

"I mean it's a copy. It's not the original. I don't know where the original is. Honestly, I don't. But my mother did—or at least she did once. When I went to my office yesterday, I was reminded of an archive project my mother had started years ago."

"An archive? Like the one in Alexandria?"

"Yes, only with photos. Photos are like—"

"I know what photos are," he said, thinking of Reynolds and his blackguardly image of Joss.

"Well, there are ways to store photos in little tiny spaces called bits and bytes, and to make them large again whenever you need them."

He shook his head. "Your world is an amazing place."

"So this is a photo of the map my mother stored."

He gazed at the parchment and the ink. "But it looks so real."

"That's only because I happen to have some really old paper in the map room. I mean, I guess it's not really old to you. Nor should it be if we want the ruse to work, but it's sure old where I come from. Look closely at the printing, though. Can you see it's made up of dots? Can you see it looks different from printing of your time?"

He brought the map into the light. She was right: there were bits of the map that didn't quite ring true. Still, it was so close, and if one wasn't an expert—especially at twenty-first-century technology . . .

"I think we could risk it," he said at last.

"Risk it? Risk what?"

"I don't know how things like this are dealt with in your time. But in 1706, forgery is crime. Punishable by hanging."

Before she could reply, he pounded on the roof of the chaise. "Driver!" he shouted. "Take the Andover Road. We're going to London, not Portsmouth."

CHAPTER FORTY-ONE

It had been a long night in the carriage followed by a long day in London, and Joss was grateful for even a moderately clean bed on the third floor of the Grey Lamb Inn. Hugh's landlady, Mrs. Kenney, had been surprised to see him, and he had asked for her discretion in keeping his presence in London as quiet as possible. Mrs. Kenney's gaze had traveled to Joss, and she'd agreed.

Mrs. Kenney had given Joss the last room available in the inn, a tiny space usually reserved for a surveyor when he was in town, but the man's rent was three months past due, and Mrs. Kenney said, "If he thinks I'm going to pass up a night of income while I wait for his three crowns ten, he is quite mistaken."

The carriage had delivered them directly to the door of the Lord Keeper's office just before noon, and they spent hours waiting for an opportunity to talk to him. None came. At seven, the man's secretary gave them the news that Sir William had left for the country and suggested they return a week hence.

Dejected, Hugh had brought her to the place he kept

rooms. Then he'd excused himself, saying he needed to send a note to a contact who might be of some help, and Joss begged for a fire and a basin of hot water, which Mrs. Kenney promptly provided. She had also promised to bring Joss something to eat.

Joss drew the washcloth along her shoulders, letting the water run down her back as she scrubbed. The warmth felt wonderful on this November night, and she stood by the fire in nothing but her chemise, thinking how differently the last week had turned out compared to what she'd been expecting. Last Monday, she'd awakened fretting as always about work and looking forward to her wedding. A week and a day later, she stood in another country, in another time, on a quest she now shared, and her wedding seemed like something old and forgotten, like a story from a book.

She looked at the bed. Tonight would have been her wedding night. Tonight she and Rogan would have finished what they'd started so many times. When she closed her eyes to try to imagine it, what she saw instead was Hugh—Hugh taking her in his arms; Hugh laying her on a bed of pillows; Hugh pressing his body slowly against hers.

A knock sounded, rousing Joss from her thoughts, and her mouth watered. She hoped Mrs. Kenney was as good a cook as she was a housekeeper. Joss hadn't eaten anything since this morning, when she had a bun and some cheese for breakfast in the carriage.

She flew to the door and opened it.

Hugh stood before her in his gleaming blue wool coat and shining brass buttons, clutching a black tricorn hat.

It was the first time she had seen him in his uniform, and the sight took her breath away. The gold trim made his shoulders look twice as broad as usual.

His eyes widened at the sight of the chemise. "I beg your pardon. Am I interrupting?"

She crossed her arms, hoping the places where the chemise clung were not too revealing. "No, I was just, er, well, perhaps I should get a blanket." She grabbed the coverlet from the bed and threw it over her shoulders. "There. Is this better?"

He gave her a crooked smile. "If I'm being honest, no. Nevertheless, I bow to propriety."

She laughed, but a pleasant charge ran through her. "I thought you were trying to be discreet."

He cocked his head for a moment, then realized what she meant. "Ah, the uniform. Aye, well, instead of writing, I decided to drop by the home of my acquaintance. 'Tis only a five-minute walk. He was not there, though I left my card. I'm afraid my luck today has not changed— that is, unless you would agree to join me for dinner. Mrs. Kenney has anticipated my stratagem, I think, having delivered both of our meals to my room. Come. It's just across the hall."

He held out his arm, and she laid her hand on it.

His rooms were not much larger than her own—a small bedroom off a slightly larger sitting room in which a small table and chairs had been placed before the fire— though Joss did notice that, unlike hers, his bed was large enough for two.

The table was set and an enormous roast chicken surrounded by turnips, peas and beets sat like a crown jewel in the center. She was so hungry she could have eaten it without silverware, but she allowed him to help her into the chair and placed the napkin in her lap. The heat from the fire curled pleasantly up her back.

He poured the wine. The red sparkled in the thick-walled goblet like a pool of rubies. He held up his glass. "To forgetting the past."

She thought of Rogan. She didn't want to forget him, but she had some misgivings about him, imagined or not, that she was going to have to deal with when she returned. For once, though, she wanted to lose herself in the moment before her, with no worries and no regrets.

"To forgetting the future," she said, and he laughed. She clinked his outstretched glass and they drank. The wine ran over her tongue like dry velvet, and she could feel his eyes on her as the heat ran down her throat and radiated out to her fingers and toes.

"Would you like to eat?" He gestured to the platter.

The question appeared perfectly innocent, but for some reason she heard an unspoken alternative behind the words.

"I-I— Yes, of course. I'm starving."

"Good."

He carved the meat, which smelled delicious. She took another long draft of wine. The fire was growing warmer. "So this is where you live. Are you here a lot?"

"Almost never." He piled a leg and several slices of breast on her plate. "Though we were forced to spend a number of weeks here preparing for the trip to the islet."

We. He and Fiona.

"You seem to work well together, you and Fiona."

He ladled peas on her plate and smiled. "Is there a question there?"

Damn those emerald eyes. "No."

"Because if there is, there's no harm in asking."

"There's not."

He laughed and served himself. "Tomorrow, I'll try my friend again. If he's not there, perhaps we can press Sir William's secretary for his whereabouts. I apologize for delaying you further."

She lifted her fork and paused, thinking of the chiton and simple bouquet of sunflowers. "Today was my wedding day."

"Aye," he said sadly. "I'm sorry."

The vision of Rogan with the gun appeared in her head, and she stole a glance at Hugh. "Perhaps it was not meant to be."

He touched her arm. "What do you mean?"

His skin was warm and the scars on his hand reminded her of how different his life had been from hers. "I mean," she said, afraid to meet his eyes, "perhaps I was meant for something else today. This adventure." She could barely speak. She had never negotiated something that seemed quite as risky as what they seemed to be negotiating now. She thought of the virginity she had protected for so long and the knight for whom she'd saved it. What if the story that had guided her all her life had never been meant to be a guide? She let the spread fall from her shoulders, wishing she had not sat so close to the flames.

His hand lifted, then stopped, a hairsbreadth above hers, and the movement of air seemed to send an explosion of invisible sparks across her skin. He was making an unspoken offer, and she shifted, hoping the wine and the warmth, a different warmth, that had spread through her belly would help her decide. She concentrated on the burnished skin of his arm, where the crisscross of scars and whorls of hair spread out before her like lines on a map. What path would she take?

"This adventure?" He repeated her words but added his own question.

She turned her palm up and threaded her fingers into his. He grasped her hand unhesitatingly, his hold neither demanding nor uncertain. The beating of her heart was as loud as the ticking of his clock. He leaned forward and their lips met. The kiss made her dizzy with longing, and the soft noise she made when they parted made her realize how much she really cared for him.

"You are engaged, milady."

"I know there are choices I have to make."

"What we do will be unforgivable in his eyes—and perhaps in your own as well."

She tugged and his fingers opened. She nearly withdrew her hand, but the steadiness of his own, open-palmed above hers, made her hesitate.

"I have always done what one person or another wants. Shouldn't I be given one night—one night—when I can do exactly what *I* want?"

"Aye, you should—though, for my own part, I hope it is more than one."

"I want this."

He closed his hand around hers. "Then you shall have it."

In an instant, their mouths were joined, and Joss felt the explosion of fireworks in her veins.

A sharp knock, and Joss pulled away as the door opened. Standing in the entry was a man in an elegant brocade coat and a pristine ruffled shirt. He was as tall as Hugh but with an air of pleasant but unmistakable entitlement that filled the room like a galleon's worth of gold. He gazed at them, mortified.

"Good Lord! I beg your pardon. Your landlady told me you were waiting for me."

Hugh leapt to his feet, and Joss scrambled for the coverlet. "'Tis nothing, Your Grace," Hugh said. "The lady was seeking my advice."

The man smiled affably. "I do hope you give it."

Hugh coughed. "Silverbridge, may I introduce Miss O'Malley. Miss O'Malley, this is His Grace, the Duke of Silverbridge."

A duke!

Hugh met Joss's eye and made a low bow. Joss followed his lead, standing to bend a knee just as Lizzy Bennet had done in *Pride and Prejudice*. She buried herself in the coverlet.

"An honor, Miss O'Malley. How do you know my friend?"

Her eyes shifted. "Um . . ."

Silverbridge lifted his palms, laughing. "Ignore my question. I have clearly interrupted. Let me slink away and leave you to this noble transmission of advice."

"No, Your Grace, please." Hugh held up a staying hand. "'Tis but a small favor. I am sorry to have caused you to venture out of your way. I left my card only so that your housekeeper might let you know I would come by tomorrow."

"She did. But I was making my way in this direction in any case. What favor do you seek?"

"We need to see the Lord Keeper on the matter of a map."

"A map?"

"A map, aye. It concerns the transfer of property between two families."

"Yours?"

Hugh shook his head. "No."

"And why, if I might ask, would a navy captain be concerned about the transfer of property between two families to which he is not related?"

"One family is mine," Joss said, she hoped helpfully.

"Ah, the plot thickens."

Hugh said, "But Sir William won't be back for a week. He has left London for—"

"Cambridgeshire, aye. He's gone to the Quarley estate. Why?"

"We would dearly love a chance to sit down with him to plead our case."

"Then you are in luck, my friend. The duchess and I are heading to the same place later this evening. Lord Quarley is hosting a rather extravagant week of hunting and dining. The largest dinner is tomorrow night. We should be happy to include you in our party if you are prepared to make the journey on such short notice."

"I am," Hugh said, then his face clouded. "But Miss O'Malley will need clothes."

"Well, she will certainly need something beyond a chemise and coverlet," Silverbridge said with a twinkle.

"I . . . We don't have time, and she has but one dress here."

"Hmm." An apparently unflappable Silverbridge declined to question why a woman in an upstanding inn would have no clothes and instead tapped a thumb against his thigh. "I have a thought. The lady is about the size and height of Kit, my wife. Kit has trunks full of gowns. More than I could count. More than any man should have to count. Would you be willing to borrow one or two from her?" he asked Joss. "She's at our town house now, overseeing the preparations for the trip."

"Will she mind?" Not every woman was willing to share a dress, no matter how many they owned.

"Kit? No. She was a reluctant entrant into the world of nobility. It took a good deal of persuasion on my part to convince her to marry. I think you will find her more than happy to share her largesse. I will send you with a note. I would go myself, but I am on my way to—late for, in fact—a meeting at Westminster, from which I hope to extract myself by one. We shall leave immediately after that."

Joss looked at Hugh. Was he in? Hugh bowed.

"Thank you, Your Grace," she said.

"John," the duke corrected. "I should never hold a woman in bedclothes to such a standard of formality."

CHAPTER FORTY-TWO

"I hope you've brought a book," said the duchess, a dark-haired woman of hardly more than nineteen or twenty. "Either that or a soft pillow."

Joss laughed. They had settled in the sitting room, where Joss was an amazed observer of the parade of food-stuffs, clothes, gifts and even bedding being brought before the mistress of the house for approval before being packed into a dozen waiting trunks. The town house was huge and exquisitely decorated. It made Joss obscurely melancholy for her own youth.

"Your husband said there would be a fancy dinner tomorrow."

"The dinner will be lovely, I think—they bring in families from around the neighborhood—but the rest of the week . . ." Kit shook her head. "The men are shooting or talking politics or smoking cigars. I should prefer to suffer a lecture on the divine right of royalty by Queen Anne rather than sit through it all, though with my unhappy luck that will happen, too."

"But surely the wives . . . ?"

"Oh, there are one or two who are all right—and I know I should try harder for John's sake—but for the most part they are as dull as their husbands. The best we can do is hope for a scandal. Last year Lord Tanger and his wife were found in bed with not one but two footmen. Or at least that's what I was told. And to think his wife spent most of the dinner at Viscount Maitland's house last week bemoaning the quality of country servants."

Joss laughed and Kit smiled.

"Come," she said. "Let us find you something to wear."

Joss fell in love with a red gown with embroidered bat-wing sleeves and bodice and a high open collar that framed her neck.

"Very oriental, aye," the duchess said. "This is quite good."

There was a decided lack of enthusiasm in her voice. "But?" Joss asked.

"But I should like to see you in something a little more daring. Try the one at the end. Aye, that one. It almost matches Captain Hawksmoor's eyes, and I can assure you he won't bother with a cigar after dinner with you in that."

The dress was a gorgeous, shimmering Cinderella blue with mutton-leg sleeves, an A-line skirt, and a low-cut bodice edged with ruffles in a drape of pearls that swung sensuously under each breast. It was the most beautiful thing she'd ever seen, but it wasn't until she'd been laced into it that she fully understood the reason it would turn heads.

"I don't mean to complain," Joss said, "but I think something's missing."

With the bodice laced tight, she saw the ruffles weren't

decorative so much as the entirety of what was meant to shield her breasts from sight.

"You need to lace it tighter, my dear." Kit pulled the laces even tighter and retied the bow. "There's the something you were missing."

And there they were, like two hot cross buns on ruffled blue doilies.

"I think," Joss said, pulling the neckline higher, "this can't be right. I mean, some of the nipple shows."

"I told you the cigar would be no match. 'Tis very French. And look. There is a certain way you can turn— lift your shoulder, that's right—in which it *all* shows."

Joss's jaw dropped. "And you have worn this . . . in public?"

"Well, only for a moment or two. Lord Tanger had begun one of his interminable speeches about Marlborough or the Spanish or the state of the red fox in Hampshire, so I bent to reach the gravy boat, and John, who was across the table, immediately excused us both with headaches."

"Two headaches at once? My goodness, that is unusual."

"We felt much better after lying down."

Joss laughed. She looked at the embroidered red gown, then back to the lovely ice blue that sizzled when she moved. "I don't know. Perhaps one must be an aristocrat to make this work."

"That's what I thought, too, but I'm only a poor soldier's daughter and it worked for me."

Joss looked at the expanse of blue and smiled. "You think I can pull this off?"

"If I am correct, 'twill be pulled off without you even lifting a finger."

Their giggles were interrupted by a knock.

"Come," Kit said.

It was Hugh, and Joss immediately readjusted the bodice. When he saw the gown, his eyes widened. "I beg your pardon," he said to Joss. "I just wanted to let you know I am going to head back to the Grey Lamb for a bit to collect our things. Is there anything else you'll need for the journey?"

Yes. Dinner, a nap, a bath, a mug of hot chocolate with peppermint schnapps and time to think about what just happened in your sitting room. "No. Thank you."

He gave her a look that said he had not forgotten what they'd begun. Then he bowed and stepped back into the hall.

"No, wait," Kit called. "We have narrowed our choices down to two. The one Miss O'Malley wears and this lovely red silk from the Far East. I prefer the red. What do you say, good sir?" She caught Joss's eye and winked.

Poor Hugh. He was a man divided. The wife of his host was suggesting the red gown, but every particle of his being quivered perceptibly for the blue.

"I think both would do," he said at last. "Why, I have often seen ladies make use of two gowns: one for day and—"

"Another for night?" The duchess angled her head innocently.

"Aye. Exactly."

"Then two it shall be." To Joss she remarked, "I suggest you keep the gravy boat close."

CHAPTER FORTY-THREE

Despite the weariness and pain that seemed to be his constant companions, Hugh floated down the dark London street, buoyed as much by the vision of Joss in that gown as by the still-tingling spot where their hands had touched over dinner. It was like two ships navigating closer and closer on a windswept sea. A moment later and Silverbridge would have blundered into something far more delicate.

His feelings for Joss had changed so much in the last week, but the moment he spotted that lifeless body in the water, he was shocked into realizing that she'd captured his heart in a way no other woman ever had. Their days together had shown him what a remarkably brave and spirited woman she was—protective of her father, deeply attached to her mother, willing to help him despite the personal cost to herself. He thought—believed? hoped?—that her feelings for him had deepened during their time together. He believed she was on the verge of two important decisions, perhaps the most important decisions of her life, and he knew her decisions were not yet set in stone. His mind galloped ahead of the facts to a cottage filled with her voice and the laughter of their children. It was a foolish thought, he realized, for a man to have about a woman whose birth had occurred three centuries after his and who wore the ring of a man she had shown no inclination to abandon on her finger. And yet, in that at the Grey Lamb, when her fingers threaded into his, he had felt his life beginning to transform.

Dangerous, dangerous.

He rued the fact that Silverbridge had chosen that moment to appear. Her offer—for offer it had been—had been a test, even if she had not seen it as such. And he would have needed several more minutes with her in his arms to decide if he would guide her toward faithfulness in her engagement or possess her. He knew which he would choose for himself, but he was keenly aware he would be choosing for her, too.

As he drew closer to the inn, he spotted a familiar profile and, in shock, broke into a half run. "Nathaniel," he called. "How on earth . . . ?"

"A very unpleasant plunge into a river. 'Tis good to see you, my friend."

"From the lions at the bank?" Hugh couldn't imagine how he had discovered the portal as well.

"Aye." Nathaniel gave his friend a look. "Fiona was following you."

Hugh thought of the scene with Joss that Fiona must have observed and felt his cheeks warm.

"Fiona's upstairs in your rooms, waiting," Nathaniel said. "We weren't sure you'd survived until we got here. And the girl is . . . ?"

"Fine. She's at the home of a friend."

"Your landlady mentioned seeing you with a companion."

The warmth turned into a full flush. Hugh was glad it was night out. "Aye. I brought her here first. But how did you survive the river? Joss and I barely made it out alive."

"A very welcome branch. We nearly didn't make it. I don't know how anyone could have survived those rapids. And we walked several miles past the bridge when we got out, and try as we might, we didn't see your friend."

Hugh felt the skin on his neck prickle. "What do you mean, 'my friend'?"

Nathaniel's eyes widened. "I thought you knew, especially as he followed so closely on your heels. Fiona wasn't the only one following you. Reynolds disappeared behind the lion a moment or two after you and Joss."

"Reynolds has known everything all along," Fiona said. "We were right."

Hugh had related the story of the map he and Joss had found secured in Reynolds's office as Fiona sat tight-lipped. The London, Edinburgh and Manchester maps were spread on the table before her.

"We don't know if he knew about the lions at the bank. It's possible Brand told him, but it's equally possible that the only reason he knows about them is from watching Joss and me tumble away behind them."

"Why do you defend the villain?" she said. "Especially since it's clear it would be very convenient for you if he were out of the way."

"Ours are not the only feelings to be considered in this situation."

Fiona snorted. "You're being led around by your nose, and you don't even see it."

The door creaked as Nathaniel entered.

Hugh felt his irritation with Fiona rise. "She saved my life. And she gave me this for you." He pulled the last map from the tube, the one of East Fenwick, and unrolled it on top of the others.

Fiona took one look at the map and threw her arms around him. "My God! It's the map!"

"It's a copy. Joss found it in an archive."

Fiona stepped back and looked from him to the map. "A copy is no different than the original," she said carefully.

"In this case, it is. The copy was stored as a very small version. It involves magic of the sort I cannot explain. When Joss found it, she had it put back on the most authentic paper she could find, but if you look closely, you'll see it's not been rendered in the same ink."

Fiona and Nathaniel examined the map.

"I think it's close enough," she said.

"Close enough to risk hanging?"

"But be fair," Nathaniel said. "Who will know?"

"Joss, for one." Fiona crossed her arms.

"For God's sake, Fiona. She gave it to me. Why would she reveal it's a copy?"

Fiona gave him a long look.

"You're wrong," Hugh said. "She won't. She's not in league with him."

"Reynolds, for another."

"Reynolds is the least of our problems. What are the odds he even survived the river?"

"Rather high," Nathaniel said. "I was asking some discreet questions downstairs. A man fitting his description was spotted in the street outside a quarter hour ago."

Hugh felt the world moving under his feet. They couldn't be so close to getting this map filed and fail now. Another part of his mind went to Joss. Was Reynolds here for her? Would he hurt her? "How did he make it to London? How did he find us?"

"He may have gold ingots, the same as we do. For all we know, he was on a post chaise, too."

Aye, probably the one that left right after yours. Reynolds had probably followed Nathaniel and Fiona right to the door of the inn downstairs.

"We have to kill him," Fiona said.

"No."

"The time for compromise is over. He's a risk we cannot bear."

"No, I say!" If it was possible to keep Joss ignorant of the darker side of her fiancé, Hugh knew he must do it. For Joss, but also to serve his own selfish interests. If Reynolds died and Joss could trace a path, direct or indirect, to Hugh, his chances of winning her would be gone forever. "Swear to me you will not touch him," he said, willing his hands not to throttle Fiona as he said it. "Swear to me, or *I* will reveal the map's a copy."

The door creaked again, and Joss stepped inside dressed in that eye-catching blue gown under a long wrap. Hugh backed away from Fiona, and the three shipmates gazed wordlessly at the addition to their party.

Joss took in the room and the maps. Hugh knew how it must look to her: a conspiracy unfolding behind her back. He saw her shoulders stiffen. He also saw the calculation in Fiona's eyes as she appraised the expensive gown.

"How . . . ?"

"Fiona and Nathaniel came the same way we did," Hugh said quickly. "A branch saved them from our fate. They were here at the inn when I arrived. How did you get here?" He wondered if Reynolds had seen her.

"Silverbridge's carriage. They're outside." She turned to Fiona. "Did you see what I brought?"

Hugh gave Fiona a scorching glare, and Fiona hesitated. "I did," she said with some effort. "Thank you."

"Do you understand I did it knowing what it would do to my family?"

"Aye." Fiona shifted her weight from foot to foot. "I appreciate it."

"I hope it works. I am sorry for your grandfather."

Fiona ducked her chin, which Hugh hoped would be enough. It was more gratitude than he had expected from her.

"I think it should work," Fiona said. "You can hardly tell the difference."

Joss said, "Well, let's just hope my mother didn't put any trap streets on it—" She started and clapped a hand over her mouth. "Trap streets!" She ran to the maps, handed the East Fenwick one to Fiona and gathered the three that shared the same cartouche into her arms.

"I should have thought of this ages ago. Bring the lantern closer."

As he collected the lamp, Hugh said, "You'll have to enlighten us. What is a trap street?"

"I run a map company, you see. And we have competitors." She arranged the maps in her hands so that the edges of all three were lined up. "In the map world, the worst thing you can do is copy your competitor's map without doing your own surveying. To guard against that, we put a couple streets on our maps that don't exist in the real world. They don't do any harm. None of our customers look for them on the map, and if they happen to stumble across them on a map while looking for a street that *does* exist, they just assume we made a mistake."

Hugh had placed the lamp in the center of the table, and Joss turned the flame up.

"But we can see if a competitor has copied our map without doing his own surveys," Joss said, "because without a survey, he won't know the fake street is fake. That's why we call it a trap."

Hugh said, "But we're not in competition for the making of these maps."

"No, but the way we spot the copying may very well be how my mother chose to hide a clue." She held the three maps up to the light. "You see, to find the trap street, all you do is overlay one map on top of the next—or, in our case, on top of the next two—and look at them either projected through a strong light source or with a strong light source behind them."

She tried turning the flame in the lamp higher, but it was as high as it would go. "I wish this were brighter, but we'll have to make do."

Hugh watched her eyes flicker back and forth across

the cartouche. "Look!" she cried. "These are words! The dashes and slashes and arcs and upside-down Vs make words when you put them all together and line up the edges!"

Hugh looked where she was pointing.

"'An arrow for the fire, a warrin' man's tower,'" Hugh read, "'safe may you find it, a reluctant bride's dower.'"

She looked at Hugh. "What does it mean?"

"I don't know. Is it one of your mother's puzzles?"

Nathaniel said, "Archers sometimes light their arrows when they're firing at a stronghold."

"That fits with the 'warrin' man,'" Hugh said.

Fiona touched the last line on the cartouche. "Who was the reluctant bride?"

Hugh saw Joss's eyes soften, and his heart tightened.

Joss said, "My mother, I'm sure of it. Do any of you recognize the tower? It must refer to the tower in the cartouche."

The three of them looked.

"They're all over Northumberland," Nathaniel said. "I was there once, visiting my cousin. A savage place. A man'll kill you as soon as say good day. Bloody good thing they have that wall there. Keeps 'em penned off from the rest of us."

Hugh laughed. "I suggest you not mention that to my friend, the duke of Silverbridge. His castle is within sight of the wall."

"Speaking of the duke," Fiona said, "why is he waiting?"

"I called on the Lord Keeper today," Hugh said, "but he was engaged and then left for a hunting party at Lord

Quarley's home in Cambridgeshire before I could see him. Seeing no other option, I asked Silverbridge for help. It turns out he, too, is attending the hunting party, and has asked us to join his party as a way of getting our case before Sir William as soon as possible."

Fiona quickly began to roll up the East Fenwick map. "When do we leave?"

"Fiona, the invitation is for Joss and me only."

Her eyes glowed green fire. "Why is *she* involved?"

Joss was tired of being referred to as "she." "You know, this affects *my* family, too."

"She doesn't know the details of—"

"*I* know the details!" Hugh boomed. "*I* can recite the story of the transfer that James Brand and your grandfather intended to execute. For God's sake, I've heard it a hundred times. The duke has been generous enough to allow us to join him. Let it be, Fiona. You and Nathaniel can stay here. Joss and I will return in a day or two, and with any bit of luck, we'll return with good news."

"If you're not hanged," Nathaniel added with a wry smile.

"Thank you, Nathaniel. Joss, I'll gather what we need here. Would you tell Silverbridge I'll be down in a moment?"

She nodded. "Did you tell them about the Trojan Horse?"

"Not yet."

"Hugh and I have seen the original Manchester map," Joss said to Fiona and Nathaniel. "Something was added to it. Several lines from the *Aeneid*. The part about the Trojan Horse. In Latin. It's a direct quotation, as near I can tell: the priest Laocoön's warning not to admit the horse."

"What does it mean?"

"I don't know." She shrugged.

Fiona looked at Joss. "Perhaps one of us is not what we seem?"

Joss raised her hand. "I admit it. I'm a horse."

Hugh gave Joss a look. "Perhaps you'd better see to Silverbridge."

She exited.

"You bloody bastard," Fiona said to Hugh.

Nathaniel cleared his throat. "I think I'll take a walk up the street, to see what's about."

"No," Fiona said. "You wait. This involves you, too."

She turned to Hugh, who had begun putting what they'd need into a valise and refused to be drawn in.

"Are you going to say something?"

"No," he said. "The plan is set." He took the East Fenwick map from her hand and began to fold it.

"You're a fool."

He ignored her, hoping to divert the gathering storm, and deposited the map in his coat pocket. He gazed down at the remaining maps, the ones sharing the mysterious cartouche. "These seem to have led us nowhere. We may never know what the rhyme means—if it means anything at all."

"Leave them, if you would," Nathaniel said. "I should like to ponder them more."

"As you wish." He scanned the room to see if there was anything else he should take to Cambridgeshire. He could feel Fiona's eyes burning into his back. She had not given up on this.

"Hugh," she said, voice brimming with fury, "do you not see she has done everything she can to set this up so that she controls the outcome? This is *her* map. She has divided you from your colleagues. She has contrived it so that she goes to Cambridgeshire with you."

"You're wrong," he said. "She's on our side."

Resigned to defeat at last, Fiona shook her head sadly. "Oh, Hugh, what temptation has she conjured to bewitch you like this?"

The question surprised him and he flushed. He turned his face away, but it was too late.

"Dear God." Fiona clapped her hands together and laughed a short, bitter laugh. "You are to be her 'Mr. Mistake.' Rogan Reynolds's fiancée is not quite the innocent we thought."

Hugh didn't understand what "Mr. Mistake" meant and certainly didn't like the sound of it, but he refused to dignify her attempts to manipulate him by asking her to clarify. That didn't stop her from spotting the curiosity on his face.

"'Mr. Mistake?'" she said with obvious relish. "You haven't heard? 'Tis the man a woman chooses to be her last lover before she marries."

He wished she would stop. "That's disgusting."

"You do not care for the idea? Pray, then, tell *her*. They talked about it in the tailor shop, she and her friend. A Mr. Mistake is to be chosen as incautiously as possible so that during the many years of marriage that follow, when a woman reflects upon her far superior choice of husband, she will congratulate herself on her wisdom."

Hugh felt ill. Was that what Joss's invitation tonight

had been about? Was that what she'd meant when she said, "Perhaps I was meant for something else today. This adventure"? Was he to be a diversion on the way to the Reynolds's marriage bed? "You're lying."

"Nathaniel?" Fiona prompted.

Hugh turned to his shipmate, and Nathaniel looked at him, stricken.

"I'm sorry, my friend," he said. "I heard it, too. I was outside the curtain."

Hugh felt a vast empty space open inside him as if some vital organ had just been torn from his body.

"I-I—"

Fiona crossed her arms, triumphant. "The man she chooses for this illustrious assignment is to be a stallion in bed and a fool everywhere else. 'Twill suit you perfectly."

She slammed the door as she left.

CHAPTER FORTY-FOUR

The lurch of the wheels as he leaned against the exquisitely made seat of the duke's carriage did nothing to tame the thoughts tumbling wildly through Hugh's head. Joss lay against his shoulder, asleep, and he felt each of her inhalations as an unintended tease. She had fallen asleep with the duke's small game table on her lap, and a handful of dice in the table's well clinked every time the carriage hit a rut or stone. Across the box, Silverbridge had his feet up on an ottoman and was snoring, and the duchess lay curled against him.

Joss did not want him. She wanted only what he might offer in a liaison. It pained him to think of the cruel sobriquet she and her friend had used, but it pained him more to feel the destruction of his hopes.

In truth, he had long wished to bed her. From the moment she'd struggled in his arms outside the tailor shop, he'd imagined her wrapping those long, shapely legs around him and forgetting everything she knew about a fiancé careless enough to let her wander into his base of operations.

He thought about the tiny slip of lace and wire he'd found under Reynolds's office couch and the look on Joss's face when she spotted it in his hand. He could almost feel her twist and move on his lap, taste the faint salt of her flesh, smell the perfume of her breasts as he brought his lips to them.

Would Hugh enjoy such an adventure? Aye, he would. And if she had searched a year for a more able man for the task, she wouldn't have found one. But he thought, perhaps, he had reached the time of his life when such interludes would be more than lustful joinings. Other women had used him as such, but none until Joss had led him to believe it would be something else.

He did not know what he would choose if she offered herself. In his heart, lust and pride did battle. If she wanted a stallion, oh, there were things he could do. He could slake his burning desire, but he also knew every kiss would be a blow, every thrust a humiliating reminder that he was no more to her than a carnal back scratch.

She moved. The wrap had fallen from her shoulders, and in the light of the moon he saw the snowy orbs of her breasts and the torturous shadow of her aureoles. Even in her sleep she taunted him. His belly ached for her, and his cock was casting a firm vote for action.

Tell me, Joss, he thought. *Is it Rogan you want, or it is me?*

Joss shifted and mewled, and Hugh hoped she was waking to pull him into a kiss, but instead she resettled herself, brought her fingers to that obnoxious diamond ring and sighed.

Blood roared in his ears. He knew whom she would pick. But he wanted her anyway

In Joss's dream, Hugh caressed her breast and she inhaled lustily. Only this wasn't a dream. His mouth was on hers and she kissed him in the dark, sleepy carriage, happy to feel the embers that had flickered between them for so long rise into flames. He tasted of desire and the duke's whisky, and she savored every morsel.

"I want you," he whispered in her ear.

"And I, you."

He kissed her again, gently squeezing where he'd grazed before, and as quiet as they were, she knew they were making too much noise.

"Not here."

"Not here," he agreed. "But as soon as we arrive."

"Yes."

"No breakfast, no basins of hot water. Just straight to your bed, do you understand?"

"Yes." She could feel her heart pounding in her chest.

His fingertips brushed her peaked flesh casually. "You want an adventure, is that not so?"

"Not here. Please," she said, though she had thrown back her shoulders.

"Ah, there is a point at which your courage fails you. 'Tis but proper, I suppose. From what else do you shrink? Let me hear."

"Nothing," she said boldly.

He chuckled. "Nothing, is it?"

"Nothing." Her determination rose, piqued by his

goading. She prided herself on adventurousness in this area, and if he didn't believe it, he would live to eat his words. With a skilled hand, she caressed the thickening length along his thigh. His groan made her smile. "Do you doubt me?"

"Shall we raise the stakes in this adventure, then?"

The touch of his fingers on her straining flesh was agony. "I don't know. How much are you willing to risk?"

"You have mistaken me, milady, for a man with something to lose. Count the dice," he commanded.

"What?"

"Count the dice in the well."

She removed her hand from his trousers and spread the dice on the lap tray. "Six," she said.

"Six, eh? I have a timepiece that will chime every ten minutes if it is set so. Ten minutes is enough for a worthy adventure into pleasure, is it not? Let us imagine each die represents one-sixth of an hour. We shall roll the dice to see who commands the other for each ten-minute part. And the only rule is that there are no rules. Nothing is beyond the boundaries. Do you accept?"

"I want to be even," she said, though what she wanted was to be on an even keel. His words made her dizzy.

"As you wish. Roll. One at a time."

The first roll was a one, and he shifted his bulk, pleased. She could almost hear the machinations of his imagination. "That is one for you," she managed to say without her voice cracking.

"Indeed."

The next was a six. She exhaled, and in addition to relief, which she expected, several surprising ideas popped into her head—ideas with which she would have never credited herself, almost certainly inspired by the vision of him on the security camera monitor. A delectable heat swept through her as she wondered if this might be how nights with Hugh would always be.

"We are even," she said, and he made a low snort.

She rolled again. This roll was a five, and it was followed by another five. Her hands began to tremble. Twenty minutes of whatever mischief he could think of. . . .

He laid a finger on her knee, and in that touch she could feel the hold he would take of her and the triumphant plunge— Her heart stopped racing and jumped with a jolt. *He* would take her virginity. *He* would be the one for whom she'd saved this treasure. Had it been what she'd planned? No. Had it been what her mother seemed to have wanted for her? She no longer knew or cared. She wanted to feel Hugh's arms around her as she made this leap, and, more importantly, she wanted Hugh to carry this gift with him forever, no matter what happened to them next.

"Almost done," she said.

"The sooner to begin."

The fifth roll showed a two. She might be a virgin, but she was not unaccomplished. He would forget every other woman who had ever shared his bed.

He took the last die from her hand and tossed it himself. A three. He brushed the dice into the well and brought his mouth to hers. The scent of his hair and clothes was making her woozy. If they weren't careful, their hour's adventure would begin in full force on the finely upholstered seat of His Grace's carriage.

As if on cue, the duchess stirred, and Hugh and Joss jerked apart. Joss prayed their hosts hadn't seen anything. She leaned against the seat back, eyes shut, pretending she was asleep for what seemed like hours, and when real heavy-liddedness found its way through her agitated thoughts, the last thing she apprehended was Hugh staring out the window, tapping his hand distractedly against his thigh.

CHAPTER FORTY-FIVE

"Joss. Joss, wake up. 'Tis time."

In her dream, the voice had been Hugh's, and Joss hoped Kit didn't see the disappointment on her face when she opened her eyes.

The sun was high in the sky. It was one of those unexpectedly warm fall days that make you regret not appreciating summer more while you had it, and Joss kicked off the carriage blanket. The fresh breeze coming in through the windows felt good on her skin.

"Where are the men?" The carriage was making its way up a long curved drive to a sweeping estate, and Kit, who looked to be newly awake herself, was her only companion.

"They got out at the other end of the park. Lord Quarley was there with a group of hunters."

And Sir William, she hoped, which would keep Hugh busy for the better part of the afternoon. She found the notion of the liaison they'd planned more unnerving in the stark light of day.

"Unfortunately," said Kit, who knew Joss's reasons for

coming, "Sir William does not arrive until later this afternoon. You will have to wait a bit for your meeting."

Nonetheless, Joss thought quickly, Hugh would have some duties to perform with Lord Quarley—making introductions, commenting favorably on his dogs and estate, perhaps walking the grounds. Surely she would have a little time to collect herself.

Something on the floor caught a ray of the sun. It was one of the duke's dice. They lay scattered from one door to the other, and the little table lay overturned as well.

Joss bent to collect the items, and the duchess cleared her throat meaningfully. A wave of heat passed over Joss's cheeks. "I hope," Joss said, still bent, "we did not wake you with our game."

Kit laughed. "Perhaps a little."

"Oh, I'm so sorry."

The duchess's eyes twinkled. "Your fiancé is a very good player. I hope you did not bet too much."

"I'm afraid I did. Oh dear, I'm so embarrassed."

"Pray, do not trouble yourself. Have you not heard the story of my courtship with Silverbridge? You would have to run naked through the streets of Windsor to put a shine on that. What did you bet?"

"Oh dear. I really don't think I should say."

Kit clapped her hands. "How wonderful!"

But Kit must have seen that the expression on Joss's face did not quite deliver on the merriment such frivolity deserved, and she touched Joss's arm.

"What is it?"

"I am engaged."

"My dear Joss, I hope you do not think you are the first

woman who sampled the pudding before she finished the pork. There's hardly a woman in my circle who did not anticipate her vows. In truth, there's hardly a woman in my circle who did not anticipate the second ball."

"I am not engaged to Hugh."

Kit's smile transformed instantly from one of pleasure to one of deeply felt sympathy. "Oh, Joss. That does make it more difficult."

Joss gazed at her ring forlornly. "I don't think I love him, but I'm not sure."

"The man of the ring or the man of the seas?"

"The man of the ring. I'm sure I love Hugh." She was surprised to hear herself say it, but she knew it was true. When he'd taken her in his arms after she'd nearly drowned, and she could feel the raw relief in his every muscle, she'd felt treasured and protected. It was a wonderful feeling, and the first time in her adult life she'd felt like she could let go and someone else would be there to catch her.

"Then you must return the ring. Or," the duchess added with a pragmatic shrug, "at least send a note."

"He has done nothing, really, to make me stop loving him. He is just not Hugh."

"But a more earth-shattering fault you could not have named. Have you and Hugh . . . .?"

Joss shook her head. "Not yet. Today, I think."

"The dice, aye."

"It's worse than that."

"I have heard of Hugh's reputation. Perhaps you don't know the definition of 'worse.' "

"I am a virgin."

Kit jerked upright. The carriage was drawing to a stop,

and footmen leapt on the outside steps and opened the doors. "Close these at once," Kit commanded. "Do you not know when to knock?"

The horrified men, who had surely never thought to knock on a carriage, shut the doors and retreated.

"I don't know why I jumped," Kit said. "It's not as if it's the yellow fever, after all. Many survive virginity. It's just that I assumed that if you were with Hugh . . ."

"I know."

"Hugh Hawksmoor is one of the best men I know—though, now that I know you're a virgin, I might wonder at your rather reckless challenge last night. I believe you had him dry swallowing. I know I was."

"But—"

"I understand. 'Tis a momentous thing. I think a large glass of whisky might be in order."

The doors reopened, but this time it was the duke.

"What, might I ask, are you at, my love?" he said, frowning. "The footmen are cowering in fear. They warned me to approach at my own risk."

"They did no such thing. 'Tis a tête-à-tête. We are nearly done."

"Good. Hugh has sent word for the lady to meet him at the stables. 'Tis a matter of a stallion, he said."

Kit met Joss's eyes. "John," she said to her husband, "give me your flask."

"Might I point out it is barely noon."

"No, you may not."

He withdrew it immediately and handed it to her.

"Thank you."

He gave an easy nod and waited.

"As I said, we are nearly done."

Silverbridge ducked his head in pardon and exited the carriage.

"Drink up," Kit said, putting the flask in Joss's hand. "And no more betting. The stakes are high enough."

"Yes. Thank you. Thank you for everything."

"I would say to put yourself in Hugh's hands, but that seems inevitable."

Joss laughed. She pulled off her ring. "Would you hold this for me?"

The duchess slipped it on her finger, directly above a sapphire about as large as Joss's knuckle. "Happily."

CHAPTER FORTY-SIX

Hugh was waiting for her by a horse tacked for riding. The horse was black and sleek and tall, but Joss only had eyes for the man in the handsome naval coat, with his broad back to her, who seemed almost to paw the ground with simmering energy. She felt a kick of heat in her belly.

He turned when he heard her steps on the gravel, and it took all her strength to keep her chin up. The sun was warm, but the look in those gray-green eyes was warmer. He raked her from head to foot. By the time she reached his side, she felt as if she'd crossed the Sahara barefoot. Her hair was a mess from sleeping, and she touched it self-consciously.

"You look lovely," he said. "But then, you knew that."

He caught her by the waist and tipped her back into a scorching kiss. Desire pulsed like a current through her body, and she could feel her nerve endings light up like a thousand tiny lightbulbs. He reawakened her desire with ease.

Breathless, she said, "There are people in the stable."

"No rules," he said, and kissed her again. "Been drinking, have you?" He released her and lifted himself easily onto the horse, using only his good arm. He was a natural horseman. She hadn't known that about him.

"Yes."

He slipped off his coat and laid it over his knees. "There is a punishment for relying on false courage."

He did not elaborate on the punishment, which made it worse, for Joss's imagination was very vivid. "I do not require false courage," she said, hardly above a whisper.

He chuckled and held out his arm.

"I know how to ride," she said. "I can have my own horse."

"Not today."

He pulled her onto the blankets behind him. She had to ruck her skirts and wrap her arms around his waist to keep herself upright. He gave the impression of being built out of barrel staves, so sinewy were his waist and back.

He geed the horse to a trot. The blankets were coarse, and the wool rubbed her thighs.

Within a moment or two, they had reached the bottom of the prospect the house had been built on and were on level parkland half a mile long, edged with gardens that ended at a long reflecting pool, behind which stood the entrance to an ancient stand of oaks. The sun's rays danced on the gold and red foliage. A dog bayed in the distance.

He pulled the horse to a stop. "Loosen your bodice," he said.

It was useless to protest. She knew the terms she had agreed to. With shaking fingers, she pulled the ruffles lower. Her nipples tightened as the air hit her. She prayed none of the lord's guests were taking an afternoon walk.

"Now pull my shirt free."

She tugged the snowy linen from his trousers, releasing his warmth.

She knew what he wanted, and she wanted it herself. Without a bodice, this was the only cover she would have. She lifted the fabric and pressed herself against him. In an instant, they were off at a hard gallop. The ride pummeled her bones, and she clung giddily to his chest as the horse's hooves threw up chunks of Lord Quarley's turf. Faster and faster Hugh drove the creature, straight down the center of the park until Joss realized he was going to take the horse over the pool.

"No!" she cried as she felt him urge the horse forward.

The pounding stopped, and for an endless instant the horse rose in the air, carried upward by an unearthly power, Hugh flung himself low over the its neck and Joss flung herself low over Hugh, until the creature reached its apex and descended with a thump, thump once more to the ground. The jolt shook her spine.

Hugh drove the horse through the forest, narrowly avoiding the stout trunks and gnarled roots until they emerged into the sun again on the other side. The flat parkland was gone now, replaced by rolling hills, scattered copses of elms and patches of verdant ferns and ivy.

He pulled to a stop next to a dilapidated fence and lowered her to the ground with a sweep of his arm. As she tugged her bodice higher, he swung himself down and tied the lead. If he noticed her movements, he said nothing. Instead he spread the blanket on a mound of green near a picket, then turned to her and waited. She reclined reluctantly, knowing the next time she stood, the world would be a different place.

He undid his stock and dropped it. Then he stretched out beside her. Without a word, he pulled his timepiece from his pocket and turned the stem. When it rang, he held it so she could see the face, then laid it on a rock. "The time," he said, "has come, and may I say, 'tis long overdue. This will ring every ten minutes until we are done."

He lowered his mouth to hers and supped there. She embraced him hungrily, her hips still tingling from the thrilling ride. He stopped for a moment to draw a caressing knuckle down her shoulder, then picked up his stock and dangled it before her.

"Wrists or eyes?"

Her heart nearly jumped out of her chest. "What do you mean?"

"You understand how this works, surely? With the wrists held immobile, a woman convinces herself she is unable to stop what the man is doing and is thus relieved of any guilt she might otherwise—"

"I *know* what it's for."

"Then I repeat my question: wrists or eyes?"

She dared not let him see the flurry of terror he was stirring in her. "Eyes," she said, and damned him for the curve that rose at the corner of his mouth.

He wound the fabric around her head and fastened the fabric with a quick knot. With the world plunged into a dim blankness, the sounds as he moved on the blanket and the loamy smell of the ivy seemed to grow more distinct. He kissed her, this time sweetly and slowly, skimming his lips over her cheek before settling at her mouth. She took in the scent of his clean-smelling hair.

His hand trailed down her neck, past her collarbone

and over her breasts. She was covered now, and he teased the tight flesh through the fabric. The feel of his hands on her was exhilarating. She thought about those sturdy shoulders and that hard, hard waist, lost herself in the heat of his soft, probing tongue.

Lacking the canvas of his face, her sense of him came entirely through the touch of his hands and the way his body seemed to mold around her. He was a swirling eddy of need and desire, but there was a filter somewhere—something he was holding back. She caressed the rough stubble of his cheek, and he seemed to withdraw, but that must have been an illusion, for his arms held her tight.

"It *is* an adventure," she murmured. "Isn't it?"

"One you shall never forget."

"I hope not."

He found her knee and then the inside of her thigh. His long strokes made her sigh with pleasure. Then he found her bud and rolled it slowly. She could feel his breath on her cheek, like the wings of a butterfly. Even though she couldn't see him, she knew he was watching her closely.

In the distance, on her right, she heard the thumping of many hooves. "What is it?" she whispered, wary. The hoofbeats dissipated, only to return a moment later.

He chuckled. "Fearful, are you?" His fingers continued their slow circle.

"What is it?"

He bent to her ear. "Hunters, lass. Don't fret yourself. They have seen this sort of larking before."

The place where he touched her burned with a steady fire. She rolled her hips to keep pace with his movements.

"Is it really hunters?"

"Oh, they've spotted us," he said, amused. The hoof-beats slowed and stopped.

They couldn't be more than thirty yards away. "Hugh, please."

"Please what?" His rhythm quickened, and she braided her fingers into the ivy to hold herself steady. "They're a good distance away," he said. "I very much doubt they could identify your face, though they have certainly identified what we are doing. 'Tis a matter of some interest, it appears." His mouth hovered outside her ear. "Lower your bodice."

"Hugh!"

"We are trespassing on their land. The least we can do is give them something for it."

She strained her ears for the sound of voices. Nothing carried on this very clear day. "You're lying," she said. "There *are* no hunters."

"In that case, the dress shall come down to your waist."

Breathless, unknowing who if anyone was watching, she guided her arms out of the sleeves and drew the bodice below her breasts.

"They approve," he whispered. "And so do I." He caught one of the dress's hanging strings of pearl trim and rolled it over a nipple. " 'Tis very fine," he said, admiring, "like a large, tawny pearl itself."

He tugged her bodice. "Lower."

She brought the fabric to her waist, then lifted her arms above her head, determined not to let the unseen eyes of a pack of hunters, or, more specifically, of Hugh's conjured pack of hunters, deter her.

She was moving now, her hips undulating to a regular

beat. He was a practiced guide, and his fingers slowed and quickened in breathtaking rhythms.

"Shall we give them what they've been waiting for?"

"Yes," she whispered, her mouth like a desert.

"Then you don't mind their eyes upon you?" He began pulling her nipple with his free hand, bringing a small gasp with each tug.

"No." She wanted him to do more. The wave was rising in her, but she needed more, more.

"Perhaps you rather like it. They see, but they cannot possess. Oh, you will haunt their dreams tonight. They will take their wives in their arms, but when they plunge, it will be between your tender thighs. Do you like that? A dozen men longing for your—"

His fingers moved faster and faster, and she cried, her body racked with a storm of lightning and heat. She clutched his hair, not wanting that hand to stop. And it moved and moved, drawing the final bolt into a scorching, unending charge of pleasure.

She tore off the stock and scrabbled to her elbows. A half dozen horses chewed grass in a corral on the next hill and a dozen more ran in bounding half circles. There was not a human being in sight. "Liar."

He rolled onto his back, grinning, his desire unhidden. "Had the story not had such a salutary effect on you, I might apologize."

A tiny bell sounded.

"Your ten minutes is up," she said haughtily, pulling up her bodice at least far enough to be proper. "It's my time now."

"How may I serve?"

Damn the laughter in those eyes.

"Take off your clothes," she said.

"This time you speak for yourself."

"Slowly," she added. "There. Near the rock. So you are available for the viewing pleasure of those in as many directions as possible."

He kicked off one boot and then the other. The socks followed. She had to admit, she was sorry to see those boots go.

He grabbed the collar on the back of his shirt, then pulled the whole thing over his head and tossed it to the side. She gazed at the wide back lined with scars, and the muscular chest.

"I do believe you've traversed this land before," he said.

"Not quite like this."

He loosened the trouser buttons with a single hand. The flap dropped and the buff-colored fabric fell to the ground.

And there he was, just like that day on the security camera monitor. With one very big difference.

The generous swath of chestnut hair on his chest narrowed to a tight dark line that traveled down his muscled belly to an extraordinary patch between two firm, tan thighs. That he was uncircumcised didn't surprise her. That he was considerably larger than even Rogan did.

He was a ruggedly handsome man, and the hard-muscled arms and back reminded her he was also a man of action. If only the eyes weren't so guarded. A small voice warned, *Be careful what you bestow on a man who hides a part of himself from you.*

"If this is the only use you are to make of me," he said, "may I suggest you are wasting your ten minutes?"

As far as she was concerned, ten minutes of gazing at this maritime Adonis could never be considered wasted. "What do you look for in a woman?"

He blinked at the question, unprepared for the game to take this new direction, but apparently reflecting on the rule of no rules, he answered. "Honesty," he said coolly. "Faithfulness. Relationships with others that aren't motivated solely by self-interest."

She squirmed at "faithfulness." She had hoped for "spirited" and "courageous." That's what he had called her before. And there had been the hint of something else in his words. . . .

"Did you sleep with Fiona?"

"Aye." His eyes flashed, and she wondered if she'd dare ask more.

"She is driven almost entirely by self-interest."

"You asked what I look for, not what I'd take."

"Sounds like a bit of self-interest at work to me."

He said nothing, and the obscuring haze across his eyes got thicker.

"Perhaps you could use a lesson in altruism," she said. "Is your mouth as capable as that hand?"

The haze lifted, and he dropped to a crouch. "Better."

She crossed her arms behind her head and shivered as he spread her legs. She had just finished and thought it unlikely she'd reach a second peak so soon, but the sight of him as a supplicant made her wonder.

"So close," she said, seeing the look in his eyes and the quiver of his hardened flesh. "It's too bad, really, I'm the only one who shall enjoy this."

He bent to her dark, willing triangle and laved it. The

touch sent a divine tingle through her still-sensitive flesh. Then he lowered his body to the grass, groaning as his erection bent under him.

"If you do well, I might help you with that," she said happily. "Otherwise, I'll make you take care of it yourself." *That should hold the horses' attention. I know it would hold mine.*

She raised her skirt until she had both the sun on her belly and an unobstructed view of Hugh's dark waves as he bobbed.

Up and down, she thought, imagining the moment he would take her virginity. *He will disappear into my thighs and those luscious, hard hips will do their work.* She pushed aside the worry—both for the pain and the thought she might be making a mistake—and let his mouth lead her on a starkly imagined journey. In her mind, he laid her on a gleaming white bed among a hundred white pillows, whispering words of love in the candlelight.

But the eyes . . . The eyes made her hesitate. She closed her mind to the vision and took comfort in the now.

His mouth was exquisite. Her narrow field of experience had not included a lover with such skill. Rogan's reluctant craft in this area paled next to Hugh's.

She could command it. She could command their joining, right now. But the words of her mother's story echoed in her head. *The princess-girl, now an able woman, waited for the man who would share with her all he possessed—his help and his heart.* But was he sharing all?

The chime of the timepiece roused her from her reverie. Ten minutes had passed? No, it wasn't possible. He laughed at the look of wronged surprise on her face.

"You, milady, are inexhaustible. Which is as it should be, for my twenty minutes has begun."

He climbed to his feet and gave her a hungry look. "I want you to serve me with your mouth."

When got to her knees, he touched her chin. She lifted it defiantly, and he raised a brow. "You are practiced at this, I see."

"The best you'll ever have."

"I shall have to take your word on that—at least for now." He struggled into his breeks and slipped his shirt over his head. "I have a different notion of how your mouth may serve."

He stretched out again on the blanket and motioned for her to join him. She lay with her head in the crook of his arm. When she settled herself, he slipped his hands down her dress, caught her nipples and began to caress them again, fanning the still-glowing embers between her legs. She pressed her eyes shut. *Oh, God, this is torture.*

"Do you like it?" he asked.

"Very much." She shifted, trying to release some of the heat.

"If I chose to do this until the timepiece rings, would you like that?"

"Yes," she said, breathless.

"Have you ever done this to yourself?"

A flame of heat went through her. "Yes."

"Have you ever done more?"

Her cheeks stung with rushing blood, though why she should be ashamed, she didn't know. "Yes."

She could feel him nod.

"Have you lain with a woman?"

She started. "Aren't I supposed to be serving you with my mouth now?"

He laughed. "What do you think you're doing, lass? I want to hear your secrets."

She shivered.

"Have you lain with a woman?" he repeated.

"Why do you want to know?" She knew the answer but wanted to hear the words.

"The woman from whom I learned what I just did to you said she learned it from another woman. The vision has stayed with me." He brushed her flesh with his palms, circling and circling. "I have imagined you with her."

"I see." At the center of his fantasies. She liked that.

"What about two men?" he asked. "Have you lain with two?"

The thought of Hugh's mouth between her legs with Rogan cupping her breasts was quickly supplanted with the thought of two Hughs instead.

"No," she said, holding that last picture in her head.

"Have you ever imagined it?"

"No."

"You're lying," he said. "You're imagining it now."

She prayed he would not make her say more. In the tangle of bodies in her mind's eye she could feel Hugh conquering her in every way imaginable.

"When we were in Reynolds's office that night—"

"When you robbed me of the key?" Even then, as he turned her roughly and made her surrender it, she'd sensed she'd wanted him to possess her. She'd wanted him to be the one. But was this the way she'd wanted it?

"Aye. I found a corset there. All of lace."

She flushed. "Yes. It's called a bra."

"What had you been doing there with him?"

"What do you think?"

"I should like to hear." He stroked one nipple and then the other. "In this game, I have the right."

"It was essentially a lap dance. I needed his help. It was my way of making it worthwhile."

" 'Lap dance'? I am not familiar with the term, though I admit it is quite descriptive."

"Well, it wasn't a lap dance, really. That's just short-hand for what I did."

"I see. And this 'lap dance,' it is . . . ?"

"About as you'd guess," she said. "The woman strad-dles the man's lap. She is naked, or nearly so, and he is fully clothed. And she teases him."

"Teases?"

"Yes. Like this. Now." Her nipples burned with plea-sure. Oh, how she wanted him between her legs.

"And he takes her?"

"No. He is not allowed to touch her. If he touches her, the dance is over."

"I want one," he said, getting to his feet. "Show me."

He pulled her to a standing position, and led her to the stone wall, where he seated himself near the stile. She had never done anything like a real lap dance before, though she had a good idea of what was involved. He leaned against the wooden rails of the stile and waited.

She stood between his legs and clasped his thighs. She could feel the long, coiled strength there. This part of the wall was low and her breasts were at the height of his face. "The objective is to make you hard."

"You're being imprecise," he said, and lifted his mouth to hers. When they parted, he said, "Come to me."

He helped her place a knee on either side of him, then she lowered herself to his lap. She could feel his erection strain his breeks beneath her. The flap of his trousers was loose and moved when she did. The cool brass buttons brushed her skin. She had no underclothes save a chemise, and she knew that was the way lap dances were done, but it felt very wicked to be rubbing his clothes like this.

She ground her hips, and he leaned against the stile, watching her move. She liked the look in his eyes, liked the way his fingers stretched and curled on the stone as she shifted her weight, liked the way the thickness moved beneath her. She saw the desire there so clearly, but wished she could see more. He hid more than he revealed.

He extended a hand to brush away her bodice.

"Ah ah ah," she warned.

"But—"

"Patience." She crossed her arms over her head and moved to the music in her head. The bodice and chemise slipped lower and lower until the only thing holding either aloft was the tip of a nipple. With one final shimmy, the dress fell to her waist, and he made a gurgling noise.

"Where is that whisky?" he asked hoarsely.

She fished the flask out of the gown's pocket, and he took it from her hand. He downed a generous gulp, the muscles of his throat moving eagerly, then wiped his mouth, his eyes pasted to her the entire time. She rose upward, brushing her breasts across his mouth and cheeks.

"I thought touching was forbidden."

"I may touch. Not you."

"Bugger that." He brought his mouth to her ear. "I want you ride me. I want to see you squirm like this on the end of my pike."

"Not during this."

He was so close, the heat from his body warmed her chest and neck. It must torture him to be so close and not be able to touch her. He lifted his hand again, and she caught it.

"I can't help it," he said. "It just moves on its own."

She opened his palm and wove so that only the barest touch of nipple grazed it.

"Cruel," he said, and she smiled at the power she held over him. His erection had doubled in hardness. It was the hammer of a Greek god now, poised for battle. Every move made him sway and she wanted to tease him the way he'd teased her. What she really wanted to do was break through that reserve, stir his heart, not his hunger.

"I will let you lower your trousers now," she said, "if you promise to remain absolutely still."

He nodded wordlessly and shifted the fabric to his knees. The hammer rose triumphantly, and Joss felt omnipotent as she pressed it slowly underneath her, letting its impressive length rake her, yet ensuring he was no more sheathed now than he had been a moment earlier.

He moaned, an animal noise that sent a shock through her.

"This is an abomination." His words were choked. "I must have you."

"You may not move." She took the flask from his hand and dribbled the whisky over her breasts.

"A taste. Please."

"Not now. Perhaps when we finish." She lifted the flask and drank. The movement arched a breast almost to his mouth.

"May I finish?"

She rocked across him, as slowly and firmly as the stroke of a hand. "Yes."

"In you!" he demanded.

"No. That's not how the game is played."

She could see the struggle on his face. "Poor Samson. You have been shorn of your power. And yet, for this"— she dribbled more liquid on her nipples and a timely breeze hardened them into whisky-soaked rubies—"it might be worth it."

She was playing with fire, and she knew it. A danger when she had only one thing left to lose.

"You are wanton," he whispered.

She crushed him in accelerating circles, a lascivious stirring of flesh and fire. He gripped the stones harder and lifted his hips, straining for friction. He entered her in his thoughts—she could see it in those eyes, though the object in question got no closer to its goal than the top of her thigh. He grunted in agony.

Then he grabbed her shoulders and crushed her hips into his lap, pressing his erection against her thigh and bucking them both nearly off the wall. Again he pressed, and again he groaned. She could feel the warmth of his seed spilling against her leg.

Then he clutched her to him, suckling one nipple and then the other, as if his empty stores could be filled from their fount.

She cradled his cheek, hoping he would give her one of his warm, reassuring smiles. "I really like this," she said softly, "and like you." But he seemed not to hear.

"You have been far too reckless. And you shall pay the price." He scooped her into his arms and brought her again to the blanket. In an instant she was on her back, and he was on his knees, breathing with the anticipation of a conqueror. "Samson, am I?" Not an inch had been lost from his steely length, and he lowered himself between her legs.

No, she thought, *no.* Not with those guarded eyes. Not with that hardened heart.

"No!" she cried. "I don't want to."

"No?" He stopped, dizzy but hearing the agitation in her voice.

"This isn't right."

The timepiece chimed and she slid from under him.

CHAPTER FORTY-SEVEN

Not right? He was still in shock—shock and a state of such unparalleled shame he could hardly speak.

They had dressed in awkward silence, and now he stood stiffly by the stile, his hands tucked under his arms as if he could ward off the self-rebuke. He watched her brush the dirt and grass from her gown, afraid to say a word.

He shook his head. "Are you all right?"

"Yes, fine. I'm sorry. It just . . . isn't right."

He felt the sting of the words, though they didn't surprise him. She was saving herself for her husband. Hurt and ill at ease, he scanned the horizon, though he had seen or heard nothing of Reynolds since their carriage left London. If he was near, he was keeping his distance. If he was near, Hugh hoped he hadn't seen what had just transpired.

"I'm sorry," she said. "I know it's foolish, given what we already did."

"And this?" He swept his arm over the blanket, still on the ivy, hoping the gesture would save him from having to put words to the acts they'd just committed. "Were all of these things unhappy for you?"

She flushed, and he saw she regretted them already.

"No, no, no. It was quite beyond anything I've ever experienced," she said. "Honestly."

Meaningless praise. He knew he was nothing if not a skilled stud horse. But this was one time he had hoped to be more. As the circumstance seemed to require it, he bowed. "'Twas my pleasure." That, at least, was not a lie.

"I won't ever forget this," she said, though she looked as if she would give anything if she could.

"Nor I." He gestured to the horse, the mute witness to their misplaced passion. "Shall we . . . ?"

Her face filled with . . . Was it relief? Regret? Sadness? It had been a long time since he'd been clumsy or thoughtless enough to drive a woman to tears. He hoped this would not mark a new milestone for him.

"Yes. If you wish." She adjusted her sleeves. "Do I look all right?"

"Beautiful. The gown is fine."

"I doubt the duchess will want it back at this point."

He considered a jest about the duchess's earthy sense of humor, but abandoned it as poorly timed and gave Joss a weak smile.

He refolded the blanket, then mounted the horse and extended his arm. Her touch was torture. He pulled her up before him so that she could ride a proper sidesaddle back to the house. It would be the last time he would hold her in his arms.

"I've never ridden like this," she said.

"'Tis a day for firsts." He decided he would rather

spend a lifetime with his open palm a quarter of an inch from her breast than endure the scent of her hair like this. He'd been foolish to place her in front of him.

Just as he shook the reins, the timepiece chimed.

He drew the chased gold from his pocket, pulled the stem to disable the bell and, with a silent sigh, began the long journey back to the house.

Chapter Forty-eight

Hugh hurried the horse forward at the sight of a servant boy running through the Quarley gardens, waving wildly in their direction. Joss was glad for a distraction from the heavy silence that had stretched over their return. It had been obvious Hugh had found her putting a premature end to their lovemaking off-putting, and his strained courtesy only made her feel worse. From the garden, they had a sweeping view of the entry courtyard, and she noted the presence of several well-appointed carriages at the top of the long drive that hadn't been there when they'd left. Perhaps this hell would be over sooner than she thought, and she could return, shamefaced, to both the company she'd put in jeopardy and the man she'd left at the altar.

"Are you Captain Hawksmoor?" asked the boy, breathless, when he reached them.

"Aye."

"You are to come inside. The Duke of Silverbridge requests your presence immediately."

"Where is he?" Hugh slipped off the horse, and Joss felt his warmth evaporate.

"Outside the dining room. Begging your pardon, Mrs. Hawksmoor."

Hugh's gaze went to his boots. "This is Miss O'Malley," he said, handing the boy the leads. "See that she gets to the house safely."

Hugh adjusted his coat, gave her a low bow and strode toward the house.

Silverbridge was waiting for him in the entry hall, and Hugh labored to dispel the dour look he knew must be on his face. Careful formality replaced the wry ducal smile.

"Where is Miss O'Ma—"

"In the stable, I believe. Has Sir William arrived?"

"Aye, and I have laid the groundwork for your case. You need to gather the map and your other papers and share them with him."

"They were taken to my room, I believe," Hugh said. "Let me retrieve them and I will join you."

He hurried down the grand hallway. At long last, the chance to do something to avenge his brother's death had come.

Joss gazed into the looking glass in her well-appointed bedroom, wondering how an afternoon that should have been so perfect could have turned out so poorly. Stopping Hugh had hurt him and it had certainly not pleased her, but there had been something cold and mechanical in the way he'd moved, and if she couldn't trust her instincts, what could she trust? She was gazing at her wrinkled gown, wondering what if anything she could do to make herself presentable, when a voice sounded at the open door.

"Given the particular placement of that grass stain, I must strongly suggest changing before dinner." It was Kit, hands on her hips, grinning. "Can I assume everything has changed?"

"Everything has changed," Joss said sadly. "Only not for the better."

"Where are we?" Fiona asked, roused from a deep sleep when the carriage pulled to a stop.

"Our destination is Thetford," Nathaniel said, "a place of my youth. 'Tis still a distance of ten miles or so. I am stopping to pick up some provisions."

"I would thank you if I had asked our destination. What I asked was our location."

He sighed. "We are outside Cambridge."

"Cambridge! Then we are near Lord Quarley's home."

"'Tis a quarter hour in that direction," he said, jerking his thumb, "but we are not here for that, I told you—"

"Aye, aye, aye. I know what you told me. We are here on a lark, though you refuse to share the details."

"That's not the only reason we're here. Despite his protestations to the contrary, I do not intend to leave Hugh's safety to fate. Especially now, when he's—" He stopped.

"Distracted?" She made a sour face. "I do not care for that woman."

"As I said, I would have been happy to leave you at the Grey Lamb."

"Oh, I'm certain you would have." She gazed out the

post chaise window toward the hills he'd indicated. Somewhere beyond them Hugh would be sharing his bed with that damnable wench. Fiona felt the reassuring weight of the pistol she had hidden in her cloak, right next to the maps of London and Edinburgh. "Where's the Manchester map?" she asked.

Nathaniel, who had been examining one or the other of them throughout the better part of their trip, pointed to the place on the bench where he'd been sitting.

"Do not leave the carriage," Nathaniel said. "Hugh doesn't want us here. An unwelcome appearance will only endanger his chances of being able to help your family. As I said, I'm stopping only to gather some provisions. I'll be back in a quarter hour."

Fiona heaved her disgust. "Do you mind if I take a piss? Or is that forbidden as well?"

Nathaniel opened the door and jumped to the street amid passing riders and carriages. "If your idea of an appropriate facility is a field behind a whorehouse, you may take your chances. Otherwise, there's a commode under the seat."

Damned old fornicator, she thought. There was a word for what he was getting, and it wasn't "provisions."

She waited until he'd disappeared, then slipped out of the carriage. Cambridge was a sizeable town, and they were on its outskirts, a largely unpopulated street with as many empty fields as businesses. Other than a smith, a dilapidated inn and what she supposed was the aforementioned whorehouse, a two-storey affair with sooty windows and a porch with two cheerless chairs, the prospects were bleak.

She stepped toward the inn, uncertain if she wanted a drink, a rest or just the satisfaction of knowing she was doing exactly what she had been told not to. She waited at the corner for a wagon to pass. When the vehicle cleared, she spotted Rogan Reynolds talking to the driver of another carriage.

In a flash, she realized he must have followed them. She turned to hide her face, though she was uncertain he knew who she was, and kept walking. *Was he here for them? Was he here for Joss? Or was he here for the map?*

The map, according to Joss, was virtually an exact copy. Could Reynolds have known such a thing had been so meticulously produced? Fiona bet he didn't know about the map and had come only on the suspicion that his fiancée and her new lover were getting close to the truth. If Reynolds had been following them closely enough to discover them kissing by the statue of the lion, it undoubtedly meant he already had his doubts about Hugh. Fiona was certain she had a man on her hands desperate to protect both his fortune and his claim on his fiancée.

Would he recognize her? The time he'd come to the shop, Fiona had been gone. The question was, had he been following Joss and Hugh or had he been following her and Nathaniel? She prayed it was the former, as this would allow her some small element of surprise.

She crossed the road. She could feel his eyes upon her, but that in itself was not relevant, as she was frequently the object of men's attentions. He was surprisingly handsome in person, especially in the black coat he wore. She wondered from whom it had been stolen. She considered killing him on the spot, but somehow the notion of strip-ping him of the Brand Industries wealth gave her more pleasure. Hugh had better succeed in their petition to Sir William.

She decided to take the offensive. She turned, choos-ing the moment when their eyes would meet, then nod-ded. Reynolds bowed. "Are you lost?" she asked. "You look a trifle uncertain."

"I am not lost. I'm on my way to Scotland."

She nearly laughed. No one in their right mind would hire a post chaise to Scotland. "Gretna?" she asked with a smile. "Do you have your bride stowed in there?" Let the bastard twist a little.

"No," he said. "My bride is decidedly not inside."

"*Tsk-tsk.* 'Tis a shame." Then it struck her. Allowing Reynolds to walk into Lord Quarley's home now, while Hugh and that woman pleaded her case, would be tan-tamount to throwing their family's chances of recover-ing their fortunes into the Thames, but allowing him to discover Joss a moment *after* the Lord Keeper put his signature on the transfer would be poetry indeed. Reyn-olds could drag Joss back to the future—a very changed future—and Hugh . . . well, Hugh could find comfort in the arms of the woman who remained.

Reynolds turned as she passed and, like many men before him, was swept along in her wake. "What about you?" he asked, jogging a step or two to catch up to her. "You talk of Gretna as if you have personal knowledge of it. Where is your husband?"

"I am unmarried, sir. I'm afraid I find most men about as enticing as o'ertight shoes." She looked over her shoulder to see if Nathaniel was about. "I wonder," she said, "if you would like to consider an exchange, Mr. Reynolds."

He paled upon hearing his name.

"Aye, sir, I am quite aware of who you are. And I think we can effect an exchange that would be beneficial to both of us."

His face broke into an interested smile. After casting a look in both directions, he led her around the corner of the inn into the quiet of a barrel-strewn alley. "Tell me more."

She gazed at the long shadows in the street. It must be close on five. Hugh had said he would see the Lord Keeper today. If he signed the deed by sundown, then delivering Reynolds to his fiancée at midnight ought to be a fitting end to a successful day.

"Provide me with a nice hot supper," she said, "and I shall take you to your fiancée." In fact, she thought, if he continued to look at her with those glittering blue eyes, she might allow him to provide her with more than supper. It was all in the name of service, after all, and if Joss was going to bed Fiona's lover, Fiona certainly wasn't going to hesitate to bed Joss's.

"You know where she is?"

"I believe I might." She smiled.

"Then tell me now." He caught her by the throat and squeezed.

She couldn't breathe. His hands were as cold and strong as steel, and he backed her hard into the wall. She clawed at his grasp but couldn't loosen it. He lifted her slowly off the ground. Spots appeared at the edges of her vision. The gun was in her cloak. She could feel it banging against her thigh. "I'll tell!" she croaked. "I'll tell!"

He held his grip. "Where?" he said coolly.

"The home of Lord Quarley," she said, kicking against his bulk. "Let me down!"

The corners of his mouth rose in an apologetic smile, and he tightened his grip.

Chapter Forty-nine

"Sir William is finishing his lunch," Silverbridge said when Hugh returned, holding up a palm to stop him from bursting through the closed doors of the Quarley dining hall. "Might I suggest you have a seat? Might I also suggest that a pleasant demeanor will do more for your case than the scowl currently residing there?"

Hugh dropped into a chair, clutching his papers, abashed. He took a deep breath. "I beg your pardon. You are quite right. I am a bit, well . . . let us say today has not gone as well as I had hoped."

Silverbridge picked a small leaf of ivy out of the gold rope at Hugh's shoulder. "Anything you'd care to speak of, Captain?"

Hugh flushed. "I . . . no."

"Miss O'Malley, is it? Kit is quite fond of her."

Hugh shook his head. "Delicacy forbids . . ."

Silverbridge clapped him on the shoulder. "Keep at it, Hugh. Do not give up. 'Tis like navigating a maze with mortars at every turn, but if you don't press on, you will be obliterated where you stand. That's the one thing I learned with Kit. The only thing harder than persevering was giving up. I would have died without her."

Hugh hung his head. "Miss O'Malley belongs to another."

"You and I know that doesn't always matter. Your brother, I think, would counsel you to think otherwise."

"You knew him?"

"My father knew him. I knew *of* him. But I remember hearing a dinner guest at our home criticize him for leaving the navy. My father, who knew a thing or two about war, said, 'Sometimes love is the only battle worth winning.'"

"Thank you."

"And does this have something to do with Miss O'Malley?" Silverbridge tapped the map.

"No. Well . . ." Hugh thought of Bart in that awful pool of blood and all the steps Hugh had taken over the last twenty years that had brought him here to avenge his brother's death. "Did you know I went into the navy to impress my brother? Lord, I was a miserable recruit. The only thing I had the slightest bit of talent for was climbing to the top of the mast. Bart was twenty years older, you know, and I thought of him as this noble, untouchable hero—like a knight from a child's tale."

Silverbridge laughed. "You are hardly the first man to follow the model set by a family hero. Good God, the way they revered my father . . ."

Hugh knew Silverbridge's father had been a much decorated general in the army prior to his death at the hands of a Scottish clan chief in the borderlands—a clan who was now Silverbridge's grandfather-in-law.

Silverbridge said, "For many years, I measured myself against my father. Everything I did was either to honor him or make him furious. It works for a randy youth in London, but it seemed rather foolish for a grown man, especially after my father was dead."

"How do you bear it?" Hugh asked, then quickly held up a hand. "I beg your pardon. 'Tis none of my business."

"You mean my father's murder?"

"Aye."

"'Tis kind of you not to add, 'at the hand's of your wife's grandfather.' I know you know it. Everyone does. Kit is part Scot. 'Tis an odd thing, I'm sure, to outsiders, especially since I spent half my life before I fell in love with Kit trying to avenge my father. He did die in a legitimate battle—and battle, as you know, is different—but I think what happened is that one day, not long before I'd met Kit, I got down on my knees at my father's grave and asked him what he wanted me to do. I was angry. I felt I'd been under his bridle my whole life, both before and after he died. I was fighting a bloody no-win battle with the Scots that had been his battle and undoubtedly will be my son's battle and my grandson's as well. The queen was cutting me off at the ankles. I felt penned in on all sides. I believe my words were 'Speak up, old man. You were never afraid to tell me what I needed to do before. Tell me now.'"

"And what happened?"

Silverbridge chuckled. "Nothing. Not a damned thing. I think I realized then the only person who can guide me is me. My decisions are my responsibility. Of course, it wasn't long after that when I first noticed Kit—really noticed her, if you follow—and if you care to interpret that as a reward for accepting my burden, I will not disagree. Life could not have made it clearer that I should put my father's death behind me than by making me fall in love with the granddaughter of the man who killed him."

Hugh shook his head, amazed. "You are at peace, then?"

"Aye. Though," he added with a cocked brow, "if I do not get Kit out of here by Tuesday, I will withdraw the statement."

Hugh laughed despite his turmoil. If Sir William accepted his map, all that Hugh could rightfully do would be done. And then what? He wouldn't have Joss. He wouldn't have his brother. He would have a profession he had approached only as a means to an end. And he wouldn't even have revenge. Alfred Brand had died a lonely, sick, rich old man, and if Hugh reversed the future, Brand would die without ever knowing what hell he had once caused. Restoring the wealth to the McPhersons was the right thing to do, and Bart would have approved. But revenge? The only person he would hurt is Joss.

He gazed at the thick sheet of paper, tracing his finger over the new property line it had been drawn up to display. A few tiny acres. So much unhappiness. So much bloodshed. When he looked hard, he could see the disconnected dots that revealed it as a mere ghost of the original, dots that could put him in prison or on a gallows. Would Bart have wanted that?

The dining hall door opened. Hugh and Silverbridge got to their feet. Sir William bowed to Silverbridge. Hugh bowed to Sir William. Silverbridge said, "This is my acquaintance, Captain Hugh Hawksmoor of Her Majesty's Navy. Thank you for agreeing to hear this matter, Sir William. It is of grave concern to the captain."

The man blotted his mouth with a napkin. "I am familiar with the case," he said. "When I heard you were to ask my help, I sent for my assistant. He was in Cambridge, so it was no great hardship for him to bring the relevant casebooks. And given the fact that these are lands that have been confiscated by the Crown, it is a fairly serious matter."

Hugh saw the man sitting at the dining table with his books and several magnifying glasses and swallowed.

"Come," Sir William said. "Let us begin."

CHAPTER FIFTY

"And?" Kit said eagerly, passing Joss the flask.

Joss lifted her chin only long enough to down the last of the whisky. "And so we came back just the way we came."

"Not quite the way you came."

"I meant on the horse. Only no one said anything." Joss collapsed back against the pillows and closed her eyes ruefully. *What a mess of a day.*

Kit leaned back on an elbow, watching the fire from her perch at the far end of the bed. "Poor Hugh."

"Poor *Hugh*?"

"Whose pennant flag ended up beating in the wind?"

Kit was a little tipsy, and so was Joss. "That's supposed to be a secret."

"I will carry it with me to my dying day—the image most certainly. And 'twas like a squash, you say?"

Joss choked. "I most certainly did *not* say that."

"That's right. Your words were something like 'a breath-taking garden delight.' I was the one who said 'squash.'" Kit flopped on her back. "But which kind? John keeps a hothouse, you know. I have seen a fair number. Did it have stripes? Maybe the *courge*? Or the one like a turban?" She adjusted an invisible swath of fabric around her head and began to snort. "Or the one like a swan's neck? Not the one they call an acorn, I hope. Oh dear, that would be quite embarrassing."

Joss couldn't help but laugh. "I think that's all the squash talk a girl can bear for one afternoon," she said, rolling onto her stomach and clutching the dress to keep her breasts from tumbling over the top, "though I did see one once that was round and as big as a bale of straw. It was orange, with teeth and eyes carved into it."

Kit let out a hoot. "I'm afraid the only one I ever see is toothless and blind, like a cranky old man."

"Can't blame him for being cranky. He's got a stiff back and too-tight shoes."

They dissolved into peals of giggles.

When Joss caught her breath, she laid her head on her arms. "Oh, Kit. What am I going to do?"

"I know exactly what you're going to do. You're going to march right down to his bedchamber and finish this up."

"Oh, no I'm not."

"Aye, you are," Kit said. "It's like falling off a horse. You have to get right back on."

"These metaphors are starting to make me nervous."

"But only in the best possible way. As soon as you finish the whisky." She took the flask from Joss's hand and shook it. "Uh-oh. Looks like the time has come. And just to make sure he understands exactly what you're there for, I think we shall send you down in your chemise."

"That is *not* going to happen."

"Oh, gather your courage. I shall let you keep a wrap on, but only until I leave you at the door. Then—"

"No, it won't do. I don't want to give my virginity to a man whose heart is not open to me."

" 'Not open'?"

"He guards so much. There are things he doesn't reveal."

Kit pursed her lips. "And this openness—you say it is a necessity?"

"Of course. How can any sort of affection grow without it? I was about to give my virginity to him."

"I agree. I damn any man who aims to carry the mantle of such an honor yet behaves so shoddily. He's a brute."

"But he didn't *know* I was a virgin. I hadn't told him yet—" Joss saw the duchess's spreading grin. "Oh. I get it."

"Come, now. A chemise and the truth: 'tis the best cure for a broken heart—and virginity, too, come to think of it."

CHAPTER FIFTY-ONE

Hugh paced the length of the library. He had been sent here to await word from Sir William. The carriages of Lord Quarley's guests had been arriving all evening, issuing their well-dressed passengers into the waiting arms of Quarley's footmen. He wondered what Joss was doing now, and what, if anything, she was thinking about him.

"Sir?"

One of Quarley's footmen had opened the door and stepped inside.

"Aye?"

"I am to inform you the Lord Keeper has come to a decision. He wishes to see you at once."

Hugh inhaled and followed the man out.

The dining room doors were open, and Hugh knew his future as soon as he saw Sir William's face. He prayed he had not also besmirched Silverbridge's reputation in the process. Hugh stepped into the room, straight as a mast, to accept his fate.

"We've been examining the map closely," Sir William

said. "It will come as no surprise to you that there is very little that some men will do to defraud the Crown."

Hugh tried to keep his face expressionless as he felt his liberty and possibly his life evaporate.

"This map caused us a good deal of consternation, especially given your reputation."

Hugh bowed his head. Sir William's assistant had pushed the map as far away from him as his arm would reach.

"But I am sorry to say," Sir William went on, "we cannot accept it. While I'm certain it reflects the will of both parties, the time for contesting the decision is too far passed. The Crown will not reverse its decision. Please give my sympathies to the family."

He would not be hanged, but the realization that his lifelong quest—the only thing that had given his life meaning these last twenty years—had failed wrapped his heart in a heavy darkness.

"I-I thank you for your consideration," Hugh said, barely seeing the table before him. "I will let the family know."

He closed the door behind him, the roar of defeat in his ears. There was nothing left. Everything he had hoped to do for Bart was gone. Everything that had guided his life since the age of eleven, swept away. And there was nothing but a vast unknown before him, an unknown he had not an inkling how to navigate.

He returned to the far end of the garden wing, to the small bedchamber he'd been assigned, and stood at the window. It had been a day of reckoning for him. He had hurt the woman he loved and failed his brother. He had nothing left.

His hand went to the timepiece in his pocket, and he closed his eyes.

Bart, I am abject before you. You gave everything for me, and now I have failed you. I wish . . . He wiped away the wetness gathering in his eyes, ashamed for his weakness. *I wish there was something I could do, something to set things to rights, something to honor the good you did and wash away the evil that was done to you and to Maggie, but there is nothing, nothing I can—*

A knock at the door lifted him from his thoughts.

"Who goes?"

"Joss," came the quiet reply.

He ran to the door and opened it. She stood in her chemise, a vision in diaphanous white. She looked small and cold and more than a little uncertain.

"Good God, what are you doing?" he whispered fiercely, looking down the hall and pulling her inside. "Someone might see you. Think of your reputation!"

"My reputation." She gave him a weak smile. "I would not care to have anyone characterize my reputation at this moment—especially not you."

He closed the door. The garment was barely buttoned. He could see the outline of her breasts and hips through the lightweight linen. There could be no mistaking her purpose in coming. The only question now was, would he do it?

"I thought," he said in a voice barely audible, "you did not care to betray your fiancé. I thought that was why you stopped me this afternoon."

"Oh, Hugh, if that had been my concern, don't you think my actions betrayed him long ago?"

Hugh stood unmoving, afraid to even breathe.

"I chose you that night in the inn," she said, "because I want to be with you. I haven't been truthful. I've had feelings about you since the first time we met—before, really, if you count when you picked me up and carried me through the sparks. At first, I thought it was just a crush, but the first time you wrapped me in that chiton, I knew I was mistaken. I was in trouble."

He gave her a smile tinged with fear. His heart was expanding in his chest faster than he could control it, and if this turned into another disappointment, he would be destroyed.

"After you left me at Rogan's house, I told him I wanted to delay the wedding."

Hugh's heart was like an Oriental hot-air lantern filled with joy, and he was clinging to the edge, trying to keep it from lifting him off the ground. But he had heard the nuance of that word.

"Delay?" he said carefully. "You did not cancel it?"

"No." Her voice shook, and he watched the blood creep up her cheeks. "I wasn't sure."

Not sure? The words were like the stab of an arrow. The lantern collapsed and shuddered to earth. His shoulders fell.

"But I *am* sure *now*!" she cried.

"You are not. I can see the disquiet on your face."

"No! The disquiet isn't for Rogan—or you. It's for me. I'm a virgin."

He blinked. *Virgin?* He felt as if he'd lost his footing in a complicated dance.

"I'm sorry," she said. "I should have told you."

She grazed his hand, and his heart pulsed.

"He will know," Hugh said wildly, pulling his hand free.

Her eyes flickered, fearful. "No he won't."

"He *will*. He's not a fool, and neither am I. I will have no part in . . . in preparing you for his bed."

Glimmering drops appeared in her eyes.

"There will not be a marital bed," she said. "At least not with Rogan. I can't marry him. Not when you're the only man in my head. What kind of a woman do you think I am?" A tear fell and then a second.

"Oh, Joss." He swept her into his arms. If this was his punishment for failing his brother, he hoped his life was one long failure. "You've made me so happy. I don't know what I've done to deserve it. And what a day for it to happen."

She hugged him tighter. He tilted her in his arms and for a long, long moment they kissed.

"Where is your ring?" he asked when they had stopped, lightly touching his forehead to hers.

"With the duchess."

"I cannot afford another like it. I suggest you keep it close."

She laughed through her tears. "I was told you are a very successful captain. Have I been misinformed?"

"I can manage a bauble or two," he said, then added with a sly smile, "Anything more would have to be earned."

"Earned, is it?" She lifted her unadorned fingers and gave him a smile. "I do have a great taste for jewelry."

He whispered the going price into her ear and heard her inhale.

"Is that all?" she said.

"That is per jewel, of course."

"In that case, I shall have a neck collar fit for a queen."

He put out his hand to her. "And what is the price for a virgin queen?"

She laid her quaking palm on his. "A bracelet," she said, "of tawny pearls."

He led her to the bed. "You set your price too low, milady. You are worth far more. You are worth a band of gold." He wrapped that thick dark hair around his hand and gazed with amazed joy into those eyes of cornflower blue. "Do you wish it?"

"Yes."

He married his mouth to hers, savoring the sweet wine of her kiss. "Then demand it."

"Possess me," she whispered. "And the price is a wedding ring on my finger."

"A fair price at that."

His tongue was warm and undemanding, and she reveled in the confection of joy and pleasure he stirred.

He proceeded slowly, caressing her shoulders and breasts, his great, strong arms encompassing her.

"Have you done this before?" she asked, and pursed her lips when he smiled. "I mean *this*." She gestured vaguely to the virgin territory below her navel.

"Once or twice," he said, in a way that made her think the number was considerably higher. "You are in capable hands, Joss. I promise I will see you safely to the other side."

"Why didn't you marry *them*?" This sense of being taken care of was new to her and she wanted some reassurance it wasn't a mistake.

"All of them?" He rose to his feet and slipped out of his coat.

"Hugh."

He grinned. "None touched my heart. 'Twas my own fault, though. I don't think I had a heart to touch until I met you." He loosened his stock—the stock that had played such a heated role in their afternoon—and dropped it on the floor.

"I wonder if they think about you." If she was to wear his ring, she wanted no ghosts lurking in the shadows.

"I should very much doubt it. As I said, I was not much of a prize—am not, still, though I will strive to become one for you."

He pulled off his shirt, and she was taken once more with the broad expanse of his chest and the back streaked with scars of battle, including the bullet wound he had taken in Pittsburgh. "I know Fiona thinks about you."

His face clouded for an instant. "I hope not," he said, removing a boot. "Our exchange was a fair one, and I do not think either of us expected more." The second boot followed, then the socks.

He placed his timepiece on the nightstand, then loosened his breeks and let them fall. She gathered the sheets nervously in her fingers. He was considerably larger than a tongue or a finger. Her palms began to sweat.

His eyes glittered. "You have called upon me to guide you. You must trust me. The tool is irrelevant."

"Irrelevant" was the last word she would have chosen.

He stretched out beside her, and she twined her leg over his, feeling the power in his long limbs. Their mouths joined easily, and he braided his hand in her hair.

"How is it," he murmured, "you are yet unplucked? The men before me have been foolish indeed."

"My mother," she said as he brought a hand to her hip. "Her *Tale of the Beautiful Mapmaker* and the young girl in it whose mother warns her to wait for the man who will love and protect her."

"Today is a day of many surprises," he said, falling back onto the pillows. "That tale inspired me, too. 'Tis one of the reasons I wanted to come to your time. I thought I was the knight who would save her daughter."

"And I thought Rogan was my knight!"

"*Oof.* I should prefer it if you were not quite so exuberant about that fact."

"Don't you see? Because I waited for Rogan, I was here for you. Do you think my mother planned it that way? Do you think she told the story to you so you'd come and to me so I'd wait?"

He smiled. "With Maggie, anything would have been possible."

"She laid it out for us like a maze, and we met in the middle."

"Then let us not disappoint."

He brought his hand between her legs, and the fire was different now—the flames were flames of joy, and her heart pounded at the difference. She ached for him in a way that carnality could not satisfy. But she wanted that, too. He had come to her unguarded. How had she ever imagined he had held back part of himself?

He lifted himself gingerly on an elbow and shifted his hips over hers. She could tell his shoulder pained him. Nonetheless, he took her hands and clasped them. "Are you ready?"

"Yes."

He pressed himself against her and she opened herself to him, savoring the heft of his weight on her thighs. With a pinch she would remember the rest of her life, he was inside her.

"Oh, God," he whispered. "You are so beautiful. Are you all right?"

"Yes." She longed to move but was fearful as well. It was different from what she'd imagined, more intimate. His eyes were so warm.

He slipped a hand free and brought it to her bud. She felt herself tighten around him.

"Careful, lass. 'Tis all I can do to be still."

He had the fingers of a piano prodigy and she squirmed. "Move," she begged. "Just a little."

He moved, slowly. When she gasped, he stopped. "Joss?"

"Go," she said. "More. Please." Whether it was him or the act, she didn't know, but she felt as if she might burst with the pleasure that burned between her legs.

"If I am hesitant, 'tis only because I don't know where your experience ends and mine begins."

"This is all new," she mused. "So, so wonderful. Am I bleeding?"

He checked his fingers in the light. "Aye. A bit. Should I stop?"

"Do you want to stop?"

"God, no."

She smiled. "I know how to . . . But with this . . ." Her thoughts were so scattered. She laid a hand on his arm, feeling the coiled power there.

"God, I want to bury myself in you," he said, slowly rocking. "I want to batter you. Tell me I will someday."

"Oh yes."

"And you will be round with my child."

She flushed, thinking of the power of his act. "Someday, yes."

"Today, if I have my way. And you will long for my touch even then."

"Yes."

"And I will plow you each night and each morn."

"Yes. Yes."

He cupped her breast, moaning as he kneaded the weight.

The rocking increased in tempo and pressure. She felt the same slow, driving rhythm sweep through her limbs, but this felt more momentous than anything she'd ever known. It could have been the unfamiliar pleasure between her legs, or the sloughing off of her virginity, or this new flavor of desire, but she thought instead it was the clear spring green of his eyes and the way he strained to hold himself from hurting her and the matchless communion she felt in his arms.

She pulled him closer, feeling his long muscles move. "More," she whispered. "Harder."

"Are you sure?"

"Yes."

He pressed himself slowly into her. It felt as if he reached her lungs.

He groaned and allowed himself a small thrust. "God, you're as tight as a drum."

"More."

He thrust again. She could feel his shoulders tremble, and she pressed her hips against him.

"Do not, milady," he begged, "do not."

But her hips were moving on their own. She moaned, heedless of nothing but the tide rising in her. He joined the heated tempo with short, anchored strokes that made her bones shake.

The minutes could have been hours. She rode the momentous joy, clutching his back and taking in his salty scent.

Then the tide took her. She cried out, and he moved just enough to catch her in its crashing ferocity and hold her there. She clutched his shoulders, writhing, calling. Then he caught her hands again, pinning them over her head, and sheathed himself hard, groaning her name as he shuddered.

He collapsed beside her, his body damp with sweat, and pulled her into his arms. "Oh, Joss."

She curled beside him, awash in the happiness of her new status. "I liked it."

He laughed. "I could tell."

"Can we do it again?"

"Aye." He threw an arm over his eyes and exhaled. "If I can ever stand."

"I don't need you to stand."

"You do for what I'm planning."

She laid her head on his chest and marveled at the joy she felt. She had no idea how they'd live or where they'd live, and she knew she would have to have an awkward conversation with Rogan to let him know of her decision before she could be completely content, but somehow she knew it would all work out.

Poor Rogan. He was a good man. Whatever she had imagined she'd seen in that dome had to be just that—something she'd imagined.

"When will you get to see the Sir William?" she asked.

The joy in his eyes flickered briefly.

"What?" she asked. "What happened with Sir William?"

"He cannot accept the map."

Joss felt the world turn over again. For her it meant the life she had known would not disappear like a thief in the night. She would be the daughter of a murderer, but her memories would reflect what had truly happened, and in some strange way she was grateful for that. But for Hugh it meant something else, something worse. "I'm sorry," she said.

He squeezed her closer. "As am I. I had thought . . . Oh, I suppose it doesn't matter what I thought now."

"No, tell me."

"I thought it was the one thing I could do for my brother, since I was powerless to do anything else. But maybe the one thing I was supposed to do for my brother was to fall in love with the girl he loved as a daughter, the girl whose mother he loved truly and proudly."

"Oh, Hugh." She hugged him. "I-I had another thought about the Trojan Horse."

"You did?"

"We thought my mother put it there as another clue, but what if it's just meant to be what it is?"

"Which is what?"

"A warning that what you see isn't what you get."

He smiled. "It makes sense, but knowing that doesn't seem to help us unless we know what the what is. It could be the map itself, a symbol in the map, someone involved in the quest." He touched her nose. "Maybe your mother just wanted to ensure you had a reason to study Latin."

They heard the sound of violins coming from somewhere in the house.

She looked at him, confused.

"Dinner, milady. The party is about to begin." He slid from the bed and pulled on his breeks.

"What? Now?"

He pulled back the drapes an inch or two to gaze at the evening shadows in the garden. "Aye, we cannot lie abed all day. At some point, we shall have to thank the man who has generously provided the setting for our happy adventures here."

Dinner? It hardly seemed possible. She grabbed the timepiece off the nightstand and popped open the cover. But before she could even register the time on the clock-face, the words inscribed on the inside cover struck her like ice water.

Hugh turned. His face fell when he saw her. "Oh, Joss, no!"

"What does this mean, 'His blood for yours. A brother's promise'?" She felt as if air were stuck in her lungs, and had trouble keeping the words in focus.

"I-I—"

"*Whose* blood, Hugh? *Whose?*"

"I was a young man then," he said weakly, "and fool-ish."

"When you came to that alley the first time, what did you want?"

"Joss . . ."

A siren rang in her head. She'd been so stupid, so ready to believe. She felt like an idiot for not having seen this before now. "What did you want?"

Their gazes held in an embrace of righteous anger and sorrow. At last he said, "I wanted to find Bart's murderer."

"Whom you knew to be my father?"

His shirt hung loosely in his hand, as if he'd forgotten its purpose. "Aye."

"So that you could trade his blood for Bart's?"

He sighed and nodded.

"So that you could kill him?"

"Aye. But he was already dead."

"And was that the end of your hunger for vengeance?"

He gazed at the floor, silent.

"Tell me, Hugh. At least be man enough to tell me that."

A tremor ran over him, as if he had been slipped into a suit of armor. When he lifted his head and looked into her eyes, she barely recognized him. "No," he said, "'twas not the end. I settled on destroying you—that is, until I found out you were Maggie Brand's daughter, and then I settled on destroying Reynolds, the heir to the ill-gotten gains from your father's abominable crime."

And nothing could have destroyed Rogan more easily than his fiancée's betrayal. She had served willingly as the dagger of revenge in Hugh's black quest. Had Hugh actually planned on marrying her? Of course he had. No betrayal is complete without the total destruction of one's enemy. Hugh had seduced her, torn her from her friends and would steal her forever from Rogan's world as surely as Zeus had abducted Europa.

"Leave me," she said, and flung the timepiece onto the bed.

A terrible sadness appeared in his eyes, then it was gone, replaced by something awful and determined. "I cannot. He is here."

"Rogan?" she asked, shocked.

Hugh nodded.

"Where?" She hoped her seeming eagerness pained Hugh as much as he had pained her. The truth was, she wasn't sure if she cared if Rogan was there or not, but she knew she was about to cry and she would die before she'd do it in front of Hugh.

"I do not know, milady. But he's here, in 1706, and he is a danger, perhaps to you. He's the one who shot me."

She gasped, but knew in an instant that had to be the truth. She hated that she'd been lied to, hated that her instincts about Rogan had been correct, hated that Hugh was the one to make her see this.

"You're a liar! I wouldn't believe you if you said the moon was round. Get out!" she cried. *"Get out!"*

She buried her face in her hands while he dressed, and the last thing she heard before the sound of the French doors opening and closing was a long sigh and the rustle of bedsheets as he swept the timepiece into his hand.

CHAPTER FIFTY-TWO

Hugh stepped into the gloomy twilight, his world in pieces at his feet. She was right, he thought as he stumbled blindly away from the house. He had come to her world with the sole purpose of destroying what she held dear. How could he have expected that sin to be borne away like smoke from a doused fire just because they had fallen in love?

He had lived a life of anger and cold-blooded determination, and now he had lost his only chance for happiness. The punishment was just, but that did not make the coup de grâce any less painful.

He found himself in a thick copse of oaks, though how he had gotten there he could not say. He felt the darkness envelop him, and he wanted to be lost; but just as the last bits of light disappeared, the call of duty stopped him. He couldn't abandon her. Not when Rogan prowled the land. Even if she did not wish to see him, Hugh must stay where he could see *her*. He turned as if pulled by a powerful magnet and in the distance found the French doors, still lit by the lamp that had shone on their lovemaking.

He had just settled against a gnarled trunk when an arm as strong as iron bent around his throat and the cold steel of a knife pierced his shirt.

Joss cried silently, curled into a ball on a bed still alive with the perfume of their joining. How fleeting her joy had been. She'd thrown herself into Hugh's arms, trusting those wry green-gray eyes and that warm, hungry mouth. She'd saved herself this long, and for what? A man whose lies were as numerous as his charms. All that was left for her was to slink back to Pittsburgh, a place she should never have left, and pick up the pieces of her company, if indeed there would be any left without Rogan's help.

There was a knock at the hallway door. She ignored it, but it came again, more urgently.

"Captain Hawksmoor?" said a young footman. "There is a visitor here who insists—"

"Dammit, Hugh!" a louder voice called. "Open the door if you're in there!"

There was no mistaking Nathaniel's voice and he sounded desperate. Joss slipped a blanket over her shoulders and opened the door. Nathaniel's face was awash in excitement.

"I beg your pardon, m'um," the footman said, horrified at having roused a woman from the bed of one of his master's guests. "The man here claimed an acquaintance—"

"That's fine," Joss said. "I know him." She gestured Nathaniel in, closing the door on the young footman with an apologetic *click*. Nathaniel's eyes flickered over the blanket and the chemise beneath but his face betrayed nothing—nothing, that is, except the thrill of apparent news. His hands were stuffed furtively in his pockets.

"What is it?" she asked.

"Is Hugh about?" He kept his eyes from the tousled bedsheets.

"No. He went that way, if you'd like to look for him." She pointed to the French doors.

Her tone lessened the look of happiness on his face, but not enough to keep him from pulling his hands free and dumping two handfuls of gold coins on the bedside table.

"Gold," he whispered. "And there's more where that came from."

The coins gleamed in the candlelight like a heavenly visitation. There were coins of every type, small and large, highly engraved and plain, new and tinged with the dirt of ages past.

"Where? How?" she asked, mesmerized.

"There's a share for you, too," he said happily. "'Twas your map, after all—or should I say, your *maps*."

She looked at him strangely. "My maps?"

"Done by your mother. You put them together and the marks made words, do you remember? 'An arrow for the fire, a warrin' man's tower / Safe may you find it, a reluctant bride's dower'?"

She nodded, still not understanding.

"The map showed a pele tower," he said.

"The cartouche, yes. They were each the same."

"But it wasn't a pele tower. 'Twas a warrener's lodge," he said triumphantly. "W-A-R-R-E-N-E-R. Do you see? 'A warrin' man's tower.'"

"A warrener's lodge?"

" 'Tis a place where a gentleman's warrener lives, the man who protects the rabbits on his estate. I recognized the lodge. 'Tis square, not round. I lived in Cambridgeshire as a lad, and when I saw that tower in the map"—he pulled the papers from his pocket and unfolded them—"something tickled my memory."

"But the gold . . . ?"

" 'A reluctant bride's dower'!" He clapped his hands. "It's too lovely! Your mother's verse led me there. I wasn't sure, of course. The notion came to me in the carriage. That's when I remembered I'd played near such a tower in my boyhood. It wasn't until I found the dilapidated old thing again that I knew."

"Knew what?"

"The bricks over the hearth. They are placed in an arrow pattern."

She looked at him, and he grinned.

" 'An arrow for the fire,' " she repeated excitedly, her mother's riddle finally untangling.

"Aye, milady! And 'Safe may you find it.' There were safes! Dozens of them! Between the inner walls and outer ones! Filled with gold! More than we could carry! It will take a wagon and four strong horses!"

Then it hit her—the beauty of her mother's story! This was the gold from the man who came to the mapmaker to make a map to remind him where he'd hidden his treasure; the man who never collected the maps because he didn't need them to win the hand of the woman he loved; the man who told her mother the gold was hers!

"Of course, we'll have to do the moving by night. I don't know the man who owns the land now, but I doubt—"

"The gold doesn't belong to him."

"Pardon?" It was Nathaniel's turn to be surprised.

"It belongs to me—well, all of us. Fiona can buy her grandfather out of prison, help her people." Joss felt a wave of relief she wouldn't have expected. She couldn't restore Fiona's lands to her family or bring back Hugh's brother, but perhaps, in some small way, the gold would help atone for what her father had done.

Then she saw the flash of worry on Nathaniel's face.

"Where's Fiona?" he asked.

"With you, isn't she?"

He shook his head, and she could see his worry grow. "Well, perhaps she's with—" Then he stopped himself.

"Hugh?"

"Aye."

"She might be. I haven't seen her."

"She disappeared in Cambridge. I told her not to come to the estate here."

"One can hardly count on Fiona to obey those sorts of commands, though, I'm sure." She smiled, hoping to relieve his concern.

"You have spoken the God's honest truth there, lass."

"What made you follow us?"

"Pardon?"

"You said the notion concerning the warrener's lodge came to you in the carriage. Why were you coming to Cambridgeshire?"

An air of guardedness came over him, and she knew the answer. *Rogan.*

"Seemed wiser to keep you close," he said obscurely, and turned his face.

"Shouldn't you find Hugh?" She pointed again to the doors.

Nathaniel' eyes swept over the chemise again and he shook his head. "I think," he said carefully, "I will not interrupt. You may tell him the news yourself, lass. I will be in the inn down the road if I'm wanted." He put a hand on the hallway door.

"Will you take your gold?" she said.

"It's been lucky for me," he said. "I should like to think it might be the same for you."

The door closed, and she touched the pile of coins absently. She supposed she ought to try to sneak back to her room. There she would wait for Hugh so that they might begin the excruciating process of traveling to Portsmouth, posting themselves on a ship that could take them to Mr. Roark, who could in turn take her to the islet so that she might enter the cave for the very last time. It would be a long, long way to go in silence.

The French doors creaked. She turned.

"Hello, Joss."

It was Rogan, standing there with the same charming smile he might have worn if he had run into her on the elevator. He was wearing a suit of clothes from 1706. How he might have gotten it, she couldn't guess. She was so shocked, she didn't know what to do or say. "Rogan."

"A lot's changed since we last saw each other, I guess." He gave her a regretful smile. "I saw you kiss him outside Dollar Bank. I had to follow."

Was this a man who would shoot another in cold blood? Her instincts were confused. Part of her saw the possibility, but another part of her saw the man who had stood outside her father's hospital, waiting for her with flowers in his hand.

"I'm sorry," she said. "I'm sorry you saw that."

"Do you love him?"

"I thought I did."

"Because I don't care what you did. I want you if you'll have me." He extended an uncertain hand.

Had her suspicions about him been real or had they been a projection of her ego, giving herself a way out of the guilt she was feeling over her attraction to Hugh? Would she know if she touched him, the knight who had saved her and her company when she'd needed help? Surely the sense of the man would come through.

She turned toward him tentatively.

"Joss, please."

When she put out her hand, she saw the blood splattered on his trousers and nearly jumped. Whom had he hurt? How had he found her?

"I-I want some time," she said as she took his hand, heart pounding.

He pulled her close. "Of course. As much as you want."

She felt ill, as if she were clasping a giant viper. It took all her willpower not to fling his arms away, but something told her that would be the worst move of all.

His cheek brushed her hair. She could feel his breath on her skin. "Did you see these?" She broke free and gestured to the coins.

"My God! No, I didn't." He took a step closer and brought his fingers to them.

"Wait here," she said. "There's something else I want to show you."

She padded out the French doors, wrapping the blanket around her shoulders, and as soon as she reached the far end of the courtyard, she began to run.

The gravel moved under her bare feet, hiding the sounds behind her. Was Rogan there? Was he following? She scoured the view ahead, desperate for a place to hide. She had to put distance between them, as much as she could. Her feet were cold, aching. She didn't care.

"Joss!" Rogan cried.

The word went through her like a blade. Was he calling for her because he saw her or because he didn't see her? She turned her head and saw his figure racing into the garden in the distance.

Now she had only time on her side, and little of that. Had she gotten a good enough start to lose him in the woods ahead?

The ground was filled with acorns and stones, and they stung her feet. She could hear him pelting behind her. She spotted an oak large enough to hide her and was swerving to the right to reach it when her foot caught on a root and she hit the ground, smacking her elbow on a rock. When she opened her eyes, she saw a pair of booted legs sticking out from behind a fallen tree, and she almost screamed. The legs were Hugh's.

She scrabbled over the trunk. He was gagged and bound, but alive. His shirt was wet with blood, and she flung herself toward him, but he shook his head roughly, terror in his eyes.

Rogan's footsteps neared, and she had only enough time to loosen the rope around Hugh's ankles before she flattened herself against him in the darkness and threw the blanket over both of them.

Rogan ran past them, and Joss thought they were safe, but then he slowed, stopped, and turned around.

"So you found him."

Joss got to her knees and reached for Hugh's gag.

"Don't touch that."

"Go to hell." She untied it and ran her hands over the wetness at his collar. "Where are you bleeding?"

"Shoulder," he said. "It's all right."

"Look at me," Rogan demanded.

She ignored him. She felt Hugh's chest and abdomen. They were solid. Then she found more bleeding behind his ear. Rogan must have knocked him out.

"Look at me!"

"What?" She spun around angrily.

"I don't have a weapon." Rogan held out his hands. "I want to talk."

"Bully for you." Hugh was shivering, and she wondered how much blood he'd lost. She tucked the blanket around his legs, then reached for the rope binding his wrists.

Rogan shoved her back. "That I must insist you stop."

"I'm fine, Joss," Hugh said. "Don't worry."

"He's bleeding and cold." She caught the knot and continued.

Rogan bent to grab her, but he flew over her instead, crashing hard into the bushes. Hugh had booted him off his feet.

"He has a pistol!" Hugh cried. "Run!"

Joss spotted the gun sticking out of the back of Rogan's

trousers, and she lunged for him, hoping to grab it first. But he caught her and rolled on top of her, pinning her while he found the weapon. He cocked the hammer and pointed it at her, then climbed to his feet. "Now, get up. We're going."

"I'm not leaving Hugh."

"Here's the deal: I won't hurt him, and I won't hurt you. We'll return to Pittsburgh. I know the way. I want you, Joss. That's the deal."

She looked at Hugh. "Go," he said. "That's the best offer we could get."

"I'm not going to go." She swiped a tear from her eye.

"Please," Hugh said. "I don't like our other choices."

"Will you come back?"

"No, Joss," Rogan interjected. "That's part of the deal. Your friend will understand. No more travel to the future. No more travel to the past. And you both live."

Hugh looked at her, eyes clouded in sorrow. "Do it."

She trembled, the anger and sadness too much to bear. "I'm going to untie him."

"Fine. Yes." Rogan waved his gun. "You can untie his hands if you say you'll leave."

"I hate you."

"I hope that changes."

She untied the rope, and Hugh lifted a hand to her cheek. "Thank you, milady. I know I failed you, and I'm sorry."

She laid her hand over his, and tears filled her eyes.

Rogan took her other hand and pulled her roughly to her feet. He said to Hugh, "I trust you'll stay where you are until we leave the estate."

The muscle in Hugh's jaw flexed, but he nodded. "Take the blanket, Joss."

She bent to collect it, and when she unfolded herself, Rogan's face had changed.

"Your dress . . ." he said.

She turned to see what he had seen. Dried blood streaked the skirt of her chemise, right down the center of the back.

Rogan made a noise like a dying animal. "You slept with him? You made *me* wait, and you slept with him?"

"Jesus, Rogan—"

"Did he rape you? Did you rape her?" He swung the gun toward Hugh.

"No, he didn't rape me."

Rogan's hand began to shake. "You take it all?" he said to Hugh. "You take the map—and don't lie. I know she printed one for you. You take the company I've worked so hard to buy and make it so it never existed. You steal her away in the night like a thief, and then you take her virginity?"

"She doesn't love me, Reynolds."

He lifted the gun to aim it. Hugh's shoulders stiffened.

"No, Rogan!" Joss cried. "Listen to me. The map didn't work. I know that's why you came, but the Lord Keeper wouldn't accept it. The transfer won't go through. Nothing's changed. The company is still yours."

"Oh, something's changed." Rogan wiped the sweat from his brow. "Something has definitely changed."

He tightened his arm and closed his eyes.

"No!"

The shot exploded into the forest, filling it for an instant with light. And then a red spot appeared on Rogan's chest, growing bigger as stunned incomprehension filled his face. "Joss?"

She turned. Fiona stood with a pistol in her hand, a look of crazed fury on her face. Her neck was bruised and her eyes were puffed and red.

"That," Fiona said, "is for my grandfather. And this"—she spat on him—"is for me."

CHAPTER FIFTY-THREE

PITTSBURGH, PRESENT DAY

One day, a knight came to visit the beautiful mapmaker's daughter. He didn't want to court her. He admired her maps. He asked her about the places she drew. He looked at copies of the maps she'd made and made her tell the stories of the men who had asked for them to be made. He wanted to take her to lands outside her shop. He told her she looked sad and asked what he could do to make her happy. And the girl knew that he was the man she would marry, because, among all her many suitors, he was the only one who had offered to help her put things to rights.

—The Tale of the Beautiful Mapmaker

"Exactly what sort of man does it take to convince you to take a leave of absence from work?" Di straightened the sheaf of papers before her and slipped them into the drawer.

Joss flushed and turned to gaze out the office window. It was weird to be sitting on the other side of her desk. "C'mon. You've met him."

"I've met him, and he's charming and handsome and

all, but that's not what I'm talking about. Don't forget, I caught a glimpse of your last boyfriend. This guy has to be as big as—"

"The Gulf Tower, actually," LaWren said, opening the door and ushering Hugh in. "That's what it's called. It's forty-four storeys tall and has a weather beacon on the top that turns red or blue depending on the forecast. Red's better."

"Red, you say?" Hugh made a quick bow to Joss and Di, then angled his head to try to observe this phenomenon.

"Only when the forecast is *really* good," Di said, and Joss bit her lip to keep from laughing.

"And when something big's gonna happen," LaWren added, demonstrating with her hands, "it starts to pulse."

Di said, "And that's when you'd really better watch out."

"I'm Hugh Hawksmoor," he said, extending his hand to LaWren. "Have we met before?"

LaWren shook it. "Ah, no. Not exactly." She looked at Joss and smiled. "Let's just say I'm pretty familiar with you."

"Excellent." Hugh rubbed his hands. "How is the meeting going, miladies?"

" 'Miladies'?" Di lifted an impressed brow in Joss's direction.

LaWren gazed at him in gleeful wonder. "Oh, say it again."

"What? 'Miladies'?"

"Do you know Colin Firth?"

Hugh shook his head.

"Hugh Grant? Sean Connery? Seal?"

"None. Are they friends of yours?"

"I wish." LaWren sighed sadly, and closed the door behind her.

Joss said to Di, "So we're having LaWren escort visitors in now?"

"LaWren," Di said, "is going to be my new executive assistant."

"Really?"

"She seems to know where the bodies are buried. It's a good quality in an assistant. How are you this morning, Hugh?"

"Very well, thank you." He pulled up the seat next to Joss. "Are you almost done with the bride-to-be?"

"If I can get her to peel her fingers off next year's marketing plan, then yes. You'll be ready to go."

Joss pursed her lips and handed the last file over to her friend.

LaWren opened the door again. "Sorry. The chairman of the board of Brand Industries wants to see this month's cash flow. He's in the conference room."

"Thanks," Joss said.

"Thanks," Di said at the same time, and gave Joss a look. "Tell him I'll be in in a minute."

Di stood and gathered her calculator and a report from the top of the stack. "So this six-month voyage is— what?—a prewedding honeymoon?"

Hugh cleared his throat. "*I'll* be working."

"They need tailors on sailboats?"

"I do a little navigating, too. It's one of my other interests."

Di narrowed her eyes. "Uh-huh. And what about you? I thought you were terrified of water?"

"Only of looking at it," Joss said. "I'm planning to spend a good deal of time in the cabin."

"A very good deal," Hugh added.

"Hm."

"Did you ever read *The Little Prince*?" Joss asked.

"Once," Di said. "A long time ago."

"Do you remember when the prince goes to the asteroid where the geologist lives?"

"Vaguely."

"Well, the geologist is someone who sits behind his desk all day, making maps. He never leaves his tiny planet. And when the prince describes *his* asteroid to the geologist so the geologist can draw its volcanoes and the little flower the little prince loves and cares for, the geologist says, 'We don't record flowers because they are only ephemeral.' Well, I was afraid I was becoming that geologist. Hugh is going to take me to see some flowers."

"And maybe some volcanoes as well." He smiled.

"Hmmm." Di tucked the report under her arm. "And what are you going to do with all that time in the cabin, not looking at the water?"

"You know. Read, relax, sightsee. The usual stuff." Joss smiled at Hugh, who said, "There's a dice game I intend to finish as well."

"But this ship has no phone and no radio?" Di asked.

Joss shrugged. "You know I'll check in whenever I can."

"Isn't it going to be a little dangerous?"

Joss took Hugh's hand. "I guess. But it seems like a worthwhile risk."

"Well, we're certainly not facing too much in the way of financial difficulties," Di said, "not since you sold your mother's maps. Who knew they'd be worth so much?"

"It was almost like finding a pot of gold."

"Several," Hugh said.

Di made her way to the door. "But you're not going to get married before you get back? I have my Casual Friday outfit all picked out."

"Ha-ha." Joss looked at Hugh. "I'm not sure I can promise that," she said. "Captains can do some surprising things at sea."

Di looked from one to the other. "Well, I guess I should be grateful the ceremony's not in the Founders Room. Just promise me you'll wear something other than a blouse and skirt."

Hugh said, "Oh, I've got something else in mind entirely. It's a lovely white dress. Nathaniel has it waiting on board."

Joss turned to him. "He made it? Really?"

"I told you. It's been ready since the day of your party. I'm a man of my word, you know. You'll be the goddess I always imagined."

"Well . . ." Di ran to Joss and gave her a hug. Hugh offered his hand. Di popped onto her toes and kissed him on the cheek. "Take care of her."

" 'Tis my only desire."

Di paused at the door. "Be safe. Oh, and keep your eye on that Gulf Tower," she added to Joss, then closed the door behind her.

Hugh returned his gaze to the building in question. "For what are you looking?"

The red light shone clear and steady.

"Nothing," Joss said. "That's just her way of wishing us luck."

He took her in his arms. "A good captain never turns

down luck in any form, though I hope she doesn't think we need it."

"No, I think she thinks you're pretty good for me."

A silence came over Hugh, and Joss knew he was remembering the last man Di had thought that about.

He searched for words. "I-I—"

"You have nothing to be sorry about," Joss said. "Rogan was going to kill you. I'm grateful Fiona arrived when she did. Besides saving you, she saved him from having to become a murderer."

"Even if it meant losing his life?"

Joss had thought a long time about this. "Yes. I can see now what it did to my father."

Hugh ran a hand over his chin, considering. "'Tis a high price to pay."

"It is," she agreed sadly. "I hope Fiona can find peace. Her act will be a burden to her as well."

"Her grandfather is free. They will not be the tin merchants they'd hoped, but I suspect the gold will find another good use. I do not think you need to worry about Fiona."

"The board has found some irregularities in the Brand Industries balance sheet since Rogan took over. They think that's why he's disappeared. So does his family. I-I think that's better. They think that's why I put the wedding on hold. My leave from work is supposed to be a time for me to recover from being abandoned."

He gazed at her closely. "Is it?"

"I'm sad Rogan wasn't the man I thought he was. He was a good man. Once."

"If it's any comfort," Hugh said, "I think he was a good man when you met him and fell in love. I think your father wanted to leave his terrible secret with someone when he was dying, and I think he sensed he couldn't do that with you. His family fortune was gone, but the business empire could be saved under Reynolds. That was your father's legacy. He told Reynolds everything: that all the Brand success and fortune depended on the changes he'd made back in 1684 never being reversed. He probably also told him to be on the lookout for anyone odd who came asking questions. Fortune—especially ill-gotten fortune—does strange things to men, Joss. I've seen it happen. I do think he loved you. I'm afraid the glory of Brand Industries clouded his thinking."

She laid her head on Hugh's shoulder and said a small prayer for the man she had once loved.

"What about you?" she asked, fingering the notch in his lapel. "You're a rich man now."

He chuckled, his broad chest rumbling under her touch. "I was never a man driven by money. I should be just as happy with nothing."

"Oh, I don't like the sound of that."

He laughed and pulled her tighter. "Which is not to say I'm a man without faults. Far from it. My faults were anger and a lack of forgiveness—worse than greed, I think." He lifted her chin. "I came to Pittsburgh to do a terrible thing. I'm sorry. I hope someday I can earn the right to be as happy as you've made me. I know I don't deserve it now."

She smiled. "You did it for your brother. I don't know what it's like to have a brother murdered, but if you felt even a tenth as upset as I felt about my mother and the unhappiness she had to bear, it must have been an awful burden. I wish I had known what she was like before my father changed her."

An almost childlike earnestness came over him, and he took a step back from Joss and clasped her hands. "I should like . . . I mean, if it pleases you, I should like to take you to the cottage where we lived in Wych Cross— you and I and Bart and your mother. I can show you where we played bowls, and the branch where we sat— you and I—while Maggie told us stories. I knew her well, Joss. I can tell you everything I know."

She felt her eyes begin to sting. "I would love that."

"In fact, I wish I had known my brother as well. I told you he was older, and he was a very reserved man. I think it came from years of running a ship. I find myself becoming that way, too. But I know he cared for me. Ah, Bartholomew." He shook his head sadly. "You are still such a cipher to me."

Joss blinked. "Bartholomew? That was his name?"

"Aye. The sailors called him Granite. Not to his face, of course. I'm sure the townsfolk who used the services of the poor, unassuming clerk never suspected he was once one of the most vaunted men in the English navy."

She put a hand to her cheek. "I-I know a story. It's called 'Bartholomew the Clerk.'"

"What an odd coincidence."

"It's not a coincidence. The story came from my mother. She gave it to me while she was dying. It wasn't a fairy tale she told. It was a long story, written down, about a man who loved a woman so much, he gave up his riches to live with her. So many chapters. I thought she was insane to work so hard when she was ill. I haven't thought about it in years. Oh my God, Hugh. I have it in my things in storage! It's *their* story!"

She could see the longing in the clear gray-green of his eyes, feel his need to belong again to that which he'd lost.

"We have so much to give each other," he whispered.

"Thanks to your brother and my mother."

"I have one more thing," he said, taking her left hand. "I know it's what Bart would have wanted. 'Tis what I want as well. And you have Nathaniel to thank for it. He took my timepiece to the armorer." Hugh slipped a hand in his pocket and pulled out a small circlet of gold. "I'm certain it's the only way to exorcise it. Will you carry it—until such time I've earned the right to ask you to wear it on your finger?"

She threw her arms around him. "I will."

And as the beacon on the Gulf Tower began an inexplicable shower of sparks, he said, "Blood. In the end it's all we have. Share mine."

The mapmaker's daughter told the knight who had come to help her that she had no gold, and that she was very poor. But instead of giving her gold—for he had gold to give—he told her they did not need money to be happy. She said, "You have given me your help and your heart. You have won my hand." They married and they were very happy, traveling to places she had only imagined before—the places she'd drawn on her maps.

—The Tale of the Beautiful Mapmaker